HE 02/20

Margaret Atwood is the author of more than forty books of fiction, poetry and critical essays, including the Booker Prize-winning *The Blind Assassin*. Her work has received many awards around the world, and her novel *The Handmaid's Tale* was adapted into an award-winning television series. She has also been a cartoonist, illustrator, librettist, playwright and puppeteer. She lives in Toronto.

You can discover more about the author at www.margaretatwood.ca

THE TESTAMENTS

Over fifteen years after the events of *The Handmaid's Tale*, the Republic of Gilead has maintained its grip on power. Yet there are signs it is beginning to rot from within. And, as it does, the lives of these three radically different women will converge.

Agnes, the cosseted child of a high-status Wife, recalls only the barest fragments of the time before Gilead. Now she desperately seeks to escape being married off to an ageing Commander.

Canadian teenager Daisy's only connection to Gilead is through school studies, protests, and the pamphlets of their Pearl Girl missionaries. Or so she thinks.

Meanwhile, within the bastions of Ardua Hall, the notorious Aunt Lydia has taken up a pen and begun to write . . .

*Books by Margaret Atwood
Published by Ulverscroft:*

THE BLIND ASSASSIN
ORYX AND CRAKE
MORAL DISORDER
HAG-SEED

MARGARET ATWOOD

THE TESTAMENTS

Complete and Unabridged

CHARNWOOD
Leicester

First published in Great Britain in 2019 by
Chatto & Windus
an imprint of Vintage
London

First Charnwood Edition
published 2020
by arrangement with
Vintage
Penguin Random House
London

Interior case art by Suzanne Dean (fountain pen)
and Noma Bar (girl profiles)

A catalogue record for this book is available
from the British Library.

ISBN 978–1–4448–4309–5

Published by
F. A. Thorpe (Publishing)
Anstey, Leicestershire

Set by Words & Graphics Ltd.
Anstey, Leicestershire
Printed and bound in Great Britain by
T. J. International Ltd., Padstow, Cornwall

This book is printed on acid-free paper

'Every woman is supposed to have the same set of motives, or else to be a monster.'

— GEORGE ELIOT, *DANIEL DERONDA*

'When we look one another in the face, we're neither of us just looking at a face we hate — no, we're gazing into a mirror . . . Do you really not recognize yourselves in us . . . ?'

— OBERSTURMBANNFÜHRER LISS TO OLD BOLSHEVIK MOSTOVSKOY, VASILY GROSSMAN, *LIFE AND FATE*

'Freedom is a heavy load, a great and strange burden for the spirit to undertake . . . It is not a gift given, but a choice made, and the choice may be a hard one.'

— URSULA K. LE GUIN, *THE TOMBS OF ATUAN*

Contents

I

Statue

The Ardua Hall Holograph

1

Only dead people are allowed to have statues, but I have been given one while still alive. Already I am petrified.

This statue was a small token of appreciation for my many contributions, said the citation, which was read out by Aunt Vidala. She'd been assigned the task by our superiors, and was far from appreciative. I thanked her with as much modesty as I could summon, then pulled the rope that released the cloth drape shrouding me; it billowed to the ground, and there I stood. We don't do cheering here at Ardua Hall, but there was some discreet clapping. I inclined my head in a nod.

My statue is larger than life, as statues tend to be, and shows me as younger, slimmer, and in better shape than I've been for some time. I am standing straight, shoulders back, my lips curved into a firm but benevolent smile. My eyes are fixed on some cosmic point of reference understood to represent my idealism, my unflinching commitment to duty, my determination to move forward despite all obstacles. Not that anything in the sky would be visible to my statue, placed as it is in a morose cluster of trees and shrubs beside the footpath running in front of Ardua

Hall. We Aunts must not be too presumptuous, even in stone.

Clutching my left hand is a girl of seven or eight, gazing up at me with trusting eyes. My right hand rests on the head of a woman crouched at my side, her hair veiled, her eyes upturned in an expression that could be read as either craven or grateful — one of our Handmaids — and behind me is one of my Pearl Girls, ready to set out on her missionary work. Hanging from a belt around my waist is my Taser. This weapon reminds me of my failings: had I been more effective, I would not have needed such an implement. The persuasion in my voice would have been enough.

As a group of statuary it's not a great success: too crowded. I would have preferred more emphasis on myself. But at least I look sane. It could well have been otherwise, as the elderly sculptress — a true believer since deceased — had a tendency to confer bulging eyes on her subjects as a sign of their pious fervour. Her bust of Aunt Helena looks rabid, that of Aunt Vidala is hyperthyroid, and that of Aunt Elizabeth appears ready to explode.

At the unveiling the sculptress was nervous. Was her rendition of me sufficiently flattering? Did I approve of it? Would I be *seen* to approve? I toyed with the idea of frowning as the sheet came off, but thought better of it: I am not without compassion. 'Very lifelike,' I said.

That was nine years ago. Since then my statue has weathered: pigeons have decorated me, moss has sprouted in my damper crevices. Votaries

4

have taken to leaving offerings at my feet: eggs for fertility, oranges to suggest the fullness of pregnancy, croissants to reference the moon. I ignore the breadstuffs — usually they have been rained on — but pocket the oranges. Oranges are so refreshing.

★   ★   ★

I write these words in my private sanctum within the library of Ardua Hall — one of the few libraries remaining after the enthusiastic book-burnings that have been going on across our land. The corrupt and blood-smeared finger-prints of the past must be wiped away to create a clean space for the morally pure generation that is surely about to arrive. Such is the theory.

But among these bloody fingerprints are those made by ourselves, and these can't be wiped away so easily. Over the years I've buried a lot of bones; now I'm inclined to dig them up again — if only for your edification, my unknown reader. If you are reading, this manuscript at least will have survived. Though perhaps I'm fantasizing: perhaps I will never have a reader. Perhaps I'll only be talking to the wall, in more ways than one.

That's enough inscribing for today. My hand hurts, my back aches, and my nightly cup of hot milk awaits me. I'll stash this screed in its hiding place, avoiding the surveillance cameras — I know where they are, having placed them myself. Despite such precautions, I'm aware of the risk I'm running: writing can be dangerous. What betrayals, and then what denunciations, might lie in store for me? There are several within Ardua Hall who would love to get their hands on these pages.

Wait, I counsel them silently: it will get worse.

II

PRECIOUS FLOWER

Transcript of Witness Testimony 369A

2

You have asked me to tell you what it was like for me when I was growing up within Gilead. You say it will be helpful, and I do wish to be helpful. I imagine you expect nothing but horrors, but the reality is that many children were loved and cherished, in Gilead as elsewhere, and many adults were kind though fallible, in Gilead as elsewhere.

I hope you will remember, too, that we all have some nostalgia for whatever kindness we have known as children, however bizarre the conditions of that childhood may seem to others. I agree with you that Gilead ought to fade away — there is too much of wrong in it, too much that is false, and too much that is surely contrary to what God intended — but you must permit me some space to mourn the good that will be lost.

★ ★ ★

At our school, pink was for spring and summer, plum was for fall and winter, white was for special days: Sundays and celebrations. Arms covered, hair covered, skirts down to the knee before you were five and no more than two inches above the ankle after that, because the urges of men were terrible things and those urges needed to be curbed. The man eyes that were always roaming here and there like the eyes of tigers, those searchlight eyes, needed to be shielded from the alluring and indeed blinding power of us — of our shapely or skinny or fat legs, of our graceful or knobbly or sausage arms, of our peachy or blotchy skins, of our entwining curls of shining hair or our coarse unruly pelts or our straw-like wispy braids, it did not matter. Whatever our shapes and features, we were snares and enticements despite ourselves, we were the innocent and blameless causes that through our very nature could make men drunk with lust, so that they'd stagger and lurch and topple over the verge — The verge of what? we wondered. Was it like a cliff? — and go plunging down in flames, like snowballs made of burning sulphur hurled by the angry hand of God. We were custodians of an invaluable treasure that existed, unseen, inside us; we were precious flowers that had to be kept safely inside glass houses, or else we would be ambushed and our petals would be torn off and our treasure would be stolen and we would be ripped apart and trampled by the ravenous men who might lurk around any corner, out there in the wide sharp-edged sin-ridden world.

That was the kind of thing runny-nosed Aunt Vidala would tell us at school while we were doing petit-point embroidery for handkerchiefs and footstools and framed pictures: flowers in a vase, fruit in a bowl were the favoured patterns.

10

But Aunt Estée, the teacher we liked the best, would say Aunt Vidala was overdoing it and there was no point in frightening us out of our wits, since to instill such an aversion might have a negative influence on the happiness of our future married lives.

'All men are not like that, girls,' she would say soothingly. 'The better kind have superior characters. Some of them have decent self-restraint. And once you are married it will seem quite different to you, and not very fearsome at all.' Not that she would know anything about it, since the Aunts were not married; they were not allowed to be. That was why they could have writing and books.

'We and your fathers and mothers will choose your husbands wisely for you when the time comes,' Aunt Estée would say. 'So you don't need to be afraid. Just learn your lessons and trust your elders to do what is best, and everything will unfold as it should. I will pray for it.'

But despite Aunt Estée's dimples and friendly smile, it was Aunt Vidala's version that prevailed. It turned up in my nightmares: the shattering of the glass house, then the rending and tearing and the trampling of hooves, with pink and white and plum fragments of myself scattered over the ground. I dreaded the thought of growing older — older enough for a wedding. I had no faith in the wise choices of the Aunts: I feared that I would end up married to a goat on fire.

★ ★ ★

11

The pink, the white, and the plum dresses were the rule for special girls like us. Ordinary girls from Econofamilies wore the same thing all the time — those ugly multicoloured stripes and grey cloaks, like the clothes of their mothers. They did not even learn petit-point embroidery or crochet work, just plain sewing and the making of paper flowers and other such chores. They were not pre-chosen to be married to the very best men — to the Sons of Jacob and the other Commanders or their sons — not like us; although they might get to be chosen once they were older if they were pretty enough.

Nobody said that. You were not supposed to preen yourself on your good looks, it was not modest, or take any notice of the good looks of other people. Though we girls knew the truth: that it was better to be pretty than ugly. Even the Aunts paid more attention to the pretty ones. But if you were already pre-chosen, pretty didn't matter so much.

I didn't have a squint like Huldah or a pinchy built-in frown like Shunammite, and I didn't have barely-there eyebrows like Becka, but I was unfinished. I had a dough face, like the cookies my favourite Martha, Zilla, made for me as a treat, with raisin eyes and pumpkin-seed teeth. But though I was not especially pretty, I was very, very chosen. Doubly chosen: not only pre-chosen to marry a Commander but chosen in the first place by Tabitha, who was my mother.

That is what Tabitha used to tell me: 'I went for a walk in the forest,' she would say, 'and then I came to an enchanted castle, and there were a lot of little girls locked inside, and none of them had any mothers, and they were under the spell of the wicked witches. I had a magic ring that unlocked the castle, but I could only rescue one little girl. So I looked at them all very carefully, and then, out of the whole crowd, I chose you!'

'What happened to the others?' I would ask. 'The other little girls?'

'Different mothers rescued them,' she would say.

'Did they have magic rings too?'

'Of course, my darling. In order to be a mother, you need to have a magic ring.'

'Where's the magic ring?' I would ask. 'Where is it now?'

'It's right here on my finger,' she would say, indicating the third finger of her left hand. The heart finger, she said it was. 'But my ring had only one wish in it, and I used that one up on you. So now it's an ordinary, everyday mother ring.'

At this point I was allowed to try on the ring, which was gold, with three diamonds in it: a big one, and a smaller one on either side. It did look as if it might have been magic once.

'Did you lift me up and carry me?' I would ask. 'Out of the forest?' I knew the story off by heart, but I liked to hear it repeated.

'No, my dearest, you were already too big for that. If I had carried you I would have coughed, and then the witches would have heard us.' I could see this was true: she did cough quite a lot. 'So I took you by the hand, and we crept out of the castle so the witches wouldn't hear us. We

13

both said *Shh, shh'* — here she would hold her finger up to her lips, and I would hold my finger up too and say *Shh, shh* delightedly — 'and then we had to run very fast through the forest, to get away from the wicked witches, because one of them had seen us going out the door. We ran, and then we hid in a hollow tree. It was very dangerous!'

I did have a hazy memory of running through a forest with someone holding my hand. Had I hidden in a hollow tree? It seemed to me that I had hidden somewhere. So maybe it was true.

'And then what happened?' I would ask.

'And then I brought you to this beautiful house. Aren't you happy here? You are so cherished, by all of us! Aren't we both lucky that I chose you?'

I would be nestled close to her, with her arm around me and my head against her thin body, through which I could feel her bumpy ribs. My ear would be pressed to her chest, and I could hear her heart hammering away inside her — faster and faster, it seemed to me, as she waited for me to say something. I knew my answer had power: I could make her smile, or not.

What could I say but yes and yes? Yes, I was happy. Yes, I was lucky. Anyway it was true.

3

How old was I at that time? Perhaps six or seven. It's hard for me to know, as I have no clear memories before that time.

I loved Tabitha very much. She was beautiful although so thin, and she would spend hours playing with me. We had a dollhouse that was like our own house, with a living room and a dining room and a big kitchen for the Marthas, and a father's study with a desk and bookshelves. All the little pretend books on the shelves were blank. I asked why there was nothing inside them — I had a dim feeling that there were supposed to be marks on those pages — and my mother said that books were decorations, like vases of flowers.

What a lot of lies she had to tell for my sake! To keep me safe! But she was up to it. She had a very inventive mind.

We had lovely big bedrooms on the second floor of the dollhouse, with curtains and wallpaper and pictures — nice pictures, fruit and flowers — and smaller bedrooms on the third floor, and five bathrooms in all, though one was a powder room — Why was it called that? What was 'powder'? — and a cellar with supplies.

We had all the dolls for the dollhouse that you

might need: a mother doll in the blue dress of the Commanders' Wives, a little girl doll with three dresses — pink, white, and plum, just like mine — three Martha dolls in dull green with aprons, a Guardian of the Faith with a cap to drive the car and mow the lawn, two Angels to stand at the gate with their miniature plastic guns so nobody could get in and hurt us, and a father doll in his crisp Commander's uniform. He never said much, but he paced around a lot and sat at the end of the dining table, and the Marthas brought him things on trays, and then he would go into his study and close the door.

In this, the Commander doll was like my own father, Commander Kyle, who would smile at me and ask if I had been good, and then vanish. The difference was that I could see what the Commander doll was doing inside his study, which was sitting at his desk with his Computalk and a stack of papers, but with my real-life father I couldn't know that: going into my father's study was forbidden.

What my father was doing in there was said to be very important — the important things that men did, too important for females to meddle with because they had smaller brains that were incapable of thinking large thoughts, according to Aunt Vidala, who taught us Religion. It would be like trying to teach a cat to crochet, said Aunt Estée, who taught us Crafts, and that would make us laugh, because how ridiculous! Cats didn't even have fingers!

So men had something in their heads that was like fingers, only a sort of fingers girls did not have. And that explained everything, said Aunt Vidala, and we will have no more questions about it. Her mouth clicked shut, locking in the other words that might have been said. I knew there must be other words, for even then the notion about the cats did not seem right. Cats did not want to crochet. And we were not cats.

Forbidden things are open to the imagination. That was why Eve ate the Apple of Knowledge, said Aunt Vidala: too much imagination. So it was better not to know some things. Otherwise your petals would get scattered.

★   ★   ★

In the dollhouse boxed set, there was a Handmaid doll with a red dress and a bulgy tummy and a white hat that hid her face, though my mother said we didn't need a Handmaid in our house because we already had me, and people shouldn't be greedy and want more than one little girl. So we wrapped the Handmaid up in tissue paper, and Tabitha said that I could give her away later to some other little girl who didn't have such a lovely dollhouse and could make good use of the Handmaid doll.

I was happy to put the Handmaid away in the box because the real Handmaids made me nervous. We would pass them on our school outings, when we'd walk in a long double line with an Aunt at each end of it. The outings were to churches, or else to parks where we might play circle games or look at ducks in a pond. Later we would be allowed to go to Salvagings and

17

Prayvaganzas in our white dresses and veils to see people being hanged or married, but we weren't mature enough for that yet, said Aunt Estée.

There were swings in one of the parks, but because of our skirts, which might be blown up by the wind and then looked into, we were not to think of taking such a liberty as a swing. Only boys could taste that freedom; only they could swoop and soar; only they could be airborne.

I have still never been on a swing. It remains one of my wishes.

⋆ ⋆ ⋆

As we marched along the street, the Handmaids would be walking two by two with their shopping baskets. They would not look at us, or not much, or not directly, and we were not supposed to look at them because it was rude to stare at them, said Aunt Estée, just as it was rude to stare at cripples or anyone else who was different. We were not allowed to ask questions about the Handmaids either.

'You'll learn about all of that when you're old enough,' Aunt Vidala would say. *All of that*: the Handmaids were part of *all of that*. Something bad, then; something damaging, or something damaged, which might be the same thing. Had the Handmaids once been like us, white and pink and plum? Had they been careless, had they allowed some alluring part of themselves to show?

You couldn't see very much of them now. You

18

couldn't even see their faces because of those white hats they wore. They all looked the same.

In our dollhouse at home there was an Aunt doll, although she didn't really belong in a house, she belonged in a school, or else at Ardua Hall, where the Aunts were said to live. When I was playing with the dollhouse by myself, I used to lock the Aunt doll in the cellar, which was not kind of me. She would pound and pound on the cellar door and scream, 'Let me out,' but the little girl doll and the Martha doll who'd helped her would pay no attention, and sometimes they would laugh.

I don't feel pleased with myself while recording this cruelty, even though it was only a cruelty to a doll. It's a vengeful side of my nature that I am sorry to say I have failed to subdue entirely. But in an account such as this, it is better to be scrupulous about your faults, as about all your other actions. Otherwise no one will understand why you made the decisions that you made.

★ ★ ★

It was Tabitha who taught me to be honest with myself, which is somewhat ironic in view of the lies she told me. To be fair, she probably was honest when it came to herself. She tried — I believe — to be as good a person as was possible, under the circumstances.

Each night, after telling me a story, she would tuck me into bed with my favourite stuffed animal, which was a whale — because God made whales to play in the sea, so it was all right for a whale to be something you could play with — and then we would pray.

The prayer was in the form of a song, which we would sing together:

Now I lay me down to sleep,
I pray the Lord my soul to keep;
If I die before I wake,
I pray the Lord my soul to take.

Four angels standing round my bed,
Two to feet and two to head;
One to watch and one to pray,
And two to carry my soul away.

Tabitha had a beautiful voice, like a silver flute. Every now and then, at night when I am drifting off to sleep, I can almost hear her singing.

There were a couple of things about this song that bothered me. First of all, the angels. I knew they were supposed to be the kind of angels with white nightgowns and feathers, but that was not how I pictured them. I pictured them as our kind of Angels: men in black uniforms with cloth wings sewn onto their outfits, and guns. I did not like the thought of four Angels with guns standing around my bed as I slept, because they were men after all, so what about the parts of me that might stick out from under the blankets? My feet, for instance. Wouldn't that inflame their urges? It would, there was no way around it. So the four Angels were not a restful thought.

Also, it was not encouraging to pray about dying in your sleep. I did not think I would, but what if I did? And what was my soul like — that thing the angels would carry away? Tabitha said it was the spirit part and did not die when your body did, which was supposed to be a cheerful idea.

But what did it look like, my soul? I pictured it as just like me, only much smaller: as small as the little girl doll in my dollhouse. It was inside me, so maybe it was the same thing as the invaluable treasure that Aunt Vidala said we had to guard so carefully. You could lose your soul, said Aunt Vidala, blowing her nose, in which case it would topple over the verge and hurtle down and endlessly down, and catch on fire, just like the goatish men. This was a thing I very much wished to avoid.

21

4

At the beginning of the next period I am about to describe, I must have been eight at first, or possibly nine. I can remember these events but not my exact age. It's hard to remember calendar dates, especially since we did not have calendars. But I will continue on in the best way I can.

My name at that time was Agnes Jemima. Agnes meant 'lamb,' said my mother, Tabitha. She would say a poem:

Little lamb, who made thee?
Dost thou know who made thee?

There was more of this, but I have forgotten it.

As for Jemima, that name came from a story in the Bible. Jemima was a very special little girl because her father, Job, was sent bad luck by God as part of a test, and the worst part of it was that all Job's children were killed. All his sons, all his daughters: killed! It sent shudders through me every time I heard about it. It must have been terrible, what Job felt when he was told that news.

But Job passed the test, and God gave him some other children — several sons, and also three daughters — so then he was happy again.

And Jemima was one of those daughters. 'God gave her to Job, just as God gave you to me,' said my mother.

'Did you have bad luck? Before you chose me?'

'Yes, I did,' she said, smiling.

'Did you pass the test?'

'I must have,' said my mother. 'Or I wouldn't have been able to choose a wonderful daughter like you.'

I was pleased with this story. It was only later that I pondered it: how could Job have allowed God to fob off a batch of new children on him and expect him to pretend that the dead ones no longer mattered?

★   ★   ★

When I wasn't at school or with my mother — and I was with my mother less and less, because more and more she would be upstairs lying down on her bed, doing what the Marthas called 'resting' — I liked to be in the kitchen, watching the Marthas make the bread and the cookies and pies and cakes and soups and stews. All the Marthas were known as Martha because that's what they were, and they all wore the same kind of clothing, but each one of them had a first name too. Ours were Vera, Rosa, and Zilla; we had three Marthas because my father was so important. Zilla was my favourite because she spoke very softly, whereas Vera had a harsh voice and Rosa had a scowl. It wasn't her fault though, it was just the way her face was made. She was older than the other two.

'Can I help?' I would ask our Marthas. Then they would give me scraps of bread dough to play with, and I would make a man out of dough, and they would bake it in the oven with whatever else they were baking. I always made dough men, I never made dough women, because after they were baked I would eat them, and that made me feel I had a secret power over men. It was becoming clear to me that, despite the urges Aunt Vidala said I aroused in them, I had no power over them otherwise.

'Can I make the bread from scratch?' I asked one day when Zilla was getting out the bowl to start mixing. I'd watched them do it so often that I was convinced I knew how.

'You don't need to bother with that,' said Rosa, scowling more than usual.

'Why?' I said.

Vera laughed her harsh laugh. 'You'll have Marthas to do all of that for you,' she said. 'Once they've picked out a nice fat husband for you.'

'He won't be fat.' I didn't want a fat husband.

'Of course not. It's just an expression,' said Zilla.

'You won't have to do the shopping either,' said Rosa. 'Your Martha will do that. Or else a Handmaid, supposing you need one.'

'She may not need one,' said Vera. 'Considering who her mother — '

'Don't say that,' said Zilla.

'What?' I said. 'What about my mother?' I knew there was a secret about my mother — it had to do with the way they said *resting* — and it frightened me.

24

'Just that your mother could have her own baby,' said Zilla soothingly, 'so I'm sure you can too. You'd like to have a baby, wouldn't you, dear?'

'Yes,' I said, 'but I don't want a husband. I think they're disgusting.' The three of them laughed.

'Not all of them,' said Zilla. 'Your father is a husband.' There was nothing I could say about that.

'They'll make sure it's a nice one,' said Rosa. 'It won't be just any old husband.'

'They have their pride to keep up,' said Vera. 'They won't marry you down, that's for sure.'

I didn't want to think about husbands any longer. 'But what if I want to?' I said. 'Make the bread?' My feelings were hurt: it was as if they were closing a circle around themselves, keeping me out. 'What if I want to make the bread myself?'

'Well, of course, your Marthas would have to let you do that,' said Zilla. 'You'd be the mistress of the household. But they'd look down on you for it. And they'd feel you were taking their rightful positions away from them. The things they know best how to do. You wouldn't want them to feel that about you, would you, dear?'

'Your husband wouldn't like it either,' said Vera with another of her harsh laughs. 'It's bad for the hands. Look at mine!' She held them out: her fingers were knobby, the skin was rough, the nails short, with ragged cuticles — not at all like my mother's slender and elegant hands, with their magic ring. 'Rough work — it's all bad for

25

the hands. He won't want you smelling of bread dough.'

'Or bleach,' said Rosa. 'From scrubbing.'

'He'll want you to stick to the embroidery and such,' said Vera.

'The petit point,' said Rosa. There was derision in her voice.

Embroidery was not my strong suit. I was always being criticized for loose and sloppy stitches. 'I hate petit point. I want to make bread.'

'We can't always do what we want,' said Zilla gently. 'Even you.'

'And sometimes we have to do what we hate,' said Vera. 'Even you.'

'Don't let me, then!' I said. 'You're being mean!' And I ran out of the kitchen.

By this time I was crying. Although I'd been told not to disturb my mother, I crept upstairs and into her room. She was under her lovely white coverlet with blue flowers. Her eyes were closed but she must have heard me because she opened them. Every time I saw her, those eyes looked larger and more luminous.

'What is it, my pet?' she said.

I crawled under the coverlet and snuggled up against her. She was very warm.

'It's not fair,' I sobbed. 'I don't want to get married! Why do I have to?'

She didn't say *Because it's your duty*, the way Aunt Vidala would have, or *You'll want to when the time comes*, which was what Aunt Estée would say She didn't say anything at first. Instead she hugged me and stroked my hair.

26

'Remember how I chose you,' she said, 'out of all the others.'

But I was old enough now to disbelieve the choosing story: the locked castle, the magic ring, the wicked witches, the running away 'That's only a fairy tale,' I said. 'I came out of your stomach, just like other babies.' She did not affirm this. She said nothing. For some reason this was frightening to me.

'I did! Didn't I?' I asked. 'Shunammite told me. At school. About stomachs.'

My mother hugged me tighter. 'Whatever happens,' she said after a while, 'I want you to always remember that I have loved you very much.'

5

You have probably guessed what I am going to tell you next, and it is not at all happy.

My mother was dying. Everyone knew, except me.

I found out from Shunammite, who said she was my best friend. We weren't supposed to have best friends. It wasn't nice to form closed circles, said Aunt Estée: it made other girls feel left out, and we should all be helping one another be the most perfect girls we could be.

Aunt Vidala said that best friends led to whispering and plotting and keeping secrets, and plotting and secrets led to disobedience to God, and disobedience led to rebellion, and girls who were rebellious became women who were rebellious, and a rebellious woman was even worse than a rebellious man because rebellious men became traitors, but rebellious women became adulteresses.

Then Becka spoke up in her mouse voice and asked, What is an adulteress? We girls were all surprised because Becka so seldom asked any questions. Her father was not a Commander like our fathers. He was only a dentist: the very best dentist, and our families all went to him, which was why Becka was allowed into our school. But it did mean the other girls looked down on her and expected her to defer to them.

Becka was sitting beside me — she always tried to sit beside me if Shunammite did not shoulder her away — and I could feel her trembling. I was afraid that Aunt Vidala would punish her for being impertinent, but it would have been hard for anyone, even Aunt Vidala, to accuse her of impertinence.

Shunammite whispered across me at Becka: *Don't be so stupid!* Aunt Vidala smiled, as much as she ever did, and said she hoped Becka would never find that out through personal experience, since those who did become adulteresses would end up being stoned or else hanged by their neck with a sack over their heads. Aunt Estée said there was no need to frighten the girls unduly; and then she smiled and said that we were precious flowers, and who ever heard of a rebellious flower?

We looked at her, making our eyes as round as possible as a sign of our innocence, and nodding to show we agreed with her. No rebellious flowers here!

★   ★   ★

Shunammite's house had just one Martha and mine had three, so my father was more important than hers. I realize now that this was why she wanted me as her best friend. She was a stubby girl with two long thick braids that I envied, since my own braids were skinny and shorter, and black eyebrows that made her look

29

more grown up than she was. She was belligerent, but only behind the Aunts' backs. In the disputes between us, she always had to be right. If you contradicted her, she would only repeat her first opinion, except louder. She was rude to many other girls, especially Becka, and I am ashamed to tell you that I was too weak to overrule her. I had a weak character when dealing with girls my own age, though at home the Marthas would say I was headstrong.

'Your mother's dying, isn't she?' Shunammite whispered to me one lunchtime.

'No she's not,' I whispered back. 'She just has a condition!' That was what the Marthas called it: *your mother's condition*. Her condition was what caused her to rest so much, and to cough. Lately our Marthas had been taking trays up to her room; the trays would come back down with hardly anything eaten from the plates.

I wasn't allowed to visit her much anymore. When I did, her room would be in semi-darkness. It no longer smelled like her, a light, sweet smell like the lily-flowered hostas in our garden, but as if some stale and dirtied stranger had crept in and was hiding under the bed.

I would sit beside my mother where she lay huddled under her blue-flower-embroidered bedspread and hold her thin left hand with the magic ring on it and ask when her condition would be gone, and she would say she was praying for her pain to be over soon. That would reassure me: it meant she would get better. Then she would ask me if I was being good, and if I was happy, and I would always say yes, and she would squeeze my hand and ask me to pray with her, and we would sing the song about the angels standing around her bed. And she would say thank you, and that was enough for today.

'She really is dying,' Shunammite whispered. 'That's what her condition is. It's dying!'

'That's not true,' I whispered too loudly. 'She's getting better. Her pain will be over soon. She prayed for it.'

'Girls,' said Aunt Estée. 'At lunchtime our mouths are for eating, and we can't talk and chew at the same time. Aren't we lucky to have such lovely food?' It was egg sandwiches, which ordinarily I liked. But right then the smell of them was making me feel sick.

'I heard it from my Martha,' Shunammite whispered when Aunt Estée's attention was elsewhere. 'And your Martha told her. So it's true.'

'Which one?' I said. I couldn't believe any of our Marthas would be so disloyal as to pretend that my mother was dying — not even scowling Rosa.

'How should I know which one? They're all just Marthas,' said Shunammite, tossing her long thick braids.

★   ★   ★

That afternoon when our Guardian had driven me home from school, I went into the kitchen. Zilla was rolling pie dough; Vera was cutting up a chicken. There was a soup pot simmering on the back of the stove: the extra chicken parts would

31

go into it, and any vegetable scraps and bones. Our Marthas were very efficient with food, and did not waste supplies.

Rosa was over at the large double sink rinsing off dishes. We had a dishwasher, but the Marthas didn't use it except after Commanders' dinners at our house because it took too much electricity, said Vera, and there were shortages because of the war. Sometimes the Marthas called it the watched-pot war because it never boiled, or else the Ezekiel's Wheel war because it rolled around without getting anywhere; but they only said such things among themselves.

'Shunammite said one of you told her Martha that my mother is dying,' I blurted out. 'Who said that? It's a lie!'

All three of them stopped doing what they were doing. It was as if I'd waved a wand and frozen them: Zilla with the lifted rolling pin, Vera with a cleaver in one hand and a long pale chicken neck in the other, Rosa with a platter and a dishcloth. Then they looked at one another.

'We thought you knew,' Zilla said gently. 'We thought your mother would have told you.'

'Or your father,' said Vera. That was silly, because when could he have done that? He was hardly ever at our house nowadays, and when he was, he was either eating dinner by himself in the dining room or shut inside his study doing important things.

'We're very sorry,' said Rosa. 'Your mother is a good woman.'

'A model Wife,' said Vera. 'She has endured

her suffering without complaint.' By this time I was slumped over at the kitchen table, crying into my hands.

'We must all bear the afflictions that are sent to test us,' said Zilla. 'We must continue to hope.'

Hope for what? I thought. What was there left to hope for? All I could see in front of me was loss and darkness.

★ ★ ★

My mother died two nights later, though I didn't find out until the morning. I was angry with her for being mortally ill and not telling me — though she had told me, in a way: she had prayed for her pain to be over soon, and her prayer was answered.

Once I'd finished being angry, I felt as if a piece of me had been cut off — a piece of my heart, which was surely now dead as well. I hoped that the four angels round her bed were real after all, and that they had watched over her, and that they had carried her soul away, just as in the song. I tried to picture them lifting her up and up, into a golden cloud. But I could not really believe it.

III

Hymn

The Ardua Hall Holograph

6

Readying myself for bed last night, I unpinned my hair, what is left of it. In one of my bracing homilies to our Aunts some years ago, I preached against vanity, which creeps in despite our strictures against it. 'Life is not about hair,' I said then, only half jocularly. Which is true, but it is also true that hair is about life. It is the flame of the body's candle, and as it dwindles the body shrinks and melts away. I once had enough hair for a topknot, in the days of topknots; for a bun, in the age of buns. But now my hair is like our meals here at Ardua Hall: sparse and short. The flame of my life is subsiding, more slowly than some of those around me might like, but faster than they may realize.

I regarded my reflection. The inventor of the mirror did few of us any favours: we must have been happier before we knew what we looked like. It could be worse, I told myself: my face betrays no signs of weakness. It retains its leathery texture, its character-bestowing mole on the chin, its etching of familiar lines. I was never frivolously pretty, but I was once handsome: that can no longer be said. *Imposing* is the best that might be ventured.

How will I end? I wondered. Will I live to a

gently neglected old age, ossifying by degrees? Will I become my own honoured statue? Or will the regime and I both topple and my stone replica along with me, to be dragged away and sold off as a curiosity, a lawn ornament, a chunk of gruesome kitsch?

Or will I be put on trial as a monster, then executed by firing squad and dangled from a lamppost for public viewing? Will I be torn apart by a mob and have my head stuck on a pole and paraded through the streets to merriment and jeers? I have inspired sufficient rage for that.

Right now I still have some choice in the matter. Not whether to die, but when and how. Isn't that freedom of a sort?

Oh, and who to take down with me. I have made my list.

★   ★   ★

I am well aware of how you must be judging me, my reader; if, that is, my reputation has preceded me and you have deciphered who I am, or was.

In my own present day I am a legend, alive but more than alive, dead but more than dead. I'm a framed head that hangs at the backs of classrooms, of the girls exalted enough to have classrooms: grimly smiling, silently admonishing. I'm a bugaboo used by the Marthas to frighten small children — *If you don't behave yourself, Aunt Lydia will come and get you!* I'm also a model of moral perfection to be emulated — *What would Aunt Lydia want you to do?* — and a judge and arbiter in the misty inquisition of the imagination — *What would Aunt Lydia have to say about that?*

I've become swollen with power, true, but also nebulous with it — formless, shape-shifting. I am everywhere and nowhere: even in the minds of the Commanders I cast an unsettling shadow. How can I regain myself? How to shrink back to my normal size, the size of an ordinary woman?

But perhaps it is too late for that. You take the first step, and to save yourself from the consequences, you take the next one. In times like ours, there are only two directions: up or plummet.

⋆　⋆　⋆

Today was the first full moon after March 21. Elsewhere in the world, lambs are being slaughtered and eaten; Easter eggs, too, are consumed, for reasons having to do with Neolithic fertility goddesses nobody chooses to remember.

Here at Ardua Hall we skip the lamb flesh but have kept the eggs. As a special treat I allow them to be dyed: baby pink and baby blue. You have no idea what delight this brings to the Aunts and Supplicants assembled in the Refectory for supper! Our diet is monotonous and a little variation is welcome, even if only a variation in colour.

After the bowls of pastel eggs had been brought in and admired but before our meagre feast began, I led the usual Prayer of Grace — *Bless this food to our service and keep us on the Path, May the Lord open* — and then the special Spring Equinox Grace:

As the year unfolds into spring, may our
hearts unfold; bless our daughters, bless
our Wives, bless our Aunts and Suppli-
cants, bless our Pearl Girls in their mission
work beyond our borders, and may
Fatherly Grace be poured out upon our
fallen Handmaid sisters and redeem them
through the sacrifice of their bodies and
their labour according to His will.

And bless Baby Nicole, stolen away by
her treacherous Handmaid mother and
hidden by the godless in Canada; and bless
all the innocents she represents, doomed to
be raised by the depraved. Our thoughts
and prayers are with them. May our Baby
Nicole be restored to us, we pray; may
Grace return her.

Per Ardua Cum Estrus. Amen.

It pleases me to have concocted such a slippery
motto. Is *Ardua* 'difficulty' or 'female progenitive
labour'? Does *Estrus* have to do with hormones
or with pagan rites of spring? The denizens of
Ardua Hall neither know nor care. They are
repeating the right words in the right order, and
thus are safe.

Then there is Baby Nicole. As I prayed for
her return, all eyes were focused on her picture
hanging on the wall behind me. So useful, Baby
Nicole: she whips up the faithful, she inspires
hatred against our enemies, she bears witness to
the possibility of betrayal within Gilead and to
the deviousness and cunning of the Handmaids,
who can never be trusted. Nor is her usefulness

40

at an end, I reflected: in my hands — should she end up there — Baby Nicole would have a brilliant future.

Such were my thoughts during the closing hymn, sung in harmony by a trio of our young Supplicants. Their voices were pure and clear, and the rest of us listened with rapt attention. Despite what you may have thought, my reader, there was beauty to be had in Gilead. Why would we not have wished for it? We were human after all.

I see that I have spoken of us in the past tense.

The music was an old psalm melody, but the words were ours:

Under His Eye our beams of truth shine out,
We see all sin;
We shall observe you at your goings-out,
Your comings-in.
From every heart we wrench the secret vice,
In prayers and tears decree the sacrifice.

Sworn to obey, obedience we command,
We shall not swerve!
To duties harsh, we lend a willing hand,
We pledge to serve.
All idle thoughts, all pleasures we must quell,
Self we renounce, in selflessness we dwell.

Banal and without charm, those words: I can say that, since I wrote them myself. But such hymns are not meant to be poetry. They are meant simply to remind those singing them of the high price they would pay for deviation from the set path. We are not forgiving towards one another's lapses, here at Ardua Hall.

After the singing, the festal munching began. I noted that Aunt Elizabeth took one more egg than was her share and that Aunt Helena took one fewer, making sure that everyone noticed it. As for Aunt Vidala, snuffling into her serviette, I saw her red-rimmed eyes flicking from one of them to the other, and then to me. What is she planning? Which way will the cat jump?

⋆ ⋆ ⋆

After our little celebration, I made my nocturnal pilgrimage to the Hildegard Library at the far end of the Hall, along the silent moonlit walk and past my shadowy statue. I entered, I greeted the night librarian, I traversed the General section, where three of our Supplicants were grappling with their recently acquired literacy. I walked through the Reading Room, for which a higher authorization is required and where the Bibles brood in the darkness of their locked boxes, glowing with arcane energy.

Then I opened a locked door and threaded my way through the Bloodlines Genealogical Archives with their classified files. It's essential to record who is related to whom, both officially and in fact: due to the Handmaid system, a couple's child may not be biologically related to the elite mother or even to the official father, for a desperate Handmaid is likely to seek impregnation however she may. It is our business to inform ourselves, since incest must be prevented: there are enough Unbabies already. It is also the business of Ardua

Hall to guard that knowledge jealously: the Archives are the beating heart of Ardua Hall.

Finally I reached my inner sanctum, deep in the Forbidden World Literature section. On my private shelves I've arranged my personal selection of proscribed books, off-limits to the lower ranks. *Jane Eyre*, *Anna Karenina*, *Tess of the d'Urbervilles*, *Paradise Lost*, Lives of Girls and Women — what a moral panic each one of them would cause if set loose among the Supplicants! Here I also keep another set of files, accessible only to a very few; I think of them as the secret histories of Gilead. All that festers is not gold, but it can be made profitable in non-monetary ways: knowledge is power, especially discreditable knowledge. I am not the first person to have recognized this, or to have capitalized on it when possible: every intelligence agency in the world has always known it.

★ ★ ★

Once sequestered, I took my nascent manuscript out of its hiding place, a hollow rectangle cut inside one of our X-rated books: Cardinal Newman's *Apologia Pro Vita Sua: A Defence of One's Life*. No one reads that weighty tome anymore, Catholicism being considered heretical and next door to voodoo, so no one is likely to peer within. Though if someone does, it will be a bullet in the head for me; a premature bullet, for I am far from ready to depart. If and when I do, I plan to go out with a far bigger bang than that.

I have chosen my title advisedly, for what else

am I doing here but defending my life? The life I have led. The life — I've told myself — I had no choice but to lead. Once, before the advent of the present regime, I gave no thought to a defence of my life. I didn't think it was necessary. I was a family court judge, a position I'd gained through decades of hardscrabble work and arduous professional climbing, and I had been performing that function as equitably as I could. I'd acted for the betterment of the world as I saw that betterment, within the practical limits of my profession. I'd contributed to charities, I'd voted in elections both federal and municipal, I'd held worthy opinions. I'd assumed I was living virtuously; I'd assumed my virtue would be moderately applauded.

Though I realized how very wrong I had been about this, and about many other things, on the day I was arrested.

IV

THE CLOTHES HOUND

Transcript of Witness Testimony 369B

7

They say I will always have the scar, but I'm almost better; so yes, I think I'm strong enough to do this now. You've said that you'd like me to tell you how I got involved in this whole story, so I'll try; though it's hard to know where to begin.

I'll start just before my birthday, or what I used to believe was my birthday. Neil and Melanie lied to me about that: they'd done it for the best of reasons and they'd meant really well, but when I first found out about it I was very angry at them. Keeping up my anger was difficult, though, because by that time they were dead. You can be angry at dead people, but you can never have a conversation about what they did; or you can only have one side of it. And I felt guilty as well as angry, because they'd been murdered, and I believed then that their murder was my fault.

I was supposed to be turning sixteen. What I was most looking forward to was getting my driver's licence. I felt too old for a birthday party, though Melanie always got me a cake and ice cream and sang 'Daisy, Daisy, give me your answer true,' an old song I'd loved as a child and was now finding embarrassing. I did get the cake, later — chocolate cake, vanilla ice cream, my favourites — but by then I couldn't eat it. By that time Melanie was no longer there.

That birthday was the day I discovered that I was a fraud. Or not a fraud, like a bad magician: a fake, like a fake antique. I was a forgery, done on purpose. I was so young at that moment — just a split second ago, it seems — but I'm not young anymore. How little time it takes to change a face: carve it like wood, harden it. No more of that wide-eyed daydream gazing I used to do. I've become sharper, more focused. I've become narrowed.

★   ★   ★

Neil and Melanie were my parents; they ran a store called The Clothes Hound. It was basically used clothing: Melanie called it 'previously loved' because she said 'used' meant 'exploited.' The sign outside showed a smiling pink poodle in a fluffy skirt with a pink bow on its head, carrying a shopping bag. Underneath was a slogan in italics and quotation marks: *'You'd Never Know!'* That meant the used clothes were so good you'd never know they were used, but that wasn't true at all because most of the clothes were crappy.

Melanie said she'd inherited The Clothes Hound from her grandmother. She also said she knew the sign was old-fashioned, but people were familiar with it and it would be disrespectful to change it now.

Our store was on Queen West, in a stretch of blocks that had once all been like that, said

Melanie — textiles, buttons and trims, cheap linens, dollar stores. But now it was going upmarket: cafés with fair trade and organic were moving in, big-brand outlets, name boutiques. In response, Melanie hung a sign in the window: *Wearable Art*. But inside, the store was crowded with all kinds of clothes you would never call wearable art. There was one corner that was kind of designer, though anything really pricey wouldn't be in The Clothes Hound in the first place. The rest was just everything. And all sorts of people came and went: young, old, looking for bargains or finds, or just looking. Or selling: even street people would try to get a few dollars for T-shirts they'd picked up at garage sales.

Melanie worked on the main floor. She wore bright colours, like orange and hot pink, because she said they created a positive and energetic atmosphere, and anyway she was part gypsy at heart. She was always brisk and smiling, though on the lookout for shoplifting. After closing, she sorted and packed: this for charity, this for rags, this for Wearable Art. While doing the sorting she'd sing tunes from musicals — old ones from long ago. 'Oh what a beautiful morning' was one of her favourites, and 'When you walk through a storm.' I would get irritated by her singing; I'm sorry about that now.

Sometimes she'd get overwhelmed: there was too much fabric, it was like the ocean, waves of cloth coming in and threatening to drown her. Cashmere! Who was going to buy thirty-year-old cashmere? It didn't improve with age, she would say — not like her.

Neil had a beard that was going grey and wasn't always trimmed, and he didn't have much hair. He didn't look like a businessman, but he handled what they called 'the money end': the invoices, the accounting, the taxes. He had his office on the second floor, up a flight of rubber-treaded stairs. He had a computer and a filing cabinet and a safe, but otherwise that room wasn't much like an office: it was just as crowded and cluttered as the store because Neil liked to collect things. Wind-up music boxes, he had a number of those. Clocks, a lot of different clocks. Old adding machines that worked with a handle. Plastic toys that walked or hopped across the floor, such as bears and frogs and sets of false teeth. A slide projector for the kind of coloured slides that nobody had anymore. Cameras — he liked ancient cameras. Some of them could take better pictures than anything nowadays, he'd say. He had one whole shelf with nothing on it but cameras.

One time he left the safe open and I looked inside. Instead of the wads of money I'd been expecting, there was nothing in it but a tiny metal-and-glass thing that I thought must be another toy like the hopping false teeth. But I couldn't see where to wind it up, and I was afraid to touch it because it was old.

'Can I play with it?' I asked Neil.

'Play with what?'

'That toy in the safe.'

'Not today,' he said, smiling. 'Maybe when you're older.' Then he shut the safe door, and I forgot about the strange little toy until it was time for me to remember it, and to understand what it was.

Neil would try to repair the various items, though often he failed because he couldn't find the parts. Then the things would just sit there, 'collecting dust,' said Melanie. Neil hated throwing anything out.

On the walls he had some old posters: LOOSE LIPS SINK SHIPS, from a long-ago war; a woman in overalls flexing her biceps to show that women could make bombs — that was from the same olden-days war; and a red-and-black one showing a man and a flag that Neil said was from Russia before it was Russia. Those had belonged to his great-grandfather, who'd lived in Winnipeg. I knew nothing about Winnipeg except that it was cold.

I loved The Clothes Hound when I was little: it was like a cave full of treasures. I wasn't supposed to be in Neil's office by myself because I might 'touch things,' and then I might break them. But I could play with the wind-up toys and the music boxes and the adding machines, under supervision. Not the cameras though, because they were too valuable, said Neil, and anyway there was no film in them, so what would be the point?

We didn't live over the store. Our house was a long distance away, in one of those residential neighbourhoods where there were some old bungalows and also some newer, bigger houses that had been built where the bungalows had been torn down. Our house was not a bungalow — it had a second floor, where the bedrooms

51

were — but it was not a new house either. It was made of yellow brick, and it was very ordinary. There was nothing about it that would make you look at it twice. Thinking back, I'm guessing that was their idea.

8

I was in The Clothes Hound quite a lot on
Saturdays and Sundays because Melanie didn't
want me to be in our house by myself. Why not?
I began to ask when I was twelve. Because what
if there was a fire, said Melanie. Anyway, leaving
a child in a house alone was against the law.
Then I would argue that I was not a child, and
she would sigh and say I didn't really know what
was and was not a child, and children were a big
responsibility, and I would understand later.
Then she'd say I was giving her a headache, and
we would get into her car and go to the store.

I was allowed to help in the store — sorting
T-shirts by size, sticking the prices on them,
setting aside those that needed to be either cleaned
or discarded. I liked doing that: I sat at a table in
the back corner, surrounded by the faint smell of
mothballs, watching the people who came in.

They weren't all customers. Some of them
were street people who wanted to use our staff
washroom. Melanie let them do it as long as she
knew them, especially in winter. There was one
older man who came in quite frequently. He
wore tweed overcoats that he got from Melanie
and knitted vests. By the time I was thirteen, I
was finding him creepy, since we'd done a

module on pedophiles at school. His name was George.

'You shouldn't let George use the washroom,' I said to Melanie. 'He's a perv.'

'Daisy, that's unkind,' said Melanie. 'What makes you think so?' We were at our house, in the kitchen.

'He just is. He's always hanging around. He's bothering people for money right outside the store. Plus, he's stalking you.' I might have said he was stalking me, which would have caused serious alarm, but that wasn't true. George never paid any attention to me.

Melanie laughed and said, 'No he isn't.' I decided she was naive. I was the age at which parents suddenly transform from people who know everything into people who know nothing.

★   ★   ★

There was another person who was in and out of the store quite a lot, but she wasn't a street person. I guessed she was forty, or maybe closer to fifty: I couldn't tell with older people. She usually had on a black leather jacket, black jeans, and heavy boots; she kept her long dark hair pulled back, and she didn't wear makeup. She looked like a biker, but not a real biker — more like an ad of a biker. She wasn't a customer — she came in through the back door to pick up clothes for charity. Melanie said the two of them were old friends so when Ada asked, it was difficult to say no. Anyway Melanie claimed that she only gave Ada items that would be hard to sell, and it was good that people would get some use out of them.

Ada didn't look to me like the charitable type. She wasn't soft and smiling, she was angular, and when she walked she strode. She never stayed long, and she never left without a couple of cardboard boxes of castoffs, which she stowed in whatever car she'd parked in the alleyway behind the store. I could see these cars from where I sat. They were never the same.

⋆   ⋆   ⋆

There was a third kind of person who came into The Clothes Hound without buying anything. These were the young women in long silvery dresses and white hats who called themselves Pearl Girls and said they were missionaries doing God's work for Gilead. They were a lot creepier than George. They worked the downtown, talking to street people and going into shops and making pests of themselves. Some people were rude to them, but Melanie never was because she said it served no purpose.

They always appeared in twos. They had white pearl necklaces and smiled a lot, but not real smiling. They would offer Melanie their printed brochures with pictures of tidy streets, happy children, and sunrises, and titles that were supposed to lure you to Gilead: 'Fallen? God Can Still Forgive You!' 'Homeless? There Is a Home for You in Gilead.'

There was always at least one brochure about Baby Nicole. 'Give Back Baby Nicole!' 'Baby

Nicole Belongs in Gilead!' We'd been shown a documentary about Baby Nicole at school: her mother was a Handmaid, and she'd smuggled Baby Nicole out of Gilead. Baby Nicole's father was a top-brass super-nasty Gilead Commander, so there had been a huge uproar, and Gilead had demanded her return, so she could be reunited with her legal parents. Canada had dragged its feet and then caved in and said they would make every effort, but by that time Baby Nicole had disappeared and had never been found.

Now Baby Nicole was the poster child for Gilead. On every Pearl Girls brochure there was the same picture of her. She looked like a baby, nothing special, but she was practically a saint in Gilead, said our teacher. She was an icon for us too: every time there was an anti-Gilead protest in Canada, there would be the picture, and slogans like BABY NICOLE! SYMBOL OF FREE-DOM! Or BABY NICOLE! LEADING THE WAY! As if a baby could lead the way on anything, I would think to myself.

I'd basically disliked Baby Nicole since I'd had to do a paper on her. I'd got a C because I'd said she was being used as a football by both sides, and it would be the greatest happiness of the greatest number just to give her back. The teacher had said I was callous and should learn to respect other people's rights and feelings, and I'd said people in Gilead were people, and shouldn't their rights and feelings be respected too? She'd lost her temper and said I needed to grow up, which was maybe true: I'd been aggravating on pur-pose. But I was angry about the C.

Every time the Pearl Girls came, Melanie would accept the brochures and promise to keep a pile of them at point of sale. Sometimes she would even give some of the old brochures back to them: they collected the leftover ones for use in other countries.

'Why do you do that?' I asked her when I was fourteen and taking a greater interest in politics. 'Neil says we're atheists. You're just encouraging them.' We'd had three modules in school on Gilead: it was a terrible, terrible place, where women couldn't have jobs or drive cars, and where the Handmaids were forced to get pregnant like cows, except that cows had a better deal. What sort of people could be on the side of Gilead and not be some kind of monsters? Especially female people. 'Why don't you tell them they're evil?'

'There's no point arguing with them,' said Melanie. 'They're fanatics.'

'Then I'll tell them.' I thought I knew what was wrong with people then, especially adult people. I thought I could set them straight. The Pearl Girls were older than me, it isn't as if they were children: how could they believe all that crap?

'No,' said Melanie quite sharply. 'Stay in the back. I don't want you talking to them.'

'Why not? I can deal — '

'They try to con girls your age into going to Gilead with them. They'll say the Pearl Girls are helping women and girls. They'll appeal to your idealism.'

'I would never fall for that!' I said indignantly. 'I'm not fucking brain-dead.' I didn't usually swear around Melanie and Neil, but sometimes those words just slipped out.

'Watch the potty mouth,' said Melanie. 'It makes a bad impression.'

'Sorry. But I'm not.'

'Of course not,' said Melanie. 'But just leave them alone. If I take the brochures, they go away.'

'Are their pearls real?'

'Fake,' said Melanie. 'Everything about them is fake.'

9

Despite all that she did for me, Melanie had a distant smell. She smelled like a floral guest soap in a strange house I was visiting. What I mean is, she didn't smell to me like my mother.

One of my favourite books at the school library when I was younger was about a man who got himself into a wolf pack. This man could never take a bath because the wolf pack scent would wash off and then the wolves would reject him. With Melanie and me, it was more like we needed to add on that layer of pack-scent, the thing that would tag us as us — us-together. But that never happened. We were never very snuggly.

Also, Neil and Melanie weren't like the parents of the kids I knew. They were too careful around me, as if I was breakable. It was like I was a prize cat they were cat-sitting: you'd take your own cat for granted, you'd be casual about it, but someone else's cat would be another story because if you lost that cat you would feel guilty about it in a completely different way.

Another thing: the kids from school had pictures of themselves — a lot of pictures. Their parents documented every minute of their lives. Some of the kids even had photos of themselves being born, which they'd brought to Show and Tell. I used to think that was gross — blood and great big legs, with a little head coming out from between them. And they had baby pictures of themselves, hundreds of them. These kids could hardly burp without some adult pointing a camera at them and telling them to do it again — as if they lived their lives twice, once in reality and the second time for the photo.

That didn't happen to me. Neil's collection of antique cameras was cool, but cameras that actually worked were non-existent in our house. Melanie told me that all the early pictures of me had been burnt up in a fire. Only an idiot would have believed this, so I did.

★　★　★

Now I'm going to tell you about the stupid thing I did, and the consequences of it. I'm not proud of how I behaved: looking back, I realize how dumb it was. But I couldn't see that at the time.

A week before my birthday, there was going to be a protest march about Gilead. Footage of a new batch of executions had been smuggled out of Gilead and broadcast on the news: women being hanged for heresy and apostasy and also for trying to take babies out of Gilead, which was treason under their laws. The two oldest grades in our school had been given time off so we could go to the protest as part of World Social Awareness.

We'd made signs: NO TRADE WITH GILEAD! JUSTICE FOR GILIBAD WOMEN! BABY NICOLE,

GUIDING STAR! Some kids had added green signs: GILEAD, CLIMATE SCIENCE DE-LIAR! GILEAD WANTS US TO FRY!, with pictures of forest fires and dead birds and fish and people. Several teachers and some volunteer parents were going to come with us to make sure nothing violent happened to us. I was excited because it would be my first-ever protest march. But then Neil and Melanie said I couldn't go.

'Why not?' I said. 'Everyone else is going!'

'Absolutely not,' said Neil.

'You're always saying how we should defend our principles,' I said.

'This is different. It's not safe, Daisy,' said Neil.

'Life isn't safe, you say that yourself. Anyway lots of teachers are coming. And it's part of school — if I don't go, I'll lose marks!' This last part wasn't exactly true, but Neil and Melanie liked me to have good grades.

'Maybe she could go,' said Melanie. 'If we ask Ada to go with her?'

'I'm not a baby, I don't need a babysitter,' I said.

'Are you hallucinating?' Neil said to Melanie. 'That thing will be crawling with press! It'll be on the news!' He was tugging at his hair, what was left of it — a sign that he was worried.

'That is the *point*,' I said. I'd made one of the posters we'd be carrying — big red letters and a black skull. GILEAD=DEATH OF THE MIND. 'The whole idea is to be on the news!'

Melanie put her hands over her ears. 'I'm getting a headache. Neil is right. No. I'm saying

61

no. You will spend the afternoon at the store helping me out, period.'

'Fine, lock me up,' I said. I stomped off to my room and slammed the door. They couldn't make me.

★ ★ ★

The school I went to was called the Wyle School. It was named after Florence Wyle, a sculptor of olden times whose picture was in the main entrance hall. The school was supposed to encourage creativity, said Melanie, and understanding democratic freedom and thinking for yourself, said Neil. They said that was why they'd sent me there, though they didn't agree with private schools in general; but the standards of the public schools were so low, and of course we should all work to improve the system, but meanwhile they did not want me getting knifed by some junior drug pusher. I think now they chose the Wyle School for another reason. Wyle took strict attendance: it was impossible to skip school. So Melanie and Neil could always know where I was.

I didn't love the Wyle School, but I didn't hate it either. It was something to get through on my way to real life, the shape of which would become clear to me soon. Not long before, I'd wanted to be a small-animal vet, but that dream came to seem childish to me. After that I'd decided to be a surgeon, but then I saw a video of a surgery at school and it made me nauseous. Some of the other Wyle School students wanted

62

to be singers or designers or other creative things, but I was too tone-deaf and clunky for that.

I had some friends at school: gossiping friends, girls; homework-trading friends, some of each. I made sure that my marks were stupider than I was — I didn't want to stand out — so my own homework didn't have a high trading value. Gym and sports, though — it was all right to be good at those, and I was, especially any sports favouring height and speed, such as basketball. That made me popular when it came to teams. But outside of school I led a constricted life, since Neil and Melanie were so jumpy. I wasn't allowed to stroll around in shopping malls because they were infested by crack addicts, said Melanie, or hang out in parks, said Neil, because of the strange men lurking there. So my social life was pretty much a zero: it consisted entirely of things I would be allowed to do when I was older. Neil's magic word in our house was *No*.

This time, though, I wasn't going to back down: I was going to that protest march no matter what. The school had hired a couple of buses to take us. Melanie and Neil had tried to head me off by phoning the principal and denying permission, and the principal had asked me to stay behind, and I'd assured her that of course I understood, no problem, and I would wait for Melanie to come and pick me up in her car. But it was only the bus driver checking off the kids' names and he didn't know who was who, and everyone was milling around, and the parents and teachers weren't paying attention

63

and didn't know I wasn't supposed to come, so I switched identity cards with a member of my basketball team who didn't want to go and made it onto the bus, feeling very pleased with myself.

10

The protest march was thrilling at first. It was downtown, near the Legislature Building, though it wasn't really a march because nobody marched anywhere, they were too jammed together. People made speeches. A Canadian relative of a woman who'd died in the Gilead Colonies cleaning up deadly radiation talked about slave labour. The leader of the Survivors of Gilead National Homelands Genocide told about the forced marches to North Dakota, where people had been crowded like sheep into fenced-in ghost towns with no food and water, and how thousands had died, and how people were risking their lives walking north to the Canadian border in winter, and he held up a hand with missing fingers and said, Frostbite.

Then a speaker from SanctuCare — the refugee organization for escaped Gilead women — spoke about those whose babies had been taken away from them, and how cruel that was, and how if you tried to get your baby back they would accuse you of disrespecting God. I couldn't hear all the speeches because sometimes the sound system cut out, but the meaning was clear enough. There were a lot of Baby Nicole posters: ALL GILEAD BABIES ARE BABY NICOLE!

Then our school group shouted things and held up our signs, and other people had different signs: DOWN WITH GILIBAD FASCISTS! SANCTUARY NOW! Right then some counter-marchers turned up with different signs: CLOSE THE BORDER! GILEAD KEEP YOUR OWN SLUTS AND BRATS, WE GOT ENOUGH HERE! STOP THE INVASION! HANDJOBS GO HOME! Among them there was a group of those Pearl Girls in their silvery dresses and pearls — with signs saying DEATH TO BABY STEALERS and GIVE BACK BABY NICOLE. People on our side were throwing eggs at them and cheering when one hit, but the Pearl Girls just kept smiling in their glassy way.

Scuffles broke out. A group of people dressed in black with their faces covered started smashing store windows. Suddenly there were a lot of police in riot gear. They seemed to come out of nowhere. They were banging their shields and moving forward, and hitting kids and other people with their batons.

Up to that time I'd been elated, but now I was scared. I wanted to get out of there, but it was so jam-packed I could hardly move. I couldn't find the rest of my class, and the crowd was panicking. People surged this way and that, screaming and shouting. Something hit me in the stomach: an elbow, I think. I was breathing fast and I could feel tears coming out of my eyes.

'This way,' said a gravelly voice behind me. It was Ada. She grabbed me by the collar and dragged me behind her. I'm not sure how she cleared a path: I'm guessing she kicked legs. Then we were in a street behind the riot, as they called it later on TV. When I saw the footage I thought, Now I know what it feels like to be in a riot: it feels like drowning. Not that I'd ever drowned.

'Melanie said you might be here,' said Ada. 'I'm taking you home.'

'No, but — ' I said. I didn't want to admit that I was scared.

'Right now. Toot sweet. No ifs and buts.'

★ ★ ★

I saw myself on the news that night: I was holding up a sign and shouting. I thought Neil and Melanie would be furious with me, but they weren't. Instead they were anxious. 'Why did you do that?' said Neil. 'Didn't you hear us?'

'You always said a person should stand up against injustice,' I said. 'The school says that too.' I knew I'd crossed a line, but I wasn't about to apologize.

'What's our next move?' said Melanie, not to me but to Neil. 'Daisy, could you get me a water? There's some ice in the fridge.'

'It might not be so bad,' said Neil.

'We can't take the chance,' I heard Melanie saying. 'We need to get moving, like yesterday. I'm calling Ada, she can arrange a van.'

'There's no fallback ready,' said Neil. 'We can't . . . '

I came back into the room with the glass of water. 'What's going on?' I said.

'Don't you have homework?' said Neil.

11

Three days later there was a break-in at The Clothes Hound. The store had an alarm, but the burglars were in and out before anyone could get there, which was the problem with alarms, said Melanie. They didn't find any money because Melanie never kept cash there, but they took some of the Wearable Art, and they trashed Neil's office — his files were scattered over the floor. They also took some of his collectibles — a few clocks and old cameras, an antique wind-up clown. They set a fire, but in an amateur way, said Neil, so the fire was quickly put out.

The police came around and asked if Neil and Melanie had any enemies. They said that no they didn't, and everything was okay — probably it was only some street people after drug money — but I could tell they were upset because they were talking in that way they had when they didn't want me to hear.

'They got the camera,' Neil was saying to Melanie as I was coming into the kitchen.

'What camera?' I said.

'Oh, just an old camera,' Neil said. More hair-tugging. 'A rare one, though.'

From then on, Neil and Melanie got more and more jittery. Neil ordered a new alarm system for the store. Melanie said we might be moving to a different house, but when I started asking questions she said it was just an idea. Neil said *No harm done* about the break-in. He said it several times, which left me wondering what sort of harm actually had been done, besides the disappearance of his favourite camera.

The night after the break-in, I found Melanie and Neil watching TV. They didn't usually really watch it — it was just always on — but this time they were intent. A Pearl Girl identified only as 'Aunt Adrianna' had been found dead in a condo that she and her Pearl Girls companion had rented. She'd been tied to a doorknob with her own silvery belt around her neck. She'd been dead for a number of days, said the forensic expert. It was another condo owner who'd detected the smell and alerted the police. The police said it was a suicide, self-strangulation in this manner being a common method.

There was a picture of the dead Pearl Girl. I studied it carefully: sometimes it was hard to tell Pearl Girls apart because of their outfits, but I remembered she'd been in The Clothes Hound recently, handing out brochures. So had her partner, identified as 'Aunt Sally,' who — said the news anchor — was nowhere to be found. There was a picture of her too: police were asking that sightings be reported. The Gilead Consulate had made no comment as yet.

'This is terrible,' said Neil to Melanie. 'The poor girl. What a catastrophe.'

'Why?' I said. 'The Pearl Girls work for Gilead. They hate us. Everyone knows that.'

They both looked at me then. What's the word for that look? *Desolate*, I think. I was baffled: why should they care?

★ ★ ★

The really bad thing happened on my birthday. The morning started as if things were normal. I got up, I put on my green plaid Wyle School uniform — did I say we had a uniform? I added my black lace-up shoes to my green-socked feet, pulled my hair back into the ponytail that was among the prescribed school looks — no dangling locks — and headed downstairs.

Melanie was in the kitchen, which had a granite island. What I would have liked instead was one of the resin-and-recycled tops like those in our school cafeteria — you could see down through the resin to the objects inside, which in one counter included a raccoon skeleton, so there was always something to focus on.

The kitchen island was where we ate most of our meals. We did have a living-dining area with a table. That was supposed to be for dinner parties, but Melanie and Neil didn't throw dinner parties; instead they threw meetings, which had to do with various causes of theirs. The night before, some people had come over: there were still several coffee cups on the table, and a plate with cracker crumbs and a few wizened grapes. I hadn't seen who these people were because I was upstairs in my room, avoiding the fallout from whatever it was I had done. That thing was evidently bigger than simple disobedience.

I went into the kitchen and sat down at the island. Melanie's back was to me; she was looking out the window. From that window you could see our yard — round cement planters with rosemary bushes in them, a patio with an outdoor table and chairs, and a corner of the street at the front.

'Morning,' I said. Melanie whipped around.

'Oh! Daisy!' she said. 'I didn't hear you! Happy birthday! Sweet sixteen!'

★ ★ ★

Neil didn't turn up for breakfast before it was time for me to leave for school. He was upstairs talking on his phone. I was slightly hurt, but not very: he was very absent-minded.

Melanie drove me, as she usually did: she didn't like me going to school by myself on the bus, even though the stop was right near our house. She said — as she always said — that she was on her way to The Clothes Hound and she might as well drop me off.

'Tonight we'll have your birthday cake, with ice cream,' she said, her voice rising at the end as if it was a question. 'I'll pick you up after school. There are some things Neil and I want to tell you, now that you're old enough.'

'Okay,' I said. I thought this was going to be about boys and what consent meant, which I'd heard enough about at school. It was bound to be awkward, but I would have to get through it.

I wanted to say I was sorry for having gone to

the protest march, but then we were at the school and I hadn't said it. I got out of the car silently; Melanie waited until I was at the entrance. I waved at her, and she waved back. I don't know why I did that — I didn't usually. I guess it was a sort of apology.

I don't remember that school day much, because why would I? It was normal. Normal is like looking out a car window. Things pass by, this and that and this and that, without much significance. You don't register such hours; they're habitual, like brushing your teeth.

A few of my homework friends sang 'Happy Birthday' to me in the cafeteria while we were having lunch. Some of the others clapped.

Then it was the afternoon. The air was stale, the clock slowed down. I sat in French class, where we were supposed to be reading a page from a novella by Colette — *Mitsou*, about a music-hall star hiding a couple of men in her wardrobe. As well as being French, it was supposed to be about how terrible life used to be for women, but Mitsou's life didn't seem so terrible to me. Hiding a handsome man in her closet — I wished I could do that. But even if I knew such a man, where could I stash him? Not in my own bedroom closet: Melanie would catch on right away, and if not, I'd have to feed him. I gave that some thought: What sort of food could I sneak without Melanie noticing? Cheese and crackers? Sex with him would be out of the question: it would be too risky to let him out of the closet, and there wasn't room for me to cram myself in there with him. This was the kind of daydreaming I often did in school: it passed the time.

Still, it was a problem in my life. I'd never gone out with anyone because I'd never met anyone I might want to go out with. There seemed to be no way that could happen. Boys from the Wyle School were not possible: I'd gone through grade school with them, I'd seen them pick their noses, and some of them had been pants-wetters. You can't feel romantic with those images in your mind.

By this time I was feeling glum, which is one of the effects a birthday can have: you're expecting a magic transformation but then it doesn't happen. To keep myself awake I pulled hairs out of my head, in behind my right ear, just two or three hairs at a time. I knew that if I pulled out that same hair too often I risked creating a bald spot, but I had only begun this habit a few weeks before.

Finally the time was up and I could go home. I walked along the polished hall towards the front door of the school and stepped outside. There was a light drizzle; I didn't have my raincoat. I scanned the street: Melanie wasn't waiting in her car.

All of a sudden Ada appeared beside me, in her black leather jacket. 'Come on. Let's get in the car,' she said.

'What?' I said. 'Why?'

'It's about Neil and Melanie.' I looked at her face, and I could tell: something really bad must have happened. If I'd been older I would've asked what it was right away, but I didn't because I wanted to postpone the moment when I would know what it was. In stories I'd read, I'd come across the words *nameless dread*. They'd just been words then, but now that's exactly what I felt.

Once we were in the car and she'd started driving, I said, 'Did someone have a heart attack?' It was all I could think of.

'No,' Ada said. 'Listen carefully and don't freak out on me. You can't go back to your house.'

The awful feeling in my stomach got worse. 'What is it? Was there a fire?'

'There's been an explosion,' she said. 'It was a car bomb. Outside The Clothes Hound.'

'Shit. Is the store wrecked?' I said. First the break-in, and now this.

'It was Melanie's car. She and Neil were both in it.'

I sat there for a minute without speaking; I couldn't make sense of this. What kind of maniac would want to kill Neil and Melanie? They were so ordinary.

'So they're dead?' I said finally. I was shivering. I tried to picture the explosion, but all I could see was a blank. A black square.

V

Van

The Ardua Hall Holograph

12

Who are you, my reader? And when are you? Perhaps tomorrow, perhaps fifty years from now, perhaps never.

Possibly you are one of our Aunts from Ardua Hall, stumbling across this account by chance. After a moment of horror at my sinfulness, will you burn these pages to preserve my pious image intact? Or will you succumb to the universal thirst for power and scuttle off to the Eyes to snitch on me?

Or will you be a snoop from outside our borders, rooting through the archives of Ardua Hall once this regime has fallen? In which case, the stash of incriminating documents I've been hoarding for so many years will have featured not only at my own trial — should fate prove malicious, and should I live to feature at such a trial — but at the trials of many others. I've made it my business to know where the bodies are buried.

★　★　★

By now you may be wondering how I've avoided being purged by those higher up — if not in the earlier days of Gilead, at least as it settled into its

77

dog-eat-dog maturity. By then a number of erstwhile notables had been hung on the Wall, since those on the topmost pinnacle took care that no ambitious challengers would displace them. You might assume that, being a woman, I would be especially vulnerable to this kind of winnowing, but you would be wrong. Simply by being female I was excluded from the lists of potential usurpers, since no woman could ever sit on the Council of the Commanders; so on that front, ironically, I was safe.

But there are three other reasons for my political longevity. First, the regime needs me. I control the women's side of their enterprise with an iron fist in a leather glove in a woollen mitten, and I keep things orderly: like a harem eunuch, I am uniquely placed to do so. Second, I know too much about the leaders — too much dirt — and they are uncertain as to what I may have done with it in the way of documentation. If they string me up, will that dirt somehow be leaked? They might well suspect I've taken backup precautions, and they would be right.

Third, I'm discreet. Each one of the top men has always felt that his secrets are safe with me; but — as I've made obliquely clear — only so long as I myself am safe. I have long been a believer in checks and balances.

Despite these security measures, I do not allow myself to be lulled. Gilead is a slippery place: accidents happen frequently. Someone has already written my funeral eulogy, it goes without saying. I shiver: whose feet are walking on my grave?

Time, I plead to the air, just a little more time. That's all I need.

⋆　⋆　⋆

Yesterday I received an unexpected invitation to a private meeting with Commander Judd. It's not the first such invitation I've received. Some of the earlier encounters were unpleasant; others, of a more recent date, have been mutually profitable.

As I set out across the swatch of feeble grass that covers the ground between Ardua Hall and the headquarters of the Eyes, and climbed — somewhat laboriously — the hillside of imposing white stairs that leads to the many-pillared main entrance, I was wondering which kind this meeting would prove to be. I must admit that my heart was beating faster than usual, and not only from the stairs: not everyone who has gone in through that particular doorway has come out again.

The Eyes hold sway in a former grand library. It now shelters no books but their own, the original contents having been either burned or, if valuable, added to the private collections of various sticky-fingered Commanders. Being now thoroughly instructed in Scripture, I can quote chapter and verse on the hazards of snatching loot forbidden by the Lord, but discretion is the better part of valour, so I do not.

I am pleased to relate that no one has erased the murals on either side of this building's interior staircase: since they depict dead soldiers, angels, and wreaths of victory, they are pious enough to have been deemed acceptable, although the flag of the erstwhile United States of America in the right-hand one has been painted over with that of Gilead.

Commander Judd has risen in the world since I first knew him. Straightening out Gilead's women offered little real scope for his ego and garnered insufficient respect. But as the Commander in charge of the Eyes, he is now universally feared. His office is at the back of the building, in a space once consecrated to book storage and research cubicles. A large Eye with a real crystal in the pupil is centred on the door. That way he can see who is about to knock.

'Come in,' he said as I was raising my hand. The two junior Eyes who'd been escorting me took this as their signal to depart.

'Dear Aunt Lydia,' he said, beaming from behind his enormous desk. 'Thank you for gracing my humble office. You are well, I hope?'

He did not hope that, but I let it pass. 'Praise be,' I said. 'And you? And your Wife?' This Wife has lasted longer than usual. His Wives have a habit of dying: Commander Judd is a great believer in the restorative powers of young women, as were King David and assorted Central American drug lords. After each respectable period of mourning, he has let it be known that he is in the market for another child bride. To be clear: he has let it be known to me.

'I and my Wife are both well, thanks be,' he said. 'I have wonderful news for you. Please sit down.' I did so, and prepared to listen attentively. 'Our agents in Canada have succeeded in identifying and eliminating two of the most active Mayday operatives. Their cover was a used clothing store in a seedy area of Toronto. A preliminary search of the premises suggested that they'd been playing a key role in aiding and abetting the Underground Femaleroad.'

'Providence has blessed us,' I said.

'Our enthusiastic young Canadian agents carried out the operation, but your Pearl Girls pointed the way. So useful of you to share their intuitive female gleanings.'

'They are observant, well trained, and obedient,' I said. The Pearl Girls were originally my idea — other religions had missionaries, so why not ours? And other missionaries had produced converts, so why not ours? And other missionaries had gathered information used in espionage, so why not ours? — but, being no fool or at least not that kind of fool, I'd let Commander Judd take credit for the plan. Officially, the Pearl Girls report only to me, as it would be unseemly for the Commander to involve himself in the details of what is essentially women's work; though of course I must pass along to him anything I deem either necessary or unavoidable. Too much and I'd lose control, too little and I'd fall under suspicion. Their attractive brochures are composed by us, and designed and printed by the small Ardua Hall press located in one of our cellars.

My Pearl Girls initiative came at a crucial moment for him, just as the folly of his National Homelands fiasco was becoming undeniable.

81

The genocide charges levied by international human rights organizations had become an embarrassment, the flow of refugee Homelanders from North Dakota across the Canadian border was an unstoppable flood, and Judd's ridiculous Certificate of Whiteness scheme had collapsed in a welter of forgeries and bribery. The launch of the Pearl Girls saved his bacon, though I have since wondered whether it was politic of me to have saved it. He owes me, but that could prove a liability. Some people do not enjoy being indebted.

Right then, however, Commander Judd was all smiles. 'Indeed, they are Pearls of Great Price. And with those two Mayday operatives out of commission, there will be less trouble for you, it is to be hoped — fewer Handmaids escaping.'

'Praise be.'

'Our feat of surgical demolition and cleansing won't be announced by us publicly, of course.'

'We'll be blamed for it anyway,' I said. 'By the Canadian and international media. Naturally.'

'And we will deny it,' he said. 'Naturally.'

There was a moment of silence as we regarded each other across his desk, like two chess players, possibly; or like two old comrades — for both of us had survived three waves of purges. That fact alone had created a bond of sorts.

'There is something that has been puzzling me, however,' he said. 'Those two Mayday terrorists must have had a counterpart here in Gilead.'

'Really? Surely not!' I exclaimed.

'We've made an analysis of all known escapes: their high success rate cannot be explained without an element of leakage. Someone in Gilead — someone with access to our security personnel deployments — must have been informing the Underground Femaleroad. Which routes are watched, which are likely to be clear, that sort of thing. As you know, the war has meant that manpower, especially in Vermont and Maine, is thin on the ground. We've needed the bodies elsewhere.'

'Who in Gilead would be so treacherous?' I asked. 'Betraying our future!'

'We're working on it,' he said. 'Meanwhile, if any ideas should occur to you . . . '

'Of course,' I said.

'There's one other thing,' he said. 'Aunt Adrianna. The Pearl Girl found dead in Toronto.'

'Yes. Devastating,' I said. 'Is there any further information?'

'We're expecting an update from the Consulate,' he said. 'I'll let you know.'

'Anything I can do,' I said. 'You know you can count on me.'

'In so many ways, dear Aunt Lydia,' he said. 'Your price is above rubies, praise be.'

I like a compliment as well as anyone. 'Thank you,' I said.

★ ★ ★

My life might have been very different. If only I'd looked around me, taken in the wider view. If only I'd packed up early enough, as some did, and left the country — the country that I still foolishly thought was the same as the country to which I had for so many years belonged.

Such regrets are of no practical use. I made choices, and then, having made them, I had fewer choices. Two roads diverged in a yellow wood, and I took the one most travelled by. It was littered with corpses, as such roads are. But as you will have noticed, my own corpse is not among them.

In that vanished country of mine, things had been on a downward spiral for years. The floods, the fires, the tornadoes, the hurricanes, the droughts, the water shortages, the earthquakes. Too much of this, too little of that. The decaying infrastructure — why hadn't someone decommissioned those atomic reactors before it was too late? The tanking economy, the joblessness, the falling birth rate.

People became frightened. Then they became angry.

The absence of viable remedies. The search for someone to blame.

Why did I think it would nonetheless be business as usual? Because we'd been hearing these things for so long, I suppose. You don't believe the sky is falling until a chunk of it falls on you.

★   ★   ★

My arrest came shortly after the Sons of Jacob attack that liquidated Congress. Initially we were told it was Islamic terrorists: a National Emergency was declared, but we were told that we should carry on as usual, that the Constitution would shortly be reinstated, and that the state of emergency would soon be over. That was correct, but not in the way we'd assumed.

It was a viciously hot day. The courts had been closed — temporarily, until a valid line of command and the rule of law could be reinstituted, we were told. Despite that, some of us had gone into work — the freed-up time could always be used to tackle the document backlog, or that was my excuse. Really I wanted company.

Oddly, none of our male colleagues had felt the same need. Perhaps they were finding solace among their wives and children.

As I was reading through some casework, one of my younger colleagues — Katie, recently appointed, thirty-six, and three months pregnant via sperm bank — came into my office. 'We need to leave,' she said.

I stared at her. 'What do you mean?' I said.

'We need to get out of the country. There's something happening.'

'Well, of course — the state of emergency — '

'No, more than that. My bank card's been cancelled. My credit cards — both of them. I was trying to get a plane ticket, that's how I know. Is your car here?'

'What?' I said. 'Why? They can't simply cut off your money!'

'It seems they can,' said Katie. 'If you're a woman. That's what the airline said. The provisional government has just passed new laws: women's money now belongs to the male next of kin.'

'It's worse than you think,' said Anita, a somewhat older colleague. She'd come into my office too. 'Way worse.'

'I don't have a male next of kin,' I said. I felt stunned. 'This is completely unconstitutional!'

'Forget the Constitution,' said Anita. 'They've just abolished it. I heard about that in the bank, when I tried to . . . ' She began crying.

'Pull yourself together,' I said. 'We need to think.'

'You'll have a male relative somewhere,' said Katie. 'They must have been planning this for years: they told me that my male next of kin is my twelve-year-old nephew.'

At that moment the main door was kicked in. Five men entered, two by two and then one on his own, submachine guns at the ready. Katie, Anita, and I came out of my office. The general receptionist, Tessa, screamed and ducked down behind her desk.

A couple of them were young — twenties, perhaps — but the other three were middle-aged. The younger ones were fit, the others had beer bellies. They were wearing camouflage gear direct from central casting, and if it hadn't been for the guns I might have laughed, not yet realizing that female laughter would soon be in short supply.

'What's this about?' I said. 'You could have knocked! The door was open!'

The men ignored me. One of them — the leader, I suppose — said to his companion, 'Got the list?'

I tried a more outraged tone. 'Who is responsible for this damage?' Shock was beginning to hit me: I felt cold. Was this a robbery? A hostage-taking? 'What do you want? We don't keep any money here.'

Anita nudged me with her elbow to get me to keep quiet: she already had a better grasp of the situation than I did.

The second-in-command held up a sheet of paper. 'Who's the pregnant one?' he said. The three of us looked at one another. Katie stepped forward. 'I am,' she said.

'No husband, right?'

'No, I . . . ' Katie was holding her hands protectively in front of her stomach. She'd chosen single motherhood, as many women did in those days.

'The high school,' the leader said. The two younger men stepped forward.

'Come with us, ma'am,' said the first.

'Why?' said Katie. 'You can't just barge in here and — '

'Come with us,' said the second younger man. They grabbed her by her arms, hauled. She screamed, but out she went through the door nonetheless.

'Stop that!' I said. We could hear her voice outside in the hall, diminishing.

'I'm giving the orders,' said the leader. He had eyeglasses and a handlebar moustache, but these did not render him avuncular. I've had cause to notice over the course of what you might call my Gilead career that underlings given sudden power frequently become the worst abusers of it.

'Don't worry, she won't be hurt,' said the second-in-command. 'She's going to a place of safety.'

He read our names off the list. There was no

point in denying who we were: they already knew. 'Where's the receptionist?' said the leader. 'This Tessa.'

Poor Tessa emerged from behind her desk. She was shivering with terror.

'What d'you think?' said the man with the list. 'Box store, high school, or stadium?'

'How old are you?' said the leader. 'Never mind, it's here. Twenty-seven.'

'Let's give her a chance. Box store. Maybe some guy might marry her.'

'Stand over there,' said the leader to Tessa.

'Christ, she's wet herself,' said the third older man.

'Don't swear,' said the leader. 'Good. A fearful one, maybe she'll do as she's told.'

'Fat chance any of them will,' said the third man. 'They're women.' I think he was making a joke.

The two young men who had disappeared with Katie now came back through the door. 'She's in the van,' said one.

'Where's the other two so-called lady judges?' said the leader. 'This Loretta? This Davida?'

'They're on lunch,' said Anita.

'We'll take these two. Wait here with her until they come back,' said the leader, indicating Tessa. 'Then lock her in the box-store van. Then bring the two lunch ones.'

'Box store or stadium? For these two here?'

'Stadium,' said the leader. 'One of them's overage, they've both got law degrees, they're lady judges. You heard the orders.'

'It's a waste though, in some cases,' said the

88

second one, nodding towards Anita.

'Providence will decide,' said the leader.

Anita and I were taken down the stairs, five flights. Was the elevator running? I don't know. Then we were cuffed with our hands in front of us and inserted into a black van, with a solid panel between us and the driver and mesh inside the darkened glass windows.

The two of us had been mute all this time, because what was there to say? It was clear that cries for help would go unanswered. There was no point in shouting or flinging ourselves against the walls of the van: it would simply have been a futile expense of energy. And so we waited.

At least there was air conditioning. And seats to sit down on.

'What will they do?' Anita whispered. We couldn't see out the windows. Nor could we see each other, except as dim shapes.

'I don't know,' I said.

★   ★   ★

The van paused — at a checkpoint, I suppose — then moved, then halted. 'Final stop,' said a voice. 'Out!'

The back doors of the van were opened. Anita clambered out first. 'Move it,' said a different voice. It was hard to get down from the van with my hands cuffed; someone took my arm and pulled, and I lurched onto the ground.

As the van pulled away, I stood unsteadily and gazed around. I was in an open space in which there were many groups of other people — other women, I should say — and a large number of men with guns.

I was in a stadium. But it was no longer that. Now it was a prison.

VI

SIX FOR DEAD

13

It has been very difficult for me to tell you about the events surrounding my mother's death. Tabitha had loved me without question, and now she was gone, and everything around me felt wavering and uncertain. Our house, the garden, even my own room — they seemed no longer real — as if they would dissolve into a mist and vanish. I kept thinking of a Bible verse Aunt Vidala had made us learn by heart:

> For a thousand years in thy sight are but
> as yesterday when it is past, and as a
> watch in the night. Thou carriest them
> away as with a flood; they are as a sleep;
> in the morning they are like grass which
> groweth up. In the morning it flourisheth,
> and groweth up; in the evening it is cut
> down, and withereth.

Withereth, withereth. It was like lisping — as if God did not know how to speak clearly. A lot of us had stumbled over that word while reciting it.

★   ★   ★

For my mother's funeral I was given a black dress. Some of the other Commanders and their Wives were in attendance, and our Marthas. There was a closed coffin with the earthly husk of my mother inside it, and my father made a short speech about what a fine Wife she had been, forever thinking of others ahead of herself, an example for all the women of Gilead, and then he said a prayer, thanking God for freeing her from pain, and everyone said Amen. They didn't make a big fuss over the funerals of women in Gilead, even high-ranking ones.

The important people came back to our house from the cemetery, and there was a small reception. Zilla had made cheese puffs for it, one of her specialties, and she'd let me help her. That was some comfort: to be allowed to put on an apron, and to grate the cheese, and to squeeze the dough out of the pastry tube onto the baking sheet, and then to watch through the glass window of the oven as it puffed up. We baked these at the last minute, once the people had come.

Then I took off the apron and went in to the reception in my black dress, as my father had requested, and was silent, as he had also requested. Most of the guests ignored me, except for one of the Wives, whose name was Paula. She was a widow, and somewhat famous because her husband, Commander Saunders, had been killed in his study by their Handmaid, using a kitchen skewer — a scandal that had been much whispered about at school the year before. What was the Handmaid doing in the study? How had she got in?

Paula's version was that the girl was insane, and had crept downstairs at night and stolen the skewer from the kitchen, and when poor Commander Saunders had opened his study door she had taken him by surprise — killed a man who had always been respectful to her and to her position. The Handmaid had run away, but they'd caught her and hanged her, and displayed her on the Wall.

The other version was Shunammite's, via her Martha, via the main Martha at the Saunders house. It involved violent urges and a sinful connection. The Handmaid must have enticed Commander Saunders in some way, and then he'd ordered her to creep downstairs during the nights when everyone was supposed to be asleep. Then she would slither into the study, where the Commander would be waiting for her, and his eyes would light up like flashlights. Who knows what lustful demands he must have made? Demands that had been unnatural, and had driven the Handmaid mad, not that it would take that much with some of them, because they were borderline as it was, but this one must have been worse than most. It did not bear thinking about, said the Marthas, who could think of little else.

When her husband hadn't turned up for breakfast, Paula had gone looking for him and had discovered him lying on the floor without his trousers. Paula had put the trousers back on him before calling the Angels. She'd had to order one of her own Marthas to help her: dead people were either stiff or floppy, and Commander

Saunders was a large and clumsily shaped man. Shunammite said the Martha said that Paula had got a lot of blood on herself while wrestling the clothes onto the dead body, and must have nerves of steel because she'd done what was right to save appearances.

I preferred Shunammite's version to Paula's. I thought about it at the funeral reception when my father was introducing me to Paula. She was eating a cheese puff; she gave me a measuring look. I'd seen a look like that on Vera when she was poking a straw into a cake to see if it was done.

Then she smiled and said, 'Agnes Jemima. How lovely,' and patted me on the head as if I was five, and said it must be nice to have a new dress. I felt like biting her: was the new dress supposed to make up for my mother being dead? But it was better to hold my tongue than to show my true thoughts. I did not always succeed in that, but I succeeded on this occasion.

'Thank you,' I said. I pictured her kneeling on the floor in a pool of blood, trying to put a pair of trousers on a dead man. This put her in an awkward position in my mind, and made me feel better.

* * *

Several months after my mother's death, my father married the widow Paula. On her finger appeared my mother's magic ring. I suppose my father didn't want to waste it, and why buy another ring when such a beautiful and

96

expensive one was already available?

The Marthas grumbled about it. 'Your mother wanted that ring to go to you,' Rosa said. But of course there was nothing they could do. I was enraged, but there was nothing I could do either. I brooded and sulked, but neither my father nor Paula paid any attention to that. They had taken to doing something they called 'humouring me,' which in practice meant ignoring any displays of mood so I would learn that I could not influence them by stubborn silences. They would even discuss this pedagogical technique in front of me while speaking about me in the third person. *I see Agnes is in one of her moods. Yes, it is like the weather, it will soon pass. Young girls are like that.*

14

Shortly after my father's wedding to Paula, something very disturbing occurred at school. I am recounting it here not because I wish to be gruesome, but because it made a deep impression on me, and may help to explain why some of us from that time and place acted as we did.

This event took place in the Religion class, which, as I have mentioned, was taught to us by Aunt Vidala. She was in charge of our school, and indeed of the other schools like ours — the Vidala Schools, they were called — but the picture of her that hung at the back of every classroom was smaller than the picture of Aunt Lydia. There were five of these pictures: Baby Nicole at the top, because we had to pray for her safe return every day. Then Aunt Elizabeth and Aunt Helena, then Aunt Lydia, then Aunt Vidala. Baby Nicole and Aunt Lydia had gold frames, whereas the other three only had silver frames.

Of course we all knew who the four women were: they were the Founders. But the founders of what we were not sure, nor did we dare to ask: we did not want to offend Aunt Vidala by calling attention to her smaller picture. Shunammite said that the eyes of the Aunt Lydia picture could follow you around the room and that it could hear what you said, but she exaggerated and made things up.

Aunt Vidala sat on top of her big desk. She liked to have a good view of us. She told us to move our desks forward and closer together. Then she said we were now old enough to hear one of the most important stories in the Bible — important because it was a message from God especially for girls and women, so we must listen carefully. This was the story of the Concubine Cut into Twelve Pieces.

Shunammite, sitting beside me, whispered, 'I already know this.' Becka, on the other side, inched her hand over to mine beneath the desktop.

'Shunammite, be silent,' said Aunt Vidala. After blowing her nose, she told us the following story.

A man's concubine — which was a sort of Handmaid — ran away from her owner, back to her father's abode. That was very disobedient of her. The man went to collect her, and being a kind and forgiving man, all he asked was to have her back. The father, knowing the rules, said yes — he was disappointed in his daughter for being so disobedient — and the two men had a dinner to celebrate their accord. But this meant that the man and his concubine were late setting out, and when it got dark they took refuge in a town where the man didn't know anyone. But a generous citizen said they could stay overnight in his house.

But some other citizens, being filled with sinful urges, came to the house and demanded that the traveller be handed over to them. They wanted to do shameful things to him. Lustful and sinful things. But that would have been especially wicked between men, so the generous man and the traveller put the concubine outside the door instead.

'Well, she deserved it, don't you think?' said Aunt Vidala. 'She shouldn't have run away. Think of all the suffering she caused to other people!' But when it was morning, said Aunt Vidala, the traveller opened the door, and the concubine was lying on the threshold. 'Get up,' the man said to her. But she did not get up because she was dead. The sinful men had killed her.

'How?' Becka asked. Her voice was barely above a whisper; she was squeezing my hand hard. 'How did they kill her?' Two tears were running down her cheeks.

'Many men doing lustful things all at once will kill a girl,' said Aunt Vidala. 'This story is God's way of telling us that we should be content with our lot and not rebel against it.' The man in charge should be honoured by the woman, she said. If not, this was the result. God always made the punishment fit the crime.

I learned the rest of the story later — how the traveller cut the concubine's body into twelve pieces and sent one to each of the Tribes of Israel, calling on them to avenge the misuse of his concubine by executing the murderers, and how the Tribe of Benjamin refused because the killers were Benjaminites. In the war of vengeance that followed, the Tribe of Benjamin was almost obliterated and their wives and children were all killed. Then the other eleven tribes reasoned that to obliterate the twelfth would be bad, so they stopped killing. The remaining Benjaminites couldn't marry any other women officially to make more children, since the rest of the tribes had taken an oath against that, but they were told they could steal some girls and marry them unofficially, which is what they did.

But we didn't hear the rest of the story at the time because Becka had burst into tears. 'That is horrible, that is horrible!' she said. The rest of us sat very still.

'Control yourself, Becka,' said Aunt Vidala. But Becka couldn't. She was crying so hard I thought she would stop breathing.

'May I give her a hug, Aunt Vidala?' I asked at last. We were encouraged to pray for other girls but not to touch one another.

'I suppose so,' said Aunt Vidala grudgingly. I put my arms around Becka, and she wept against my shoulder.

Aunt Vidala was annoyed by the state Becka was in, but she was also concerned. Becka's father was not a Commander, only a dentist, but he was an important dentist, and Aunt Vidala had bad teeth. She got up and left the room.

After several minutes, Aunt Estée arrived. She was the one called in when we needed calming down. 'It's all right, Becka,' she said. 'Aunt Vidala didn't mean to frighten you.' This was not exactly true, but Becka stopped crying and began to hiccup. 'There's another way of looking at the story. The concubine was sorry for what she had done, and she wanted to make amends, so she sacrificed herself to keep the kind traveller from being killed by those wicked men.' Becka turned her head slightly to the side: she was listening.

'That was brave and noble of the concubine, don't you think?' A small nod from Becka. Aunt Estée sighed. 'We must all make sacrifices in order to help other people,' she said in a soothing tone. 'Men must make sacrifices in war, and women must make sacrifices in other ways. That is how things are divided. Now we may all have a little treat to cheer us up. I have brought us some oatmeal cookies. Girls, you may socialize.'

We sat there eating the oatmeal cookies. 'Don't be such a baby,' Shunammite whispered across at Becka. 'It's only a story.'

Becka did not seem to hear her. 'I will never, ever get married,' she murmured, almost to herself.

'Yes you will,' said Shunammite. 'Everyone does.'

'No they don't,' said Becka, but only to me.

15

A few months after the wedding of Paula and my father, our household received a Handmaid. Her name was Ofkyle, since my father's name was Commander Kyle. 'Her name would have been something else earlier,' said Shunammite. 'Some other man's. They get passed around until they have a baby. They're all sluts anyway, they don't need real names.' Shunammite said a slut was a woman who'd gone with more men than her husband. Though we did not really know what 'gone with' meant.

And Handmaids must be double sluts, said Shunammite, because they didn't even have husbands. But you weren't supposed to be rude to the Handmaids or call them sluts, said Aunt Vidala, wiping her nose, because they were performing a service to the community by way of atonement, and we should all be grateful to them for that.

'I don't see why being a slut is performing a service,' Shunammite whispered.

'It's because of the babies,' I whispered back. 'The Handmaids can make babies.'

'So can some other women too,' said Shunammite, 'and they aren't sluts.' It was true, some of the Wives could, and some of the

Econowives: we'd seen them with their bulging stomachs. But a lot of women couldn't. Every woman wanted a baby, said Aunt Estée. Every woman who wasn't an Aunt or a Martha. Because if you weren't an Aunt or a Martha, said Aunt Vidala, what earthly use were you if you didn't have a baby?

What the arrival of this Handmaid meant was that my new stepmother, Paula, wanted to have a baby because she did not count me as her child: Tabitha was my mother. But what about Commander Kyle? I didn't seem to count as a child for him either. It was as if I had become invisible to both of them. They looked at me, and through me, and saw the wall.

★   ★   ★

When the Handmaid entered our household, I was almost of womanly age, as Gilead counted. I was taller, my face was longer in shape, and my nose had grown. I had darker eyebrows, not furry caterpillar ones like Shunammite's or wispy ones like Becka's, but curved into half-circles, and dark eyelashes. My hair had thickened and changed from a mousey brown to chestnut. All of that was pleasing to me, and I would look at my new face in the mirror, turning to take it in from all angles despite warnings against vanity.

More alarmingly, my breasts were swelling, and I had begun to sprout hair on areas of my body that we were not supposed to dwell on: legs, armpits, and the shameful part of many elusive names. Once that happened to a girl, she was no longer a precious flower but a much more dangerous creature.

We'd been prepared for such things at school — Aunt Vidala had presented a series of embarrassing illustrated lectures that were supposed to inform us about a woman's role and duty in regard to her body — a married woman's role — but they had not been very informative or reassuring. When Aunt Vidala asked if there were any questions, there weren't any, because where would you begin? I wanted to ask why it had to be like this, but I already knew the answer: because it was God's plan. That was how the Aunts got out of everything.

Soon I could expect blood to come out from between my legs: that had already happened to many of the girls at school. Why couldn't God have arranged it otherwise? But he had a special interest in blood, which we knew about from Scripture verses that had been read out to us: blood, purification, more blood, more purification, blood shed to purify the impure, though you weren't supposed to get it on your hands. Blood was polluting, especially when it came out of girls, but God once liked having it spilled on his altars. Though he had given that up — said Aunt Estée — in favour of fruits, vegetables, silent suffering, and good deeds.

The adult female body was one big booby trap as far as I could tell. If there was a hole, something was bound to be shoved into it and something else was bound to come out, and that went for any kind of hole: a hole in a wall, a hole in a mountain, a hole in the ground. There were so many things that could be done to it or go wrong with it, this adult female body, that I was left feeling I would be better off without it. I considered shrinking myself by not eating, and I did try that for a day, but I got so hungry I couldn't stick to my resolution, and went to the kitchen in the middle of the night and ate chicken scraps out of the soup pot.

★   ★   ★

My effervescent body was not my only worry: my status at school had become noticeably lower. I was no longer deferred to by the others, I was no longer courted. Girls would break off their conversations as I approached and would eye me strangely. Some would even turn their backs. Becka did not do that — she still contrived to sit beside me — but she looked straight ahead and did not slip her hand under the desk to hold mine.

Shunammite was still claiming to be my friend, partly I am sure because she was not popular among the others, but now she was doing me the favour of friendship instead of the other way around. I was hurt by all of this, though I didn't yet understand why the atmosphere had changed.

The others knew, however. Word must have been going around, from mouth to ear to mouth — from my stepmother, Paula, through our Marthas, who noticed everything, and then from them to the other Marthas they would encounter when doing errands, and then from those Marthas to their Wives, and from the Wives to their daughters, my schoolmates.

What was the word? In part, that I was out of favour with my powerful father. My mother, Tabitha, had been my protectress; but now she was gone, and my stepmother did not wish me well. At home she would ignore me, or she would bark at me — *Pick that up! Don't slouch!* I tried to keep out of her sight as much as possible, but even my closed door must have been an affront to her. She would have known that I was concealed behind it thinking acid thoughts.

But my fall in value went beyond the loss of my father's favour. There was a new piece of information circulating, one that was very harmful to me.

★   ★   ★

Whenever there was a secret to tell — especially a shocking one — Shunammite loved to be the messenger.

'Guess what I found out?' she said one day while we were eating our lunchtime sandwiches. It was a sunny noon: we were being allowed to have a picnic outside on the school lawn. The grounds were enclosed by a high fence topped with razor wire and there were two Angels at the gate, which was locked except when the Aunts' cars went in and out, so we were perfectly safe.

'What?' I said. The sandwiches were an artificial cheese mixture that had replaced real cheese in our school sandwiches because the real cheese was needed by our soldiers. The sunlight was warm, the grass was soft, I had made it out of the house that day without Paula seeing me, and for the moment I was feeling marginally content with my life.

'Your mother wasn't your real mother,' said Shunammite. 'They took you away from your real mother because she was a slut. But don't worry, it's not your fault, because you were too young to know that.'

My stomach clenched. I spat a mouthful of sandwich onto the grass. 'That's not true!' I almost shouted.

'Calm down,' said Shunammite. 'Like I said, it's not your fault.'

'I don't believe you,' I said.

Shunammite gave me a pitying, relishing smile. 'It's the truth. My Martha heard the whole story from your Martha, and *she* heard it from your new stepmother. The Wives know about things like that — some of them got their own kids that way Not me, though, I was born properly'

I really hated her at that moment. 'Then where's my real mother?' I demanded. 'If you know everything!' You are really, really mean, I wanted to say. It was dawning on me that she must have betrayed me: before telling me, she'd already told the other girls. That's why they'd become so cool: I was tainted.

'I don't know, maybe she's dead,' Shunammite said. 'She was stealing you from Gilead, she was trying to run away through a forest, she was going to take you across the border. But they caught up with her and rescued you. Lucky for you!'

'Who did?' I asked faintly. While telling me this story, Shunammite was continuing to chew. I watched her mouth, out of which my doom was emerging. There was orange cheese substitute between her teeth.

'You know, them. The Angels and Eyes and them. They rescued you and gave you to Tabitha because she couldn't have a baby. They were doing you a favour. You have a much better home now than with that slut.'

I felt belief creeping up through my body like a paralysis. The story Tabitha used to tell, about rescuing me and running away from the evil witches — it was partly true. But it hadn't been Tabitha's hand I'd been holding, it had been the hand of my real mother — my real mother, the slut. And it wasn't witches chasing us, it was men. They would've had guns, because such men always did.

Tabitha did choose me though. She chose me from among all the other children pried loose from their mothers and fathers. She chose me, and she cherished me. She loved me. That part was real.

But now I was motherless, because where was my real mother? I was fatherless as well — Commander Kyle was no more related to me than the man in the moon. He'd only tolerated me because I was Tabitha's project, her plaything, her pet.

No wonder Paula and Commander Kyle wanted a Handmaid: they wanted a real child instead of me. I was nobody's child.

⋆　⋆　⋆

Shunammite continued to chew, watching with satisfaction as her message sank in. 'I'll stick up

109

for you,' she said in her most pious and insincere voice. 'It doesn't make any difference to your soul. Aunt Estée says all souls are equal in heaven.'

Only in heaven, I thought. And this is not heaven. This is a place of snakes and ladders, and though I was once high up on a ladder propped against the Tree of Life, now I've slid down a snake. How gratifying for the others to witness my fall! No wonder Shunammite could not resist spreading such baleful and pleasing news. Already I could hear the snickering behind my back: *Slut, slut, daughter of a slut.*

Aunt Vidala and Aunt Estée must know as well. The two of them must always have known. It was the kind of secret the Aunts knew. That was how they got their power, according to the Marthas: from knowing secrets.

And Aunt Lydia — whose frown-smiling gold-framed picture with the ugly brown uniform hung at the backs of our schoolrooms — must know the most secrets of all because she had the most power. What would Aunt Lydia have to say about my plight? Would she help me? Would she understand my unhappiness, would she save me? But was Aunt Lydia even a real person? I had never seen her. Maybe she was like God — real but unreal at the same time. What if I were to pray to Aunt Lydia at night, instead of to God?

I did try, later in the week. But the idea was too unthinkable — praying to a woman — so I stopped.

16

I went through the rest of that terrible afternoon as if sleepwalking. We were embroidering sets of petit-point handkerchiefs for the Aunts, with flowers on them to go with their names — echinacea for Elizabeth, hyacinths for Helena, violets for Vidala. I was doing lilacs for Lydia, and I stuck a needle halfway into my finger without noticing it until Shunammite said, 'There's blood on your petit point.' Gabriela — a scrawny, smart-mouthed girl who was now as popular as I had once been because her father had been promoted to three Marthas — whispered, 'Maybe she's finally getting her period, out her finger,' and everyone laughed because most of them already had theirs, even Becka. Aunt Vidala heard the laughing and looked up from her book and said, 'That's enough of that.'

Aunt Estée took me to the washroom and we rinsed off the blood on my hand, and she put a bandage on my finger, but the petit-point handkerchief had to be soaked in cold water, which is the way we'd been taught that you got out blood, especially from white cloth. Getting out blood was something we would have to know as Wives, said Aunt Vidala, as it would be part of our duties: we would have to supervise our

Marthas to make sure they did it right. Cleaning up things such as blood and other substances that came out of bodies was part of women's duty of caring for other people, especially little children and the elderly, said Aunt Estée, who always put things in a positive light. That was a talent women had because of their special brains, which were not hard and focused like the brains of men but soft and damp and warm and enveloping, like . . . like what? She didn't finish the sentence.

Like mud in the sun, I thought. That's what was inside my head: warmed-up mud.

★ ★ ★

'Is anything wrong, Agnes?' Aunt Estée asked after my finger had been cleaned up. I said no.

'Then why are you crying, my dear?' It seemed that I was: tears were coming out of my eyes, out of my damp and muddy head, despite my effort to control them.

'Because it hurts!' I said, sobbing now. She didn't ask what hurt, though she must have known it wasn't really my needled finger. She put her arm around me and gave me a little squeeze.

'So many things hurt,' she said. 'But we must try to be cheerful. God likes cheerfulness. He likes us to appreciate the nice things in the world.' We heard a lot about the likes and dislikes of God from the Aunts who taught us, especially Aunt Vidala, who seemed to be on very close terms. Shunammite once said she was going to ask Aunt Vidala what God liked for breakfast, which scandalized the more timid girls, but she never actually did it.

I wondered what God thought about mothers, both real and unreal. But I knew there was no point in questioning Aunt Estée about my real mother and how Tabitha had chosen me, or even how old I'd been at the time. The Aunts at school avoided talking to us about our parents.

★   ★   ★

When I got home that day, I cornered Zilla in the kitchen, where she was making biscuits, and repeated everything that Shunammite had told me at lunchtime.

'Your friend has a big mouth,' was what she said. 'She should keep it shut more often.' Unusually harsh words, coming from her.

'But is it true?' I said. I still half-hoped, then, that she would deny the whole story.

She sighed. 'How'd you like to help me make the biscuits?'

But I was too old to be bribed with simple gifts like that. 'Just tell me,' I said. 'Please.'

'Well,' she said. 'According to your new stepmother, yes. That story is true. Or something like it.'

'So Tabitha wasn't my mother,' I said, holding back the fresh tears that were coming, keeping my voice steady.

'It depends what you mean by a mother,' said Zilla. 'Is your mother the one who gives birth to you or the one who loves you the most?'

'I don't know,' I said. 'Maybe the one who

113

loves you the most?'

'Then Tabitha was your mother,' said Zilla, cutting out the biscuits. 'And we Marthas are your mothers too, because we love you as well. Though it may not always seem so to you.' She lifted each round biscuit with the pancake flipper and placed it onto the baking sheet. 'We all have your best interests at heart.'

This made me distrust her a little because Aunt Vidala said similar things about our best interests, usually before doling out a punishment. She liked to switch us on the legs where it wouldn't show, and sometimes higher up, making us bend over and raise our skirts. Sometimes she would do that to a girl in front of the whole class. 'What happened to her?' I asked. 'My other mother? The one who was running through the forest? After they took me away?'

'I don't truly know,' said Zilla, not looking at me, sliding the biscuits into the hot oven. I wanted to ask if I could have one when they came out — I craved warm biscuits — but this seemed like a childish request to make in the middle of such a serious conversation.

'Did they shoot her? Did they kill her?'

'Oh no,' said Zilla. 'They wouldn't have done that.'

'Why?'

'Because she could have babies. She had you, didn't she? That was proof she could. They would never kill a valuable woman like that unless they really couldn't help it.' She paused to let this sink in. 'Most likely they would see if she could be . . . The Aunts at the Rachel and Leah

114

Centre would pray with her; they would talk to her at first, to see if it was possible to change her mind about things.'

There were rumours about the Rachel and Leah Centre at school, but they were vague: none of us knew what went on inside it. Still, just being prayed over by a bunch of Aunts would be scary. Not all of them were as gentle as Aunt Estée. 'And what if they couldn't change her mind?' I asked. 'Would they kill her then? Is she dead?'

'Oh, I'm sure they changed her mind,' said Zilla. 'They're good at that. Hearts and minds — they change them.'

'Where is she now, then?' I asked. 'My mother — the real — the other one?' I wondered if that mother remembered me. She must remember me. She must have loved me or she wouldn't have tried to take me with her when she was running away.

'None of us know that, dear,' said Zilla. 'Once they become Handmaids they don't have their old names anymore, and in those outfits they wear you can hardly see their faces. They all look the same.'

'She's a Handmaid?' I asked. It was true, then, what Shunammite had said. 'My mother?'

'That's what they do, over at the Centre,' said Zilla. 'They make them into Handmaids, one way or another. The ones they catch. Now, how about a nice hot biscuit? I don't have any butter right now, but I can put a little honey on it for you.'

I thanked her. I ate the biscuit. My mother

was a Handmaid. That's why Shunammite insisted she was a slut. It was common knowledge that all the Handmaids had been sluts, once upon a time. And they still were, although in a different way.

★ ★ ★

From then on, our new Handmaid fascinated me. I'd ignored her when she'd first come, as instructed — it was the kindest thing for them, said Rosa, because either she would have a baby and then be moved somewhere else, or she wouldn't have a baby and would be moved somewhere else anyway, but in any case she wouldn't be in our house for long. So it was bad for them to form attachments, especially with any young people in the household, because they would only have to give those attachments up, and think how upsetting that would be for them.

So I'd turned away from Ofkyle and had pretended not to notice her when she'd glide into the kitchen in her red dress to pick up the shopping basket and then go for her walk. The Handmaids all went for a walk every day two by two; you could see them on the sidewalks. Nobody bothered them or spoke to them or touched them, because they were — in a sense — untouchable.

But now I gazed at Ofkyle from the sides of my eyes at every chance I got. She had a pale oval face, blank, like a gloved thumbprint. I knew how to make a blank face myself, so I didn't believe she was really blank underneath. She'd

116

had a whole other life. What had she looked like when she'd been a slut? Sluts went with more than one man. How many men had she gone with? What did that mean exactly, going with men, and what sort of men? Had she allowed parts of her body to stick out of her clothing? Had she worn trousers, like a man? That was so unholy it was almost unimaginable! But if she'd done that, how daring! She must have been very different from the way she was now. She must have had a lot more energy.

I would go to the window to watch her from behind as she went out for her walk, through our garden and down the path to our front gate. Then I would take off my shoes, tiptoe along the hall, and creep into her room, which was at the back of the house, on the third floor. It was a medium-sized room with its own bathroom attached. It had a braided rug; on the wall there was a picture of blue flowers in a vase that used to belong to Tabitha.

My stepmother had put the picture in there to get it out of sight, I suppose, because she was purging the visible parts of the house of anything that might remind her new husband of his first Wife. Paula wasn't doing it openly, she was more subtle than that — she was moving or discarding one thing at a time — but I knew what she was up to. It was one more reason for me to dislike her.

Why mince words? I don't need to do that anymore. I didn't just dislike her, I hated her. Hatred is a very bad emotion because it curdles the soul — Aunt Estée taught us that — but, although I'm not proud to admit it and I used to pray to be forgiven for it, hatred is indeed what I felt.

Once I was inside our Handmaid's room and had closed the door softly, I would poke around in there. Who was she really? And what if *she* was my missing mother? I knew this was make-believe, but I was so lonely; I liked to think of how things would be if it were true. We would fling ourselves into each other's arms, we would hug each other, we would be so happy to have found each other again . . . But then what? I had no version of what might happen after that, though I had a dim idea that it would be trouble.

There was nothing in Ofkyle's room that provided any clue about her. Her red dresses were hanging in the closet in an orderly row, her plain white underthings and her sack-like nightgowns were folded neatly on the shelves. She had a second pair of walking shoes and an extra cloak and a spare white bonnet. She had a toothbrush with a red handle. There was a suitcase she'd brought these things in, but it was empty.

17

Finally our Handmaid managed to get pregnant. I knew this before I was told, because instead of treating her as if she were a stray dog they were putting up with out of pity, the Marthas began fussing over her and giving her bigger meals, and placing flowers in little vases on her breakfast trays. Because of my obsession with her, I kept track of details like that as much as I could.

I would listen to the Marthas talking excitedly in the kitchen when they thought I wasn't there, though I couldn't always hear what they said. When I was with them Zilla smiled to herself a lot, and Vera lowered her harsh voice as if she was in church. Even Rosa had a smug expression, as if she'd eaten a particularly delicious orange but was not telling anyone about it.

As for Paula, my stepmother, she was glowing. She was nicer to me on those occasions when we were together in the same room, which were not frequent if I could help it. I snatched breakfast in the kitchen before being driven to school, and I left the dinner table as quickly as I could, pleading homework: some piece of petit point or knitting or sewing, a drawing I had to finish, a watercolour I needed to paint. Paula never objected: she didn't want to see me any more than I wanted to see her.

'Ofkyle's pregnant, isn't she?' I asked Zilla one morning. I tried to be casual about it in case I was wrong. Zilla was caught off guard.

'How did you know?' she asked.

'I'm not blind,' I said in a superior voice that must have been irritating. I was at that age.

'We aren't supposed to say anything about it,' said Zilla, 'until after the third month. The first three months are the danger time.'

'Why?' I said. I didn't really know much after all, despite Aunt Vidala's runny-nosed slideshow about fetuses.

'Because if it's an Unbaby, that's when it might . . . that's when it might get born too early,' said Zilla. 'And it would die.' I knew about Unbabies: they were not taught, but they were whispered about. There were said to be a lot of them. Becka's Handmaid had given birth to a baby girl: it didn't have a brain. Poor Becka had been very upset because she'd wanted a sister. 'We're praying for it. For her,' Zilla had said then. I'd noticed the *it*.

Paula must have dropped a hint among the other Wives about Ofkyle being pregnant, though, because my status at school suddenly shot upwards again. Shunammite and Becka competed for my attention, as before, and the other girls deferred to me as if I had an invisible aura.

A coming baby shed lustre on everyone connected with it. It was as if a golden haze had enveloped our house, and the haze got brighter

120

and more golden as time passed. When the three-month mark was reached, there was an unofficial party in the kitchen and Zilla made a cake. As for Ofkyle, her expression was not so much joyful as relieved, from what I could glimpse of her face.

In the midst of this repressed jubilation, I myself was a dark cloud. This unknown baby inside Ofkyle was taking up all the love: there seemed to be none left anywhere for me. I was all alone. And I was jealous: that baby would have a mother, and I would never have one. Even the Marthas were turning away from me towards the light shining out of Ofkyle's belly. I am ashamed to admit it — jealous of a baby! — but that was the truth.

★ ★ ★

It was at this time that an event took place that I should pass over because it's better forgotten, but it had a bearing on the choice I was soon to make. Now that I am older and have seen more of the outside world, I can see that it might not seem that significant to some, but I was a young girl from Gilead, and I had not been exposed to these kinds of situations, so this event was not trivial to me. Instead it was horrifying. It was also shameful: when a shameful thing is done to you, the shamefulness rubs off on you. You feel dirtied.

The prelude was minor: I needed to go to the dentist for my yearly checkup. The dentist was Becka's father, and his name was Dr. Grove. He was the best dentist, said Vera: all the top Commanders and their families went to him. His office was in the Blessings of Health Building, which was for doctors and dentists. It had a picture of a smiling heart and a smiling tooth on the outside.

One of the Marthas always used to go with me to the doctor or the dentist and sit in the waiting room, as it was more proper that way, Tabitha used to say without explaining why, but Paula said the Guardian could just drive me there, since there was too much work to be done in the house considering the changes that had to be prepared for — by which she meant the baby — and it would be a waste of time to send a Martha.

I did not mind. In fact, going by myself made me feel very grown up. I sat up straight in the back seat of the car behind our Guardian. Then I went into the building and pressed the elevator button that had three teeth on it, and found the right floor and the right door, and sat in the waiting room looking at the pictures of transparent teeth on the wall. When it was my turn I went into the inner room, as the assistant, Mr. William, asked me to do, and sat down in the dentist chair. Dr. Grove came in and Mr. William brought my chart and then went out and closed the door, and Dr. Grove looked at my chart, and asked if I had any problems with my teeth, and I said no.

He poked around in my mouth with his picks and probes and his little mirror, as usual. As usual, I saw his eyes up close, magnified by his glasses — blue and bloodshot, with elephant-knee eyelids — and tried not to breathe in when he was breathing out because his breath smelled — as usual — of onions. He was a middle-aged man with no distinguishing features.

He snapped off his white stretchy sanitary gloves and washed his hands at the sink, which was behind my back.

He said, 'Perfect teeth. Perfect.' Then he said, 'You're getting to be a big girl, Agnes.'

Then he put his hand on my small but growing breast. It was summer, so I was wearing the summer school uniform, which was pink and made of light cotton.

I froze, in shock. So it was all true then, about men and their rampaging, fiery urges, and merely by sitting in the dentist chair I was the cause. I was horribly embarrassed — what was I supposed to say? I didn't know, so I simply pretended it wasn't happening.

Dr. Grove was standing behind me, so it was his left hand on my left breast. I couldn't see the rest of him, only his hand, which was large and had reddish hairs on the back. It was warm. It sat there on my breast like a large hot crab. I didn't know what to do. Should I take hold of his hand and move it off my breast? Would that cause even more burning lust to break forth? Should I try to get away? Then the hand squeezed my breast. The fingers found my nipple and pinched. It was like having a thumbtack stuck into me. I moved the upper part of my body forward — I needed to get out of that dentist chair as fast as I could — but the hand was locking me in. Suddenly it lifted, and then some of the rest of Dr. Grove moved into sight.

'About time you saw one of these,' he said in the normal voice in which he said everything. 'You'll have one of them inside you soon enough.' He took hold of my right hand and positioned it on this part of himself.

I don't think I need to tell you what happened next. He had a towel handy. He wiped himself off and tucked his appendage back into his trousers.

'There,' he said. 'Good girl. I didn't hurt you.' He gave me a fatherly pat on the shoulder. 'Don't forget to brush twice a day, and floss afterwards. Mr. William will give you a new toothbrush.'

I walked out of the room, feeling sick to my stomach. Mr. William was in the waiting room, his unobtrusive thirty-year-old face impassive. He held out a bowl with new pink and blue toothbrushes in it. I knew enough to take a pink one.

'Thank you,' I said.

'You're welcome,' said Mr. William. 'Any cavities?'

'No,' I said. 'Not this time.'

'Good,' said Mr. William. 'Keep away from the sweet things and maybe you'll never have any. Any decay. Are you all right?'

'Yes,' I said. Where was the door?

'You look pale. Some people have a fear of dentists.' Was that a smirk? Did he know what had just happened?

'I'm not pale,' I said stupidly — how could I

tell I wasn't pale? I found the door handle and blundered out, reached the elevator, pressed the down button.

Was this now going to happen every time I went to the dentist? I couldn't say I didn't want to go back to Dr. Grove without saying why, and if I said why I knew I would be in trouble. The Aunts at school taught us that you should tell someone in authority — meaning them — if any man touched you inappropriately, but we knew not to be so dumb as to make a fuss, especially if it was a well-respected man like Dr. Grove. Also, what would it do to Becka if I said that about her father? She would be humiliated, she would be devastated. It would be a terrible betrayal.

Some girls had reported such things. One had claimed their Guardian had run his hands over her legs. Another had said that an Econo trash collector had unzipped his trousers in front of her. The first girl had had the backs of her legs whipped for lying, the second had been told that nice girls did not notice the minor antics of men, they simply looked the other way.

But I could not have looked the other way. There had been no other way to look.

'I don't want any dinner,' I said to Zilla in the kitchen. She gave me a sharp glance.

'Did your dentist appointment go all right, dear?' she said. 'Any cavities?'

'No,' I said. I tried a wan smile. 'I have perfect teeth.'

'Are you ill?'

'Maybe I'm catching a cold,' I said. 'I just need to lie down.'

Zilla made me a hot drink with lemon and honey in it and brought it up to my room on a tray. 'I should have gone with you,' she said. 'But he's the best dentist. Everyone agrees.'

She knew. Or she suspected. She was warning me not to say anything. That was the kind of coded language they used. Or I should say: that we all used. Did Paula know too? Did she foresee that such a thing would happen to me at Dr. Grove's? Is that why she sent me by myself?

It must have been so, I decided. She'd done it on purpose so I would have my breast pinched and that polluting item thrust in front of me. She'd wanted me to be defiled. That was a word from the Bible: *defiled*. She was probably having a malicious laugh about it — about the nasty joke she'd played on me, for I could see that in her eyes it would be viewed as a joke.

After that I stopped praying for forgiveness about the hatred I felt towards her. I was right to hate her. I was prepared to think the very worst of her, and I did.

18

The months passed; my life of tiptoeing and eavesdropping continued. I worked hard at seeing without being seen and hearing without being heard. I discovered the cracks between doorframes and nearly closed doors, the listening posts in hallways and on stairs, the thin places in walls. Most of what I heard came in fragments and even silences, but I was becoming good at fitting these fragments together and filling in the unsaid parts of sentences.

Ofkyle, our Handmaid, got bigger and bigger — or her stomach did — and the bigger she got, the more ecstatic our household became. I mean the women became ecstatic. As for Commander Kyle, it was hard to tell what he felt. He'd always had a wooden face, and anyway men were not supposed to display emotions in such ways as crying or even laughing out loud; though a certain amount of laughing did go on behind the closed dining-room doors when he'd have his groups of Commanders over for dinner, with wine and one of the party desserts involving whipped cream, when obtainable, that Zilla made so well. But I suppose even he was at least moderately thrilled about the ballooning of Ofkyle.

Sometimes I wondered what my own father might have felt about me. I had some notions about my mother — she'd run away with me, she'd been turned into a Handmaid by the Aunts — but none at all about my father. I must have had one, everyone did. You'd think I'd have filled up the blank with idealized pictures of him, but I didn't: the blank remained blank.

Ofkyle was now quite a celebrity. Wives would send their Handmaids over with some excuse — borrowing an egg, returning a bowl — but really to ask how she was doing. They would be allowed inside the house; then she would be called down so they could put their hands on her round belly and feel the baby kicking. It was amazing to see the expression on their faces while they were performing this ritual: Wonder, as if they were witnessing a miracle. Hope, because if Ofkyle could do it, so could they. Envy, because they weren't doing it yet. Longing, because they really wanted to do it. Despair, because it might never happen for them. I did not yet know what might become of a Handmaid who, despite having been judged viable, came up barren through all her allotted postings, but I already guessed it would not be good.

Paula threw numerous tea parties for the other Wives. They would congratulate her and admire her and envy her, and she would smile graciously and accept their congratulations modestly, and say all blessings came from above, and then she would order Ofkyle to appear in the living room so the Wives could see for themselves and exclaim over her and make a fuss. They might even call Ofkyle 'Dear,' which they never did for an ordinary Handmaid, one with a flat stomach. Then they would ask Paula what she was going to name her baby.

Her baby. Not Ofkyle's baby. I wondered what Ofkyle thought about that. But none of them were interested in what was going on in her head, they were only interested in her belly. They would be patting her stomach and sometimes even listening to it, whereas I would be standing behind the open living-room door looking at her through the crack so I could watch her face. I saw her trying to keep that face as still as marble, but she didn't always succeed. Her face was rounder than it had been when she'd first arrived — it was almost swollen — and it seemed to me that this was because of all the tears she was not allowing herself to cry. Did she cry them in secret? Although I would lurk outside her closed door with my ear to it, I never heard her.

At these moments of lurking I would become angry. I'd had a mother once, and I'd been snatched away from that mother and given to Tabitha, just as this baby was going to be snatched away from Ofkyle and given to Paula. It was the way things were done, it was how things were, it was how they had to be for the good of the future of Gilead: the few must make sacrifices for the sake of the many. The Aunts were agreed on that; they taught it; but still I knew this part of it wasn't right.

But I couldn't condemn Tabitha, even though she'd accepted a stolen child. She didn't make the world the way it was, and she had been my mother, and I had loved her and she had loved me. I still loved her, and perhaps she still loved me. Who could tell? Perhaps her silvery spirit was with me, hovering over me, keeping watch. I liked to think so.

I needed to think so.

★ ★ ★

At last the Birth Day came. I was home from school because I'd finally got my first period and I was having bad cramps. Zilla had made a hot water bottle for me and had rubbed on some painkilling salve and had made me a cup of analgesic tea, and I was huddled in my bed feeling sorry for myself when I heard the Birthmobile siren coming along our street. I hauled myself out of bed and went to the window: yes, the red van was inside our gates now and the Handmaids were climbing down out of it, a dozen of them or more. I couldn't see their faces, but just from the way they moved — faster than they usually did — I could tell they were excited.

Then the cars of the Wives began to arrive, and they too hurried into our house in their identical blue cloaks. Two Aunts' cars also drove up, and the Aunts got out. They weren't ones I recognized. Both were older, and one was carrying a black bag with the red wings and the knotted snake and the moon on it that meant it was a Medical Services First Responder bag, female division. A number of the Aunts were trained in first response and midwifery, though they could not be real doctors.

I was not supposed to witness a Birth. Girls and marriageable young women — such as I'd just become by having my period — were not allowed to see or know what went on, because such sights and sounds were not suitable for us and might be harmful to us — might disgust us or frighten us. That thick red knowledge was for married women and Handmaids, and for the Aunts, of course, so they could teach it to the midwife Aunts in training. But naturally I repressed my own cramping pain and put on my dressing gown and slippers, and crept halfway up the stairs that led to the third floor, where I would be out of sight.

The Wives were downstairs having a tea party in the living room and waiting for the important moment. I did not know what moment exactly, but I could hear them laughing and chattering. They were drinking champagne along with their tea, as I knew from the bottles and empty glasses I saw in the kitchen later.

The Handmaids and the designated Aunts were with Ofkyle. She wasn't in her own room — that room wouldn't have been big enough for everyone — but in the master bedroom on the second floor. I could hear a groaning sound that was like an animal, and the Handmaids chanting — *Push, push, push, breathe, breathe, breathe* — and at intervals an anguished voice I didn't recognize — but it must have been Ofkyle's — saying *Oh God, Oh God*, deep and dark as if it was coming out of a well. It was terrifying. Sitting on

131

the stairs hugging myself, I began to shiver. What was happening? What torturing, what inflicting? What was being done?

These sounds went on for what seemed a long time. I heard footsteps hurrying along the hallway — the Marthas, bringing whatever had been requested, carrying things away. From snooping in the laundry later in the evening I saw that some of these things were bloody sheets and towels. Then one of the Aunts came out into the hall and started barking into her Computalk. 'Right now! As fast as you can! Her pressure's way down! She's losing too much blood!'

There was a scream, and another. One of the Aunts called down the stairs to the Wives: 'Get in here now!' The Aunts didn't usually yell like that. A crowd of footsteps, hurrying up the stairs, and a voice saying, 'Oh, Paula!'

Then there was another siren, a different kind. I checked the hallway — nobody — and scuttled to my own room to peer out the window. A black car, the red wings and the snake, but a tall gold triangle: a real doctor. He almost leapt out of the car, slamming the door, and ran up the steps.

I heard what he was saying: *Shit! Shit! Shit! Shit of a God!*

This in itself was electrifying: I had never heard a man say anything like that before.

★   ★   ★

It was a boy, a healthy son for Paula and Commander Kyle. He was named Mark. But Ofkyle died.

I sat with the Marthas in the kitchen after the Wives and the Handmaids and everyone had gone away. The Marthas were eating the leftover party food: sandwiches with the crusts cut off, cake, real coffee. They offered me some of the treats, but I said I wasn't hungry. They asked about my cramps; I would feel better tomorrow, they said, and after a while it wouldn't be so bad, and anyway you got used to it. But that wasn't why I had no appetite.

There would have to be a wet nurse, they said: it would be one of the Handmaids who'd lost a baby. That, or formula, though everyone knew formula wasn't as good. Still, it would keep life in the little mite.

'The poor girl,' Zilla said. 'To go through all of that for nothing.'

'At least the baby was saved,' said Vera.

'It was one or the other,' said Rosa. 'They had to cut her open.'

'I'm going to bed now,' I said.

★ ★ ★

Ofkyle hadn't yet been taken out of our house. She was in her own room, wrapped in a sheet, as I discovered when I went softly up the back stairs.

I uncovered her face. It was flat white: she must have had no blood left in her. Her eyebrows were blond, soft and fine, upcurved as if surprised. Her eyes were open, looking at me. Maybe that was the first time she had ever seen me. I kissed her on the forehead.

133

'I won't ever forget you,' I said to her. 'The others will, but I promise I won't.'

Melodramatic, I know: I was still a child really. But as you can see, I have kept my word: I never have forgotten her. Her, Ofkyle, the nameless one, buried under a little square stone that might as well have been blank. I found it in the Handmaid graveyard, some years later.

And when I had the power to do so, I searched for her in the Bloodlines Genealogical Archives, and I found her. I found her original name. Meaningless, I know, except for those who must have loved her and then been torn apart from her. But for me it was like finding a handprint in a cave: it was a sign, it was a message. *I was here. I existed. I was real.*

What was her name? Of course you will want to know.

It was Crystal. And that is how I remember her now. I remember her as Crystal.

★ ★ ★

They had a small funeral for Crystal. I was allowed to come to it: having had my first period, I was now officially a woman. The Handmaids who'd been present at the Birth were allowed to come too, and our entire household went as well. Even Commander Kyle was there, as a token of respect.

We sang two hymns — 'Uplift the Lowly' and 'Blessed Be the Fruit' — and the legendary Aunt Lydia gave a speech. I looked at her with wonder, as if she was her own picture come to life: she existed after all. She looked older than her picture, though, and not quite as scary.

She said that our sister in service, Handmaid Ofkyle, had made the ultimate sacrifice, and had died with noble womanly honour, and had redeemed herself from her previous life of sin, and she was a shining example to the other Handmaids.

Aunt Lydia's voice trembled a little as she was saying this. Paula and Commander Kyle looked solemn and devout, nodding from time to time, and some of the Handmaids cried.

I did not cry. I'd already done my crying. The truth was that they'd cut Crystal open to get the baby out, and they'd killed her by doing that. It wasn't something she chose. She hadn't volunteered to die with noble womanly honour or be a shining example, but nobody mentioned that.

19

At school my position was now worse than it had ever been. I had become a taboo object: our Handmaid had died, which was believed among the girls to be a sign of bad fate. They were a superstitious group. At the Vidala School there were two religions: the official one taught by the Aunts, about God and the special sphere of women, and the unofficial one, which was passed from girl to girl by means of games and songs.

The younger girls had a number of counting rhymes, such as *Knit one, purl two, Here's a husband just for you; Knit two, purl one, He got killed, here's another one.* For the small girls, husbands were not real people. They were furniture and therefore replaceable, as in my childhood dollhouse.

The most popular singing game among the younger girls was called 'Hanging.' It went like this:

Who's that hanging on the Wall? Fee Fie Fiddle-Oh!
It's a Handmaid, what's she called? Fee Fie Fiddle-Oh!
She was (here we would put in the name of one of us), *now she's not. Fee Fie Fiddle-Oh!*

She had a baby in the pot (here we would slap our little flat stomachs). *Fee Fie Fiddle-Oh!*

The girls would file under the uplifted hands of two other girls while everyone chanted: *One for murder, Two for kissing, Three for a baby, Four gone missing, Five for alive and Six for dead, And Seven we caught you, Red Red Red!*

And the seventh girl would be caught by the two counters, and paraded around in a circle before being given a slap on the head. Now she was 'dead,' and was allowed to choose the next two executioners. I realize this sounds both sinister and frivolous, but children will make games out of whatever is available to them.

The Aunts probably thought this game contained a beneficial amount of warning and threat. Why was it 'One for murder,' though? Why did murder have to come before kissing? Why not after, which would seem more natural? I have often thought about that since, but I have never found any answer.

We were allowed other games inside school hours. We played Snakes and Ladders — if you landed on a Prayer you went up a ladder on the Tree of Life, but if you landed on a Sin you went down a Satanic snake. We were given colouring books, and we coloured in the signs of the shops — ALL FLESH, LOAVES AND FISHES — as a way of learning them. We coloured the clothing of people too — blue for the Wives, stripes for the Econowives, red for the Handmaids. Becka once got in trouble with Aunt Vidala for colouring a Handmaid purple.

Among the older girls the superstitions were whispered rather than sung, and they were not games. They were taken seriously. One of them went like this:

If your Handmaid dies in your bed,
Then her blood is on your head.
If your Handmaid's baby dies,
Then your life is tears and sighs.
If your Handmaid dies in Birth,
The curse will follow you over the earth.

Ofkyle had died during a Birth, so I was viewed by the other girls as accursed; but also, since little baby Mark was alive and well and my brother, I was also viewed as unusually blessed. The other girls did not taunt me openly, but they avoided me. Huldah would squint up at the ceiling when she saw me coming; Becka would turn away, though she would slip me portions of her lunch when no one was looking. Shunammite fell away from me, whether out of fear because of the death or envy because of the Birth, or a combination of both.

At home all attention was on the baby, who demanded it. He had a loud voice. And although Paula enjoyed the prestige of having a baby — and a male one at that — she was not the motherly type at heart. Little Mark would be produced and exhibited for her friends, but a short time of that went a long way with Paula and he would soon be handed over to the wet

138

nurse, a plump, lugubrious Handmaid who had recently been Oftucker but was now, of course, Ofkyle.

When he wasn't eating or sleeping or being shown off, Mark passed his time in the kitchen, where he was a great favourite among the Marthas. They loved to give him his bath and exclaim over his tiny fingers, his tiny toes, his tiny dimples, and his tiny male organ, out of which he could project a truly astonishing fountain of pee. What a strong little man!

I was expected to join in the worship, and when I didn't show enough zeal I was told to stop sulking, because soon enough I would have a baby of my own, and then I would be happy. I doubted that very much — not the baby so much as the happiness. I spent as much time in my room as possible, avoiding the cheerfulness in the kitchen and brooding on the unfairness of the universe.

VII

Stadium

The Ardua Hall Holograph

20

The crocuses have melted, the daffodils have shrivelled to paper, the tulips have performed their enticing dance, flipping their petal skirts inside out before dropping them completely. The herbs nurtured in the Ardua Hall borders by Aunt Clover and her posse of semi-vegetarian trowel-wielders are in their prime. *But, Aunt Lydia, you must drink this mint tea, it will do wonders for your digestion!* Keep your nose out of my digestion, I want to snap at them; but they mean well, I remind myself. Is that ever a convincing excuse when there's blood on the carpet?

I meant well too, I sometimes mumble silently. I meant it for the best, or for the best available, which is not the same thing. Still, think how much worse it could have been if not for me.

Bullshit, I reply on some days. Though on other days I pat myself on the back. Whoever said consistency is a virtue?

What's next in the waltz of the flowers? Lilacs. So dependable. So frilly. So aromatic. Soon my old enemy, Aunt Vidala, will be sneezing. Maybe her eyes will swell up and she won't be able to peer at me out of their corners, hoping to detect some slippage, some weakness, some lapse in theological correctness that can be leveraged into my downfall.

Hope on, I whisper to her. I pride myself on the fact that I can keep one jump ahead of you. But why only one? Several. Topple me and I'll pull down the temple.

★ ★ ★

Gilead has a long-standing problem, my reader: for God's kingdom on earth, it's had an embarrassingly high emigration rate. The seepage of our Handmaids, for instance: too many have been slipping away. As Commander Judd's analysis of escapes has revealed, no sooner is an exit route discovered by us and blocked than another opens up.

Our buffer zones are too permeable. The wilder patches of Maine and Vermont are a liminal space not fully controlled by us, where the natives are, if not overtly hostile, prone to heresies. They are also, as I know from my own experience, densely interconnected by a network of marriages that resembles a piece of surreal knitting, and they are prone to vendettas if crossed. For this reason it's difficult to get them to betray one another. It's been suspected for some time there are guides among them, acting either from a desire to outsmart Gilead or from simple cupidity, for Mayday has been known to pay. One Vermonter who fell into our hands told us they have a saying: 'Mayday is Payday.'

The hills and swamps, the winding rivers, the long rock-strewn bays that lead to the sea with its high tides — all aid the clandestine. In the subhistory of the region, there are rum-runners, there are cigarette profiteers, there are drug smugglers, there are illicit peddlers of all kinds. Borders mean nothing to them: they slip in and out, they thumb their noses, money changes hands.

One of my uncles was active in that way. Our family having been what it was — trailer-park dwellers, sneerers at the police, consorters with the flip side of the criminal justice system — my father was proud of that. Though not of me: I was a girl and, worse, a smarty-pants girl. Nothing for it but to wallop those pretensions out of me, with fists or boots or whatever else was to hand. He got his throat cut before the triumph of Gilead, or I would have arranged to have it done for him. But enough of such folk memories.

★　★　★

Quite recently, Aunt Elizabeth, Aunt Helena, and Aunt Vidala came up with a detailed plan for better control. *Operation Dead End*, it was called. *A Plan to Eliminate the Female Emigrant Problem in the North-Eastern Seaboard Territories*. It outlined the steps necessary for the trapping of fugitive Handmaids en route to Canada, and called for the declaration of a National Emergency, plus a doubling of tracker dogs and a more efficient system of interrogation. I detected Aunt Vidala's hand in this last: it is her secret sorrow that fingernail ripping and

145

evisceration are not on our list of chastisements.

'Well done,' I said. 'This seems very thorough. I will read it with great care, and I can assure you that your concerns are shared by Commander Judd, who is taking action, although I am not free to share the details with you at this time.'

'Praise be,' said Aunt Elizabeth, though she did not sound overjoyed.

'This escape business must be crushed once and for all,' Aunt Helena declared, glancing at Aunt Vidala for reassurance. She stamped her foot for emphasis, which must have been painful considering her fallen arches: she ruined her feet in youth by wearing five-inch Blahnik stilettos. The shoes alone would get her denounced nowadays.

'Indeed,' I said suavely. 'And it does appear to be a business, at least in part.'

'We should clear-cut the entire area!' said Aunt Elizabeth. 'They're hand in glove with Mayday in Canada.'

'That is what Commander Judd believes as well,' I said.

'Those women need to do their duty to the Divine Plan like the rest of us,' said Aunt Vidala. 'Life is not a vacation.'

Although they'd concocted their plan without getting authorization from me first — an act of insubordination — I felt duty-bound to pass it along to Commander Judd; especially in view of the fact that if I did not, he would be certain to hear of it and take note of my recalcitrance.

★ ★ ★

This afternoon, the three of them paid me another visit. They were in high spirits: raids in Upstate New York had just produced a mixed haul of seven Quakers, four back-to-the-landers, two Canadian moose-hunting guides, and a lemon smuggler, each of whom was a suspected link in the Underground Femaleroad chain. Once any additional information they might possess had been wrung from them, they would be disposed of, unless they were found to have trading value: hostage exchanges between Mayday and Gilead were not unknown.

I was of course aware of these developments. 'Congratulations,' I said. 'You must each take some credit, if only under the table. Commander Judd will take centre stage, naturally.'

'Naturally,' said Aunt Vidala.

'We are happy to serve,' said Aunt Helena.

'I have some news to share with you in my turn, from Commander Judd himself. But it must not go beyond us.' They leaned in: we all love a secret. 'Two of the top Mayday operatives in Canada have been erased by our agents.'

'Under His Eye,' said Aunt Vidala.

'Our Pearl Girls were pivotal,' I added.

'Praise be!' said Aunt Helena.

'One of them was a casualty,' I said. 'Aunt Adrianna.'

'What happened to her?' Aunt Elizabeth asked.

'We are waiting for clarification.'

'We will pray for her soul,' said Aunt Elizabeth. 'And Aunt Sally?'

'I believe she is safe.'

'Praise be.'

'Indeed,' I said. 'The bad news, however, is that we have uncovered a breach in our defences. The two Mayday agents must have been getting help from traitors inside Gilead itself. Someone was passing messages to them, from here to there — informing them about our security operations, and even about our agents and volunteers within Canada.'

'Who would do that?' said Aunt Vidala. 'It's apostasy!'

'The Eyes are trying to find out,' I said. 'So if you notice anything suspicious — anything, by anyone, even anyone at Ardua Hall — do let me know.'

There was a pause while they looked at one another. *Anyone at Ardua Hall* included the three of them.

'Oh, surely not,' said Aunt Helena. 'Think of the shame it would bring upon us!'

'Ardua Hall is spotless,' said Aunt Elizabeth.

'But the human heart is devious,' said Aunt Vidala.

'We must try for heightened awareness,' I said. 'Meanwhile, well done. Let me know how you make out with the Quakers and so forth.'

★ ★ ★

I record, I record; though to no end, I often fear. The black drawing ink I've been using is running out: soon I will switch to blue. Requisitioning a bottle from the Vidala School supplies should not be difficult: they teach drawing there. We Aunts used to be able to obtain ballpoint pens through the grey market, but no longer: our New Brunswick-based supplier has been arrested, having snuck under the radar once too often.

But I was telling you about the van with darkened windows — no, looking back a page, I see we'd arrived at the stadium.

Once on the ground, Anita and I were prodded to the right. We joined a herd of other women: I describe it as a herd because we were being herded. This collection was funnelled into a section of the bleachers marked off by the kind of yellow tape typical of crime scenes. There must have been about forty of us. Once installed, we had our handcuffs removed. I assumed they were needed for others.

Anita and I sat beside each other. To my left was a woman I didn't know who said she was a lawyer; to the right of Anita was another lawyer. Behind us, four judges; in front of us, four more. All of us judges or lawyers.

'They must be sorting us by profession,' said Anita.

And so it was. In a moment of inattention by the guards, the woman at the end of our row managed to communicate across the aisle with a woman in the section next to us. Over there, all were doctors.

★　★　★

We hadn't had lunch, and we weren't given any. Throughout the following hours, vans continued to arrive and discharge their unwilling female passengers.

149

None of them was what you would call young. Middle-aged professional women, in suits and good haircuts. No handbags, though: we had not been allowed to bring those. So no combs, no lipsticks, no mirrors, no little packets of throat lozenges, no disposable tissues. It's amazing how naked you feel without those things. Or felt, once.

The sun beat down: we were without hats or sunblock, and I could picture the shade of blistering red I would be by sundown. At least the seats had backs to them. They would not have been uncomfortable if we'd been there for recreational purposes. But entertainment was not being provided, and we could not get up to stretch: attempts to do so produced shouts. Sitting without moving necessarily becomes tedious and a strain on the buttock, back, and thigh muscles. It was minor pain, but it was pain.

To pass the time I berated myself. Stupid, stupid, stupid: I'd believed all that claptrap about life, liberty, democracy, and the rights of the individual I'd soaked up at law school. These were eternal verities and we would always defend them. I'd depended on that, as if on a magic charm.

You pride yourself on being a realist, I told myself, so face the facts. There's been a coup, here in the United States, just as in times past in so many other countries. Any forced change of leadership is always followed by a move to crush the opposition. The opposition is led by the educated, so the educated are the first to be eliminated. You're a judge, so you are the educated, like it or not. They won't want you around.

I'd spent my earlier years doing things I'd been told would be impossible for me. No one in my family had ever been to college, they'd despised me for going, I'd done it with scholarships and working nights at crappy jobs. It toughens you. You get stubborn. I did not intend to be eliminated if I could help it. But none of my college-acquired polish was of any use to me here. I needed to revert to the mulish underclass child, the determined drudge, the brainy overachiever, the strategic ladder-climber who'd got me to the social perch from which I'd just been deposed. I needed to work the angles, once I could find out what the angles were.

I'd been in tight corners before. I had prevailed. That was my story to myself.

★   ★   ★

Mid-afternoon produced bottles of water, handed out by trios of men: one to carry the bottles, one to pass them out, and one to cover us with his weapon in case we began to leap, thrash about, and snap, like the crocodiles we were.

'You can't keep us here!' one woman said. 'We haven't done anything wrong!'

'We're not allowed to talk to you,' said the bottle-passer.

None of us was allowed to go to the bathroom. Trickles of pee appeared, running down the bleachers towards the playing field. This

151

treatment was supposed to humiliate us, break down our resistance, I thought; but resistance to what? We weren't spies, we had no secret information we were holding back, we weren't the soldiers of an enemy army. Or were we? If I looked deep into the eyes of one of these men, would there be a human being looking back out at me? And if not, then what?

I tried to place myself in the position of those who had corralled us. What were they thinking? What was their goal? How did they hope to accomplish it?

* ★ *

At four o'clock we were treated to a spectacle. Twenty women, of various sizes and ages, but all in business attire, were led into the centre of the field. I say led because they were blindfolded. Their hands were cuffed in front. They were arranged in two rows, ten and ten. The front row was forced to kneel down, as if for a group photo.

A man in a black uniform orated into a microphone about how sinners were always visible to the Divine Eye and their sin would find them out. An undertone of assent, like a vibration, came from the guards and attendants. *Mmmmmm . . .* like a motor revving up.

'God will prevail,' concluded the speaker.

There was a chorus of baritone Amens. Then the men who'd escorted the blindfolded women raised their guns and shot them. Their aim was good: the women keeled over.

There was a collective groan from all of us who were seated in the bleachers. I heard screams and sobbing. Some of the women leapt to their feet, shouting — I could not make out the words — but were quickly silenced by being hit on the backs of their heads with the butts of guns. There were no repeated blows: one sufficed. Again, the aim was good: these men were trained.

We were to see but not speak: the message was clear. But why? If they were going to kill us all, why this display?

⋆ ⋆ ⋆

Sundown brought sandwiches, one each. Mine was egg salad. I am ashamed to say I gobbled it up with relish. There were a few distant sounds of retching, but, under the circumstances, surprisingly few.

After that we were instructed to stand up. Then we filed out, row by row — the process was eerily silent, and very orderly — and were ushered down into the locker rooms and the corridors leading to them. That is where we spent the night.

There were no amenities, no mattresses or pillows, but at least there were bathrooms, filthy as they had already become. No guards were present to stop us from talking, though why we supposed no one was listening escapes me now. But by that time, none of us was thinking clearly.

The lights were left on, which was a mercy.

153

No, it was not a mercy. It was a convenience for those in charge. Mercy was a quality that did not operate in that place.

VIII

CARNARVON

21

I was sitting in Ada's car, trying to absorb what she'd told me. Melanie and Neil. Blown up by a bomb. Outside The Clothes Hound. It wasn't possible.

'Where are we going?' I said. It was a limp thing to say, it sounded so normal; but nothing was normal. Why wasn't I screaming?

'I'm thinking,' Ada said. She looked into the rear-view mirror, then pulled into a driveway. The house had a sign that said ALTERNA RENO-VATIONS. Every house in our area was always being renovated; then someone would buy it and renovate it again, which drove Neil and Melanie crazy. Why spend all that money on tearing the guts out of perfectly good houses? Neil would say. It was hiking up the prices and shutting poor people out of the market.

'Are we going in here?' I was suddenly very tired. It would be nice to go into a house and lie down.

'Nope,' said Ada. She took out a small wrench from her leather backpack and destroyed her phone. I watched as it cracked and slivered: the case shattered, the metal innards warped and fell apart.

'Why are you wrecking your phone?' I said.

'Because you can never be too careful.' She

put the remains into a small plastic bag. 'Wait'll this car goes past, then get out and toss it into that trash bin.'

Drug dealers did this — they used burner phones. I was having second thoughts about having come with her. She wasn't just severe, she was scary. 'Thanks for the lift,' I said, 'but I should go back to my school now. I can tell them about the explosion, they'll know what to do.'

'You're in shock. It's no wonder,' she said.

'I'm okay,' I said, though it wasn't true. 'I can just get out here.'

'Suit yourself,' she said, 'but they'll have to report you to Social Services, and those folks will put you into foster care, and who knows how that'll turn out?' I hadn't thought about that. 'So once you've ditched my phone,' she continued, 'you can either get back in the car or keep on walking. Your choice. Just don't go home. That's not a command, it's advice.'

I did as she'd asked. Now that she'd laid out my options, what choice did I have? Back in the car I began to sniffle, but except for handing me a tissue, Ada didn't react. She made a U-turn and headed south. She was a fast and efficient driver. 'I know you don't trust me,' she said after a while, 'but you have to trust me. The same people who set that car bomb could be looking for you right now. I'm not saying they are, I just don't know, but you're at risk.'

At risk — that's what they said on the news about children who'd been found battered to death despite multiple warnings by the neighbours, or women who'd hitchhiked because there was no bus and were found by someone's dog in a shallow grave with their necks broken. My teeth were chattering, though the air was hot and sticky.

I didn't quite believe her, but I didn't disbelieve her either. 'We could tell the police,' I said timidly.

'They'd be useless.' I'd heard about the uselessness of the police — Neil and Melanie regularly expressed that opinion. She turned the car radio on: soothing music with harps in it. 'Don't think about anything yet,' she said.

'Are you a cop?' I asked her.

'Nope,' she said.

'Then what are you?'

'Least said, soonest mended,' she said.

★ ★ ★

We stopped in front of a large, square-shaped building. The sign said MEETING HOUSE and RELIGIOUS SOCIETY OF FRIENDS (QUAKERS). Ada parked the car at the back beside a grey van. 'That's our next ride,' she said.

We went in through the side door. Ada nodded at the man sitting at a small desk there. 'Elijah,' she said. 'We've got errands.'

I didn't really look at him. I followed her through the Meeting House proper, with its empty hush and its echoes and its slightly chilly smell, then into a larger room, which was brighter and had air conditioning. There was a row of beds — more like cots — with women lying down on some of them, covered with blankets, all different colours. In another corner there were five armchairs and a coffee table. Several women sitting there were talking in low voices.

'Don't stare,' said Ada to me. 'It's not a zoo.'

'What is this place?' I said.

'SanctuCare, the Gilead refugee organization. Melanie worked with it, and so did Neil in a different way. Now, I want you to sit in that chair and be a fly on the wall. Don't move and don't say boo. You'll be safe here. I need to make some arrangements for you. I'll be back in maybe an hour. They'll make sure you get some sugar into you, you need it.' She went over and spoke to one of the women in charge, then walked quickly out of the room. After a while, the woman brought me a cup of hot sweet tea and a chocolate-chip cookie, and asked if I was all right and if I needed anything else, and I said no. But she came back anyway with one of the blankets, a green-and-blue one, and tucked it around me.

I managed to drink some of the tea, and my teeth stopped chattering. I sat there and watched the foot traffic, the way I used to watch it in The Clothes Hound. Several women came in, one of them with a baby. They looked really wrecked, and also scared. The SanctuCare women went over and welcomed them and said, 'You're here now, it's all right,' and the Gilead women started to cry. At the time I thought, Why cry, you should be happy, you got out. But after all that's happened to me since that day, I understand why. You hold it in, whatever it is, until you can make it through the worst part. Then, once you're safe, you can cry all the tears you couldn't waste time crying before.

Words came out of the women in snatches and gasps:

If they say I have to go back . . .
I had to leave my boy behind, isn't there
*   any way to . . .*
I lost the baby. There was no one . . .

The women in charge handed them tissues. They said calm things like *You need to be strong.* They were trying to make things better. But it can put a lot of pressure on a person to be told they need to be strong. That's another thing I've learned.

★　★　★

After an hour or so, Ada came back. 'You're still alive,' she said. If it was a joke, it was a bad one. I just stared at her. 'You have to dump the plaid.'

'What?' I said. It was like she was speaking some other language.

'I know this is tough for you,' she said, 'but we don't have time for that right now, we need to get moving fast. Not to be alarmist, but there's trouble. Now let's get some other clothes.' She took hold of my arm and lifted me up out of the chair: she was surprisingly strong.

We went past all the women, into a back room where there was a table with T-shirts and sweaters and a couple of racks with hangers. I recognized some of the items: this was where the

161

donations from The Clothes Hound ended up.

'Pick something you'd never wear in real life,' said Ada. 'You need to look like a totally different person.'

I found a black T-shirt with a white skull, and a pair of leggings, black with white skulls. I added high-tops, black and white, and some socks. Everything was used. I did think about lice and bedbugs: Melanie always asked whether the stuff people tried to sell her had been cleaned. We got bedbugs in the store once and it was a nightmare.

'I'll turn my back,' said Ada. There was no change room. I wriggled out of my school uniform and put on my new used clothes. My movements felt very slowed down. What if she was abducting me? I thought groggily. *Abducting.* It was what happened to girls who were smuggled and made into sex slaves — we'd learned about that at school. But girls like me didn't get abducted, except sometimes by men posing as real estate salesmen who kept them locked in the basement. Sometimes men like that had women helping them. Was Ada one of those? What if her story about Melanie and Neil being blown up was a trick? Right now the two of them might be frantic because I hadn't turned up. They might be calling the school or even the police, useless though they considered them.

Ada still had her back to me, but I sensed that if I even thought about making a break for it — out the side door of the Meeting House, for instance — she would know about it in advance. And supposing I ran, where could I go? The only place I wanted to go was home, but if Ada was telling the truth I shouldn't go there. Anyway, if Ada was telling the truth it would no longer be my home because Melanie and Neil wouldn't be in it. What would I do all by myself in an empty house?

'I'm done,' I said.

Ada turned around. 'Not bad,' she said. She took off her black jacket and stuffed it into a carry bag, then put on a green jacket that was on the rack. Then she pinned up her hair and added sunglasses. 'Hair down,' she told me, so I pulled off my scrunchie and shook my hair out. She found a pair of sunglasses for me: orange mirror ones. She handed me a lipstick, and I made myself a new red mouth.

'Look like a thug,' she said.

I didn't know how, but I tried. I scowled, and pouted my lips that were covered in red wax.

'There,' she said. 'You'd never know. Our secret is safe with us.'

What was our secret? That I no longer officially existed? Something like that.

22

We got into the grey van and drove for a while, with Ada paying close attention to the traffic behind us. Then we threaded through a maze of side streets, and pulled into a drive in front of a big old brownstone mansion. In the semicircle that might once have been a flower garden and even now had the remains of some tulips among the uncut grass and dandelions, there was a sign with a picture of a condo building.

'Where is this?' I said.

'Parkdale,' said Ada. I'd never been to Parkdale before, but I'd heard about it: some of the drug-head kids at school thought it was cool, which was what they said about decaying urban areas that were now re-gentrifying. There were a couple of trendy nightclubs in it, for those who wanted to lie about their age.

The mansion sat on a large scruffy lot with a couple of huge trees. Nobody had cleaned up the fallen leaves for a long time; a few stray rags of coloured plastic, red and silver, shone out from the drift of mulch.

Ada headed towards the house, glancing back to make sure I was following. 'Are you okay?' she asked.

'Yeah,' I said. I felt a little dizzy. I walked

behind her over the uneven paving; it felt spongy, as if my foot could go through it at any moment. The world was no longer solid and dependable, it was porous and deceptive. Anything could disappear. At the same time, everything I looked at was very clear. It was like one of those surrealist paintings we'd studied in school the year before. Melted clocks in the desert, solid but unreal.

Heavy stone steps led up to the front porch. It was framed by a stone archway with a name carved into it in the Celtic lettering you sometimes see on older buildings in Toronto — CARNARVON — surrounded by stone leaves and elvish faces; they were probably meant to be mischievous, but I found them malignant. Everything seemed malignant to me right then.

The porch smelled of cat piss. The door was wide and heavy, studded with black nailheads. The graffiti artists had been at work on it in red paint: that pointy writing they do, and another more legible word that might have been BARF.

Despite the slummy look of the door, the lock worked with a magnetic key fob. Inside was an old maroon hall carpet and a flight of broad stairs winding upwards, with beautiful curved banisters.

'It was a rooming house for a while,' said Ada. 'Now it's furnished apartments.'

'What was it at first?' I was leaning against the wall.

'A summer house,' said Ada. 'Rich people. Let's get you upstairs, you need to lie down.'

'What's 'Carnarvon'?' I was having a little

trouble getting up the stairs.

'Welsh place,' said Ada. 'Somebody must've been homesick.' She took my arm. 'Come on, count the steps.' Home, I thought. I was going to start sniffling again. I tried not to.

We got to the top of the stairs. There was another heavy door, another fob lock. Inside was a front room with a sofa and two easy chairs and a coffee table and a dining table.

'There's a bedroom for you,' said Ada, but I had no urge to see it. I fell onto the sofa. All of a sudden I had no strength; I didn't think I could get up.

'You're shivering again,' said Ada. 'I'll turn down the AC.' She brought a duvet from one of the bedrooms, a new one, white.

Everything in the room was realer than real. There was some kind of houseplant on the table, though it might have been plastic; it had rubbery, shiny leaves. The walls were covered with rose-coloured paper, with a darker design of trees. There were nail holes where there must have been pictures once. These details were so vivid they were almost shimmering, as if they were lit from behind.

I closed my eyes to shut out the light. I must have dozed off because suddenly it was evening, and Ada was turning on the flatscreen. I guess that was for my benefit — so I would know she'd been telling the truth — but it was brutal. The wreckage of The Clothes Hound — the windows shattered, the door gaping open. Scraps of fabric scattered over the sidewalk. In front, the shell of Melanie's car, crumpled like a burnt-out marshmallow. Two police cars visible, and the yellow tape they put around disaster areas. No sign of Neil or Melanie, and I was glad: I had a horror of seeing their blackened flesh, the ash of their hair, their singed bones.

The remote was on an end table beside the sofa. I turned off the sound: I didn't want to hear the anchor's level voice talking as if this event was the same as a politician getting onto a plane. When the car and the store vanished and the newsman's head bobbed into view like a joke balloon, I switched the TV off.

Ada came in from the kitchen. She brought me a sandwich on a plate: chicken salad. I said I wasn't hungry.

'There's an apple,' she said. 'Want that?'

'No thank you.'

'I know this is bizarre,' she said. I said nothing. She went out and came in again. 'I got you some birthday cake. It's chocolate. Vanilla ice cream. Your favourites.' It was on a white plate; there was a plastic fork. How did she know what my favourites were? Melanie must have told her. They must have talked about me. The white plate was dazzling. There was a single candle stuck into the piece of cake. When I was younger I would have made a wish. What would my wish be now? That time would move backwards? That it would be yesterday? I wonder how many people have ever wished that.

'Where's the bathroom?' I asked. She told me, and I went into it and was sick. Then I lay down on the sofa again and shivered. After a while she brought me some ginger ale. 'You need to get your blood sugar up,' she said. She went out of the room, turning off the lights.

It was like being home from school when you had the flu. Other people would cover you up and bring you things to drink; they would be the ones dealing with real life so you didn't have to. It would be nice to stay like this forever: then I would never have to think about anything again.

In the distance there were the noises of the city: traffic, sirens, a plane overhead. From the kitchen came the sound of Ada rustling around; she had a brisk, light way of moving, as if she walked on her toes. I heard the murmur of her voice, talking on the phone. She was in charge, though what she was in charge of I couldn't guess; nonetheless I felt lulled and held. Behind my closed eyes I heard the apartment door open, and then pause, and then shut.

23

When I woke up again, it was morning. I didn't know what time it was. Had I slept in, was I late for school? Then I remembered: school was done. I would never be going back there, or to anywhere else I knew.

I was in one of the Carnarvon bedrooms, with the white duvet covering me, still wearing the T-shirt and leggings, though I didn't have the socks or shoes on. There was a window, with a roller shade pulled down. I sat up carefully. I saw some red on the pillowcase, but it was only lipstick from yesterday's red mouth. I was no longer nauseous and dizzy, but I was fuzzy. I scratched my head all over and gave my hair a tug. Once when I had a headache I'd been told by Melanie that pulling your hair increased the circulation to the brain. She said that's why Neil did it.

After I stood up, I felt more awake. I studied myself in the big wall mirror. I wasn't the same person as the day before, although I looked similar. I opened the door and went along the hall to the kitchen in my bare feet.

Ada wasn't there. She was in the living room, sitting in one of the easy chairs with a mug of coffee. On the sofa was the man we'd passed when going in through the side door at SanctuCare.

'You woke up,' said Ada. Adults were in the habit of stating the obvious — *You woke up* was something Melanie might have said to me, as if it was an accomplishment — and I was disappointed to find that Ada was no exception in this way.

I looked at the man and he looked at me. He was wearing black jeans and sandals and a grey T-shirt that said TWO WORDS, ONE FINGER and a Blue Jays baseball cap. I wondered if he knew what his T-shirt actually meant.

He must have been fifty, but his hair was dark and thick, so maybe he was younger. His face was like creased leather, and he had a scar up the side of his cheek. He smiled at me, showing white teeth with a molar missing on the left. A tooth missing like that makes a person look illegal.

Ada nodded her chin over at the man: 'You remember Elijah, from SanctuCare. Friend of Neil's. He's here to help. There's cereal in the kitchen.'

'Then we can talk,' said Elijah.

The cereal was the kind I liked, round Os made from beans. I brought the bowl into the living area and sat down in the other easy chair, and waited for them to speak.

Neither of them said anything. They glanced at each other. I ate two spoonfuls, tentatively, in case my stomach was still unsettled. In my ears I could hear the crunching of the Os.

'Which end first?' said Elijah.

'The deep end,' said Ada.

'Okay,' he said and looked directly at me. 'Yesterday was not your birthday.'

I was surprised. 'Yes it was,' I said. 'The first of May. I turned sixteen.'

'In reality you're about four months younger,' said Elijah.

How do you prove your birth date? There must have been a birth certificate, but where did Melanie keep it? 'It's on my health card. My birthday,' I said.

'Try again,' said Ada to Elijah. He looked down at the carpet.

'Melanie and Neil were not your parents,' he said.

'Yes they were!' I said. 'Why are you saying that?' I felt tears building in my eyes. There was another void opening in reality: Neil and Melanie were fading, changing shape. I realized I didn't know much about them really, or about their past. They hadn't talked about it, and I hadn't asked. Nobody ever asks their parents much about themselves, do they?

'I know this is distressing for you,' said Elijah, 'but it's important, so I'll say it again. Neil and Melanie were not your parents. Sorry to be so blunt, but we don't have much time.'

'Then who were they?' I said. I was blinking. One of the tears made it out; I wiped it away.

'No relation,' he said. 'You were placed with them for safekeeping when you were a baby.'

'That can't be true,' I said. But I was less convinced.

'You should've been told earlier,' said Ada.

'They wanted to spare you the worry. They were going to tell you on the day they . . . ' She trailed off, clamped her lips shut. She'd been so silent about Melanie dying, as if they hadn't been friends at all, but now I could see that she was truly upset. It made me like her more.

'Part of their job was to protect you and keep you safe,' said Elijah. 'I'm sorry to be the messenger.'

On top of the new-furniture smell of the room, I could smell Elijah: a sweaty, solid, practical-laundry-soap smell. Organic laundry soap. It was the kind Melanie used. Had used. 'Then who were they?' I whispered.

'Neil and Melanie were very valued and experienced members of the — '

'No,' I said. 'My other parents. My real ones. Who were they? Are they dead too?'

'I'll make more coffee,' said Ada. She got up and went into the kitchen.

'They're still alive,' said Elijah. 'Or they were yesterday.'

I stared at him. I wondered if he was lying, but why would he have done that? If he'd wanted to make things up, he could have made up better things. 'I don't believe any of this,' I said. 'I don't know why you're even saying it.'

Ada came back into the room with a mug of coffee and said did anyone else want one, help yourself, and maybe I should have some time to myself to think things over.

Think what over? What was there to think? My parents had been murdered, but they weren't my real parents, and a different set of parents had appeared in their place.

'What things?' I said. 'I don't know enough to think anything.'

'What would you like to know?' said Elijah in a kind but tired voice.

'How did it happen?' I said. 'Where are my real . . . my other mother and father?'

'Do you know much about Gilead?' Elijah asked.

'Of course. I watch the news. We took it in school,' I said sullenly. 'I went to that protest march.' Right then I wanted Gilead to evaporate and leave us all alone.

'That's where you were born,' he said. 'In Gilead.'

'You're joking,' I said.

'You were smuggled out by your mother and Mayday. They'd risked their lives. Gilead made a big fuss about it; they wanted you back. They said your so-called legal parents had the right to claim you. Mayday hid you; there were a lot of people looking for you, plus a media blitz.'

'Like Baby Nicole,' I said. 'I wrote an essay about her at school.'

Elijah looked down at the floor again. Then he looked straight at me. 'You are Baby Nicole.'

IX

Thank Tank

The Ardua Hall Holograph

24

This afternoon I had another summons from Commander Judd, brought to me in person by a junior Eye. Commander Judd could have picked up the phone himself and discussed his business that way — there is an internal hotline between his office and mine, with a red telephone — but, like me, he can't be sure who else might be listening. In addition, I believe he enjoys our little tête-à-têtes, for reasons that are complex and perverse. He thinks of me as his handiwork: I am the embodiment of his will.

'I trust you are well, Aunt Lydia,' he said as I sat down across from him.

'Flourishing, praise be. And you?'

'I myself am in good health, but I fear my Wife is ailing. It weighs upon my soul.'

I was not surprised. The last time I saw her, Judd's current Wife was looking shopworn. 'That is sad news,' I said. 'What seems to be the malady?'

'It is not clear,' he said. It never is. 'An affliction of the inner organs.'

'Would you like someone at our Calm and Balm Clinic to consult?'

'Perhaps not just yet,' he said. 'Most likely it is minor, or perhaps even imaginary, as so many of these female complaints prove to be.' There was a pause while we regarded each other. Soon, I feared, he would again be a widower, and in the market for another child bride.

'Whatever I can do to help,' I said.

'Thank you, Aunt Lydia. You understand me so well,' he said, smiling. 'But that isn't the reason I asked you here. We have taken a position on the death of the Pearl Girl we lost in Canada.'

'What in fact transpired?' I already knew the answer, but had no intention of sharing it.

'The official Canadian account of the matter is suicide,' he said.

'I am devastated to hear this,' I replied. 'Aunt Adrianna was one of the most faithful and efficient . . . I placed much trust in her. She was exceptionally courageous.'

'Our own version is that the Canadians are covering up, and the depraved Mayday terrorists enabled by Canada's lax toleration of their illegal presence killed Aunt Adrianna. Though between you and me, we are baffled. Who can tell? It may even have been one of those random drug-related killings so prevalent in that decadent society. Aunt Sally was just around the corner purchasing some eggs. When she returned and discovered the tragedy, she wisely decided that a swift return to Gilead was her best option.'

'Very wisely,' I said.

       ★   ★   ★

Upon her sudden return, a shaken Aunt Sally had come straight to me. Then she'd described

178

how Adrianna had met her end. 'She attacked me. Out of nowhere, just before we were leaving for the Consulate. I don't know why! She leapt on me and tried to choke me, and I fought back. It was self-defence,' she'd sobbed.

'A momentary psychotic break,' I'd said. 'The strain of being in a strange and debilitating environment, such as Canada, can have that effect. You did the right thing. You had no choice. I see no reason for anyone else to know about this, do you?'

'Oh, thank you, Aunt Lydia. I'm so sorry it happened.'

'Pray for Adrianna's soul, then put it out of your mind,' I'd said. 'Do you have anything else to tell me?'

'Well, you asked us to be on the lookout for Baby Nicole. The couple running The Clothes Hound had a daughter who would be about the right age.'

'That is an interesting speculation,' I'd said. 'You intended to send a report, via the Consulate? Instead of waiting to speak directly with me upon return?'

'Well, I thought you should know immediately. Aunt Adrianna said it would be premature — she was strongly against it. We had words about it. I insisted that it was important,' Aunt Sally had said defensively.

'Indeed,' I'd said. 'It was. But risky. Such a report might well have started an unfounded rumour, with dire consequences. We have had so many false alarms, and everyone in the Consulate is potentially an Eye. The Eyes can be

179

so blunt; they lack finesse. There is always a reason for my instructions. My orders. It is not for the Pearl Girls to take unauthorized initiatives.'

'Oh, I didn't realize — I didn't think. But still, Aunt Adrianna shouldn't have — '

'Least said, soonest mended. I know you meant well,' I'd told her soothingly.

Aunt Sally had started to cry. 'I did, I really did.'

Hell was paved with good intentions, I'd been tempted to say. But refrained. 'Where is the girl in question now?' I'd asked. 'She must have gone somewhere after her parents were removed from the scene.'

'I don't know. Maybe they shouldn't have blown up The Clothes Hound so soon. Then we would have been able to — '

'I concur. I did advise against hastiness. Unfortunately the agents run by the Eyes in Canada are young and enthusiastic, and they do admire explosions. But how were they to know?' I'd paused, fixed her with my best penetrating gaze. 'And you have not communicated your suspicions about this potential Baby Nicole to anyone else?'

'No. Only to you, Aunt Lydia. And to Aunt Adrianna, before she . . . '

'Let's keep this to ourselves, shall we?' I'd said. 'There need not be a trial. Now, I think you need some rest and recuperation. I'll arrange a stay for you at our lovely Margery Kempe Retreat House in Walden. You'll be a different woman soon. The car will take you there in half an hour. And if Canada agitates about the unfortunate condo occurrence — if they wish to interview you or even charge you with some crime — we'll simply say you have disappeared.' I did not wish Aunt Sally dead: I simply wished her incoherent; and so it has been. The Margery Kempe Retreat House has a discreet staff.

More tearful thanks from Aunt Sally. 'Don't thank me,' I'd said. 'It is I who should be thanking you.'

⋆ ⋆ ⋆

'Aunt Adrianna did not give her life in vain,' Commander Judd was saying. 'Your Pearl Girls set us on a profitable course of action: we have made yet other discoveries.'

My heart contracted. 'I am happy that my girls were of use.'

'As always, thank you for your initiative. Since our operation involving the used clothing store indicated by your Pearl Girls, we've become certain of the means by which information has been exchanged in recent years between Mayday and their unknown contact here in Gilead.'

'And what is that means?'

'Via the burglary — via the special operation — we recovered a microdot camera. We've been doing tests with it.'

'Microdot?' I asked. 'What is that?'

'An old technology that has fallen into disuse, but that is still perfectly viable. Documents are photographed with a miniature camera that reduces them to microscopic size. Then they are printed on minute plastic dots, which can be applied to almost any surface and read by the recipient with a custom viewer small enough to be concealed in, for instance, a pen.'

'Astonishing,' I exclaimed. 'Not for nothing do we at Ardua Hall say 'Pen Is Envy.''

He laughed. 'Indeed,' he said. 'We pen-wielders must take care to avoid reproach. But it is intelligent of Mayday to have resorted to this method: not many people today would be aware of it. As they say: if you aren't looking, you don't see.'

'Ingenious,' I said.

'It's only one end of the string — the Mayday end. As I've mentioned, there's a Gilead end — those who are receiving the microdots here and reciprocating with messages of their own. We have still not identified that individual, or individuals.'

'I've asked my colleagues at Ardua Hall to keep their eyes and ears open,' I said.

'And who better placed to do that than the Aunts?' he said. 'You have access to any house you choose to enter, and with your finer women's intuition you hear things we dull men are too deaf to register.'

'We'll outfox Mayday yet,' I said, clenching my fists, thrusting out my jaw.

'I like your spirit, Aunt Lydia,' he said. 'We make a great team!'

'The truth shall prevail,' I said. I was quivering with what I hoped would pass as righteous indignation.

'Under His Eye,' he replied.

⋆   ⋆   ⋆

After this, my reader, I was in need of a restorative. I made my way to the Schlafly Café for a cup of hot milk. Then I came here to the Hildegard Library to continue my journey with you. Think of me as a guide. Think of yourself as a wanderer in a dark wood. It's about to get darker.

On the last page where we met, I'd brought you as far as the stadium, and there I will resume. As time crept by, things fell into a pattern. Sleep at night, if you could. Endure the days. Hug the weepers, though I have to say the weeping became tedious. So did the howling.

There was an attempt at music on the first evenings — a couple of the more optimistic and energetic women styled themselves sing-song leaders, and attempted versions of 'We Shall Overcome' and similar archaic chestnuts recalled from vanished summer camp experiences. There were problems remembering the words, but at least it added variety.

No guards put a stop to these efforts. However, by day three the perkiness was fading and few were joining in, and there were mutterings — 'Quiet, please!' 'For God's sake, shut up!' — so the Girl Scout leaders, after a few hurt protests — 'I was only trying to help' — ceased and desisted.

I was not one of the singers. Why waste your energy? My mood was not melodious. It was rather one of a rat in a maze. Was there a way out? What was that way? Why was I here? Was it

183

a test? What were they trying to find out?

Some women had nightmares, as you'd assume. They would groan and thrash about during them, or sit bolt upright with modified shouts. I'm not criticizing: I had nightmares myself. Shall I describe one for you? No, I will not. I'm fully aware of how easily one can become fatigued by other people's nightmares, having heard a number of recitals of these by now. When push comes to shove, only one's own nightmares are of any interest or significance.

In the mornings, wakeup was perpetrated by a siren. Those whose watches had not been taken away — watch removal had been spotty — reported that this happened at 6 a.m. Bread and water for breakfast. How superlatively good that bread tasted! Some wolfed and guzzled, but I made my portion last as long as possible. Chewing and swallowing distracts from abstract mental wheel-spinning. Also it passes the time.

Then, lineups for the foul toilets, and good luck to you if yours was clogged, since no one would come to unclog it. My theory? The guards went around at night stuffing various materials down the toilets as a further aggravation. Some of the more tidy-minded tried to clean up the washrooms, but once they saw how hopeless it was they gave up. Giving up was the new normal, and I have to say it was catching.

Did I say there was no toilet paper? What then? Use your hand, attempt to clean your sullied fingers under the dribble of water that sometimes came out of the taps and sometimes did not. I'm sure they arranged that on purpose

184

also, to raise us up and hurl us down at random intervals. I could picture the glee on the face of whatever kitten-torturing cretin was assigned this task as he flipped the power switch on the water flow system back and forth.

We had been told not to drink the water from those taps, but some unwisely did. Retching and diarrhea followed, to contribute to the general joy.

There were no paper towels. There were no towels of any kind. We wiped our hands on our skirts, whether those hands had been washed or not.

I am sorry to dwell so much on the facilities, but you would be amazed at how important such things become — basics that you've taken for granted, that you've barely thought about until they're removed from you. During my day-dreams — and we all daydreamed, as enforced stasis with no events produces daydreams and the brain must busy itself with something — I frequently pictured a beautiful, clean, white toilet. Oh, and a sink to go with it, with an ample flow of pure clear water.

Naturally we began to stink. In addition to the ordeal by toilet, we'd been sleeping in our business attire, with no change of underwear. Some of us were past menopause, but others were not, so the smell of clotting blood was added to the sweat and tears and shit and puke. To breathe was to be nauseated.

They were reducing us to animals — to penned-up animals — to our animal nature. They were rubbing our noses in that nature. We were to consider ourselves subhuman.

The rest of each day would unfurl like a toxic flower, petal by petal, agonizingly slow. We were sometimes handcuffed again, though sometimes not, then marched out in a line and slotted into the bleachers to sit under the blazing sun, and on one occasion — blissfully — in a cool drizzle. We reeked of wet clothing that night, but less of ourselves.

Hour by hour we watched vans arrive, discharge their quota of women, depart empty. The same wailings from the new arrivals, the same barking and shouts from the guards. How tedious is a tyranny in the throes of enactment. It's always the same plot.

Lunch was the sandwiches again, and on one day — the drizzle day — some carrot sticks.

'Nothing like a balanced meal,' said Anita. We had contrived to sit next to each other most days, and to sleep in proximity. She had not been a personal friend before this time, merely a professional colleague, but it gave me comfort simply to be with someone I knew; someone who personified my previous achievements, my previous life. You might say we bonded.

'You were a damn fine judge,' she whispered to me on the third day. 'Thank you. So were you,' I whispered back. Were was chilling.

★　★　★

Of the others in our section I learned little. Their names, sometimes. The names of their firms. Some firms had specialized in domestic work

186

— divorces, child custody, and so forth — so if women were now the enemy I could see why they might have been targeted; but being in real estate or litigation or estate law or corporate law appeared to offer no protection. All that was necessary was a law degree and a uterus: a lethal combination.

★ ★ ★

The afternoons were chosen for the executions. The same parade out to the middle of the field, with the blinded condemned ones. I noticed more details as time went on: how some could hardly walk, how some seemed barely conscious. What had been happening to them? And why had they been selected to die?

The same man in a black uniform exhorting into a microphone: *God will prevail!*

Then the shots, the toppling, the limp bodies. Then the cleanup. There was a truck for the corpses. Were they buried? Were they burned? Or was that too much trouble? Perhaps they were simply taken to a dumpsite and left for crows.

On the fourth day there was a variation: three of the shooters were women. They weren't in business suits, but in long brown garments like bathrobes, with scarves tied under their chins. That got our attention.

'Monsters!' I whispered to Anita.

'How could they?' she whispered back.

On the fifth day there were six women in brown among the shooters. There was also an uproar, as one of them, instead of aiming at the blindfolded ones, pivoted and shot one of the men in black uniforms. She was immediately bludgeoned to the ground and riddled with bullets. There was a collective gasp from the bleachers.

So, I thought. That's one way out.

* * *

During the days new women would be added to our group of lawyers and judges. It stayed the same size, however, since every night some were removed. They left singly, between two guards. We did not know where they were being taken, or why. None came back.

On the sixth night Anita was spirited away. It happened very quietly. Sometimes the targeted ones would shout and resist, but Anita did not, and I am ashamed to say that I was asleep when she was deleted. I woke up when the morning siren went off and she was simply not there.

'I'm sorry about your friend,' one kind soul whispered to me as we stood in line for the pullulating toilets.

'I'm sorry too,' I whispered back. But I was already hardening myself for what was almost surely to come. Sorry solves nothing, I told myself. Over the years — the many years — how true I have found that to be.

* * *

On the seventh night, it was me. Anita had been noiselessly abstracted — that silence had had a demoralizing effect all its own, since one could vanish, it seemed, with nobody noticing and not even a ripple of sound — but it was not intended that I should go quietly.

I was wakened by a boot applied to the hip. 'Shut up and get up,' said one of the barking voices. Before I was properly awake I was being yanked upright and set in motion. All around there were murmurs, and one voice said, 'No,' and another said, 'Fuck,' and another said, 'God bless,' and another said, 'Cuídate mucho.'

'I can walk by myself!' I said, but this made no difference to the hands on my upper arms, one on either side. This is it, I thought: they're going to shoot me. But no, I corrected myself: that's an afternoon thing. Idiot, I countered: shooting can happen anywhere at any time, and anyway shooting is not the only method.

All this time I was quite calm, which seems hard to believe, and in fact I no longer believe it: I was not quite calm, I was dead calm. As long as I thought of myself as already dead, untroubled by future cares, things would go easier for me.

I was steered through the corridors, then out of a back entrance and into a car. It was not a van this time but a Volvo. The back-seat upholstery was soft but firm, the air conditioning was like a breath of paradise. Unfortunately the freshness of the air reminded me of my own accumulated odours. Nevertheless I relished the luxury, despite the fact that I was squashed in between my two guards, both of them bulky. Neither said anything. I was simply a bundle to be transported.

The car stopped outside a police station. It was no longer a police station, however: the lettering had been covered over, and on the front door there was an image: an eye with wings. The logo of the Eyes, though I did not yet know that.

Up the front steps we went, my two companions striding, me stumbling. My feet hurt: I realized how out of practice they had become, and also how wrecked and filthy my shoes were, after the drenching, the baking, and the various substances to which they had been subjected.

We went along the corridor. Baritone rumblings came from behind doors; men in outfits like the ones beside me hurried past, their eyes gleaming with purpose, their voices staccato. There's something spine-stiffening about uniforms, about insignia, about shiny lapel pins. No slouchers here!

We turned into one of the rooms. There, behind a large desk, sat a man who looked faintly like Santa Claus: plump, white beard, rosy cheeks, cherry nose. He beamed at me. 'You may sit down,' he said.

'Thank you,' I replied. Not that I had a choice: my two travel buddies were inserting me into a chair and attaching me to it with plastic straps, arms to arms. Then they left the room, closing the door softly behind them. I had the impression that they went out backwards as if in the presence of some ancient god-king, but I couldn't see behind me.

'I should introduce myself,' he said. 'I am Commander Judd, of the Sons of Jacob.' This was our first meeting.

'I suppose you know who I am,' I replied.

'That is correct,' he said, smiling blandly. 'I apologize for the inconveniences you have been exposed to.'

'It was nothing,' I said, straight-faced.

It's foolish to joke with those who have absolute control over you. They don't like it; they think you don't appreciate the full extent of their power. Now that I have power myself, I do not encourage flippancy among subordinates. But I was careless back then. I have learned better.

His smile vanished. 'Are you thankful to be alive?' he said.

'Well, yes,' I said.

'Are you thankful that God made you in a woman's body?'

'I suppose so,' I said. 'I've never thought about it.'

'I am not sure you are thankful enough,' he said.

'What would thankful enough be like?' I said.

'Thankful enough to co-operate with us,' he said.

Have I mentioned that he had little oblong half-glasses? He took these off now and contemplated them. His eyes without the glasses were less twinkly.

'What do you mean by 'co-operate'?' I said.

'It's a yes or no.'

'I was trained as a lawyer,' I said. 'I'm a judge. I don't sign blank contracts.'

'You are not a judge,' he said, 'anymore.' He pressed a button on an intercom. 'Thank Tank,' he said. Then, to me: 'Let us hope you will learn to be more thankful. I will pray for that result.'

★ ★ ★

And that is how I found myself in the Thank Tank. It was a repurposed police-station isolation cell, approximately four paces by four. It had a bed shelf, though there was no mattress. It had a bucket, which I swiftly concluded was for human food by-products, as there were still some of those in it, as witnessed by the smell. It had once had a light, but no more: now it had only a socket, and this was not live. (Of course I stuck my finger into it after a while. You would have too.) Any light I had would come from the corridor outside, through the slot by which the inevitable sandwiches would shortly arrive. Gnawing in the dark, that was the plan for me.

I groped around in the dusk, found the bed slab, sat down on it. I can do this, I thought. I can get through.

I was right, but only just. You'd be surprised how quickly the mind goes soggy in the absence of other people. One person alone is not a full person: we exist in relation to others. I was one person: I risked becoming no person.

I was in the Thank Tank for some time. I don't know how long. Every once in a while an eye would view me through the sliding shutter that was there for viewing purposes. Every once in a while there would be a scream or a series of shrieks from nearby: brutalization on parade. Sometimes there would be a prolonged moaning;

sometimes a series of grunts and breathy gasps that sounded sexual, and probably were. The powerless are so tempting.

I had no way of knowing whether or not these noises were real or merely recordings, intended to shatter my nerves and wear away my resolve. Whatever my resolve might be: after some days I lost track of that plotline. The plotline of my resolve.

★   ★   ★

I was parked inside my twilit cell for an unknown length of time, but it couldn't really have been that long judging from the length of my fingernails when I was brought out of it. Time, however, is different when you're shut up in the dark alone. It's longer. Nor do you know when you're asleep and when awake.

Were there insects? Yes, there were insects. They did not bite me, so I expect they were cockroaches. I could feel their tiny feet tiptoeing across my face, tenderly, tentatively, as if my skin were thin ice. I did not slap them. After a while you welcome any kind of touch.

One day, if it was a day, three men came into my cell without warning, shone a glaring light into my blinking purblind eyes, threw me onto the floor, and administered a precise kicking, and other attentions. The noises I emitted were familiar to me: I had heard them nearby. I won't go into any further details, except to say that Tasers were also involved.

No, I was not raped. I suppose I was already

193

too old and tough for the purpose. Or it may be that they were priding themselves on their high moral standards, but I doubt this very much.

This kicking and tasing procedure was repeated two more times. Three is a magic number.

Did I weep? Yes: tears came out of my two visible eyes, my moist weeping human eyes. But I had a third eye, in the middle of my forehead. I could feel it: it was cold, like a stone. It did not weep: it saw. And behind it someone was thinking: *I will get you back for this. I don't care how long it takes or how much shit I have to eat in the meantime, but I will do it.*

★   ★   ★

Then, after an indefinite period and without warning, the door to my Thank Tank cell clanged open, light flooded in, and two black uniforms hauled me out. No words were spoken. I — by this time a shambling wreck, and even smellier than before — was marched or dragged down the corridor by which I had arrived, and out the front door by which I had entered, and into an air-conditioned van.

Next thing I knew I was in a hotel — yes, a hotel! It was not one of the grand hotels, more like a Holiday Inn, if that name will mean anything to you, though I suppose it will not. Where are the brands of yesteryear? Gone with the wind. Or rather gone with the paintbrush and the demolition team, because as I was being hauled into the lobby there were workmen

194

overhead, obliterating the lettering.

In the lobby there was no sweetly smiling reception staff to welcome me. Instead there was a man with a list. A conversation took place between him and my two tour guides, and I was propelled into an elevator, then along a carpeted corridor that was only beginning to show signs of an absence of maids. A couple more months and they'll have a serious mildew issue, I thought with my mushy brain as a door was carded open.

'Enjoy your stay,' said one of my minders. I don't believe he was being ironic.

'Three days R & R,' said the second one. 'Anything you need, phone the front desk.'

The door locked behind them. On the small table there was a tray with orange juice and a banana, and a green salad, and a serving of poached salmon! A bed with sheets! Several towels, more or less white! A shower! Above all, a beautiful ceramic toilet! I fell to my knees and uttered, yes, a heartfelt prayer, but to whom or what I could not tell you.

After I'd eaten all the food — I didn't care if it was poisoned, I was so overjoyed by it — I spent the next few hours taking showers. Just one shower was not enough: there were so many layers of accumulated grime I had to wash off. I inspected my healing abrasions, my yellowing and purpling bruises. I'd lost weight: I could see my ribs, which had reappeared after a decades-long absence due to fast-food lunches. During my legal career my body had been merely a vehicle for propelling me from one achievement to the next, but now I had a newfound tenderness for it. How pink were my toenails! How intricate the vein patterns on my hands! I could not get a good fix on my face in the bathroom mirror, however. Who was that person? The features seemed blurred.

Then I slept for a long time. When I woke up, there was another delicious meal, beef stroganoff with a side of asparagus, and peach Melba for dessert, and, Oh joy! A cup of coffee! I would have liked a martini, but I guessed that alcohol was not going to be on the women's menu in this new era.

My stinking former clothes had been removed by unseen hands: it seemed I was to live in the white terry cloth hotel bathrobe.

I was still in a state of mental disarray. I was a jigsaw puzzle thrown onto the floor. But on the third morning, or was it an afternoon, I woke in an improved state of coherence. It seemed I could think again; it seemed I could think the word *I*.

In addition to that, and as if in acknowledgement of it, there was a fresh garment laid out for me. It was not quite a cowl and it was not quite made of brown sackcloth, but close. I had seen it before, in the stadium, worn by the female shooters. I felt a chill.

I put it on. What else should I have done?

X

SPRING GREEN

Transcript of Witness Testimony 369A

25

I will now describe the preparations leading up to my proposed marriage, as there has been some interest expressed in the way such things were conducted in Gilead. Due to the twist my life took, I was able to observe the marriage process from both sides: that of the bride being prepared, and that of the Aunts responsible for the preparing.

The arrangement of my own wedding was standard. The temperaments of the parties involved, as well as their respective positions in Gilead society, were supposed to have some influence on the choices made available. But the goal in every instance was the same: girls of all kinds — those from good families as well as the less favoured — were to be married early, before any chance encounter with an unsuitable man might occur that would lead to what used to be called falling in love or, worse, to loss of virginity. This latter disgrace was to be avoided at all costs, as the consequences could be severe. Death by stoning was not a fate anyone wanted for their children, and the stain of it on a family could be next to indelible.

★ ★ ★

One evening Paula called me into the living room — she'd sent Rosa to pry me out of my shell, as she put it — and told me to stand in front of her. I did as required, as there was no point in not doing it. Commander Kyle was there, and so was Aunt Vidala. There was another Aunt there as well — one I had never seen — who was introduced to me as Aunt Gabbana. I said I was pleased to meet her, but I must have said it in a surly voice because Paula said, 'You see what I mean?'

'It is her age,' said Aunt Gabbana. 'Even formerly sweet and tractable girls go through this stage.'

'She's certainly old enough,' said Aunt Vidala. 'We have taught her all we can. If they stay in school too long, they become disruptive.'

'She's truly a woman?' said Aunt Gabbana, eyeing me shrewdly.

'Of course,' said Paula.

'None of that's padding?' said Aunt Gabbana, nodding towards my chest.

'Certainly not!' said Paula.

'You'd be amazed at what some families try. She has nice wide hips, none of these narrow pelvises. Let me see your teeth, Agnes.'

How was I supposed to do that? Open my mouth wide, as at the dentist? Paula saw I was confused. 'Smile,' she said. 'For once.' I drew back my lips in a grimace.

'Perfect teeth,' said Aunt Gabbana. 'Very healthy. Well then, we will start looking.'

'Only among the Commander families,' said Paula. 'Nothing lower.'

'That is understood,' said Aunt Gabbana. She was making some notations on a clipboard. I watched in awe as she moved her fingers, which held a pencil. What potent symbols was she inscribing?

'She's a little young,' said Commander Kyle, whom I no longer thought of as my father. 'Possibly.' I was grateful to him for the first time in a long while.

'Thirteen is not too young. It all depends,' said Aunt Gabbana. 'It does wonders for them if we can find the proper match. They settle right down.' She stood. 'Don't worry, Agnes,' she said to me. 'You'll have a choice among at least three candidates. They will consider it an honour,' she said to Commander Kyle.

'Let us know if there's anything else you need,' said Paula graciously. 'And sooner is better.'

'Understood,' said Aunt Gabbana. 'There will be the usual donation to Ardua Hall, once there are satisfactory results?'

'Of course,' said Paula. 'We'll pray for your success. May the Lord open.'

'Under His Eye,' said Aunt Gabbana. The two Aunts left, exchanging smiles and nods with my non-parents.

'You may go, Agnes,' said Paula. 'We'll keep you informed as matters develop. Entering into the blessed state of married womanhood must be done with every precaution, and your father and I will take those precautions for you. You are a very privileged girl. I hope you appreciate that.' She gave me a malicious little smirk: she knew she was talking froth. In reality I was an inconvenient lump that had to be disposed of in a socially acceptable manner.

I went back up to my room. I should have seen this coming: such things had happened to girls who'd not been much older than me. A girl would be present at school and then one day not present: the Aunts didn't like a lot of fuss and sentiment, with tearful goodbyes. Then there would be rumours of an engagement, then of a wedding. We were never allowed to go to these weddings even if the girl had been our close friend. When you were being readied for marriage, you disappeared from your former life. The next time you were seen, you'd be wearing the dignified blue dress of a Wife, and unmarried girls would have to let you go first through doorways.

This was now going to be my reality. I was to be ejected from my own house — from Tabitha's house, from the house of Zilla and Vera and Rosa — because Paula had had enough of me.

★   ★   ★

'You won't go to school today,' said Paula one morning, and that was that. Then nothing much happened for a week except some moping and fretting on my part, though since I pursued these activities alone in my room they had no influence.

I was supposed to be finishing a hateful petit-point project, to keep my mind occupied — the design was a bowl of fruit suitable for being made into a footstool, intended for my future husband, whoever he might be. In one corner of the footstool square I embroidered a small skull: it represented the skull of my stepmother, Paula, but if anyone asked me about it I planned to say that it was a *memento mori*, a reminder of the fact that we must all die someday.

This could hardly be objected to, as it was a pious motif: there were skulls like that on the gravestones of the old churchyard near our school. We were not supposed to go in there except to attend funerals: the names of the dead were on the stones, and that might lead to reading, and then to depravity. Reading was not for girls: only men were strong enough to deal with the force of it; and the Aunts, of course, because they weren't like us.

I had begun to wonder how a woman changed into an Aunt. Aunt Estée had said once that you needed to have a calling that told you God wanted you to help all women and not just a single family; but how did the Aunts get that calling? How had they received their strength? Did they have special brains, neither female nor male? Were they even women at all underneath their uniforms? Could they possibly be men in disguise? Even to suspect such a thing was unthinkable, but what a scandal if so! I wondered what the Aunts would look like if you made them wear pink.

★   ★   ★

On the third day of my idleness, Paula had the Marthas bring several cardboard boxes to my room. It was time to put away childish things, she said. My belongings could go into storage as very soon I would not be living here anymore. Then, once I was ordering my new household, I could decide which of these belongings should be donated to the poor. A less privileged girl from an Econofamily would take great joy in my old dollhouse, for instance; although it was not top quality and was in a shoddy state, some paint here and there would do wonders.

The dollhouse had stood near my window for many years. The happy hours I'd spent with Tabitha were still contained within it. There was the Wife doll, sitting at the dining table; there were the little girls, behaving themselves; there were the Marthas in the kitchen, making bread; there was the Commander, safely locked into his study After Paula had left, I plucked the Wife doll out of her chair and threw her across the room.

26

The next thing Aunt Gabbana did was to bring in a wardrobe team, as Paula put it, since I was considered incapable of choosing what I was to wear in the time leading up to my wedding, and especially at the wedding itself. You must understand that I was not anybody in my own right — although of the privileged class, I was just a young girl about to be confined to wedlock. Wedlock: it had a dull metallic sound, like an iron door clicking shut.

The wardrobe team was in charge of what you might call the stage set: the costumes, the refreshments, the decor. None of them had a dominating personality, which was why they had been relegated to these relatively menial duties; so even though all Aunts had high status, Paula — who did have a dominating personality — was able to boss the wedding-brigade Aunts around, within limits.

The three of them came up to my bedroom, Paula accompanying them, where — having finished my footstool project — I was amusing myself as best as I could by playing Solitaire.

The deck I used was normal in Gilead, but in case this deck is not known to the outside world I will describe it. Naturally there were not any letters on the Ace, King, Queen, or Jack cards, nor were there any numbers on the number cards. The Aces were a large Eye looking out of a cloud. Kings wore Commander uniforms, Queens were Wives, and Jacks were Aunts. The face cards were the most powerful cards. Of the suits, Spades were Angels, Clubs were Guardians, Diamonds were Marthas, and Hearts were Handmaids. Each face card had a border of smaller figures: a Wife of Angels would have a blue Wife with a border of small black-clad Angels, and a Commander of Handmaids would have a border of tiny Handmaids.

Later, once I had access to the Ardua Hall library, I researched these cards. Far back in history, Hearts were once Chalices. Perhaps that is why the Handmaids were Hearts: they were precious containers.

The three wardrobe-team Aunts advanced into my room. Paula said, 'Put your game away and stand up, please, Agnes,' in her sweetest voice — the voice of hers that I disliked the most because I knew how fraudulent it was. I did as I was told, and the three Aunts were introduced: Aunt Lorna, plump-faced and smiling; Aunt Sara Lee, stoop-shouldered and taciturn; and Aunt Betty, dithery and apologetic.

'They're here for a fitting,' Paula said.

'What?' I said. Nobody ever alerted me about anything; they did not see the need for it.

'Don't say *What*, say *Pardon*,' said Paula. 'A fitting for the clothes you will be wearing to your Premarital Preparatory classes.'

Paula ordered me to take off my pink school

uniform, which I was still wearing since I didn't have any other kinds of clothes, apart from my white dress for church. I stood in the middle of the room in my slip. The air wasn't cold, but I could feel the goose bumps rising on my skin, from being looked at and considered. Aunt Lorna took my measurements, and Aunt Betty wrote them down in a small notebook. I watched her carefully; I always watched the Aunts when they were writing secret messages to themselves.

Then I was told I could put my uniform back on, which I did.

There was a discussion about whether I would need new underclothing for the interim period. Aunt Lorna thought it would be nice, but Paula said it was unnecessary because the time in question would be short and what I had still fit me. Paula won.

Then the three Aunts went away. They came back several days later with two outfits, one for spring and summer and one for fall and winter. They were themed in green: spring green with white accents — pocket trims, collars — for spring and summer, and spring green with dark green accents for fall and winter. I'd seen girls my age wearing these dresses, and I knew what they meant: spring green was for fresh leaves, so the girl was ready for marriage. Econofamilies were not allowed such extravagances, however.

The clothes the Aunts brought had already been worn, but they weren't worn out, since nobody wore the green clothing for long. They'd been altered to fit me. The skirts were five inches above the ankle, the sleeves came to the wrist, the waists were loose, the collars high. Each had a matching hat, with a brim and a ribbon. I hated these outfits, though moderately: if I had to have clothes, these were not the worst. I found some hope in the fact that all the seasons had been provided for: maybe I would make it all the way through fall and winter without having to get married.

My old pink and plum clothes were taken away to be cleaned and reused for younger girls. Gilead was at war; we did not like to throw things out.

27

Once I had the green wardrobe, I was enrolled in another school — Rubies Premarital Preparatory, a school for young women of good family who were studying to be married. Its motto was from the Bible: 'Who can find a virtuous woman? For her price is far above rubies.'

This school was also run by the Aunts, but — despite the fact that they wore the same drab uniforms — these Aunts were somehow more stylish. They were supposed to teach us how to act as mistresses of high-ranking households. I say 'act' in a dual sense: we were to be actresses on the stages of our future houses.

Shunammite and Becka from the Vidala School were in the same class with me: Vidala School pupils often went on to Rubies. Not much real time had passed since I'd last seen the two of them, but they seemed much older. Shunammite had coiled her dark braids around behind her head and plucked her eyebrows. You wouldn't have called her beautiful, but she was as lively as she always had been. I note here that *lively* was a word the Wives used in a disapproving way: it meant brash.

Shunammite said she was looking forward to being married. In fact, she could talk of nothing else — what sorts of husbands were being vetted for her, what kind she would prefer, how she could hardly wait. She wanted a widower of about forty who hadn't loved his first Wife all that much and had no children, and was high-ranking and handsome. She didn't want some young jerk who'd never had sex before because that would be uncomfortable — what if he didn't know where to put his thing? She'd always had a reckless mouth, but now it was more so. Possibly she'd picked up these new, coarser expressions from a Martha.

Becka was even thinner. Her green-brown eyes, always large in proportion to her face, were if anything even larger. She told me that she was glad to be in this class with me, but she was not glad to be in the class itself. She'd begged and begged her family not to marry her yet — she was too young, she wasn't ready — but they'd received a very good offer: the eldest boy of a Son of Jacob and Commander who was well on his way to becoming a Commander himself. Her mother had told her not to be silly, she would never have an offer like this again, and if she didn't take this one the offers would become worse and worse the older she became. If she reached eighteen unmarried, she'd be considered dried goods and would be out of the running for Commanders: she'd be lucky to get even a Guardian. Her father, Dr. Grove the dentist, said it was unusual for a Commander to consider a girl of her lower rank, and it would be an insult to refuse, and did she wish to ruin him?

'But I don't want to!' she would wail to us

when Aunt Lise was out of the room. 'To have some man crawling all over you, like, like worms! I hate it!'

It occurred to me that she didn't say she would hate it, she said she already hated it. What had happened to her? Something disgraceful that she couldn't talk about? I remembered how upset she'd been by the story of the Concubine Cut into Twelve Pieces. But I didn't want to ask her: another girl's disgrace could rub off on you if you got too close to it.

'It won't hurt that much,' said Shunammite, 'and think of all the things you'll have! Your own house, your own car and Guardians, and your own Marthas! And if you can't have a baby you'll be given Handmaids, as many as it takes!'

'I don't care about cars and Marthas, or even Handmaids,' said Becka. 'It's the horrible feeling. The wet feeling.'

'Like what?' said Shunammite, laughing. 'You mean their tongues? It's no worse than dogs!'

'It's much worse!' said Becka. 'Dogs are friendly.'

I didn't say anything about what I myself felt about getting married. I couldn't share the story of my dental appointment with Dr. Grove: he was still Becka's father, and Becka was still my friend. In any case, my reaction had been more like disgust and loathing, and now seemed to me trivial in view of Becka's genuine horror. She really did believe that marriage would obliterate her. She would be crushed, she would be nullified, she would be melted like snow until nothing remained of her.

211

Away from Shunammite, I asked her why her mother wouldn't help her. Then there were tears: her mother wasn't her real mother, she'd found that out from their Martha. It was shameful, but her real mother had been a Handmaid — 'Like yours, Agnes,' she said. Her official mother had used that fact against her: why was she so afraid of having sex with a man, since her slut of a Handmaid mother hadn't had such fears? Quite the contrary!

I hugged her then, and said I understood.

28

Aunt Lise was supposed to teach us manners and customs: which fork to use, how to pour tea, how to be kind but firm with Marthas, and how to avoid emotional entanglements with our Handmaid, should it turn out that we needed a Handmaid. Everyone had a place in Gilead, everyone served in her own way, and all were equal in the sight of God, but some had gifts that were different from the gifts of others, said Aunt Lise. If the various gifts were confused and everyone tried to be everything, only chaos and harm could result. No one should expect a cow to be a bird!

She taught us elementary gardening, with an emphasis on roses — gardening was a suitable hobby for Wives — and how to judge the quality of the food that was cooked for us and served at our table. In these times of national scarcity it was important not to waste food or to spoil its full potential. Animals had died for us, Aunt Lise reminded us, and vegetables too, she added in a virtuous tone. We needed to be thankful for this, and for God's bounty. It was as disrespectful — one might even say sinful — to Divine Providence to mistreat food by cooking it badly as it was to discard it uneaten.

Therefore we learned how to poach an egg properly, and at what temperature a quiche ought to be served, and the difference between a bisque and a potage. I can't say I remember much about these lessons now, as I never was in a position to put them into practice.

She reviewed with us the proper prayers to say before meals too. Our husbands would recite the prayers when they were present, as heads of the household, but when they were absent — as they would be often, since they would have to work late hours, nor should we ever criticize their lateness — then it would be our duty to say these prayers on behalf of what Aunt Lise hoped would be our numerous children. Here she gave a tight little smile.

Through my head was running the pretend prayer that Shunammite and I used to amuse ourselves with when we were best friends at the Vidala School:

Bless my overflowing cup,
It flowed upon the floor:
That's because I threw it up,
Now Lord I'm back for more.

The sound of our giggling receded into the distance. How badly we'd thought we were behaving then! How innocent and ineffectual these tiny rebellions seemed to me now that I was preparing for marriage.

★   ★   ★

As the summer wore on, Aunt Lise taught us the basics of interior decorating, though the final choices about the style of our homes would of course be made by our husbands. She then taught us flower arrangement, the Japanese style and the French style.

By the time we got to the French style, Becka was deeply dejected. Her wedding was planned for November. The man selected for her had paid his first visit to her family. He'd been received in their living room, and had made small talk with her father while she'd sat there silently — this was the protocol, and I would be expected to do the same — and she said he'd made her flesh crawl. He had pimples and a scraggly little moustache, and his tongue was white.

Shunammite laughed and said it was probably toothpaste, he must have brushed his teeth just before coming because he wanted to make a good impression on her, and wasn't that sweet? But Becka said she wished she was ill, severely ill with something not only prolonged but catching, because then any proposed wedding would have to be called off.

On the fourth day of French-style flower-arranging, when we were learning to do symmetrical formal vases with contrasting but complementary textures, Becka slashed her left wrist with the secateurs and had to be taken to the hospital. The cut wasn't fatally deep, but a lot of blood came out nonetheless. It ruined the white Shasta daisies.

I'd been watching when she did it. I could not

forget her expression: it had a ferocity I had never seen in her before, and which I found very disturbing. It was as if she'd turned into a different person — a much wilder one — though only for a moment. By the time the paramedics had come and were taking her away, she'd looked serene.

'Goodbye, Agnes,' she'd said to me, but I hadn't known how to answer.

'That girl is immature,' said Aunt Lise. She wore her hair in a chignon, which was quite elegant. She looked at us sideways, down her long patrician nose. 'Unlike you girls,' she added.

Shunammite beamed — she was all set to be mature — and I managed a little smile. I thought I was learning how to act; or rather, how to be an actress. Or how to be a better actress than before.

XI

Sackcloth

The Ardua Hall Holograph

29

Last night I had a nightmare. I have had it before.

Earlier in this account I said that I would not try your patience with a recital of my dreams. But as this one has a bearing on what I am about to tell you, I will make an exception. You are of course fully in control of what you choose to read, and may pass over this dream of mine at will.

I am standing in the stadium, wearing the brown dressing-gown-like garment that was issued to me in the repurposed hotel during my recovery from the Thank Tank. Standing in a line with me are several other women in the same penitential garb, and several men in black uniforms. Each of us has a rifle. We know that some of these rifles contain blanks, some not; but we will all be killers nonetheless, because it's the thought that counts.

Facing us are two rows of women: one standing, one kneeling. They are not wearing blindfolds. I can see their faces. I recognize them, each and every one. Former friends, former clients, former colleagues; and, more recently, women and girls who have passed through my hands. Wives, daughters, Handmaids. Some have missing fingers, some have one foot, some have one eye. Some have ropes around their necks. I have judged them, I have passed sentence: once a judge, always a judge. But they are all smiling. What do I see in their eyes? Fear, contempt, defiance? Pity? It's impossible to tell.

Those of us with rifles raise them. We fire. Something enters my lungs. I can't breathe. I choke, I fall.

I wake up in a cold sweat, heart pounding. They say that a nightmare can frighten you to death, that your heart can literally stop. Will this bad dream kill me, one of these nights? Surely it will take more than that.

★ ★ ★

I was telling you about my seclusion in the Thank Tank and the luxurious experience in the hotel room that followed. It was like a recipe for tough steak: hammer it with a mallet, then marinate and tenderize.

An hour after I'd put on the penitential garb provided for me there was a knock at the door; a two-man escort was waiting. I was conducted along the corridor to another room. My white-bearded interlocutor from the time before was there, not behind a desk this time but seated comfortably in an armchair.

'You may sit down,' said Commander Judd. This time I was not forced into the chair: I sat down in it of my own accord.

'I hope our little regimen was not too strenuous for you,' he said. 'You were treated only to

220

Level One.' There was nothing to be said to this, so I said nothing. 'Was it enlightening?'

'How do you mean?'

'Did you see the light? The Divine Light?' What was the right answer to this? He would know if I were lying.

'It was enlightening,' I said. This seemed to be sufficient.

'Fifty-three?'

'You mean my age? Yes,' I said.

'You've had lovers,' he said. I wondered how he had found that out, and was slightly flattered that he'd bothered.

'Briefly,' I said. 'Several. No long-term successes.' Had I ever been in love? I didn't think so. My experience with the men in my family had not encouraged trust. But the body has its twitches, which it can be humiliating as well as rewarding to obey. No lasting harm was done to me, some pleasure was both given and received, and none of these individuals took their swift dismissal from my life as a personal affront. Why expect more?

'You had an abortion,' he said. So they'd been rifling through some records.

'Only one,' I said fatuously. 'I was very young.'

He made a disapproving grunt. 'You are aware that this form of person-murder is now punishable by death? The law is retroactive.'

'I was not aware of that.' I felt cold. But if they were going to shoot me, why this interrogation?

'One marriage?'

'A brief one. It was a mistake.'

'Divorce is now a crime,' he said. I said nothing.

'Never blessed with children?'

'No.'

'Wasted your woman's body? Denied its natural function?'

'It didn't happen,' I said, keeping the edge out of my voice as much as I could.

'Pity,' he said. 'Under us, every virtuous woman may have a child, one way or another, as God intended. But I expect you were fully occupied in your, ah, so-called career.'

I ignored the slight. 'I had a demanding schedule, yes.'

'Two terms as a schoolteacher?'

'Yes. But I went back to law.'

'Domestic cases? Sexual assault? Female criminals? Sex workers suing for enhanced protection? Property rights in divorces? Medical malpractice, especially by gynecologists? Removal of children from unfit mothers?' He had taken out a list and was reading from it.

'When necessary, yes,' I said.

'Short stint as a volunteer at a rape crisis centre?'

'When I was a student,' I said.

'The South Street Sanctuary, yes? You stopped because . . . ?'

'I got too busy,' I said. Then I added another truth, as there was no point in not being frank: 'Also it wore me down.'

'Yes,' he said, twinkling. 'It wears you down. All that needless suffering of women. We intend to eliminate that. I am sure you approve.' He paused, as if giving me a moment to ponder this. Then he smiled anew. 'So. Which is it to be?'

222

My old self would have said, 'Which of what?' or something similarly casual. Instead I said, 'You mean yes or no?'

'Correct. You have experienced the consequences of *no*, or some of them. Whereas *yes* . . . let me just say that those who are not with us are against us.'

'I see,' I said. 'Then it's yes.'

'You will have to prove,' he said, 'that you mean it. Are you prepared to do that?'

'Yes,' I said again. 'How?'

★   ★   ★

There was an ordeal. You have most likely suspected what it was. It was like my nightmare, except that the women were blindfolded and when I shot I did not fall. This was Commander Judd's test: fail it, and your commitment to the one true way would be voided. Pass it, and blood was on your hands. As someone once said, We must all hang together or we will all hang separately.

I did show some weakness: I threw up afterwards.

One of the targets was Anita. Why had she been singled out to die? Even after the Thank Tank, she must have said no instead of yes. She must have chosen a quick exit. But in fact I have no idea why. Perhaps it was very simple: she was not considered useful to the regime, whereas I was.

★   ★   ★

This morning I got up an hour early to steal a few moments before breakfast with you, my reader. You've become somewhat of an obsession — my sole confidant, my only friend — for to whom can I tell the truth besides you? Who else can I trust?

Not that I can trust you either. Who is more likely to betray me in the end? I will lie neglected in some spidery corner or under a bed while you go off to picnics and dances — yes, dancing will return, it's hard to suppress it forever — or to trysts with a warm body, so much more attractive than the wad of crumbling paper I will have become. But I forgive you in advance. I, too, was once like you: fatally hooked on life.

Why am I taking your existence for granted? Perhaps you will never materialize: you're only a wish, a possibility, a phantom. Dare I say a hope? I am allowed to hope, surely. It's not yet the midnight of my life; the bell has not yet tolled, and Mephistopheles has not yet turned up to collect the price I must pay for our bargain.

For there was a bargain. Of course there was. Though I didn't make it with the Devil: I made it with Commander Judd.

★   ★   ★

My first meeting with Elizabeth, Helena, and Vidala took place the day after my trial by murder in the stadium. The four of us were ushered into one of the hotel boardrooms. We all looked different then: younger, trimmer, less gnarled. Elizabeth, Helena, and I were wearing

224

the brown sack-like garments I've described, but Vidala already had on a proper uniform: not the Aunts' uniform later devised, but a black one.

Commander Judd was awaiting us. He sat at the head of the boardroom table, naturally. Before him was a tray with a coffee pot and cups. He poured ceremoniously, smiling.

'Congratulations,' he began. 'You have passed the test. You are brands snatched from the burning.' He poured his own coffee, added creamer, sipped. 'You may have been wondering why a person such as myself, successful enough under the previous corrupt dispensation, has acted in the way I have. Don't think I don't realize the gravity of my behaviour. Some might call the overthrowing of an illegitimate government an act of treason; without a doubt, many have had this thought about me. Now that you have joined us, it is the same thought that others will have about you. But loyalty to a higher truth is not treason, for the ways of God are not the ways of man, and they are most emphatically not the ways of woman.'

Vidala watched us being lectured by him, smiling a tiny smile: whatever he was persuading us about was already an accepted creed to her.

I took care not to react. It's a skill, not reacting. He looked from one blank face to another. 'You may drink your coffee,' he said. 'A valuable commodity that is increasingly difficult to obtain. It would be a sin to reject what God has provided to his favoured ones through his bounty.' At this we picked up our cups, as if at a ceremonial communion.

He continued: 'We have seen the results of too much laxity, too much hunger for material luxuries, and the absence of the meaningful structures that lead to a balanced and stable society. Our birth rate — for various reasons, but most significantly through the selfish choices of women — is in free fall. You do agree that human beings are at their most unhappy when in the midst of chaos? That rules and boundaries promote stability and thus happiness? You follow me so far?'

We nodded.

'Is that a yes?' He pointed at Elizabeth.

'Yes,' she said in a voice squeaky with fright. She was younger and still attractive then; she hadn't yet allowed her body to engorge. I have noted since that some kinds of men like to bully beautiful women.

'Yes, Commander Judd,' he admonished. 'Titles must be respected.'

'Yes, Commander Judd.' I could smell her fear from across the table; I wondered if she could smell mine. It has an acid smell, fear. It's corrosive.

She, too, has been alone in the dark, I thought. She has been tested in the stadium. She, too, has gazed into herself, and has seen the void.

'Society is best served by separate spheres for men and women,' Commander Judd continued in a sterner voice. 'We have seen the disastrous results of the attempt to meld those spheres. Any questions so far?'

'Yes, Commander Judd,' I said. 'I have a question.'

He smiled, though not warmly. 'Proceed.'

'What do you want?'

He smiled again. 'Thank you. What do we want from you in particular? We're building a society congruent with the Divine Order — a city upon a hill, a light to all nations — and we are acting out of charitable care and concern. We believe that you, with your privileged training, are well qualified to aid us in ameliorating the distressing lot of women that has been caused by the decadent and corrupt society we are now abolishing.' He paused. 'You wish to help?' This time the pointing finger singled out Helena.

'Yes, Commander Judd.' Almost a whisper.

'Good. You are all intelligent women. Through your former . . . ' He did not want to say *professions*. 'Through your former experiences, you are familiar with the lives of women. You know how they are likely to think, or let me rephrase that — how they are likely to react to stimuli, both positive and less positive. You can therefore be of service — a service that will qualify you for certain advantages. We would expect you to be spiritual guides and mentors — leaders, so to speak — within your own womanly sphere. More coffee?' He poured. We stirred, sipped, waited.

'Simply put,' he continued, 'we want you to help us to organize the separate sphere — the sphere for women. With, as its goal, the optimal amount of harmony, both civic and domestic, and the optimal number of offspring. Other questions?' Elizabeth put up her hand.

'Yes?' he said.

'Will we have to . . . pray, and so forth?' she asked.

'Prayer is cumulative,' he said. 'You'll come to understand what a lot of reasons you'll have to give thanks to a power greater than yourselves. My ah, colleague' — he indicated Vidala — 'has volunteered to be your spiritual instructor, having been part of our movement since its inception.'

There was a pause while Elizabeth, Helena, and I absorbed this information. By this greater power, did he mean himself? 'I am sure we can help,' I said finally. 'But it will take a considerable amount of work. Women have been told for so long that they can achieve equality in the professional and public spheres. They will not welcome the . . . ' I sought for a word. 'The segregation.'

'It was always a cruelty to promise them equality,' he said, 'since by their nature they can never achieve it. We have already begun the merciful task of lowering their expectations.'

I did not want to inquire about the means being used. Were they similar to those that had been applied to me? We waited while he poured more coffee for himself.

'Of course you will need to create laws and all of that,' he said. 'You'll be given a budget, a base of operations, and a dormitory. We've set aside a student residential complex for you, within the walled compound of one of the former universities we have requisitioned. It will not need much alteration. I am sure it will be comfortable enough.'

Here I took a risk. 'If it is to be a separate female sphere,' I said, 'it must be truly separate. Within it, women must command. Except in extreme need, men must not pass the threshold of our allotted premises, nor shall our methods be questioned. We shall be judged solely by our results. Though we will of course report to the authorities if and when it's necessary.'

He gave me a measuring look, then opened his hands and turned them palms up. 'Carte blanche,' he said. 'Within reason, and within budget. Subject, of course, to my final approval.'

I looked at Elizabeth and Helena, and saw grudging admiration. I'd tried for more power than they would have dared to ask for, and I'd won it. 'Of course,' I said.

'I am not convinced that's wise,' said Vidala. 'Letting them run their own affairs to that extent. Women are weak vessels. Even the strongest of them should not be allowed to — '

Commander Judd cut her off. 'Men have better things to do than to concern themselves with the petty details of the female sphere. There must be women competent enough for that.' He nodded at me, and Vidala shot me a look of hatred. 'The women of Gilead will have occasion to be grateful to you,' he continued. 'So many regimes have done these things badly. So unpleasantly, so wastefully! If you fail, you will fail all women. As Eve did. Now I will leave you to your collective deliberations.'

And so we began.

★   ★   ★

During these initial sessions, I took stock of my fellow Founders — for as Founders we would be revered in Gilead, Commander Judd had promised. If you are familiar with school playgrounds of the rougher sort, or with henyards, or indeed with any situation in which the rewards are small but the competition for them is fierce, you will understand the forces at work. Despite our pretense of amity, indeed of collegiality, the underlying currents of hostility were already building. If it's a henyard, I thought, I intend to be the alpha hen. To do that, I need to establish pecking rights over the others.

In Vidala I had already made an enemy. She had seen herself as the natural leader, but that view had been challenged. She would oppose me in every way she could — but I had an advantage: I was not blinded by ideology. This would give me a flexibility she lacked, in the long game ahead of us.

Of the other two, Helena would be the easiest to steer, as she was the most unsure of herself. She was plump at that time, though she has dwindled since; one of her former jobs had been with a lucrative weight-loss company, she told us. That was before she'd segued into PR work for a high-fashion lingerie company and had acquired an extensive shoe collection. 'Such beautiful shoes,' she mourned before Vidala shut her down with a frown. Helena would follow the prevailing wind, I decided; and that would work for me as long as I was that wind.

Elizabeth was from a higher social sphere, by which I mean very obviously higher than mine. It would lead her to underestimate me. She was a Vassar girl, and had worked as an executive assistant to a powerful female senator in Washington — presidential potential, she had confided. But the Thank Tank had broken something in her; her birthright and education had not saved her, and she was dithery.

One by one I could handle them, but if they combined into a mob of three I would have trouble. Divide and conquer would be my motto.

Keep steady, I told myself. Don't share too much about yourself, it will be used against you. Listen carefully. Save all clues. Don't show fear.

★   ★   ★

Week by week we invented: laws, uniforms, slogans, hymns, names. Week by week we reported to Commander Judd, who turned to me as the spokeswoman of the group. For those concepts he approved, he took the credit. Plaudits flowed his way from the other Commanders. How well he was doing!

Did I hate the structure we were concocting? On some level, yes: it was a betrayal of everything we'd been taught in our former lives, and of all that we'd achieved. Was I proud of what we managed to accomplish, despite the limitations? Also, on some level, yes. Things are never simple.

For a time I almost believed what I understood I was supposed to believe. I numbered myself among the faithful for the same reason that many in Gilead did: because it was less dangerous. What good is it to throw yourself in front of a steamroller out of moral principles and then be crushed flat like a sock emptied of its foot? Better to fade into the crowd, the piously praising, unctuous, hate-mongering crowd. Better to hurl rocks than to have them hurled at you. Or better for your chances of staying alive.

They knew that so well, the architects of Gilead. Their kind has always known that.

★   ★   ★

I will record here that, some years later — after I had tightened my grip over Ardua Hall and had leveraged it to acquire the extensive though silent power in Gilead that I now enjoy — Commander Judd, sensing that the balance had shifted, sought to propitiate me. 'I hope you have forgiven me, Aunt Lydia,' he said.

'For what, Commander Judd?' I asked in my most affable tone. Could it be that he might have become a little afraid of me?

'The stringent measures I was forced to take at the outset of our association,' he said. 'In order to separate the wheat from the chaff.'

'Oh,' I said. 'I am sure your intentions were noble.'

'I believe so. But still, the measures were harsh.' I smiled, said nothing. 'I spotted you as wheat, right from the beginning.' I continued to smile. 'Your rifle contained a blank,' he said. 'I thought you would like to know.'

'So kind of you to tell me,' I said. The muscles of my face were beginning to hurt. Under some conditions, smiling is a workout.

'I am forgiven, then?' he asked. If I hadn't been so keenly aware of his preference for barely nubile young women, I'd have thought he was flirting. I plucked a scrap from the grab bag of the vanished past: 'To err is human, to forgive divine. As someone once remarked.'

'You are so erudite.'

★ ★ ★

Last evening, after I'd finished writing, had tucked my manuscript away in the hollow cavern within Cardinal Newman, and was on my way to the Schlafly Café, I was accosted on the pathway by Aunt Vidala. 'Aunt Lydia, may I have a word?' she said. It is a request to which the answer must always be yes. I invited her to accompany me to the café.

Across the Yard, the white and many-pillared home base of the Eyes was brightly lit: faithful to their namesake, the lidless Eye of God, they never sleep. Three of them were standing on the white stairway outside their main building, having a cigarette. They didn't glance our way. In their view, the Aunts are like shadows — their own shadows, fearsome to others but not to them.

As we passed my statue I checked out the offerings: fewer eggs and oranges than usual. Is my popularity slipping? I resisted the urge to pocket an orange: I could come back later.

Aunt Vidala sneezed, the prelude to an important utterance. Then she cleared her throat. 'I shall take this occasion to remark that there has been some uneasiness expressed about your statue,' she said.

'Really?' I said. 'In what way?'

'The offerings. The oranges. The eggs. Aunt Elizabeth feels that this excess attention is dangerously close to cult worship. Which would be idolatry,' she added. 'A grave sin.'

'Indeed,' I said. 'What an illuminating insight.'

'Also it's a waste of valuable food. She says it's practically sabotage.'

'I do so agree,' I said. 'No one is more eager than I to avoid even the appearance of a cult of personality. As you know, I support strict rules concerning nutrient intake. We leaders at the Hall must set a high example, even in such matters as second helpings, especially of hard-boiled eggs.' Here I paused: I had video footage of Aunt Elizabeth in the Refectory, secreting these portable food items in her sleeves, but this was not the moment to share. 'As for the offerings, such manifestations on the part of others are beyond my control. I cannot prevent unknown persons from leaving tokens of affection and respect, of loyalty and thanks, such as baked goods and fruit items, at the feet of my effigy However undeserved by myself, it goes without saying.'

'Not prevent them ahead of time,' said Aunt Vidala. 'But they might be detected and punished.'

'We have no rule about such actions,' said I, 'so no rule has been broken.'

'Then we should make a rule,' said Aunt Vidala.

'I will certainly consider it,' I said. 'And the

appropriate punishment. These things need to be tactfully done.' It would be a pity to give up the oranges, I reflected: they are intermittent, given the undependable supply lines. 'But I believe you have more to add?'

By this time we had reached the Schlafly Café. We seated ourselves at one of the pink tables. 'A cup of warm milk?' I asked. 'I'll treat you.'

'I can't drink milk,' she said peevishly. 'It's mucus-forming.'

I always offer Aunt Vidala a warm milk at my expense, which displays my generosity — milk not being a part of our common rations, but an elective, paid for with the tokens we are given according to our status. She always declines irascibly.

'Oh, sorry,' I said. 'I'd forgotten. Some mint tea, then?'

Once our drinks were in front of us, she got down to her main business. 'The fact is,' she said, 'I personally have witnessed Aunt Elizabeth placing food items at the foot of your statue. Hard-boiled eggs in particular.'

'Fascinating,' I said. 'Why would she be doing that?'

'To create evidence against you,' she said. 'That is my opinion.'

'Evidence?' I'd thought Elizabeth had merely been eating those eggs. This was a more creative use for them: I was quite proud of her.

'I believe she's preparing to denounce you. To divert attention from herself and her own disloyal activities. She may be the traitor within us, here at Ardua Hall — working with the

235

Mayday terrorists. I have long suspected her of heresy,' said Aunt Vidala.

I experienced a jolt of excitement. This was a development I hadn't anticipated: Vidala snitching on Elizabeth — and to me of all people, despite her long-standing loathing of me! Wonders never cease.

'That is shocking news, if true. Thank you for telling me,' I said. 'You shall be rewarded. Though there is no proof at present, I shall take the precaution of communicating your suspicions to Commander Judd.'

'Thank you,' said Aunt Vidala in turn. 'I confess that I once had doubts as to your fitness as our leader, here at Ardua Hall, but I have prayed about it. I was wrong to have such doubts. I apologize.'

'Everyone makes mistakes,' I said magnanimously. 'We are only human.'

'Under His Eye,' she said, bowing her head.

Keep your friends close but your enemies closer. Having no friends, I must make do with enemies.

XII

CARPITZ

30

I was telling you about the moment when Elijah said that I wasn't who I thought I was. I don't like remembering that feeling. It was like having a sinkhole open up and swallow you — not only you but your house, your room, your past, everything you'd ever known about yourself, even the way you looked — it was falling and smothering and darkness, all at once.

I must have sat there for at least a minute, not saying anything. I felt I was gasping for breath. I felt chilled through.

Baby Nicole, with her round face and her unknowing eyes. Every time I'd seen that famous photo, I'd been looking at myself. That baby had caused a lot of trouble for a lot of people just by being born. How could I be that person? Inside my head I was denying it, I was screaming no. But nothing came out.

'I don't like this,' I said at last in a small voice.

'None of us likes it,' said Elijah kindly. 'We would all like reality to be otherwise.'

'I wish there was no Gilead,' I said.

'That's our goal,' said Ada. 'No Gilead.' She said it in that practical way she had, as if no Gilead was as easy as fixing a dripping tap. 'You want some coffee?'

I shook my head. I was still trying to take it in. So I was a refugee, like the frightened women I'd seen in SanctuCare; like the other refugees everyone was always arguing about. My health card, my only proof of identity, was a fake. I'd never legally been in Canada at all. I could be deported at any time. My mother was a Handmaid? And my father . . . 'So my father's one of those?' I said. 'A Commander?' The idea of part of him being part of me — being inside my actual body — made me shiver.

'Luckily not,' said Elijah. 'Or not according to your mother, though she doesn't wish to endanger your real father by saying so, as he may still be in Gilead. But Gilead is staking its claim to you via your official father. It's on those grounds they've always demanded your return. The return of Baby Nicole,' he clarified.

Gilead had never given up on the idea of finding me, Elijah told me. They'd never stopped looking; they were very tenacious. To their way of thinking I belonged to them, and they had a right to track me down and haul me across the border by whatever means, legal or illegal. I was underage, and although that particular Commander had disappeared from view — most likely in a purge — I was his, according to their legal system. He had living relatives, so if it came to a court case they might well be granted custody. Mayday couldn't protect me because it was classed internationally as a terrorist organization. It existed underground.

'We've planted a few false leads over the years,' said Ada. 'You were reported in Montreal,

240

and also in Winnipeg. Then you were said to be in California, and after that in Mexico. We moved you around.'

'Was that why Melanie and Neil didn't want me going to the march?'

'In a way,' said Ada.

'So I did it. It was my fault,' I said. 'Wasn't it?'

'How do you mean?' said Ada.

'They didn't want me *seen*,' I said. 'They got killed because they were hiding me.'

'Not exactly,' said Elijah. 'They didn't want pictures of you circulating, they didn't want you on TV. Gilead might conceivably search the images of the march, try to match them. They had your baby picture; they must have an approximate idea of what you might look like now. But as it turned out, they'd suspected independently that Melanie and Neil were Mayday.'

'They might have been following me,' said Ada. 'They might have connected me with SanctuCare, and then with Melanie. They've placed informants inside Mayday before — at least one fake escaped Handmaid, maybe more.'

'Maybe even inside SanctuCare,' said Elijah. I thought of the people who used to go to those meetings at our house. It was sickening to think one of them might have been planning to kill Melanie and Neil, even while they were eating the grapes and the pieces of cheese.

'So that part had nothing to do with you,' said Ada. I wondered if she was just trying to make me feel better.

'I hate being Baby Nicole,' I said. 'I didn't ask to be.'

'Life sucks, end of story,' said Ada. 'Now we have to work out where to go from here.'

Elijah left, saying he'd be back in a couple of hours. 'Don't go out, don't look out the window,' he said. 'Don't use a phone. I'll arrange for a different car.'

Ada opened a tin of chicken soup; she said I needed to get something inside me, so I tried. 'What if they come?' I asked. 'What do they even look like?'

'They look like anybody,' Ada said.

★　★　★

In the afternoon, Elijah came back. With him was George, the old street guy I'd once thought was stalking Melanie. 'It's worse than we thought,' said Elijah. 'George saw it.'

'Saw what?' said Ada.

'There was a CLOSED sign on the shop. It's never closed in the day, so I wondered,' said George. 'Then three guys came out and put Melanie and Neil into the car. They were kind of walking them as if they were drunk. They were talking, making it look social, like they'd been having a chat and were just saying goodbye. Melanie and Neil just sat in the car. Looking back — they were slumping, as if they were asleep.'

'Or dead,' said Ada.

'Yeah, could be,' said George. 'The three guys went off. About one minute later the car blew up.'

'That's way worse than what we thought,' said Ada. 'Like, what did they tell before, inside the store?'

'They wouldn't have said anything,' said Elijah.

'We don't know that,' said Ada. 'Depends on the tactics. Eyes are harsh.'

'We need to move out of here fast,' George said. 'I don't know if they saw me. I didn't want to come here, but I didn't know what to do so I called SanctuCare and Elijah came and got me. But what if they were tapping my phone?'

'Let's trash it,' said Ada.

'What kind of guys?' Elijah asked.

'Suits. Businessmen. Respectable-looking,' said George. 'They had briefcases.'

'I bet they did,' said Ada. 'And they stuck one of them in the car.'

'I'm sorry about this,' George said to me. 'Neil and Melanie were good people.'

'I need to go,' I said because I was going to start crying; so I went into my bedroom and shut the door.

⋆   ⋆   ⋆

That didn't last long. Ten minutes later there was a knock, then Ada opened my door. 'We're moving,' she said. 'Toot sweet.'

I was in bed with the duvet pulled up to my nose. 'Where?' I said.

'Curiosity got the cat in trouble. Let's go.'

We went down the big staircase, but instead of going outside we went into one of the downstairs apartments. Ada had a key.

The apartment was like the one upstairs: furnished with new things, nothing personal. It looked lived in, but just barely. There was a duvet on the bed, identical to the one upstairs. In the bedroom was a black backpack. There was a toothbrush in the bathroom, but nothing in the cabinet. I know because I looked. Melanie used to say that 90 percent of people looked in other people's bathroom cabinets, so you should never keep your secrets in there. Now I was wondering where she actually did keep her secrets, because she must have had a lot of them.

'Who lives here?' I asked Ada.

'Garth,' she said. 'He'll be our transport. Now, quiet as mice.'

'What are we waiting for?' I asked. 'When's something going to happen?'

'Wait long enough and you won't be disappointed,' said Ada. 'Something will happen. Only you might not like what it is.'

31

When I woke up, it was dark and a man was there. He was maybe twenty-five, tall and thin. He was wearing black jeans, a black T-shirt, no logo. 'Garth, this is Daisy,' Ada said. I said hi.

He looked at me with interest and said, 'Baby Nicole?'

I said, 'Please don't call me that.'

He said, 'Right. I'm not supposed to say the name.'

'We good to go?' Ada said.

'Far as I know,' said Garth. 'She should cover up. So should you.'

'With what?' said Ada. 'Didn't bring my Gilead veil. We'll get in the back. Best we can do.'

The van we'd come in was gone, and there was a different one — a delivery van that said SPEEDY DRAIN SNAKING, with a picture of a cute snake coming out of a drain. Ada and I climbed into the back. It held some plumbing tools but also a mattress, which was where we sat. It was dark and stuffy in there, but we were moving along quite fast as far as I could tell.

*   *   *

'How did I get smuggled out of Gilead?' I asked Ada after a while. 'When I was Baby Nicole?'

'No harm in telling you that,' she said. 'That network was blown years ago, Gilead shut down the route; it's wall-to-wall sniffer dogs now.'

'Because of me?' I said.

'Not everything is because of you. Anyway this is what happened. Your mother gave you to some trusted friends; they took you north up the highway, then through the woods into Vermont.'

'Were you one of the trusted friends?'

'We said we were deer-hunting. I used to be a guide around there, I knew people. We had you in a backpack; we gave you a pill so you wouldn't scream.'

'You drugged a baby. You could've killed me,' I said indignantly.

'But we didn't,' said Ada. 'We took you over the mountains, then down into Canada at Three Rivers. Trois-Rivières. That was a prime people-smuggling route back in the day.'

'Back in what day?'

'Oh, around 1740,' she said. 'They used to catch girls from New England, hold them hostage, trade them for money or else marry them off. Once the girls had kids, they wouldn't want to go back. That's how I got my mixed heritage.'

'Mixed like what?'

'Part stealer, part stolen,' she said. 'I'm ambidextrous.'

I thought about that, sitting in the dark among the plumbing supplies. 'So where is she now? My mother?'

'Sealed document,' said Ada. 'The less people

who know that, the better.'

'She just walked off and left me?'

'She was up to her neck in it,' said Ada. 'You're lucky you're alive. She's lucky too, they've tried to kill her twice that we know of. They've never forgotten how she outsmarted them about Baby Nicole.'

'What about my father?'

'Same story. He's so deep underground he needs a breathing tube.'

'I guess she doesn't remember me,' I said dolefully. 'She doesn't give a fuck.'

'Nobody is any authority on the fucks other people give,' said Ada. 'She stayed away from you for your own good. She didn't want to put you at risk. But she's kept up with you as much as she could, under the circumstances.'

I was pleased by this, though I didn't want to give up my anger. 'How? Did she come to our house?'

'No,' said Ada. 'She wouldn't risk making you a target. But Melanie and Neil sent her pictures of you.'

'They never took any pictures of me,' I said. 'It was a thing they had — no pictures.'

'They took lots of pictures,' said Ada. 'At night. When you were asleep.' That was creepy, and I said so.

'Creepy is as creepy does,' said Ada.

'So they sent these pictures to her? How? If it was so secret, weren't they afraid — '

'By courier,' said Ada.

'Everyone knows those courier services leak like a sieve.'

247

'I didn't say courier *service*, I said courier.'

I thought a minute. 'Oh,' I said. 'You took them to her?'

'Not *took*, not directly. I got them to her. Your mother really liked those pictures,' she said. 'Mothers always like pictures of their kids. She'd look at them and then burn them, so no matter what, Gilead wouldn't ever see them.'

★ ★ ★

After maybe an hour we ended up at a wholesale carpet outlet in Etobicoke. It had a logo of a flying carpet, and it was called Carpitz.

Carpitz was a genuine carpet wholesaler out front, with a showroom and a lot of carpets on display, but in back, behind the storage area, there was a cramped room with half a dozen cubicles along the sides. Some of them had sleeping bags or duvets in them. A man in shorts was sleeping in one, sprawled on his back.

There was a central area with some desks and chairs and computers, and a battered sofa over against the wall. There were some maps on the walls: North America, New England, California. A couple of other men and three women were busy at the computers; they were dressed like the people you see outside in the summer drinking iced lattes. They glanced over at us, then went back to what they were doing.

Elijah was sitting on the sofa. He got up and came over and asked if I was all right. I said I was fine, and could I have a drink of water please, because all of a sudden I was very thirsty.

248

Ada said, 'We haven't eaten lately. I'll go.'

'You should both stay here,' said Garth. He went out towards the front of the building.

'Nobody here knows who you are, except Garth,' Elijah said to me in a low voice. 'They don't know you're Baby Nicole.'

'We're keeping it that way,' said Ada. 'Loose lips sink ships.'

Garth brought us a paper bag with some wilted croissant breakfast sandwiches in it, and four takeouts of terrible coffee. We went into one of the cubicles and sat down on some used-furniture office chairs, and Elijah turned on the small flatscreen that was in there so we could watch the news while we were eating.

The Clothes Hound was still on the news, but nobody had been arrested. One expert blamed terrorists, which was vague because there were a lot of different kinds. Another said 'outside agents.' The Canadian government said they were exploring all avenues, and Ada said their favourite avenue was the waste bin. Gilead made an official statement saying they knew nothing about the bombing. There was a protest outside the Gilead Consulate in Toronto, but it wasn't well attended: Melanie and Neil weren't famous, and they weren't politicians.

I didn't know whether to be sad or angry. Melanie and Neil being murdered made me angry, and so did remembering nice things they'd done when they were alive. But things that should have made me angry, such as why Gilead was being allowed to get away with it, only made me sad.

Aunt Adrianna was back in the news — the Pearl Girls missionary found hanging from a doorknob in a condo. Suicide had been ruled out, the police said, and foul play was suspected. The Gilead Embassy in Ottawa had lodged a formal complaint, stating that the Mayday terrorist organization had committed this homicide and the Canadian authorities were covering up for them, and it was time for the entire illegal Mayday operation to be rooted out and brought to justice.

There was nothing on the news about me being missing. Shouldn't my school have reported it? I asked.

'Elijah fixed it,' Ada said. 'He knows people at the school, that's how we got you into it. Kept you out of the spotlight. It was safer.'

32

I slept in my clothes that night, on one of the mattresses. In the morning, Elijah called a meeting of the four of us.

'Things could be better,' said Elijah. 'We may have to get out of this place pretty soon. The Canadian government's under a lot of pressure from Gilead to crack down on Mayday. Gilead's got a bigger army and they're trigger-happy.'

'Cavemen, the Canadians,' said Ada. 'Sneeze and they fall over.'

'Worse, we've heard Gilead could target Carpitz next.'

'We know this how?'

'Our inside source,' said Elijah, 'but we got that before The Clothes Hound was burgled. We've lost contact with him or her, and with most of our rescue-line people inside Gilead. We don't know what's happened to them.'

'So where can we put her?' said Garth, nodding at me. 'Out of reach?'

'What about where my mother is?' I asked. 'You said they tried to kill her and failed, so she must be safe, or safer than here. I could go there.'

'Safer is a matter of time, for her,' said Elijah.

'Then how about another country?'

'A couple of years ago we could have got you out through Saint-Pierre,' said Elijah, 'but the French have closed that down. And after the refugee riots England's a no-go, Italy's the same, Germany — the smaller European ones. None of them want trouble with Gilead. Not to mention outrage from their own people, the mood being what it is. Even New Zealand's shut the door.'

'Some of them say they welcome woman fugitives from Gilead, but you wouldn't last a day in most of them, you'd be sex-trafficked,' said Ada. 'And forget South America, too many dictators. California's hard to get into because of the war, and the Republic of Texas is nervous. They fought Gilead to a standstill, but they don't want to be invaded. They're avoiding provocations.'

'So I might as well give up because they'll kill me sooner or later?' I didn't really think that, but it's how I felt right then.

'Oh no,' said Ada. 'They don't want to kill *you*.'

'Killing Baby Nicole would be a very bad look for them. They'll want you in Gilead, alive and smiling,' said Elijah. 'Though we no longer have any real way of knowing what they want.'

I thought about this. 'You used to have a way?'

'Our source in Gilead,' said Ada.

'Someone in Gilead was helping you?' I asked.

'We don't know who. They'd warn us of raids, tell us when a route was blocked, send us maps. The information's always been accurate.'

'But they didn't warn Melanie and Neil,' I said.

'They didn't appear to have total access to the inner workings of the Eyes,' said Elijah. 'So whoever they are, they aren't top of the food chain. A lesser functionary, we are guessing. But risking their life.'

'Why would they?' I asked.

'No idea, but it's not for money,' said Elijah.

According to Elijah, the source used microdots, which were an old technology — so old that Gilead hadn't thought of looking for them. You made them with a special camera, and they were so small they were almost invisible: Neil had read them with a viewer fitted inside a fountain pen. Gilead was very thorough in its searches of anything crossing the border, but Mayday had used the Pearl Girls brochures as their courier system. 'It was foolproof for a time,' Elijah said. 'Our source would photograph the documents for Mayday and stick them on the Baby Nicole brochures. The Pearl Girls could be counted on to visit The Clothes Hound: Melanie was on their list of possible converts to the cause, since she always accepted the brochures. Neil had a microdot camera, so he'd glue the return messages onto the same brochures, and then Melanie would return them to the Pearl Girls. They had orders to take any extra brochures back to Gilead for use in other countries.'

'But the dots can't work anymore,' said Ada. 'Neil and Melanie are dead, Gilead found their camera. Now they've arrested everyone on the Upstate New York escape route. Bunch of Quakers, a few smugglers, two hunting guides. Stand by for a mass hanging.'

I was feeling more and more hopeless. Gilead had all the power. They'd killed Melanie and Neil, they would track down my unknown mother and kill her too, they would wipe out Mayday. They would get hold of me somehow and drag me into Gilead, where the women might as well be house cats and everyone was a religious maniac.

'What can we do?' I asked. 'It sounds like there's nothing.'

'I'm coming to that,' said Elijah. 'As it turns out, there may be a chance. A faint hope, you could say.'

'Faint hopes are better than none,' said Ada.

The source had been promising to deliver a very big document cache to Mayday, said Elijah. Whatever this cache contained would blow Gilead sky-high, or so the source claimed. But he or she hadn't finished assembling it before The Clothes Hound was robbed and the link was broken.

The source had contrived a fallback plan, however, which he or she had shared with Mayday several microdots ago. A young woman claiming to have been converted to the faith of Gilead by the Pearl Girls missionaries could enter Gilead easily — many had done so. And the best young woman to transfer the cache — indeed, the only young woman acceptable to the source — would be Baby Nicole. The source did not doubt that Mayday knew where she was.

The source had made it clear: no Baby Nicole, no document cache; and if no document cache, then Gilead would continue as it was. Mayday's time would run out, and Melanie's and Neil's deaths would have been for nothing. Not to mention my mother's life. But if Gilead were to crumble, it would all be different.

'Why only me?'

'The source was firm on that point. Said you're the best chance. For one thing, if you get caught they won't dare kill you. They've made too much of an icon out of Baby Nicole.'

'I can't destroy Gilead,' I said. 'I'm just a person.'

'Not alone, of course not,' said Elijah. 'But you'd be transporting the ammunition.'

'I don't think I can,' I said. 'I couldn't be a convert. They'd never believe me.'

'We'll train you,' said Elijah. 'Praying and self-defence.' It sounded like some sort of TV skit.

'Self-defence?' I said. 'Against who?'

'Remember the Pearl Girl found dead in the condo?' said Ada. 'She was working for our source.'

'Mayday didn't kill her,' said Elijah. 'It was the other Pearl Girl, her partner. Adrianna must've been trying to block the partner's suspicions about the whereabouts of Baby Nicole. There must've been a fight. Which Adrianna lost.'

'There's a lot of people dying,' I said. 'The Quakers, and Neil and Melanie, and that Pearl Girl.'

'Gilead's not shy about killing,' said Ada. 'They're fanatics.' She said they were supposed to be dedicated to virtuous godly living, but you could believe you were living virtuously and also

255

murder people if you were a fanatic. Fanatics thought that murdering people was virtuous, or murdering certain people. I knew that because we'd done fanatics in school.

33

I somehow agreed to go to Gilead without ever
definitely agreeing. I'd said I'd think about it,
and then the next morning everyone acted as if
I'd said yes, and Elijah said how brave I was and
what a difference I would make, and that I would
bring hope to a lot of trapped people; so then
I more or less couldn't go back on it. Anyway,
I felt that I owed Neil and Melanie, and the
other dead people. If I was the only person the
so-called source would accept, then I would have
to try.

Ada and Elijah said they wanted to prepare
me as much as they could in the short time they
had. They set up a little gym in one of the
cubicles, with a punching bag, a skipping rope,
and a leather medicine ball. Garth did that part
of the training. At first he didn't talk to me much
except about what we were doing: the skipping,
the punching, tossing the ball back and forth.
But after a while he did thaw a little. He told me
he was from the Republic of Texas. They'd
declared independence at the beginning of
Gilead, and Gilead resented that; there had been
a war, which had ended in a draw and a new
border.

So right now Texas was officially neutral, and

any actions against Gilead by its citizens were illegal. Not that Canada wasn't neutral too, he said, but it was neutral in a sloppier way. *Sloppier* was his word, not mine, and I found it insulting until he said that Canada was sloppy in a good way. So he and some of his friends had come to Canada to join the Mayday Lincoln Brigade, for foreign freedom fighters. He'd been too young to be in the actual Gilead War with Texas, he'd only been seven. But his two older brothers had been killed in it, and a cousin of his had been grabbed and taken into Gilead, and they hadn't heard from her since.

I was adding in my head to figure out exactly how old he was. Older than me, but not too much older. Did he think of me as more than an assignment? Why was I even spending time on that? I needed to concentrate on what I was supposed to be doing.

★   ★   ★

At first I worked out twice a day for two hours, to build stamina. Garth said I wasn't in bad shape, which was true — I'd been good at sports in school, a time that seemed long ago. Then he showed me some blocks and kicks, and how to knee someone in the groin, and how to throw a heartstopper punch — by making a fist, wrapping your thumb across the second knuckles of your middle and index fingers, then punching while keeping your arm straight. We practised that one a lot: you should strike first if you had the chance, he said, because you'd benefit from the surprise.

'Hit me,' he'd say. Then he would brush me aside and punch me in the stomach — not too hard, but hard enough so I could feel it. 'Tighten your muscles,' he'd say. 'You want a ruptured spleen?' If I cried — either in pain or in frustration — he would not be sympathetic, he would be disgusted. 'You want to do this or not?' he'd say.

Ada brought in a dummy head made of moulded plastic, with gel eyes, and Garth tried to teach me how to poke somebody's eyes out; but the idea of squishing eyeballs with my thumbs gave me the shudders. It would be like stepping on worms in your bare feet.

'Shit. That would really hurt them,' I said. 'Thumbs in their eyes.'

'You *need* to hurt them,' said Garth. 'You need to *want* to hurt them. They'll be wanting to hurt you, bet on that.'

'Gross,' I said to Garth when he wanted me to practise the eye-poke. I could picture them too clearly, those eyes. Like peeled grapes.

'You want a panel discussion on whether you should be dead?' said Ada, who was sitting in on the session. 'It's not a real head. Now, *stab!*'

'Yuck.'

'Yuck won't change the world. You need to get your hands dirty. Add some guts and grit. Now, try again. Like this.' She herself had no scruples.

'Don't give up. You have potential,' said Garth.

'Thanks a bundle,' I said. I was using my sarcastic voice, but I meant it: I did want him to think I had potential. I had a crush on him, in a hopeless, puppyish way. But no matter how much I might fantasize, in the realistic part of my head I didn't see any future in it. Once I'd gone into Gilead, I would most likely never see him again.

'How's it going?' Ada would ask Garth every day after our workout.

'Better.'

'Can she kill with her thumbs yet?'

'She's getting there.'

⋆   ⋆   ⋆

The other part of their training plan was the praying. Ada tried to teach me that. She was quite good at it, I thought. But I was hopeless.

'How do you know this?' I asked her.

'Where I grew up, everyone knew this,' she said.

'Where?'

'In Gilead. Before it was Gilead,' she said. 'I saw it coming and got out in time. A lot of people I knew didn't.'

'So that's why you work with Mayday?' I said. 'It's personal?'

'Everything's personal, when you come right down to it,' she said.

'How about Elijah?' I asked. 'Was it personal for him too?'

'He taught in a law school,' she said. 'He was on a list. Someone tipped him off. He made it over the border with nothing but his clothes. Now let's try this again. *Heavenly Father, forgive my sins, and bless* . . . please stop giggling.'

'Sorry. Neil always said God was an imaginary friend, and you might as well believe in the fucking Tooth Fairy. Except he didn't say *fucking*.'

'You need to take this seriously,' said Ada, 'because Gilead sure does. And another thing: drop the swearing.'

'I don't swear hardly at all,' I said.

★ ★ ★

The next stage, they told me, was that I should dress up like a street person and panhandle somewhere where the Pearl Girls would see me. When they started to talk with me, I should let them persuade me to go with them.

'How do you know the Pearl Girls will want to take me?' I asked.

'It's likely,' Garth said. 'That's what they do.'

'I can't be a street person, I won't know how to act,' I said.

'Just act natural,' said Ada.

'The other street people will see I'm a fraud — what if they ask me how I got there, where are my parents — what am I supposed to say?'

'Garth will be there with you. He'll say you don't talk much because you've been traumatized,' said Ada. 'Say there was violence at home. Everyone will get that.' I thought about Melanie and Neil being violent: it was ridiculous.

'What if they don't like me? The other street people?'

'What if?' said Ada. 'Tough bananas. Not everybody in your life is going to like you.'

261

Tough bananas. Where did she get these expressions? 'But aren't some of them . . . aren't they criminals?'

'Dealing drugs, shooting up, drinking,' said Ada. 'All of that. But Garth will keep an eye on you. He'll say he's your boyfriend, and he'll run interference if anyone tries to mess with you. He'll stay right with you until the Pearl Girls pick you up.'

'How long will that be?' I asked.

'My guess is not long,' said Ada. 'After the Pearl Girls scoop you, Garth can't go along. But they'll coddle you like an egg. You'll be one more precious Pearl on their string.'

'But once you get to Gilead, it might be different,' said Elijah. 'You'll have to wear what they tell you to wear, watch what you say and be alert to their customs.'

'If you know too much to begin with, though,' Ada said, 'they'll suspect us of training you. So it'll need to be a fine balance.'

I thought about this: was I clever enough?

'I don't know if I can do that.'

'If in doubt, play dumb,' said Ada.

'Have you sent any pretend converts in there before?'

'A couple,' said Elijah. 'With mixed results. But they didn't have the protection you'll have.'

'You mean from the source?' *The source* — all I could picture was a person with a bag over their head. Who were they really? The more I heard about the source, the weirder they sounded.

'Guesswork, but we think it's one of the

Aunts,' said Ada. Mayday didn't know much about the Aunts: they weren't in the news, not even the Gilead news; it was the Commanders who gave the orders, made the laws, and did the talking. The Aunts worked behind the scenes. That's all we were told at school.

'They're said to be very powerful,' said Elijah. 'But that's hearsay. We don't have a lot of details.'

Ada had a few pictures of them, but only a few. Aunt Lydia, Aunt Elizabeth, Aunt Vidala, Aunt Helena: these were their so-called Founders. 'Pack of evil harpies,' she said.

'Great,' I said. 'Sounds like fun.'

★   ★   ★

Garth said that once we were on the street I needed to follow orders, because he was the one with the street smarts. I wouldn't want to provoke other people into fighting with him, so saying things like 'Who was your slave last year' and 'You're not the boss of me' would not be good.

'I haven't said stuff like that since I was eight,' I said.

'You said both of them yesterday,' said Garth. I should choose another name, he said. People might be looking for a Daisy, and I certainly couldn't be Nicole. So I said I'd be Jade. I wanted something harder than a flower.

'The source said she needs to get a tattoo on her left forearm,' Ada said. 'It's always been a non-negotiable demand.'

I'd tried for a tattoo when I was thirteen, but Melanie and Neil had been strongly against it. 'Cool, but why?' I asked now. 'There's no bare arms in Gilead, so who's going to see it?'

'We think it's for the Pearl Girls,' said Ada. 'When they pick you up. They'll be directed to look specially for it.'

'Will they know who I am, like, the Nicole thing?' I asked.

'They just follow instructions,' said Ada. 'Don't ask, don't tell.'

'What tattoo should I get, a butterfly?' That was a joke, but nobody laughed.

'The source said it should look like this,' said Ada. She sketched it:

L
GOD
V
E

'I can't have that on my arm,' I said. 'It's wrong for me to have it.' It was so hypocritical: Neil would have been shocked.

'Maybe it's wrong for you,' said Ada. 'But it's right for the situation.'

Ada brought in a woman she knew to do the tattoo and the rest of my street makeover. She had pastel green hair, and the first thing she did was tint my hair the same shade. I was pleased: I thought I looked like some dangerous avatar from a video game.

'It's a start,' said Ada, evaluating the results.

The tattoo wasn't just a tattoo, it was a

264

scarification: raised lettering. It hurt like shit. But I tried to act as if it didn't because I wanted to show Garth that I was up to it.

★   ★   ★

In the middle of the night I had a bad thought. What if the source was only a decoy, meant to deceive Mayday? What if there was no important document cache? Or what if the source was evil? What if the whole story was a trap — a clever way of luring me into Gilead? I'd go in, and I wouldn't be able to get out. Then there would be a lot of marching, with flags and choir singing and praying, and giant rallies like the ones we'd seen on TV, and I would be the centrepiece. Baby Nicole, back where she belonged, hallelujah. Smile for Gilead TV.

In the morning, while I was eating my greasy breakfast with Ada, Elijah, and Garth, I told them about this fear.

'We've considered the possibility,' said Elijah. 'It's a gamble.'

'It's a gamble every time you get up in the morning,' said Ada.

'This is a more serious gamble,' Elijah said.

'I'm betting on you,' Garth said. 'It'll be so amazing if you win.'

XIII

Secateurs

The Ardua Hall Holograph

34

My reader, I have a surprise for you. It was also a surprise for me.

Under cover of darkness, and with the aid of a stone drill, some pliers, and a little mortar patching, I installed two battery-run surveillance cameras in the base of my statue. I have always been good with tools. I replaced the moss carefully, reflecting that I should really get my replica cleaned. Moss adds respectability only up to a point. I was beginning to look furry.

I waited with some impatience for the results. It would be a fine thing to have a stash of irrefutable pictures of Aunt Elizabeth planting evidence in the form of hard-boiled eggs and oranges at my stone feet in an effort to discredit me. Even though I myself was not performing these acts of idolatry, the fact that others were performing them would reflect badly on me: it would be said that I had tolerated these acts, and I might even have encouraged them. Such aspersions might well be used by Elizabeth to lever me off my pinnacle. I was under no illusions as to Commander Judd's loyalty to me: if a safe means could be found — safe for him — he would not hesitate to denounce me. He's had a lot of practice in the denouncing business.

But here is the surprise. There were several days of no activity — or none to speak of, since I discount the three tearful young Wives, granted access to the grounds because they were married to prominent Eyes, who offered *in toto* a muffin, a small loaf of cornmeal bread, and two lemons — like gold these days, lemons, considering the disasters in Florida and our inability to gain ground in California. I am glad to have them, and shall make good use of them: if life gives you lemons, make lemonade. I shall also determine how these lemons were come by. It is ineffectual to try to clamp down on all grey market activities — the Commanders must have their little perks — but I naturally wish to know who is selling what, and how it is smuggled in. Women are only one of the commodities — I hesitate to call them commodities, but when money is in the picture, such they are — that are being relocated under cover. Is it lemons in and women out? I shall consult my grey market sources: they don't like competition.

These tearful Wives wished to enlist my arcane powers in their quest for fertility poor things. *Per Ardua Cum Estrus*, they intoned, as if Latin could have more effect than English. I will see what can be done for them, or rather who can be done — their husbands having proven so singularly feeble in that respect.

But back to my surprise. On the fourth day, what should loom into the camera's field of vision just as dawn was breaking but the large red nose of Aunt Vidala, followed by her eyes and mouth. The second camera provided a

270

longer shot: she was wearing gloves — cunning of her — and from a pocket she produced an egg, followed by an orange. Having looked about her to make sure no one was watching, she placed these votive offerings at my feet, along with a small plastic baby. Then, on the ground beside the statue, she dropped a handkerchief embroidered with lilacs: a well-known prop of mine, from Aunt Vidala's school project some years ago in which the girls embroidered sets of handkerchiefs for the senior Aunts with flowers signalling their names. I have lilacs, Elizabeth has echinacea, Helena has hyacinths, Vidala herself has violets; five for each of us — such a lot of embroidery. But this idea was thought to skirt dangerously close to reading and was discontinued.

Now, having previously told me that Elizabeth was trying to incriminate me, Vidala herself was placing the evidence against me: this innocent piece of handicraft. Where had she got it? From pilfering the laundry, I suppose. Facilitating the heretical worship of myself What a stellar denunciation! You can imagine my delight. Any false step by my main challenger was a gift from destiny. I filed away the photos for possible future use — it is always desirable to save whatever scraps may come to hand, in kitchens as elsewhere — and determined to await developments.

My esteemed Founder colleague Elizabeth must soon be told that Vidala was accusing her of treachery. Should I add Helena as well? Who was the more dispensable if a sacrifice must be made? Who might be the most easily co-opted if the need arose? How might I best set the members of the triumvirate eager to overthrow me against one another, all the better to pick them off one by one? And where did Helena actually stand vis-à-vis myself? She'd go with the zeitgeist, whatever that might prove to be. She was always the weakest of the three.

I approach a turning point. The Wheel of Fortune rotates, fickle as the moon. Soon those who were down will move upwards. And vice versa, of course.

I will inform Commander Judd that Baby Nicole — now a young girl — is finally almost within my grasp, and may shortly be enticed to Gilead. I will say *almost* and *may* to keep him in suspense. He will be more than excited, since he has long understood the propaganda virtues of a repatriated Baby Nicole. I will say that my plans are well under way, but that I would prefer not to share them at present: it is a delicate calculation, and a careless word in the wrong place could ruin all. The Pearl Girls are involved, and they are under my supervision; they are part of the special women's sphere, in which heavy-handed men should not meddle, I will say, wagging a finger at him roguishly. 'Soon the prize will be yours. Trust me on this,' I will warble.

'Aunt Lydia, you are too good,' he will beam.

Too good to be true, I will think. Too good for this earth. Good, be thou my evil.

★   ★   ★

For you to understand how matters are currently developing, I will now provide you with a little history. An incident that passed almost unnoticed at the time.

Nine years ago or thereabouts — it was the same year my statue was unveiled, though not in the same season — I was in my office, tracing the Bloodlines for a proposed marriage, when I was interrupted by the appearance of Aunt Lise, she of the fluttering eyelashes and the pretentious hairstyle — a modified French roll. As she was ushered into my office, she was nervously wringing her hands; I was ashamed of her for being so novelistic.

'Aunt Lydia, I am truly sorry for taking up your valuable time,' she began. They all say that, but it never stops them. I smiled in what I hoped was not a forbidding manner.

'What is the problem?' I said. There is a standard repertoire of problems: Wives at war with one another, daughters in rebellion, Commanders dissatisfied with the Wife selection proposed, Handmaids on the run, Births gone wrong. The occasional rape, which we punish severely if we choose to make it public. Or a murder: he kills her, she kills him, she kills her, and, once in a while, he kills him. Among the Econoclasses, jealous rage can take over and knives can be wielded, but among the elect, male-on-male murders are metaphorical: a stab in the back.

On slow days I catch myself longing for something really original — a case of cannibalism, for instance — but then I reprimand myself:

Be careful what you wish for. I have wished for various things in the past and have received them. If you want to make God laugh, tell him your plans, as used to be said; though in the present day the idea of God laughing is next door to blasphemy. An ultra-serious fellow, God is now.

'We've had another suicide attempt among the Premarital Preparatory students at Rubies,' said Aunt Lise, tucking back a wandering strand of hair. She had removed the ungainly babushka-like head covering we are obliged to wear in public to avoid inflaming men, although the idea of any men being inflamed either by Aunt Lise, impressive of profile but alarmingly puckered, or by me, with my greying thatchery and sack-of-potatoes body, is so ludicrous that it hardly needs articulating.

Not a suicide; not again, I thought. But Aunt Lise had said *attempt*, which meant that the suicide had not succeeded. There is always an inquiry when they do succeed, and fingers are pointed at Ardua Hall. Inappropriate mate selection is the usual accusation — we at the Hall being responsible for making the first cut, since we hold the Bloodlines information. Opinions vary, however, as to what is in fact appropriate.

'What was it this time? Anti-anxiety medication overdose? I wish the Wives wouldn't leave those pills strewn around where anyone can get hold of them. Those, and the opiates: such a temptation. Or did she try to hang herself?'

'Not hanging,' said Aunt Lise. 'She attempted

to slash her wrists with the secateurs. The ones I use for the flower-arranging.'

'That's direct, at any rate,' I said. 'What happened then?'

'Well, she didn't slash very deeply. Though there was a lot of blood, and a certain amount of . . . noise.'

'Ah.' By noise, she meant screaming: so unladylike. 'And then?'

'I called in the paramedics, and they sedated her and took her to the hospital. Then I notified the proper authorities.'

'Quite right. Guardians or Eyes?'

'Some of each.'

I nodded. 'You seem to have handled it in the best way possible. What is there left to consult me about?' Aunt Lise looked happy because I'd praised her, but she quickly changed her facial expression to deeply concerned.

'She says she will try it again, if . . . unless there's a change in plan.'

'Change in plan?' I knew what she meant, but it's best to require clarity.

'Unless the wedding is called off,' said Aunt Lise.

'We have counsellors,' I said. 'They've done their job?'

'They've tried all the usual methods, with no success.'

'You threatened her with the ultimate?'

'She says she's not afraid of dying. It's living she objects to. Under the circumstances.'

'Is it this particular candidate she objects to, or marriage in general?'

275

'In general,' said Aunt Lise. 'Despite the benefits.'

'Flower-arranging was no inducement?' I said drily. Aunt Lise sets great store by it.

'It was not.'

'Was it the prospect of childbirth?' I could understand that, the mortality rate being what it is; of newborns primarily, but also of mothers. Complications set in, especially when the infants are not normally shaped. We had one the other day with no arms, which was interpreted as a negative comment by God upon the mother.

'No, not childbirth,' said Aunt Lise. 'She says she likes babies.'

'What, then?' I liked to make her blurt it out: it's good for Aunt Lise to confront reality once in a while. She spends too much time diddling around among the petals.

She fiddled with the hair strand again. 'I don't like to say it.' She looked down at the floor.

'Go ahead,' I said. 'You won't shock me.'

She paused, flushed, cleared her throat. 'Well. It's the penises. It's like a phobia.'

'Penises,' I said thoughtfully. 'Them again.' In attempted suicides of young girls, this is often the case. Perhaps we need to change our educational curriculum, I thought: less fear-mongering, fewer centaur-like ravishers and male genitalia bursting into flame. But if we were to put too much emphasis on the theoretical delights of sex, the result would almost certainly be curiosity and experimentation, followed by moral degeneracy and public stonings. 'No chance she might be brought to see the item in

276

question as a means to an end? As a prelude to babies?'

'None whatever,' said Aunt Lise firmly. 'That has been tried.'

'Submission of women as ordained from the moment of Creation?'

'Everything we could think of.'

'You tried the sleep deprivation and twenty-hour prayer sessions, with relays of supervisors?'

'She is adamant. She also says she has received a calling to higher service, though as we know they often use that excuse. But I was hoping that we . . . that you . . . '

I sighed. 'There is little point in the destruction of a young female life for no reason,' I said. 'Will she be able to learn the reading and writing? Is she intelligent enough?'

'Oh yes. Slightly too intelligent,' said Aunt Lise. 'Too much imagination. I believe that's what happened, concerning the . . . those things.'

'Yes, the thought-experiment penises can get out of control,' I said. 'They take on a life of their own.' I paused; Aunt Lise fidgeted.

'We'll admit her on probation,' I said finally. 'Give her six months and see if she can learn. As you know, we need to replenish our numbers here at Ardua Hall. We of the older generation cannot live forever. But we must proceed carefully. One weak link . . . ' I am familiar with these exceptionally squeamish girls. It's no use forcing them: they can't accept bodily reality. Even if the wedding night is accomplished, they will soon be found swinging from a light fixture or in a coma under a rose bush, having swallowed every pill in the house.

'Thank you,' said Aunt Lise. 'It would have been such a shame.'

'To lose her, you mean?'

'Yes,' said Aunt Lise. She has a soft heart; that is why she is assigned to the flower-arranging and so forth. In her past life she was a professor of French literature of the eighteenth century, pre-Revolution. Teaching the Rubies Premarital Preparatory students is the closest she will ever come to having a salon.

I try to suit the occupations to the qualifications. It's better that way, and I am a great proponent of *better*. In the absence of *best*.

Which is how we live now.

★ ★ ★

And so I had to involve myself in the case of the girl Becka. It's always advisable for me to take a personal interest at the beginning with these suicidal girls who claim they wish to join us.

Aunt Lise brought her to my office: a thin girl, pretty in a delicate way, with large luminous eyes and her left wrist in a bandage. She was still wearing the green outfit of a bride-to-be. 'Come in,' I said to her. 'I won't bite.'

She flinched as if she doubted this. 'You may take that chair,' I said. 'Aunt Lise will be right beside you.' Hesitantly she sat down, knees together modestly, hands folded in her lap. She gazed at me mistrustfully.

'So you want to become an Aunt,' I said. She nodded. 'It's a privilege, not an entitlement. I assume you understand that. And it's not a reward for your silly attempt to end your own life. That was a mistake, as well as an affront to God. I trust it won't happen again, supposing we take you in.'

A shake of the head, a single tear, which she did not brush away. Was it a display tear, was she trying to impress me?

I asked Aunt Lise to wait outside. Then I launched into my spiel: Becka was being offered a second chance in life, I said, but both she and we needed to be sure that this was the right way for her, since the life of an Aunt was not for everyone. She must promise to obey the orders of her superiors, she must apply herself to a difficult course of studies as well as to the mundane chores assigned, she must pray for guidance every night and every morning; then, after six months, if this was indeed her true choice and if we ourselves were satisfied with her progress, she would take the Ardua Hall vow and renounce all other possible paths, and even then she would be only a Supplicant Aunt until the successful completion of her Pearl Girls missionary work abroad, which would not happen for many years. Was she willing to do all these things?

Oh yes, said Becka. She was so grateful! She would do anything that was required. We had saved her from, from . . . She stumbled to a halt, blushing.

'Did something unfortunate happen to you in your earlier life, my child?' I asked. 'Something involving a man?'

'I don't want to talk about it,' she said. She was paler than ever.

'You're afraid you'll be punished?' A nod from her. 'You can tell me,' I said. 'I have heard many disagreeable stories. I do understand some of what you may have been through.' But she was still reluctant, so I did not push it. 'The mills of the gods grind slowly,' I said, 'but they grind exceeding small.'

'Pardon?' She looked puzzled.

'I mean that whoever it was, his behaviour will be punished in time. Put it out of your mind. You will be safe with us here. You will never be troubled by him again.' We Aunts do not work openly in such cases, but we work. 'Now, I hope you'll prove that you are deserving of the trust I have placed in you,' I said.

'Oh yes,' she said. 'I will be deserving!' These girls are all like that at the beginning: limp with relief, abject, prostrate. That can change over time, of course: we've had renegades, we've had backdoor sneakings to meet ill-advised Romeos, we've had disobedient flights. The endings of such stories have not usually been happy.

'Aunt Lise will take you to get your uniform,' I said. 'Tomorrow you will have your initial reading lesson, and you will begin to learn our rules. But now you should select your new name. There is a list of suitable names available. Off you go. Today is the first day of the rest of your life,' I said as cheerfully as I could.

'I can't thank you enough, Aunt Lydia!' said Becka. Her eyes were shining. 'I'm so grateful!'

I smiled my wintry smile. 'I'm pleased to hear

that,' I said, and I was indeed pleased. Gratitude is valuable to me: I like to bank it for a rainy day. You never know when it may come in handy.

Many are called but few are chosen, I thought. Though that was not true at Ardua Hall: only a handful of the called have had to be discarded. Surely the girl Becka would be one of our keepers. She was a damaged houseplant, but cared for properly she would bloom.

'Close the door after you,' I said. She almost skipped out of the room. How young they are, how frisky! I thought. How touchingly innocent! Was I ever like that? I could not remember.

XIV

ARDUA HALL

Transcript of Witness Testimony 369A

35

After Becka cut her wrist with the secateurs and bled on the Shasta daisies and was taken to the hospital, I was very worried about her: would she recover, would she be punished? But as the autumn and then the winter seasons came and went, there was still no news. Even our Marthas did not hear anything about what might have happened to her.

Shunammite said Becka was just trying to get attention. I disagreed, and I am afraid there was a coolness between us for the remainder of the classes.

As the spring weather set in, Aunt Gabbana announced that the Aunts had come up with three candidates for Paula and Commander Kyle to consider. She visited us at our house and showed us their photographs and recited their biographies and qualifications, reading from her notebook, and Paula and Commander Kyle listened and nodded. I was expected to look at the pictures and listen to the recital, but not to say anything at present. I could have a week to consider. My own inclinations would naturally be taken into account, said Aunt Gabbana. Paula smiled at this.

'Of course,' she said. I said nothing.

The first candidate was a full Commander, and was even older than Commander Kyle. He was red-nosed, with slightly bulbous eyes — the mark, said Aunt Gabbana, of a strong personality, one who would be a reliable defender and sustainer of his Wife. He had a white beard and what looked like jowls underneath it, or possibly wattles: skin folds drooping down. He was one of the first Sons of Jacob and so was exceptionally godly, and had been essential in the early struggle to establish the Republic of Gilead. In fact, it was rumoured that he had been part of the group that had masterminded the attack on the morally bankrupt Congress of the former United States. He'd already had several Wives — dead, unhappily — and had been assigned five Handmaids but had not yet been gifted with children.

His name was Commander Judd, though I'm not sure this information is of much use if you are attempting to establish his true identity, since the leading Sons of Jacob had changed their names frequently when they were in the secret planning stages of Gilead. I knew nothing of these name changes at the time: I learned about them later, thanks to my excursions through the Bloodlines Genealogical Archives at Ardua Hall. But even there, Judd's original name had been obliterated.

The second candidate was younger and thinner. His head was pointed at the top and he had oddly large ears. He was good with numbers, said Aunt Gabbana, and intellectual, not always a desirable thing — especially not for women — but in a husband it could be tolerated. He had managed to have one child by his former Wife, who had died in an asylum for mental sufferers, but the poor infant had expired before the age of one.

No, said Aunt Gabbana, it had not been an Unbaby. There was nothing wrong with it at birth. The cause was juvenile cancer, alarmingly on the rise.

The third man, the younger son of a lower-ranking Commander, was only twenty-five. He had a lot of hair but a thick neck, and eyes that were close together. Not as excellent a prospect as the other two, said Aunt Gabbana, but the family was highly enthusiastic about the match, which meant I would be properly appreciated by the in-laws. This was not to be discounted, since hostile in-laws could make a girl's life miserable: they would criticize, and always side with the husband.

'Don't jump to any conclusions yet, Agnes,' Aunt Gabbana said. 'Take your time. Your parents want you to be happy.' This was a kind thought, but a lie: they didn't want me to be happy, they wanted me to be elsewhere.

I lay in bed that night with the three photographs of the eligible men floating in the darkness before my eyes. I pictured each one of them on top of me — for that is where they would be — trying to shove his loathsome appendage into my stone-cold body.

Why was I thinking of my body as stone cold? I wondered. Then I saw: it would be stone cold because I would be dead. I would be as wan and bloodless as poor Ofkyle had been — cut open to get her baby out, then lying still, wrapped in a sheet, staring at me with her silent eyes. There was a certain power in it, silence and stillness.

36

I considered running away from home, but how would I do that and where could I go? I had no notion of geography: we did not study it in school, since our own neighbourhood should be enough for us, and what Wife needed more? I did not even know how big Gilead was. How far did it go, where did it end? More practically, how would I travel, what would I eat, where would I sleep? And if I did run away, would God hate me? Surely I would be pursued? Would I cause a lot of suffering to others, like the Concubine Cut into Twelve Pieces?

The world was infested with men who were certain to be tempted by girls who'd strayed out of bounds: such girls would be viewed as loose in their morals. I might not get any farther than the next block before being ripped to shreds, polluted, and reduced to a pile of wilting green petals.

The week I'd been granted in which to choose my husband wore on. Paula and Commander Kyle favoured Commander Judd: he had the most power. They put on a show of persuading me, since it was better if the bride was willing. There had been gossip about high-level weddings that had gone off badly — wailing, fainting, slaps administered by the mother of the bride. I'd overheard the Marthas saying that before some weddings tranquilizing drugs had been administered, with needles. They had to be careful with the dose: mild staggering and slurred speech could be put down to emotion, a wedding being a hugely important moment in a girl's life, but a ceremony at which the bride was unconscious did not count.

It was clear that I would be married to Commander Judd whether I liked it or not. Whether I hated it or not. But I kept my aversion to myself and pretended to be deciding. As I say, I had learned how to act.

'Think what your position will be,' Paula would say. 'You couldn't ask for better.' Commander Judd was not young and would not live forever, and far though she was from wishing it, I would most likely survive much longer than he would, she said, and after he died I would be a widow, with more leeway to choose my next husband. Think what a benefit that would be! Naturally, any male relatives, including those by marriage, would play a role in my choice of second husband.

Then Paula would run down the qualifications of the other two candidates, disparaging their appearances, their characters, and their positions in life. She needn't have bothered: I detested both of them.

Meanwhile, I was pondering other actions I might take. There were the French-style flower-arranging secateurs, like the ones Becka had used — Paula had some of those — but they

290

were in the garden shed, which was locked. I'd heard of a girl who'd hanged herself with her bathrobe sash to avoid a marriage. Vera had told the story the year before, while the other two Marthas made sad faces and shook their heads.

'Suicide is a failure of faith,' Zilla said.

'It makes a real mess,' said Rosa.

'Such a slur on the family,' said Vera.

There was bleach, but it was kept in the kitchen, as were knives; and the Marthas — being no fools and having eyes in the backs of their heads — were alert to my desperation. They'd taken to dropping aphorisms, such as 'Every cloud has a silver lining' and 'The harder the shell, the sweeter the nut,' and even 'Diamonds are a girl's best friend.' Rosa went so far as to say, as if talking to herself, 'Once you're dead, you're dead forever' while looking at me out of the sides of her eyes.

There was no point in asking the Marthas to help me, not even Zilla. Sorry though they might feel for me, much as they might wish me well, they had no power to affect the outcome.

At the end of the week, my engagement was announced: it was to Commander Judd, as it was always going to be. He appeared at the house in his full uniform with medals, shook hands with Commander Kyle, bowed to Paula, and smiled at the top of my head. Paula moved over to stand beside me, put her arm around my back, and rested her hand lightly on my waist: she had never done such a thing before. Did she think I would try to get away?

'Good evening, Agnes, my dear,' said Commander Judd. I focused on his medals: it was

291

easier to look at them than at him.

'You may say good evening,' Paula said in a low voice, pinching me slightly with the hand that was behind my back. 'Good evening, *sir*.'

'Good evening,' I managed to whisper. 'Sir.'

The Commander advanced, arranged his face into a jowly smile, and stuck his mouth onto my forehead in a chaste kiss. His lips were unpleasantly warm; they made a sucking sound as they pulled away. I pictured a tiny morsel of my brain being sucked through the skin of my forehead into his mouth. A thousand such kisses later and my skull would be emptied of brain.

'I hope to make you very happy, my dear,' he said.

I could smell his breath, a blend of alcohol, mint mouthwash like that at the dentist's, and tooth decay. I had an unbidden image of the wedding night: an enormous, opaque white blob was moving towards me through the dusk of an unknown room. It had a head, but no face: only an orifice like the mouth of a leech. From somewhere in its midsection a third tentacle was waving around in the air. It reached the bed where I was lying paralyzed with horror, and also naked — you had to be naked, or at least naked enough, said Shunammite. What came next? I shut my eyes, trying to blank out the inner scene, then opened them again.

Commander Judd drew back, regarding me shrewdly. Had I shuddered while he was kissing me? I had tried not to. Paula was pinching my waist harder. I knew I was supposed to say something, such as *Thank you* or *I hope so too* or *I'm sure you will*, but I could not manage it. I felt sick to my stomach: what if I threw up, right now, on the carpet? That would be shameful.

'She's exceptionally modest,' said Paula through tight lips, glaring sideways at me.

'And that is a charming feature,' said Commander Judd.

'You may go now, Agnes Jemima,' said Paula. 'Your father and the Commander have things to discuss.' So I made my way towards the door. I was feeling a little dizzy.

'She seems obedient,' I heard Commander Judd saying as I left the room.

'Oh yes,' said Paula. 'She's always been a respectful child.'

What a liar she was. She knew how much rage was seething inside me.

★   ★   ★

The three wedding arrangers, Aunt Lorna, Aunt Sara Lee, and Aunt Betty, made a return visit, this time to measure me for my wedding dress: they'd brought some sketches. I was asked to give my opinion about which dress I liked best. I pointed to one at random.

'Is she well?' Aunt Betty asked Paula in a soft voice. 'She looks quite tired.'

'It's an emotional time for them,' Paula replied.

'Oh yes,' said Aunt Betty. 'So emotional!'

'You should have the Marthas make her a soothing drink,' said Aunt Lorna. 'Something with chamomile. Or a sedative.'

In addition to the dress, I was to have new underclothes, and a special nightgown for the wedding night, with ribbon bows down the front — so easy to open, like a gift-wrapped package.

'I don't know why we are bothering with the frills,' Paula said to the Aunts, talking past me. 'She won't appreciate them.'

'She won't be the one looking at them,' said Aunt Sara Lee with unexpected bluntness. Aunt Lorna gave a suppressed snort.

As for the wedding dress itself, it was to be 'classical,' said Aunt Sara Lee. Classical was the best style: the clean lines would be very elegant, in her opinion. A veil with a simple chaplet of cloth snow-drops and forget-me-nots. Artificial-flower-making was one of the handicrafts encouraged among the Econowives.

There was a subdued conversation about lace trim — to add it, as Aunt Betty advised because it would be attractive, or to omit it, which would be preferable in Paula's view, since attractive was not the main focus. Unspoken: the main focus was to get the thing over with and consign me to her past, where I would be tucked away, unreactive as lead, no longer combustible. No one would be able to say she had not done her duty as the Wife of her Commander and as an observant citizen of Gilead.

The wedding itself would take place as soon as the dress was ready — therefore, it was safe to plan it for two weeks from this day. Did Paula have the names of the guests she would like invited? Aunt Sara Lee asked. The two of them went downstairs to compile: Paula to recite the names, Aunt Sara Lee to write them down. The Aunts would prepare and personally deliver the verbal invitations: it was one of their roles, to be the bearer of poisoned messages.

'Aren't you excited?' said Aunt Betty as she and Aunt Lorna were packing up their sketches and I was putting my clothes back on. 'In two weeks you'll have your very own house!'

There was something wistful in her voice — she herself would never have a house — but I paid no attention to it. Two weeks, I thought. I had only fourteen scant days of life left to me on this earth. How would I spend them?

37

As the days ticked past, I became more desperate. Where was the exit? I had no gun, I had no lethal pills. I remembered a story — circulated by Shunammite at school — about someone's Handmaid who had swallowed drain cleaner.

'The whole bottom part of her face came off,' Shunammite had whispered with delight. 'It just . . . dissolved! It was, like, fizzing!' I hadn't believed her at the time, though now I did.

A bathtub filled with water? But I would gasp and splutter and come up for air, and I couldn't attach a stone to myself in the bath, unlike in a lake or a river or the sea. But there was no way I could get to a lake or a river, or the sea.

Maybe I would have to go through with the ceremony and then murder Commander Judd on the wedding night. Stick a purloined knife into his neck, then into mine. There would be a lot of blood to get out of the sheets. But it wouldn't be me doing the scrubbing. I pictured the dismay on Paula's face when she walked into the slaughter chamber. Such a butcher shop. And there went her social standing.

These scenarios were fantasies, of course. Underneath this web-spinning, I knew I could never kill myself or murder anyone. I remembered Becka's fierce expression when she'd slashed her wrist: she'd been serious about it, she'd really been prepared to die. She was strong in a way that I was not. I would never have her resolve.

★ ★ ★

At night when I was falling asleep, I fantasized about miraculous escapes, but all of them required help from other people, and who would help me? It would have to be someone I didn't know: a rescuer, the warden of a hidden door, the keeper of a secret password. None of that seemed possible when I woke up in the morning. I went round and round in my head: what to do, what to do? I could barely think, I could scarcely eat.

'Wedding nerves, bless her soul,' said Zilla. I did want my soul to be blessed, but I could see no way of that happening.

★ ★ ★

When there were only three days left, I had an unexpected visitor. Zilla came up to my room to call me downstairs. 'Aunt Lydia is here to see you,' she said in hushed tones. 'Good luck. We all wish you that.'

Aunt Lydia! The main Founder, the gold-framed picture at the back of every schoolroom, the ultimate Aunt — come to see me? What had I done? I was shaking as I made my way down the stairs.

Paula was out, which was a lucky thing;

297

though after I came to know Aunt Lydia better, I realized that luck had nothing to do with it. Aunt Lydia was sitting on the sofa in the living room. She was smaller than she'd been at the funeral of Ofkyle, but perhaps that was because I'd grown. She actually smiled at me, a wrinkly, yellow-toothed smile.

'Agnes, my dear,' she said. 'I thought you might like to hear some news about your friend Becka.' I was in such awe of her that it was hard for me to talk.

'Is she dead?' I whispered, my heart sinking.

'Not at all. She is safe and happy.'

'Where is she?' I managed to stammer.

'She is at Ardua Hall, with us. She wishes to become an Aunt and is enrolled as a Supplicant.'

'Oh,' I said. A light was dawning, a door was opening.

'Not every girl is suitable for marriage,' she continued. 'For some it is simply a waste of potential. There are other ways a girl or woman may contribute to God's plan. A little bird has told me that you may agree.' Who had told her? Zilla? She'd sensed how violently unhappy I was.

'Yes,' I said. Perhaps my prayers of long ago to Aunt Lydia had finally been answered, though in a different way than I'd expected.

'Becka has received a call to higher service. If you yourself have such a calling,' she said, 'you still have time to tell us.'

'But how do I . . . I don't know how . . . '

'I myself cannot be seen to be proposing this course of action directly,' she said. 'It would contravene the prime right of the father to arrange the marriage of his daughter. A calling can override the paternal right, but you must make the first approach to us. I suspect Aunt Estée would be willing to listen. If your calling proves strong enough, you will devise a way of contacting her.'

'But what about Commander Judd?' I asked timorously. He was so powerful: if I ducked the wedding, surely he would be very angry, I thought.

'Oh, Commander Judd always has lots of choices,' she said with an expression I couldn't read.

⋆　⋆　⋆

My next task was to find a pathway to Aunt Estée. I could not declare my intention outright: Paula would stop me. She'd lock me in my room, she'd resort to drugs. She was hell-bent on this marriage. I use the expression *hell-bent* advisedly: she was risking her soul for it; although, as I later learned, her soul was already in flames.

The day after Aunt Lydia's visit, I made a request of Paula. I wanted to talk to Aunt Lorna about my wedding dress, which had already been tried on twice and was being altered. I wanted everything to be perfect for my special day, I said. I smiled. I thought the dress looked like a lampshade, but it was my plan to appear cheerful and appreciative.

Paula gave me a sharp glance. I doubt that she believed in my smiling face; but if I was putting on an act so much the better, as long as it was the kind of act she wanted.

'I'm pleased you're taking an interest,' she said drily. 'It's a good thing Aunt Lydia paid you a visit.' Naturally she'd heard about that, though not about what was actually said.

But it would be a nuisance for Aunt Lorna to come to our house, said Paula. It wasn't convenient, as I ought to have known — there was the food to be ordered, there were the flowers to be arranged, Paula couldn't deal with such a time-wasting visit.

'Aunt Lorna is at Shunammite's,' I said. I knew that from Zilla: Shunammite's own wedding was also shortly to take place. In that case, our Guardian could drive me over there, said Paula. I felt my heart quicken, partly in relief, partly in fear: now I would have to carry through my risky plan.

How did the Marthas know who was where? They weren't allowed Computalks and couldn't receive letters. They must have known from other Marthas, though possibly from the Aunts as well, and some of the Wives. The Aunts, the Marthas, the Wives: despite the fact that they were frequently envious and resentful, and might even hate one another, news flowed among them as if along invisible spiderweb threads.

★   ★   ★

Our Guardian driver was summoned and given instructions by Paula. I expect she was glad to have me out of the house: my unhappiness must

300

have given off a sour smell that was irritating to her. Shunammite used to say that they put happy pills into the warm milk of girls who were about to get married, but no one had been putting happy pills in mine.

I climbed into the back seat of our car while our Guardian held the door open for me. I took a deep breath, half exhilaration, half terror. What if my attempt at deception should fail? And what if it should succeed? Either way I was heading into the unknown.

I did consult Aunt Lorna, who was indeed at Shunammite's house. Shunammite said it was fun to see me, and once we were married we could visit a lot! She hurried me inside and took me to inspect her wedding dress, and to hear all about the husband she would soon have, who (she whispered, giggling) looked like a carp, with a receding chin and goggly eyes, but who was medium-high up among the Commanders.

Wasn't that exciting, I said. I admired the dress, which — I told Shunammite — was much fancier than mine. Shunammite laughed, and said she'd heard I was practically marrying God, my new husband was so important, and wasn't I lucky; and I gazed downwards and said but anyway her dress was nicer. She was pleased by that, and said she was sure we would both get through the sex part and not make a fuss. We would follow Aunt Lise's instructions and think about arranging flowers in a vase, and it would all be over quickly, and maybe we would even have real babies, by ourselves, without Hand-maids. She asked if I would like an oatmeal cookie, and she sent the Martha for some. I took one and nibbled at it, though I was not hungry.

I couldn't stay long, I said, because there was so much to do, but could I see Aunt Lorna? We found her across the hall in one of the spare rooms, poring over her notebook. I asked her to add something or other to my dress — a white bow, a white frill, I can't remember. I said goodbye to Shunammite, and thanked her for the cookie, and said again how lovely her dress was. I went out the front door, waving cheerfully just like a real girl, and walked to our car.

After that, heart hammering, I asked our driver if he wouldn't mind stopping by my old school, since I wished to thank my former teacher Aunt Estée for everything she had taught me.

He was standing beside the car, holding the back door open for me. He gave me a suspicious frown. 'Those aren't my instructions,' he said.

I smiled in what I hoped was a charming way. My face felt stiff, as if it was covered with hardening glue. 'It's quite safe,' I said. 'Commander Kyle's Wife won't mind. Aunt Estée is an *Aunt*! It's her job to take care of me!'

'Well, I don't know,' he said dubiously.

I looked up at him. I'd never paid much attention to him before, since usually I had only the back view. He was a torpedo-shaped man, small at the top end, thick in the middle. He had not shaved carefully, and had bristles and a rash.

'I'll be married soon,' I said. 'To a very powerful Commander. More powerful than Paula — than Commander Kyle's Wife.' I paused to let this sink in, and then I am ashamed to say I placed my hand lightly on top of his, where it was holding the car door. 'I'll make sure you're rewarded,' I said.

He flinched slightly and pinkened. 'Well, then,' he said, though he didn't smile.

So this is how women get things done, I thought. If they are prepared to wheedle, and lie, and go back on their word. I was disgusted with myself, but you'll notice this didn't stop me. I smiled again, and pulled my skirt up just a little, displaying an ankle as I swivelled my legs into the car. 'Thank you,' I said. 'You won't be sorry'

He drove me to my old school as I'd requested, and talked to the Angels guarding it, and the double gates swung open, and I was driven inside. I told the driver to wait for me: I wouldn't be long. Then I walked sedately into the school building, which now seemed much smaller than when I'd left it.

It was after hours; I was lucky that Aunt Estée was still there, though again it may not have been luck. She was sitting at her desk in her usual classroom, writing in her notebook. She looked up when I came in.

'Why, Agnes,' she said. 'You're all grown up!'

I hadn't planned beyond this moment. I wanted to throw myself on the floor in front of her and burst into tears. She'd always been kind to me.

'They're making me marry a horrible, disgusting man!' I said. 'I'll kill myself first!' Then I really did burst into tears and crumpled onto her desk. It was acting in a way, and probably bad acting, but it was real acting if you see what I mean.

Aunt Estée lifted me up and walked me to a chair. 'Sit down, my dear,' she said, 'and tell me all about it.'

She asked me the questions she was duty-bound to ask. Had I considered how this marriage might affect my future positively? I told her that I knew about the benefits, but I didn't care about them because I had no future, not of that kind. What about the other candidates? she asked. Would anyone else be preferable? They were not any better, I said, and anyway Paula had made up her mind about Commander Judd. Was I in earnest about killing myself? I said I was, and that if I didn't manage it before the wedding I would be sure to do it afterwards, and I would kill Commander Judd the first time he laid a finger on me. I would do it with a knife, I said. I would cut his throat.

I said this with conviction so she would see that I was capable of it, and for that moment I believed I was. I could almost feel the blood as it came pouring out of him. And then my own blood as well. I could almost see it: a haze of red.

Aunt Estée didn't say I was very wicked, as Aunt Vidala might have done. Instead she said that she understood my distress. 'But is there another way you feel you might contribute to the greater good? Have you perhaps had a call?'

I'd forgotten about that part, but now I remembered. 'Oh yes,' I said. 'Yes I have. I'm called to higher service.'

Aunt Estée gave me a long and searching look.

Then she asked me if she could pray silently: she needed guidance about what to do. I watched while she folded her hands, closed her eyes, and bowed her head. I held my breath: Please, God, send her the right message, I prayed in my turn.

Finally she opened her eyes and smiled at me. 'I will speak with your parents,' she said. 'And with Aunt Lydia.'

'Thank you,' I said. I was beginning to cry again, this time with relief.

'Do you want to come with me?' she said. 'To talk with your parents?'

'I can't,' I said. 'They'll get hold of me and lock me in my room, and then they'll give me a drug. You know they will.'

She didn't deny it. 'That's sometimes best,' she said, 'but for you, I think not. You can't stay here at the school, however. I couldn't stop the Eyes from entering, and removing you, and changing your mind. You don't want the Eyes doing that. You'd better come with me.'

She must have evaluated Paula, and judged that she'd be capable of anything. I didn't know then how Aunt Estée had come by this information about Paula, but I know now. The Aunts had their methods, and their informants: no walls were solid for them, no doors locked.

We went outside and she told my driver to let his Commander's Wife know that she was sorry for having kept Agnes Jemima so long, and she hoped that no undue worry had been caused. Also he should say that she, Aunt Estée, was about to pay Commander Kyle's Wife a visit, to decide an important matter.

'What about her?' he said, meaning me.

Aunt Estée said she would take responsibility for me, so he need not concern himself. He gave me a reproachful look — actually a filthy look: he knew that I'd tricked him, and that he was now in trouble. But he got into the car and drove out through the gates. The Angels were Vidala School Angels: they obeyed Aunt Estée.

Then Aunt Estée used her pager to call her own Guardian driver, and we got into her car. 'I'm taking you to a safe place,' she said. 'You must stay there while I talk to your parents. When we get to the safe place, you must promise me you'll eat something. Promise?'

'I won't be hungry,' I said. I was still holding back tears.

'You will be, once you settle in,' she said. 'A glass of warm milk, at any rate.' She took my hand and squeezed it. 'All will be well,' she said. 'All manner of things will be well.' Then she let go of my hand and patted it lightly.

This was comforting to me as far as it went, but I was on the verge of crying again. Kindness sometimes has that effect. 'How?' I said. 'How can it ever be well?'

'I don't know,' said Aunt Estée. 'But it will be. I have faith.' She sighed. 'Having faith is hard work sometimes.'

38

The sun was setting. The springtime air was filled with the golden haze that can often appear at that time of year: dust, or pollen. The leaves of the trees had that glossy sheen, so fresh and newly unfolded; as if they were gifts, each one, unwrapping itself, shaken out for the first time. As if God had just made them, Aunt Estée used to tell us during Nature Appreciation, conjuring up a picture of God waving his hand over the dead-looking winter trees, causing them to sprout and unfurl. Every leaf unique, Aunt Estée would add, just like you! It was a beautiful thought.

Aunt Estée and I were driven through the golden streets. Would I ever see these houses, these trees, these sidewalks again? Empty sidewalks, quiet streets. Lights were coming on in the houses; inside there must have been happy people, people who knew where they belonged. Already I felt like an outcast; but I'd cast myself out, so I had no right to feel sorry for myself.

'Where are we going?' I asked Aunt Estée.

'Ardua Hall,' she said. 'You can stay there while I visit your parents.'

I'd heard Ardua Hall mentioned, always in hushed tones because it was a special place for the Aunts. Whatever the Aunts did when we

307

weren't looking was not our concern, said Zilla. They kept themselves to themselves and we should not poke our noses in. 'But I wouldn't want to be *them*,' Zilla would add.

'Why not?' I asked her once.

'Nasty business,' said Vera, who was running pork through the meat grinder for a pie. 'They get their hands dirty.'

'So we don't have to,' said Zilla mildly, rolling pie crust.

'They dirty up their minds too,' said Rosa. 'Whether they want to or not.' She was chopping onions with a large cleaver. 'Reading!' She gave an extra-loud chop. 'I never liked it.'

'I didn't either,' said Vera. 'Who knows what they're forced to dig around in! Filthiness and muck.'

'Better them than us,' said Zilla.

'They can never have husbands,' said Rosa. 'Not that I'd want one myself, but still. Or babies either. They can't have those.'

'They're too old anyway,' said Vera. 'All dried up.'

'The crust's ready,' said Zilla. 'Have we got any celery?'

Despite this discouraging view of the Aunts, I'd been intrigued by the idea of Ardua Hall. Ever since I'd learned that Tabitha wasn't my mother, anything secret had attracted me. When I was younger I'd ornamented Ardua Hall in my mind, made it enormous, given it magic properties: surely the location of so much subterranean but ill-understood power must be an imposing construction. Was it a huge castle, or was it more like a jail? Was it like our school? Most likely it had a lot of large brass locks on the doors that only an Aunt would be able to open.

Where there is an emptiness, the mind will obligingly fill it up. Fear is always at hand to supply any vacancies, as is curiosity. I have had ample experience with both.

★ ★ ★

'Do you live there?' I asked Aunt Estée now. 'Ardua Hall?'

'All the Aunts in this city live there,' she said. 'Though we come and go.'

As the streetlights began to glow, turning the air a dull orange, we reached a gateway in a high, red-brick wall. The barred iron gate was closed. Our car paused; then the gate swung open. There were floodlights; there were trees. In the distance, a group of men in the dark uniforms of the Eyes were standing on a wide stairway in front of a brightly lit brick palace with white pillars, or it looked like a palace. I was soon to learn it had once been a library.

Our car pulled in and stopped, and the driver opened the door, first for Aunt Estée, then for me.

'Thank you,' said Aunt Estée to him. 'Please wait here. I'll be back shortly.'

She took me by the arm, and we walked along the side of a large grey stonework building, then past a statue of a woman with some other women posed around her. You didn't usually see statues of women in Gilead, only of men.

'That is Aunt Lydia,' said Aunt Estée. 'Or a statue of her.' Was it my imagination, or did Aunt Estée give a little curtsy?

'She's different from real life,' I said. I didn't know if Aunt Lydia's visit to me was supposed to be a secret, so I added, 'I saw her at a funeral. She's not that big.' Aunt Estée did not answer for a moment. I see in retrospect that it was a difficult question: you don't want to be caught saying that a powerful person is small.

'No,' she said. 'But statues aren't real people.'

We turned onto a paved pathway Along one side of it was a long three-storey building of red brick punctuated by a number of identical doorways, each with a few steps going up to it and a white triangle over the top. Inside the triangle was some writing, which I could not yet read. Nonetheless I was surprised to see writing in such a public place.

'This is Ardua Hall,' said Aunt Estée. I was disappointed: I'd been expecting something much grander. 'Come in. You will be safe here.'

'Safe?' I said.

'For the moment,' she said. 'And, I hope, for some time.' She smiled gently 'No man is allowed inside without the permission of the Aunts. It's a law. You can rest here until I come back.' I might be safe from men, I thought, but what about women? Paula could barge in and drag me out, back into a place where there were husbands.

Aunt Estée led me through a medium-sized room with a sofa. 'This is the common sitting area. There's a bathroom through that door.' She ushered me up a flight of stairs and into a little

310

room with a single bed and a desk. 'One of the other Aunts will bring you a cup of warm milk. Then you should have a nap. Please don't worry. God has told me it will be all right.' I didn't have as much confidence in this as she appeared to, but I felt reassured.

She waited until the warm milk arrived, carried in by a silent Aunt. 'Thank you, Aunt Silhouette,' she said. The other one nodded and glided out. Aunt Estée patted my arm, then left, closing the door behind her.

I had only a sip of the milk: I didn't trust it. Would the Aunts give me drugs before kidnapping me and delivering me back into Paula's hands? I didn't think Aunt Estée would do that, though Aunt Silhouette looked as if she might. The Aunts were on the side of the Wives, or that's what the girls had said at school.

I paced around the small room; then I lay down on the narrow bed. But I was too overwrought to go to sleep, so I got up again. There was a picture on the wall: Aunt Lydia, smiling an inscrutable smile. On the opposite wall was a picture of Baby Nicole. They were the same familiar pictures that had been in the classrooms at the Vidala School, and I found them oddly comforting.

On the desk there was a book.

I'd thought and done so many forbidden things that day that I was ready to do one more. I went over to the desk and stared down at the book. What was inside it that made it so dangerous to girls like me? So flammable? So ruinous?

311

39

I reached out my hand. I picked up the book.

I opened the front cover. No flames shot out.

There were many white pages inside, with a lot of marks on them. They looked like small insects, black broken insects arranged in lines, like ants. I seemed to know that the marks contained sounds and meaning, but I couldn't remember how.

'It's really hard at first,' said a voice behind me.

I hadn't heard the door open. I startled and turned. 'Becka!' I said. I'd last seen her at Aunt Lise's flower-arranging class with blood spurting out of her cut wrist. Her face had been very pale then, and resolved, and forlorn. She looked much better now. She was wearing a brown dress, loose on top, belted at the waist; her hair was parted in the middle and pulled back.

'My name isn't Becka anymore,' she said. 'I'm Aunt Immortelle now; I'm a Supplicant. But you can call me Becka when we're alone.'

'So you didn't get married after all,' I said. 'Aunt Lydia told me you have a higher calling.'

'Yes,' she said. 'I won't have to marry any man, ever. But what about you? I heard you're going to marry someone highly important.'

'I'm supposed to,' I said. I started to cry. 'But I can't. I just can't!' I wiped my nose on my sleeve.

'I know,' she said. 'I told them I'd rather die. You must have said the same thing.' I nodded. 'Did you say you had a calling? To be an Aunt?' I nodded again. 'Do you really have one?'

'I don't know,' I said.

'Neither do I,' said Becka. 'But I passed the six-month trial period. After nine years — when I'm old enough — I can apply for Pearl Girls missionary work, and once I've done that I'll be a full Aunt. Then maybe I'll get a real calling. I'm praying for one.'

I'd finished crying. 'What do I have to do? To pass the trial?'

'At first you have to wash dishes and scrub floors and clean toilets and help with the laundry and cooking, just like Marthas,' said Becka. 'And you have to start learning how to read. Reading's way harder than cleaning toilets. But I can read some now.'

I handed her the book. 'Show me!' I said. 'Is this book evil? Is it full of forbidden things, the way Aunt Vidala said?'

'This?' said Becka. She smiled. 'Not this one. It's only the *Ardua Hall Rule Book*, with the history, the vows, and the hymns. Plus the weekly schedule for the laundry.'

'Go on! Read it!' I wanted to see if she could really translate the black insect marks into words. Though how would I know they were the right words, since I couldn't read them myself?

She opened the book. 'Here it is, on the first

313

page. 'Ardua Hall. Theory and Practice, Protocols and Procedures, *Per Ardua Cum Estrus.*'' She showed me. 'See this? It's an *A*.'

'What's an *A*?'

She sighed. 'We can't do this today because I have to go to the Hildegard Library, I'm on night duty, but I promise I'll help you later if they let you stay. We can ask Aunt Lydia if you can live here, with me. There are two bedrooms empty.'

'Do you think she'll allow it?'

'I'm not sure,' said Becka, lowering her voice. 'But don't ever say anything bad about her, even if you think you're in a safe place such as here. She has ways of knowing about it.' She whispered, 'She is truly the scariest one, of all the Aunts!'

'Scarier than Aunt Vidala?' I whispered back.

'Aunt Vidala wants you to make mistakes,' said Becka. 'But Aunt Lydia . . . it's hard to describe. You get the feeling she wants you to be better than you are.'

'That sounds inspirational,' I said. *Inspirational* was a favourite word of Aunt Lise's: she used it for flower arrangements.

'She looks at you as if she really sees you.'

So many people had looked past me. 'I think I'd like that,' I said.

'No,' said Becka. 'That's why she's so scary.'

40

Paula came to Ardua Hall to try to get me to change my mind. Aunt Lydia said it was only proper that I should meet with her and assure her in person of the rightness and holiness of my decision, so I did.

Paula was waiting for me at a pink table in the Schlafly Café, where we at Ardua Hall were permitted to receive visitors. She was very angry.

'Have you no idea of the trouble your father and I went to in order to secure the connection with Commander Judd?' she said. 'You have dishonoured your father.'

'Membership in the Aunts is far from dishonourable,' I said piously. 'I had a call to higher service. I could not refuse it.'

'You're lying,' said Paula. 'You are not the kind of girl God would ever single out. I demand that you return home immediately.'

I stood up suddenly and smashed my teacup on the floor. 'How dare you question the Divine Will?' I said. I was almost shouting. 'Your sin will find you out!' I didn't know what sin I meant, but everyone has a sin of some kind.

'Act crazy,' Becka had told me. 'Then they won't want you marrying anyone: it will be their responsibility if you do anything violent.'

Paula was taken aback. For a moment she had no answer, but then she said, 'The Aunts need Commander Kyle's agreement, and he will never give it. So pack up because you're leaving, now.'

At that moment, however, Aunt Lydia came into the café. 'May I have a word with you?' she said to Paula. The two of them moved to a table at some distance from me. I strained to hear what Aunt Lydia was saying, but I could not. When Paula stood up, however, she looked sick. She left the café without a word to me, and later that afternoon Commander Kyle signed the formal permission granting authority over me to the Aunts. It was many years before I was to learn what Aunt Lydia had said to Paula to force her to relinquish me.

★ ★ ★

Next I had to go through the interviews with the Founding Aunts. Becka had advised me on the best way to behave with each of them: Aunt Elizabeth went in for dedication to the greater good, Aunt Helena would want to get it over quickly, but Aunt Vidala liked grovelling and self-humiliation, so I was prepared.

The first interview was with Aunt Elizabeth. She asked whether I was against marriage, or just against marriage to Commander Judd? I said I was against it in general, which seemed to please her. Had I considered how my decision might hurt Commander Judd — hurt his feelings? I almost said that Commander Judd didn't seem to have any feelings, but Becka had warned me not to say anything disrespectful because the Aunts wouldn't put up with it.

I said I'd prayed for the emotional well-being of Commander Judd and he deserved every happiness, which I was positive some other Wife would bring him, but Divine Guidance had told me I would not be able to provide that sort of happiness for him, or indeed for any man, and I wanted to consecrate myself in service to all the women of Gilead rather than to one man and one family.

'If you really mean that, you are well positioned, spiritually, to get on very well here at Ardua Hall,' she said. 'I will vote for your conditional acceptance. After six months we will see whether this life is truly the path you have been chosen to follow.' I thanked her repeatedly, and said how grateful I was, and she appeared to be pleased.

My interview with Aunt Helena was nothing much. She was writing in her notebook and did not look up. She said that Aunt Lydia had already made up her mind, so of course she would have to agree. She implied I was boring and a waste of her time.

My interview with Aunt Vidala was the most difficult. She'd been one of my teachers, and she hadn't liked me then. She said I was shirking my duty, and any girl who'd been gifted with a woman's body was obligated to offer this body up in holy sacrifice to God and for the glory of Gilead and mankind, and also to fulfill the function that such bodies had inherited from the moment of Creation, and that was nature's law.

I said that God had given women other gifts as well, such as the ones he had bestowed on her. She said what might those be? I said the gift of being able to read, since all Aunts were gifted in that way. She said that the reading the Aunts did was holy reading and in the service of all the things she had said before — she said them over again — and did I presume to be sufficiently sanctified myself?

I said I was willing to do any kind of hard work in order to become an Aunt like her, because she was a shining example, and I wasn't yet sanctified at all, but perhaps through grace and prayer I would receive enough sanctification, though I could never hope to achieve the level of sanctification that she herself had reached.

Aunt Vidala said I was displaying an appropriate meekness, which boded well for a successful integration into the service community of Ardua Hall. She even gave me one of her pinched-in smiles before I left.

* * *

My final interview was with Aunt Lydia. I'd been anxious about the others, but as I stood outside the door to Aunt Lydia's office I was terrified. What if she'd thought better of it? She had a reputation for being not only fearsome but unpredictable. While I was lifting my hand to knock, her voice came from inside: 'Don't stand there all day. Come in.'

Was she looking at me through a miniature hidden camera? Becka had told me that she

318

deployed a lot of those, or that was the rumour. As I was soon to discover, Ardua Hall was an echo chamber: the rumours fed back into one another so you could never be certain where they had come from.

I entered the office. Aunt Lydia was sitting behind her desk, which was stacked high with file folders. 'Agnes,' she said. 'I must congratulate you. Despite many obstacles, you have succeeded in making your way here, and have answered the call to join us.' I nodded. I was afraid she would ask me what that call had been like — had I heard a voice? — but she did not.

'You are very positive that you do not wish to marry Commander Judd?' I shook my head for no.

'Wise choice,' she said.

'What?' I was surprised: I'd thought she might give me a moral lecturing about the true duties of women or something of the sort. 'I mean, pardon?'

'I am sure you would not have made him a fitting Wife.'

I breathed out in relief. 'No, Aunt Lydia,' I said. 'I would not. I hope he will not be too disappointed.'

'I have already proposed a more appropriate choice for him,' she said. 'Your former school-mate Shunammite.'

'Shunammite?' I said. 'But she's going to marry someone else!'

'These arrangements can always be altered. Would Shunammite welcome the change of husbands, do you think?'

I remembered Shunammite's barely concealed envy of me and her excitement over the material advantages her wedding would bring. Commander Judd would confer ten times as many of those. 'I am sure she would be deeply grateful,' I said.

'I agree.' She smiled. It was like an old turnip smiling: the dried-up kind our Marthas used to put in soup stock. 'Welcome to Ardua Hall,' she continued. 'You have been accepted. I hope you are grateful for the opportunity, and for the help I have given you.'

'I am, Aunt Lydia,' I managed to get out. 'I am truly grateful.'

'I am glad to hear it,' she said. 'Perhaps one day you will be able to help me as you yourself have been helped. Good should be repaid with good. That is one of our rules of thumb, here at Ardua Hall.'

XV

Fox and Cat

The Ardua Hall Holograph

41

All things come to she who waits. Time wounds all heels. Patience is a virtue. Vengeance is mine.

These hoary chestnuts are not always true, but they are sometimes true. Here's one that is always true: everything's in the timing. Like jokes.

Not that we have many jokes around here. We would not wish to be accused of bad taste or frivolity. In a hierarchy of the powerful, the only ones allowed to make jokes are those at the top, and they do so in private.

But to the point.

It has been so crucial for my own mental development to have had the privilege of being a fly on the wall; or, to be more exact, an ear inside the wall. So instructive, the confidences shared by young women when they believe no third party is listening. Over the years I increased the sensitivity of my microphones, I attuned them to whispers, I held my breath to see which of our newly recruited girls would provide me with the sort of shameful information I both craved and collected. Gradually my dossiers filled up, like a hot-air balloon getting ready for liftoff.

In the matter of Becka, it took years. She'd always been so reticent about the primary cause of her distress, even to her school friend Agnes. I had to wait for sufficient trust to develop.

It was Agnes who finally broached the question. I use their earlier names here — Agnes, Becka — since it was these names they used among themselves. Their transformation into perfect Aunts was far from complete, which pleased me. But then, no one's is when push comes to shove.

'Becka, what really happened to you?' Agnes said one day when they were engaged in their Bible studies. 'To make you so set against marriage.' Silence. 'I know there was something. Please, wouldn't you like to share it with me?'

'I can't say.'

'You can trust me, I won't tell.'

Then, in bits and pieces, it came out. The wretched Dr. Grove had not stopped at the fondling of his young patients in the dentist's chair. I had known about this for some time. I had even collected photographic evidence, but I had passed over it, since the testimonies of young girls — if testimonies can be extracted from them, which in this case I doubted — would count for little or nothing. Even with grown women, four female witnesses are the equivalent of one male, here in Gilead.

Grove had depended on that. Also, the man had the confidence of the Commanders: he was an excellent dentist, and much latitude is given by those in power to professionals who can relieve them of pain. The doctors, the dentists, the lawyers, the accountants: in the new world of Gilead, as in the old, their sins are frequently forgiven them.

But what Grove had done to the young Becka — the very young Becka, and then the older but still young Becka — that, to my mind, demanded retribution.

Becka herself could not be relied upon to exact it. She would not testify against Grove, of that I was certain. Her conversation with Agnes confirmed this.

AGNES: We have to tell someone.

BECKA: No, there's no one.

AGNES: We could tell Aunt Lydia.

BECKA: She'd say he was my parent and we should obey our parents, it's God's plan. That's what my father said himself.

AGNES: But he isn't your parent really. Not if he did that to you. You were stolen from your mother, you were handed over as a baby . . .

BECKA: He said he was set in authority over me by God.

AGNES: What about your so-called mother?

BECKA: She wouldn't believe me. Even if she did, she'd say I led him on. They'd all say that.

AGNES: But you were four!

BECKA: They'd say it anyway. You know they would. They can't start taking the word of . . . of people like me. And suppose they did believe me, he'd be killed, he'd be ripped apart by the Handmaids at a Particicution, and it would be my fault. I couldn't live with that. It would be like murder.

I haven't added the tears, the comfortings by Agnes, the vows of eternal friendship, the prayers. But they were there. It was enough to melt the hardest heart. It almost melted mine.

The upshot was that Becka had decided to offer up this silent suffering of hers as a sacrifice to God. I am not sure what God thought of this, but it did not do the trick for me. Once a judge, always a judge. I judged, I pronounced the sentence. But how to carry it out?

After pondering for some time, I decided last week to make my move. I invited Aunt Elizabeth for a cup of mint tea at the Schlafly Café.

She was all smiles: she had been singled out for my favour. 'Aunt Lydia,' she said. 'This is an unexpected pleasure!' She had very good manners when she chose to use them. Once a Vassar girl, always a Vassar girl, as I sometimes said snidely to myself while watching her beating to a pulp the feet of some recalcitrant Handmaid prospect in the Rachel and Leah Centre.

'I thought we should have a confidential talk,' I said. She leaned forward, expecting gossip.

'I'm all ears,' she said. An untruth — her ears were a small part of her — but I let that pass.

'I've often wondered,' I said. 'If you were an animal, what animal would you be?'

She leaned back, puzzled. 'I can't say I've given it any thought,' she said. 'Since God did not make me an animal.'

'Indulge me,' I said. 'For instance: fox or cat?'

★   ★   ★

Here, my reader, I owe you an explanation. As a child I'd read a book called *Aesop's Fables*. I'd got it from the school library: my family did not spend money on books. In this book was a story I have often meditated upon. Here it is.

Fox and Cat were discussing their respective ways of evading the hunters and their dogs. Fox said he had a whole bag of tricks, and if the hunters came with their dogs he would employ them one by one — doubling back on his own tracks, running through water to destroy his scent, diving into a den with several exits. The hunters would be worn out by Fox's cleverness and would give up, leaving Fox to continue his career of theft and barnyard muggings. 'And what about you, dear Cat?' he asked. 'What are your tricks?'

'I have only one trick,' Cat replied. 'When in extremis, I know how to climb a tree.'

Fox thanked Cat for the entertaining pre-prandial conversation and declared that it was now dinnertime and Cat was on the menu. Snapping of fox teeth, clumps of cat fur. A name tag was spat out. Posters of missing Cat were stapled to telephone poles, with heartfelt pleas from woebegone children.

Sorry. I get carried away. The fable continues as follows:

The hunters and their dogs arrive on the scene. Fox tries all his tricks, but he runs out of ruses and is killed. Cat, meanwhile, has climbed a tree and is watching the scene with equanimity. 'Not so clever after all!' she jeers. Or some such mean-spirited remark.

In the early days of Gilead, I used to ask myself whether I was Fox or Cat. Should I twist and turn, using the secrets in my possession to manipulate others, or should I zip my lip and rejoice as others outsmarted themselves? Obviously I was both, since — unlike many — here I still am. I still have a bag of tricks. And I'm still high in the tree.

★ ★ ★

But Aunt Elizabeth knew nothing of my private musings. 'I honestly don't know,' she said. 'Maybe a cat.'

'Yes,' I said. 'I'd have pegged you as a cat. But now perhaps you must draw upon your inner fox.' I paused.

'Aunt Vidala is attempting to incriminate you,' I continued. 'She claims that you are accusing me of heresy and idolatry by planting eggs and oranges on my own statue.'

Aunt Elizabeth was distraught. 'That is untrue! Why would Vidala say that? I have never harmed her!'

'Who can fathom the secrets of the human soul?' I said. 'None of us is exempt from sin. Aunt Vidala is ambitious. She may have detected that you are de facto second-in-command to me.' Here Elizabeth brightened, as this was news to her. 'She will have deduced that you are thus next in the line of succession here at Ardua Hall. She must resent this, as she considers herself your senior, and indeed mine, having been an early believer in Gilead. I am not young, nor in the best of health; she must feel that, in order to claim her rightful position, it is necessary to eliminate you. Hence her desire for new rules outlawing the offerings at my statue. With punishments,' I added. 'She must be angling for my expulsion from the Aunts and for yours as well.'

Elizabeth was weeping by now. 'How could she be so vindictive?' she sobbed. 'I thought we were friends.'

'Friendship, alas, can be skin deep. Don't worry. I will protect you.'

'I'm immensely grateful, Aunt Lydia. You have such integrity!'

'Thank you,' I said. 'But there is one little thing I want you to do for me in return.'

'Oh yes! Of course,' she said. 'What is it?'

'I want you to bear false witness,' I said.

This was not a trivial request: Elizabeth would be risking much. Gilead takes a stern view of bearing false witness, though it is nonetheless done frequently.

XVI

PEARL GIRLS

Transcript of Witness Testimony 369B

42

My first day as the runaway Jade was a Thursday. Melanie used to say that I was born on a Thursday and that meant I had far to go — this was an old nursery rhyme that also says Wednesday's child is full of woe, so when I was feeling grumpy I'd say she got the day wrong and it was really Wednesday, and she would say no, of course not, she knew exactly when I was born, how could she ever forget it?

Anyway, it was a Thursday. I was sitting cross-legged on the sidewalk with Garth, wearing black tights with a rip in them — Ada had supplied them, but I had made the rip myself — and magenta shorts over them, and worn-out silver gel shoes that looked as if they'd been through the digestive system of a raccoon. I had a dingy pink top — it was sleeveless because Ada said I should display my new tattoo. I had a grey hoodie tied around my waist and a black baseball cap. None of the clothes fit: they had to look as if I'd grabbed them out of dump bins. I'd dirtied up my new green hair to give the impression that I'd been sleeping rough. The green was already fading.

'You look amazing,' said Garth once he saw me in the full costume and ready to go.

'Amazingly like shit,' I said.

'Great shit,' said Garth. I thought he was only trying to be nice to me, and I resented that. I wanted him to actually mean it. 'But once you're in Gilead, you'll really have to cut the swearing. Maybe even let them convert you out of it.'

There were a lot of instructions to remember. I was feeling nervous — I was sure I would mess up — but Garth said just act stupid, and I'd said thanks for saying *act*.

I wasn't very good at flirting. I'd never done it before.

★ ★ ★

The two of us were set up outside a bank, which Garth said was a prime location if you were angling for free cash: people coming out of banks are more likely to give you some. Another person — a woman in a wheelchair — usually had this space, but Mayday had paid her to relocate for as long as we needed it: the Pearl Girls had a route they followed, and our spot was on it.

The sun was blazing so we were backed against the wall, in a little slice of shade. I had an old straw hat in front of me with a cardboard sign in crayon: HOMELESS PLEASE HELP. There were a few coins in the hat: Garth said that if people saw someone else had put money in they'd be more likely to do it themselves. I was supposed to be acting lost and disoriented, which wasn't hard to do, since I really felt that way.

A block to the east, George was set up on

334

another corner. He'd call Ada and Elijah if there was any trouble, either with the Pearl Girls or the police. They were in a van, cruising the area.

Garth didn't talk much. I decided he was a cross between a babysitter and a bodyguard, so he wasn't there to make conversation and there was no rule that said he had to be nice to me. He was wearing a black sleeveless T-shirt that showed his own tattoos — a squid on one biceps, a bat on the other, both of them in black. He had one of those knitted caps, also in black.

'Smile at the people if they toss in,' he said after I'd failed to do this for a white-haired old lady. 'Say something.'

'Like what?' I asked.

'Some people say 'God bless you.''

Neil would've been shocked if I'd ever said such a thing. 'That would be a lie. If I don't believe in God.'

'Okay then. 'Thanks' will do,' he said patiently. 'Or 'Have a nice day.''

'I can't say those,' I said. 'It's hypocritical. I don't feel thankful, and I don't care what kind of an asshole day they have.'

He laughed. 'Now you're worried about lying? Then why not change your name back to Nicole?'

'It's not my name of choice. It's bottom of the freaking list, you know that.' I crossed my arms on my knees and turned away from him. I was getting more childish by the minute: he brought it out in me.

'Don't waste your anger on me,' said Garth. 'I'm just furniture. Save it for Gilead.'

'You all said I had to have attitude. So, this is my attitude.'

'Here come the Pearl Girls,' he said. 'Don't stare at them. Don't even see them. Act like you're stoned.'

I don't know how he'd spotted them without seeming to look, they were way down the street. But soon they were level with us: two of them, in their silvery grey dresses with long skirts, their white collars, their white hats. A redhead, from the wisps of her hair that were showing, and a brunette, judging from the eyebrows. They smiled down on me where I sat against the wall.

'Good morning, dear,' the redhead said. 'What's your name?'

'We can help you,' said the brunette. 'No homeless in Gilead.' I gazed up at her, hoping I looked as woeful as I felt. They both were so prim and groomed; they made me feel triple grubby.

Garth put his hand on my right arm, gripped it possessively. 'She's not talking to you,' he said.

'Isn't that up to her?' said the redhead. I looked sideways at Garth as if asking for permission.

'What's that on your arm?' said the taller one, the brunette. She peered down.

'Is he abusing you, dear?' the redhead asked.

The other one smiled. 'Is he *selling* you? We can make things so much better for you.'

'Fuck off, Gilead bitches,' Garth said with impressive savagery. I looked up at the two of them, neat and clean in their pearly dresses and their white necklaces, and, believe it or not, a

336

tear rolled down my cheek. I knew they had an agenda and didn't give a shit about me — they just wanted to collect me and add me to their quota — but their kindness made me go a little wobbly. I wanted to have someone lift me up, then tuck me in.

'Oh my,' said the redhead. 'A real hero. At least let her take this.' She thrust a brochure at me. It said 'There Is a Home in Gilead for *You*!' 'God bless.' The two of them left, glancing back once.

'Wasn't I supposed to let them pick me up?' I said. 'Shouldn't I go with them?'

'Not the first time. We can't make it too easy for them,' said Garth. 'If anyone's watching from Gilead — it would be too suspicious. Don't worry, they'll be back.'

43

That night we slept under a bridge. It crossed a ravine, with a creek at the bottom. A mist was rising: after the hot day it was chilly and damp. The earth stank of cat piss, or maybe a skunk. I put on the grey hoodie, easing the arm down over my tattoo scar. It was still a little painful.

There were four or five others under the bridge with us, three men and two women, I think, though it was dark and it was hard to tell. George was one of the men; he acted as if he didn't know us. One of the women offered cigarettes, but I knew better than to try to smoke one — I would cough and give myself away. A bottle was being passed around too. Garth had told me not to smoke or drink anything, because who knew what might be in it?

He'd also told me not to talk to anyone: any of these people could be a Gilead plant, and if they tried to ferret out my story and I slipped up, they'd smell a rat and warn the Pearl Girls. He did the talking, which was mostly grunts. He seemed to know a couple of them. One of them said, 'What is she, retarded? How come she doesn't talk?' and Garth said, 'She only talks to me,' and the other one said, 'Nice work, what's your secret?'

We had several green plastic garbage bags to lie down on. Garth wrapped his arms around me, which made it warmer. At first I pushed his top arm away, but he whispered into my ear, 'Remember, you're my girlfriend,' so I stopped wriggling. I knew his hug was acting, but at that moment I didn't care. I really did feel almost as if he was my first boyfriend. It wasn't much, but it was something.

The next night Garth got into a fight with one of the men under the bridge. It was a quick fight and Garth won. I didn't see how — it was a short, swift move. Then he said we should relocate, so the next night we slept inside a downtown church. He had a key; I don't know where he got it. We weren't the only people sleeping in there, judging by the junk and crap under the pews: discarded backpacks, empty bottles, the odd needle.

We ate in fast-food places, which cured me of junk food. I used to think it was slightly glamorous, probably because Melanie disapproved of it, but if you eat it all the time you get a sickly bloated feeling. That's also where I went to the washroom, in the daytime, when I wasn't squatting in one of the ravines.

The fourth night was a cemetery. Cemeteries were good, said Garth, but there were often too many people in them. Some of them thought it was entertaining to jump up at you from behind a tombstone, but those were just kids running away from home for the weekend. The street people knew that scaring someone like that in the dark was likely to get you knifed, because not everyone roaming in cemeteries was completely stable.

'Such as you,' I said. He didn't react. I was probably getting on his nerves.

I should mention here that Garth didn't take advantage, even though he must have realized that I had a puppy-love crush on him. He was there to protect me, and he did, including protecting me from himself. I like to think he found that hard.

44

'When are the Pearl Girls going to show up again?' I asked on the morning of the fifth day. 'Maybe they've rejected me.'

'Be patient,' said Garth. 'As Ada said, we've sent people into Gilead this way before. Some of them made it in, but a couple were too eager, they let themselves be scooped on the first pass. They got flushed before they even crossed the border.'

'Thanks,' I said dolefully. 'That makes me feel confident. I'm going to screw this up, I know it.'

'Keep cool, you'll be fine,' said Garth. 'You can do it. We're all counting on you.'

'No pressure, right?' I said. 'You say jump, I say how high?' I was being a pain, but I couldn't stop myself.

★   ★   ★

Later that same day the Pearl Girls came our way again. They loitered around, passing by, then crossed the street and walked in the other direction, looking in store windows. Then, when Garth went off to get us some burgers, they came over and started talking to me.

They asked what my name was, and I said

Jade. Then they introduced themselves: Aunt Beatrice was the brunette, Aunt Dove was the freckled redhead.

They asked if I was happy, and I shook my head no. Then they looked at my tattoo, and said I was a very special person to have undergone all that suffering for God, and they were glad I knew God cherished me. And Gilead would cherish me too because I was a precious flower, every woman was a precious flower, and especially every girl of my age, and if I was in Gilead I would be treated like the special girl I was, and protected, and no one — no man — would ever be able to hurt me. And did that man who was with me — did he hit me?

I hated to lie about Garth like that, but I nodded.

'And does he make you do bad things?'

I looked stupid, so Aunt Beatrice — the taller one — said, 'Does he make you have sex?' I gave the tiniest nod, as if I was ashamed of those things.

'And does he pass you around to other men?'

That was going too far — I couldn't imagine Garth doing anything like that — so I shook my head no. And Aunt Beatrice said maybe he hadn't tried that yet, but if I stayed with him he would, because that's what men like him did — they got hold of young girls and pretended to love them, but soon enough they were selling them to whoever would pay.

'Free love,' Aunt Beatrice said scornfully. 'It's never free. There's always a price.'

'It's never even love,' said Aunt Dove. 'Why are you with him?'

'I didn't know where else to go,' I said and burst into tears. 'There was violence at home!'

'There is never violence in our homes in Gilead,' said Aunt Beatrice.

Then Garth came back and acted angry. He grabbed my arm — the left one, with the scarification on it — and pulled me to my feet, and I screamed because it hurt. He told me to shut up and said we were going.

Aunt Beatrice said, 'Could I have a word with you?' She and Garth moved away out of hearing, and Aunt Dove handed me a tissue because I was crying and said, 'May I hug you on behalf of God?' and I nodded.

Aunt Beatrice came back and said, 'We can go now,' and Aunt Dove said, 'Praise be.' Garth had walked away. He didn't even look back. I didn't get to say goodbye to him, which made me cry more.

'It's all right, you're safe now,' said Aunt Dove. 'Be strong.' Which was the kind of thing the refugee women from Gilead were told at SanctuCare, except that they were going in the other direction.

* * *

Aunt Beatrice and Aunt Dove walked very close to me, one on either side, so nobody would bother me, they said.

'That young man sold you,' said Aunt Dove with contempt.

'He did?' I asked. Garth hadn't told me he'd intended to do that.

'All I had to do was ask. That's how much he valued you. You're lucky he sold you to us and not some sex ring,' said Aunt Beatrice. 'He wanted a lot of money, but I got him down. In the end, he took half.'

'Filthy infidel,' said Aunt Dove.

'He said you were a virgin, which would make your price higher,' said Aunt Beatrice. 'But that's not what you told us, is it?'

I thought fast. 'I wanted you to feel sorry for me,' I whispered, 'so you would take me with you.'

The two of them glanced at each other, across me. 'We understand,' said Aunt Dove. 'But from now on you must tell the truth.'

I nodded, and said I would.

★ ★ ★

They took me back to the condo where they were staying. I wondered whether it was the same condo that the dead Pearl Girl had been found in. But my plan right then was to say as little as possible; I didn't want to blow it. I also didn't want to be found attached to a doorknob.

The condo was very modern. It had two bathrooms, each with a bathtub and a shower, and huge glass windows, and a big balcony with real trees growing on it in concrete planters. I soon found out that the door to the balcony was locked.

I was dying to get into the shower: I reeked, of my own layers of dirty skin flakes and sweat and feet in old socks, and the stinky mud under the bridge, and the frying fat smell of the fast-food places. The condo was so clean and filled with citrus air freshener that I thought my smell must really stand out.

When Aunt Beatrice asked if I wanted a shower, I nodded quickly But I should be careful, said Aunt Dove, because of my arm: I shouldn't get it wet because the scabs might come off. I must admit I was touched by their concern, phony though it was: they didn't want to take a festering mess to Gilead instead of a Pearl.

When I came out of the shower, wrapped up in a white fluffy towel, my old clothes were gone — they were so filthy there was no point in even washing them, said Aunt Beatrice — and they'd laid out a silvery grey dress just like theirs.

'I'm supposed to wear this?' I said. 'But I'm not a Pearl Girl. I thought the Pearl Girls were you.'

'The ones who gather the Pearls and the Pearls who are gathered are all Pearls,' said Aunt Dove. 'You are a precious Pearl. A Pearl of Great Price.'

'That's why we've gone to such risks for you,' said Aunt Beatrice. 'We have so many enemies here. But don't worry, Jade. We'll keep you safe.'

In any case, she said, even though I wasn't an official Pearl Girl, I would need to wear the dress in order to get out of Canada because the Canadian authorities were clamping down on the export of underage converts. They were viewing it as human trafficking, which was quite wrong of them, she added.

Then Aunt Dove reminded her that she should not use the word *export* as girls were not commodities; and Aunt Beatrice apologized and said she had meant to say 'the facilitating of cross-border movement.' And they both smiled.

'I'm not underage,' I said. 'I'm sixteen.'

'Do you have any identification?' Aunt Beatrice asked. I shook my head no.

'We didn't think so,' said Aunt Dove. 'So we will arrange that for you.'

'But to avoid any problems, you'll have papers identifying you as Aunt Dove,' said Aunt Beatrice. 'The Canadians know she came in, so when you cross the border they'll think you are her.'

'But I'm a lot younger,' I said. 'I don't look like her.'

'Your papers will have your picture,' said Aunt Beatrice. The real Aunt Dove, she said, would stay in Canada, and leave with the next girl who was gathered, taking the name of an incoming Pearl Girl. They were used to switching around like that.

'The Canadians can't tell us apart,' said Aunt Dove. 'We all look the same to them.' Both of them laughed, as if they were delighted at having played such pranks.

Then Aunt Dove said that the most important extra reason for wearing the silvery dress was to smooth my entrance into Gilead because women didn't wear men's clothing there. I said leggings weren't men's clothing, and they said — calmly but firmly — that yes, they were, and it was in the Bible, they were an abomination, and if I wanted to join Gilead I would have to accept that.

I reminded myself not to argue with them, so I

346

put on the dress; also the pearl necklace, which was fake, just as Melanie had said. There was a white sunhat, but I only needed to put it on to go outside, they said. Hair was permitted inside a dwelling unless there were men around, because men had a thing about hair, it made them spin out of control, they said. And my hair was particularly inflammatory because it was greenish.

'It's only a tint, it will wear off,' I said apologetically so they'd know I'd already renounced my rash hair-colour choice.

'It's all right, dear,' said Aunt Dove. 'No one will see it.'

The dress actually felt quite good after my dirty old clothes. It was cool and silky.

Aunt Beatrice ordered in pizza for lunch, which we had with ice cream from their freezer. I said I was surprised that they were eating junk food: wasn't Gilead against it, especially for women?

'It's part of our test as Pearl Girls,' said Aunt Dove. 'We're supposed to sample the fleshpot temptations of the outside world in order to understand them, and then reject them in our hearts.' She took another bite of pizza.

'Anyway it will be my last chance to try them,' said Aunt Beatrice, who had finished off the pizza and was eating her ice cream. 'I honestly don't see what's wrong with ice cream, as long as it has no chemicals.' Aunt Dove gave her a reproachful look. Aunt Beatrice licked her spoon.

I said no to the ice cream. I was too nervous.

Also I no longer liked it. It reminded me too much of Melanie.

That night before going to bed I examined myself in the bathroom mirror. Despite the shower and the food, I was wrecked. I had dark circles under my eyes; I'd lost weight. I really did look like a waif who needed to be rescued.

It was wonderful to sleep in a real bed instead of under a bridge. I missed Garth though.

Each night I was inside that bedroom, they locked my door. And they took care that during my waking hours I was never alone.

⋆ ⋆ ⋆

The next couple of days were spent in getting my Aunt Dove papers ready. I had my picture and fingerprints taken so they could make me a passport. The passport was certified at the Gilead Embassy in Ottawa, then sent back to the Consulate by special courier. They'd put in Aunt Dove's identifying numbers, but with my picture and physical data, and they'd even infiltrated the Canadian immigration database where Aunt Dove had been recorded coming in, removed the real Aunt Dove from it temporarily, and posted my own data plus my iris scan and thumbprint.

'We have many friends inside the Canadian government infrastructure,' said Aunt Beatrice. 'You'd be amazed.'

'So many well-wishers,' said Aunt Dove. Then both of them said, 'Praise be.'

They'd put an embossed stamp on one of the pages that said PEARL GIRL. That meant I would be let into Gilead immediately, no questions asked: it was like being a diplomat, said Aunt Beatrice.

Now I was Aunt Dove, but a different Aunt Dove. I had a Pearl Girls Missionary Temporary Canadian Visa that I had to give back to the border authorities when exiting. It was simple, said Aunt Beatrice.

'Look down a lot when you're going through,' said Aunt Dove. 'It hides the features. Anyway it's the modest thing to do.'

★   ★   ★

Aunt Beatrice and I were driven to the airport in a black Gilead government car, and I passed border control with no trouble. We didn't even get body-searched.

The plane was a private jet. It had an eye with wings on it. It was silver, but it looked dark to me — like a huge dark bird, waiting to fly me where? Into a blank. Ada and Elijah had tried to teach me as much as possible about Gilead; I'd seen the documentaries and the TV footage; but I still could not picture what might be waiting for me there. I didn't feel ready for this at all.

I remembered SanctuCare, and the women refugees. I'd looked at them but I hadn't really seen them. I hadn't considered what it was like to leave a place you knew, and lose everything, and travel into the unknown. How hollow and dark that must feel, except for maybe the little glimmer of hope that had allowed you to take such a chance.

Very soon I, too, was going to feel like that. I would be in a dark place, carrying a tiny spark of light, trying to find my way.

45

We were late taking off, and I worried that I had been found out and we would be stopped after all. But once we were in the air, I felt lighter. I'd never been in a plane before — I was very excited at first. But it clouded over, and the view became monotonous. I must have gone to sleep, because soon Aunt Beatrice was nudging me gently and saying, 'We're almost there.'

I looked out the little window. The plane was flying lower, and I could see some pretty-looking buildings down below, with spires and towers, and a winding river, and the sea.

Then the plane landed. We went down a set of steps they lowered from the door. It was hot and dry, with a wind blowing; our long silvery skirts were pushed against our legs. Standing on the tarmac there was a double line of men in black uniforms, and we walked between the lines, arm in arm. 'Don't look at their faces,' she whispered.

So I focused on their uniforms, but I could sense eyes, eyes, eyes, all over me like hands. I'd never felt so much at risk in that way — not even under the bridge with Garth, and with strangers all around.

Then all these men saluted. 'What is this?' I

murmured to Aunt Beatrice. 'Why are they saluting?'

'Because my mission was successful,' said Aunt Beatrice. 'I brought back a precious Pearl. That's you.'

★   ★   ★

We were taken to a black car and driven into the city. There weren't very many people on the street, and the women all had those long dresses in different colours just like in the documentaries. I even saw some Handmaids walking two by two. There was no lettering on the stores — only pictures on the signs. A boot, a fish, a tooth.

The car paused in front of a gate in a brick wall. We were waved through by two guards. The car went in and stopped, and they opened the doors for us. We got out, and Aunt Beatrice linked her arm through mine and said, 'There isn't time to show you where you'll sleep, the plane was too late. We need to go straight to the chapel, for the Thanks Giving. Just do what I say.'

I knew this would be some kind of ceremony about the Pearl Girls — Ada had warned me about it, Aunt Dove had explained it to me — but I hadn't paid close attention so I didn't really know what to expect.

We went into the chapel. It was already full: older women in the brown uniforms of the Aunts, younger ones in Pearl Girls dresses. Each Pearl Girl had a girl around my age with her, also in a temporary silver dress like me. Right up at the front there was a big gold-framed Baby Nicole picture, which did not cheer me up at all.

As Aunt Beatrice steered me down the aisle, everyone was singing:

Bringing in the Pearls,
Bringing in the Pearls,
We will come rejoicing,
Bringing in the Pearls.

They smiled and nodded at me: they seemed really happy. Maybe this won't be so bad, I thought.

We all sat down. Then one of the older women went up to the pulpit.

'Aunt Lydia,' Aunt Beatrice whispered. 'Our main Founder.' I recognized her from the picture that Ada had shown me, though she was quite a lot older than the picture, or so it seemed to me.

'We are here to give thanks for the safe return of our Pearl Girls from their missions — from wherever they have been in the world, going to and fro in it, and doing Gilead's good work. We salute their physical bravery and their spiritual courage, and we offer the thanks of our hearts. I now declare that our returning Pearl Girls are no longer Supplicants, but full Aunts, with all the powers and privileges associated thereto. We know they will do their duty, wherever and however that duty calls.' Everyone said, 'Amen.'

'Pearl Girls, present the Pearls you have gathered,' said Aunt Lydia. 'First, the mission to Canada.'

'Stand up,' Aunt Beatrice whispered. She led

me up to the front, holding me by the left arm. Her hand was on GOD/LOVE, and it hurt.

She took off her string of pearls, laid it in a big shallow dish in front of Aunt Lydia, and said, 'I return these pearls to you pure as the state in which I received them, and may they be blessed to the service of the next Pearl Girl who wears them with pride during her mission. Thanks to the Divine Will, I have added to Gilead's treasure trove of valuable gems. May I present Jade, a precious Pearl of Great Price, saved from certain destruction. May she be purified from worldly pollution, cleansed of unchaste desires, cauterized from sin, and consecrated to whatever service is allotted to her in Gilead.' She put her hands on my shoulders and pushed me into a kneeling position. I hadn't been expecting this — I almost fell over sideways. 'What're you doing?' I whispered.

'Shhh,' said Aunt Beatrice. 'Be quiet.'

Then Aunt Lydia said, 'Welcome to Ardua Hall, Jade, and may you be blessed in the choice you have made, Under His Eye, *Per Ardua Cum Estrus*.' She placed her hand on my head, then took it off again, nodded at me, and gave a dry smile.

Everyone repeated, 'Welcome to the Pearl of Great Price, *Per Ardua Cum Estrus*, Amen.'

What am I doing here? I thought. This place is weird as fuck.

XVII

Perfect Teeth

The Ardua Hall Holograph

46

My bottle of blue drawing ink, my fountain pen, my notebook pages with their margins trimmed to fit within their hiding place: through these I entrust my message to you, my reader. But what sort of message is it? Some days I see myself as the Recording Angel, collecting together all the sins of Gilead, including mine; on other days I shrug off this high moral tone. Am I not, au fond, merely a dealer in sordid gossip? I'll never know your verdict on that, I fear.

My larger fear: that all my efforts will prove futile, and Gilead will last for a thousand years. Most of the time, that is what it feels like here, far away from the war, in the still heart of the tornado. So peaceful, the streets; so tranquil, so orderly; yet underneath the deceptively placid surfaces, a tremor, like that near a high-voltage power line. We're stretched thin, all of us; we vibrate; we quiver, we're always on the alert. *Reign of terror,* they used to say, but terror does not exactly reign. Instead it paralyzes. Hence the unnatural quiet.

⋆　⋆　⋆

But there are small mercies. Yesterday I viewed — on the closed-circuit television in Commander

357

Judd's office — the Particicution presided over by Aunt Elizabeth. Commander Judd had ordered in some coffee — excellent coffee of a kind not normally available; I avoided asking him how he had come by it. He added a shot of rum to his and asked if I would like some. I declined. He then said that he had a tender heart and weak nerves and needed to brace himself, as he found it a strain on his system to watch these blood-thirsty spectacles.

'I do understand,' I said. 'But it is our duty to see justice done.' He sighed, drank up, and poured himself another shot.

Two condemned men were to be Particicuted: an Angel who'd been caught selling grey market lemons smuggled in through Maine, and Dr. Grove, the dentist. The Angel's real crime was not the lemons, however: he'd been accused of taking bribes from Mayday and aiding several Handmaids in their successful flights across our various borders. But the Commanders did not want this fact publicized: it would give people ideas. The official line was that there were no corrupt Angels, and certainly no fleeing Hand-maids; for why would one renounce God's kingdom to plunge into the flaming pit?

Throughout the process that was now about to end Grove's life, Aunt Elizabeth had been magnificent. She'd been in college dramatics, and had played Hecuba in The Trojan Women — a factoid I'd gathered during our early conferences when she and Helena and Vidala and I had been hammering out the shape of the special women's sphere in the nascent Gilead.

Camaraderie is fostered under such circumstances, past lives are shared. I took care not to share too much of mine.

Elizabeth's onstage experience had not failed her. She'd booked an appointment with Dr. Grove, as per my orders. Then, at the appropriate moment, she'd scrambled out of the dentist's chair, ripped her clothing, and shrieked that Grove had tried to rape her. Then, weeping distractedly, she'd staggered out into the waiting room, where Mr. William, the dental assistant, was able to witness her dishevelled appearance and ravaged state of soul.

The person of an Aunt is supposed to be sacrosanct. No wonder Aunt Elizabeth was so upset by this violation, was the general opinion. The man must be a dangerous lunatic.

I'd obtained a photographic sequence secured through the mini-camera I had positioned within an attractive diagram of a full set of teeth. Should Elizabeth ever attempt to slip the leash, I could threaten to produce it as proof that she had lied.

Mr. William testified against Grove at the trial. He was no fool: he'd seen immediately that his boss was doomed. He described Grove's rage at the moment of discovery. *Fucking bitch* was the epithet applied to Aunt Elizabeth by the fiendish Grove, he claimed. No such words had been uttered — in fact, Grove had said, 'Why are you doing this?' — but William's account was effective at the trial. Gasps from the listeners, which included the entire population of Ardua Hall: to call an Aunt such vulgar words was next door to blasphemy! Under questioning, William reluctantly admitted that he'd had some reason to suspect his employer of irregularities in the past. Anaesthetics, he said sadly, could be such a temptation in the wrong hands.

What could Grove say in his own defence except that he was innocent of the charge and then quote the Bible on the subject of that well-known false-rape accuser, Potiphar's wife? Innocent men denying their guilt sound exactly like guilty men, as I am sure you have noticed, my reader. Listeners are inclined to believe neither.

Grove could hardly admit that he would never have laid a lecherous finger on Aunt Elizabeth since he was only aroused by underage girls.

⋆ ⋆ ⋆

In view of Aunt Elizabeth's exceptional performance, I felt it more than fair that she be allowed to conduct the Particicution proceedings at the stadium. Grove was the second to be dispatched. He had to watch as the Angel was kicked to death and then literally torn apart by seventy shrieking Handmaids.

As he was led out to the field, arms pinioned, he screamed, 'I didn't do it!' Aunt Elizabeth, the picture of outraged virtue, sternly blew the whistle. In two minutes Dr. Grove was no more. Fists were raised, clutching clumps of bloodied hair torn out by the roots.

The Aunts and Supplicants were all present, to support the vindication of one of Ardua Hall's revered Founders. Off to one side were the newly recruited Pearls; they'd arrived only the day before, so this was a baptismal moment for them. I scanned their young faces but at that distance could not read them. Revulsion? Relish? Repugnance? It is always good to know. The Pearl of the greatest price was among them; right after the sporting event we were about to witness, I would place her in the dwelling unit that would be best for my purposes.

While Grove was being reduced to a slurry by the Handmaids, Aunt Immortelle fainted, which was to be expected: she was always sensitive. I expect she will now blame herself in some way: however despicably he behaved, Grove was nevertheless cast in the role of her father.

Commander Judd switched off the television and sighed. 'A pity,' he said. 'He was a fine dentist.'

'Yes,' I said. 'But sins must not be overlooked simply because the sinner is skilled.'

'Was he really guilty?' he asked with mild interest.

'Yes,' I said, 'but not of that. He would not have been capable of raping Aunt Elizabeth. He was a pedophile.'

Commander Judd sighed again. 'Poor man,' he said. 'It is a severe affliction. We must pray for his soul.'

'Indeed,' I said. 'But he was ruining too many young girls for marriage. Rather than accepting wedlock, the precious flowers were deserting to the Aunts.'

'Ah,' he said. 'Was that the case with the girl

Agnes? I thought there must have been something like that.'

He wanted me to say yes because then her aversion would not have been to him personally. 'I can't be sure,' I said. His face fell. 'But I believe so.' It doesn't do to push him too far.

'Your judgment can always be relied on, Aunt Lydia,' he said. 'In this matter of Grove, you've made the best choice for Gilead.'

'Thank you. I pray for guidance,' I said. 'But, to change the subject, I am happy to inform you that Baby Nicole has now been safely imported into Gilead.'

'What a coup! Well done!' he said.

'My Pearl Girls were very effective,' I said. 'They followed my orders. They took her under their wings as a new convert, and convinced her to join us. They were able to buy off the young man who'd acquired an influence over her. Aunt Beatrice did the bargaining, although she was, of course, not aware of Baby Nicole's real identity.'

'But you were, dear Aunt Lydia,' he said. 'How did you manage to identify her? My Eyes have been trying for years.' Did I detect a note of envy or, worse, of suspicion? I breezed past it.

'I have my little ways. And some helpful informants,' I lied. 'Two and two do sometimes add up to four. And we women, myopic as we are, often notice the finer details that may escape the broader and loftier views of men. But Aunt Beatrice and Aunt Dove were told only that they should be on the watch for a specific tattoo that the poor child had inflicted upon herself. And

362

luckily, they found her.'

'A self-inflicted tattoo? Depraved, like all those girls. On what part of her body?' he asked with interest.

'Only the arm. Her face is unmarked.'

'Her arms will be covered in any public presentation,' he said.

'She is going by the name of Jade; she may even believe that to be her real name. I did not wish to enlighten her about her true identity until I had consulted with you.'

'Excellent decision,' he said. 'May I inquire — what was the nature of her relationship with this young man? It would be better if she is, as it were, untouched, but in her case we would overlook the rules. She would be wasted as a Handmaid.'

'Her virginity status is as yet unconfirmed, but I believe her to be pure in that respect. I have placed her with two of our younger Aunts, who are kind and sympathetic. She will share her hopes and fears with them, no doubt; as well as her beliefs, which I am sure can be moulded to accord with ours.'

'Again, excellent, Aunt Lydia. You are indeed a gem. How soon may we reveal Baby Nicole to Gilead and the world?'

'We must first assure that she is a true-believer convert,' I said. 'Firm in the faith. That will take some care and tact. These newcomers have been swept up in enthusiasm, they have such unrealistic expectations. We must bring her down to earth, we must inform her of the duties that await: it is not all hymn-singing and exaltation here. In addition to that, she must be made acquainted with her own personal history: it will be a shock to her to discover that she is the well-known and well-loved Baby Nicole.'

'I will leave these matters in your capable hands,' he said. 'Are you sure you won't take a drop of rum in your coffee? It helps the circulation.'

'Maybe a teaspoon,' I said. He poured. We lifted our mugs, clinked them together.

'May our efforts be blessed,' he said. 'As I am convinced they will be.'

'In the fullness of time,' I said, smiling.

★   ★   ★

After her exertions in the dentist's office, at the trial, and at the Particicution, Aunt Elizabeth suffered a nervous collapse. I went with Aunt Vidala and Aunt Helena to visit her where she was recuperating at one of our Retreat Houses. She greeted us tearfully.

'I don't know what's wrong with me,' she said. 'I am drained of energy.'

'After all you've been through, it's no wonder,' said Helena.

'You are considered practically a saint at Ardua Hall,' I said. I knew what was truly agitating her: she'd perjured herself irrevocably; which, if discovered, would signal her end.

'I'm so grateful to you for your guidance, Aunt Lydia,' she said to me while glancing sideways at Vidala. Now that I was her firm ally — now that she had fulfilled my unorthodox request — she

364

must have felt that Aunt Vidala was powerless against her.

'I was happy to help,' I said.

XVIII

READING ROOM

47

Becka and I first saw Jade at the Thanks Giving held to welcome back the returning Pearl Girls and their converts. She was a tall girl, somewhat awkward, and kept gazing around her in a direct way that verged on being too bold. Already I had a feeling that she would not find Ardua Hall an easy fit, not to mention Gilead itself. But I did not think much more about her because I was caught up in the beautiful ceremony.

Soon that would be us, I thought. Becka and I were completing our training as Supplicants; we were almost ready to become full Aunts. Very soon we would receive the silver Pearl Girls dresses, so much prettier than our habitual brown. We would inherit the strings of pearls; we would set out on our mission; we would each bring back a converted Pearl.

For my first few years at Ardua Hall, I'd been entranced by the prospect. I was still a full and true believer — if not in everything about Gilead, at least in the unselfish service of the Aunts. But now I was not so sure.

★ ★ ★

We did not see Jade again until the next day. Like all the new Pearls, she'd attended an all-night vigil in the chapel, engaged in silent meditation and prayer. Then she would have exchanged her silver dress for the brown one we all wore. Not that she was destined to become an Aunt — the recently arrived Pearls were observed carefully before being assigned as potential Wives or Econowives, or Supplicants, or, in some unhappy cases, Handmaids — but while among us they dressed like us, with the addition of a large imitation-pearl brooch in the shape of a new moon.

Jade's introduction to the ways of Gilead was somewhat harsh, as the next day she was present at a Particicution. It may have been a shock to her to witness two men being literally ripped apart by Handmaids; it can be shocking even to me, although I've seen it many times over the course of the years. The Handmaids are usually so subdued, and the display of so much rage on their part can be alarming.

The Founder Aunts devised these rules. Becka and I would have opted for a less extreme method.

One of those eliminated at the Particicution was Dr. Grove, Becka's erstwhile dentist father, who'd been condemned for raping Aunt Elizabeth. Or almost raping her: considering my own experience with him, I didn't much care which. I am sorry to say I was glad he was being punished.

Becka took it very differently. Dr. Grove had treated her shamefully when she was a child, and

370

I could not excuse that, though she herself was willing to. She was a more charitable person than I was; I admired her in that, but I could not emulate her.

When Dr. Grove was torn apart at the Particicution, Becka fainted. Some of the Aunts put this reaction down to filial love — Dr. Grove was a wicked man, but he was still a man, and a high-status man. He was also a father, to whom respect was due by an obedient daughter. However, I knew otherwise: Becka felt responsible for his death. She believed that she should never have told me about his crimes. I assured her that I hadn't shared her confidences with anyone, and she said she trusted me, but Aunt Lydia must have found out somehow. It was how the Aunts got their power: by finding things out. Things that should never be talked about.

*   *   *

Becka and I had returned from the Particicution. I'd made her a cup of tea and suggested she should lie down — she was still pale — but she'd said that she'd controlled her feelings and would be fine. We were engaged in our evening Bible readings when there was a knock at the door. We were surprised to find Aunt Lydia standing outside; with her was the new Pearl, Jade.

'Aunt Victoria, Aunt Immortelle, you have been chosen for a very special duty,' she said. 'Our newest Pearl, Jade, has been assigned to you. She will sleep in the third bedroom, which I understand is vacant. Your task will be to help her in every way possible, and instruct her in the details of our life of service here in Gilead. Do you have enough sheets and towels? If not, I will arrange for some.'

'Yes, Aunt Lydia, praise be,' I said. Becka echoed me. Jade smiled at us, a smile that managed to be both tremulous and stubborn. She was not like the average new convert from abroad: these were likely to be either abject or filled with zeal.

'Welcome,' I said to Jade. 'Please come in.'

'Okay,' she said. She crossed our threshold. My heart fell: already I knew that the outwardly placid life Becka and I had been leading at Ardua Hall for the past nine years was at an end — change had come — but I did not yet grasp how wrenching that change would be.

★   ★   ★

I have said our life was placid, but perhaps that is not the right word. It was at any rate orderly, albeit somewhat monotonous. Our time was filled, but in a strange way it did not seem to pass. I'd been fourteen when I'd been admitted as a Supplicant, and although I was now grown up, I did not appear to myself to have grown much older. It was the same with Becka: we seemed to be frozen in some way; preserved, as if in ice.

The Founders and the older Aunts had edges to them. They'd been moulded in an age before Gilead, they'd had struggles we had been spared, and these struggles had ground off the softness that might once have been there. But we hadn't been forced to undergo such ordeals. We'd been protected, we hadn't needed to deal with the harshness of the world at large. We were the beneficiaries of the sacrifices made by our forebears. We were constantly reminded of this, and ordered to be grateful. But it's difficult to be grateful for the absence of an unknown quantity. I'm afraid we did not fully appreciate the extent to which those of Aunt Lydia's generation had been hardened in the fire. They had a ruthlessness about them that we lacked.

48

Despite this feeling of time standing still, I had in fact changed. I was no longer the same person I'd been when I'd entered Ardua Hall. Now I was a woman, even if an inexperienced one; then I had been a child.

'I'm very glad the Aunts let you stay,' Becka had said on that first day. She'd turned her shy gaze full upon me.

'I'm glad too,' I said.

'I always looked up to you at school. Not just because of your three Marthas and your Commander family,' she said. 'You lied less than the others. And you were nice to me.'

'I wasn't all that nice.'

'You were nicer than the rest of them,' she said.

Aunt Lydia had given permission for me to live in the same residence unit as Becka. Ardua Hall was divided into many apartments; ours was marked with the letter *C* and the Ardua Hall motto: *Per Ardua Cum Estrus.*

'It means, Through childbirth labour with the female reproductive cycle,' Becka said.

'It means all that?'

'It's in Latin. It sounds better in Latin.'

I said, 'What is Latin?'

Becka said it was a language of long ago that nobody spoke anymore, but people wrote mottoes in it. For instance, the motto of everything inside the Wall used to be *Veritas*, which was the Latin for 'truth.' But they'd chiselled that word off and painted it over.

'How did you find that out?' I asked. 'If the word is gone?'

'In the Hildegard Library,' she said. 'It's only for us Aunts.'

'What's a library?'

'It's where they keep the books. There are rooms and rooms full of them.'

'Are they wicked?' I asked. 'Those books?' I imagined all that explosive material packed inside a room.

'Not those I've been reading. The more dangerous ones are kept in the Reading Room. You have to get special permission to go in there. But you can read the other books.'

'They let you?' I was amazed. 'You can just go in there and read?'

'If you get permission. Except for the Reading Room. If you did that without permission, there would be a Correction, down in one of the cellars.' Each Ardua Hall apartment had a soundproofed cellar, she said, which used to be for things like piano practising. But now the R cellar was where Aunt Vidala did the Corrections. Corrections were a kind of punishment, for straying beyond the rules.

'But punishments are done in public,' I said. 'For criminals. You know, the Particicutions, and hanging people and displaying them on the Wall.'

'Yes, I know,' said Becka. 'I wish they wouldn't leave them up so long. The smell gets into our bedrooms, it makes me feel sick. But the Corrections in the cellar are different, they're for our own good. Now, let's get you an outfit, and then you can choose your name.'

There was an approved list of names, put together by Aunt Lydia and the other senior Aunts. Becka said the names were made from the names of products women had liked once and would be reassured by, but she herself did not know what those products were. Nobody our age knew, she said.

She read the list of names out to me, since I could not yet read. 'What about Maybelline?' she said. 'That sounds pretty. Aunt Maybelline.'

'No,' I said. 'It's too frilly.'

'How about Aunt Ivory?'

'Too cold,' I said.

'Here's one: Victoria. I think there was a Queen Victoria. You'd be called Aunt Victoria: even at the Supplicant level we're allowed the title of Aunt. But once we finish our Pearl Girls missionary work in other countries outside Gilead, we'll graduate to full Aunts.' At the Vidala School we hadn't been told much about the Pearl Girls — only that they were courageous, and took risks and made sacrifices for Gilead, and we should respect them.

'We go outside Gilead? Isn't it scary to be that far away? Isn't Gilead really big?' It would be like falling out of the world, for surely Gilead had no edges.

'Gilead is smaller than you think,' said Becka.

'It has other countries around it. I'll show you on the map.'

I must have looked confused because she smiled. 'A map is like a picture. We learn to read maps here.'

'Read a picture?' I said. 'How can you do that? Pictures aren't writing.'

'You'll see. I couldn't do it at first either.' She smiled again. 'With you here, I won't feel so alone.'

★　★　★

What would happen to me after six months? I worried. Would I be allowed to stay? It was unnerving to have the Aunts looking at me as if inspecting a vegetable. It was hard to direct my gaze at the floor, which was what was required: any higher and I might be staring at their torsos, which was impolite, or into their eyes, which was presumptuous. It was difficult never to speak unless one of the senior Aunts spoke to me first. Obedience, subservience, docility: these were the virtues required.

Then there was the reading, which I found frustrating. Maybe I was too old to ever learn it, I thought. Maybe it was like fine embroidery: you had to start young; otherwise you would always be clumsy. But little by little I picked it up. 'You have a knack,' said Becka. 'You're way better than I was when I began!'

The books I was given to learn from were about a boy and a girl called Dick and Jane. The books were very old, and the pictures had been altered at Ardua Hall. Jane wore long skirts and sleeves, but you could tell from the places where the paint had been applied that her skirt had once been above her knees and her sleeves had ended above her elbows. Her hair had once been uncovered.

The most astonishing thing about these books was that Dick and Jane and Baby Sally lived in a house with nothing around it but a white wooden fence, so flimsy and low that anyone at all could climb over it. There were no Angels, there were no Guardians. Dick and Jane and Baby Sally played outside in full view of everyone. Baby Sally could have been abducted by terrorists at any moment and smuggled to Canada, like Baby Nicole and the other stolen innocents. Jane's bare knees could have aroused evil urges in any man passing by, despite the fact that everything but her face had been covered over with paint. Becka said that painting the pictures in such books was a task that I'd be asked to perform, as it was assigned to the Supplicants. She herself had painted a lot of books.

It wasn't a given that I'd be allowed to stay, she said: not everyone was suitable for the Aunts. Before I'd arrived at Ardua Hall she'd known two girls who'd been accepted, but one of them changed her mind after only three months and her family had taken her back, and the marriage arranged for her had gone ahead after all.

'What happened to the other one?' I said.

'Something bad,' said Becka. 'Her name was Aunt Lily. There didn't seem to be anything wrong with her at first. Everyone said she was getting along well, but then she was given a Correction for talking back. I don't think it was one of the worst Corrections: Aunt Vidala can have a mean streak. She says, 'Do you like this?' when she does the Correction, and there isn't any right answer.'

'But Aunt Lily?'

'She wasn't the same person after that. She wanted to leave Ardua Hall — she said she was not suited for it — and the Aunts said that if so her planned marriage would have to take place; but she didn't want that either.'

'What did she want?' I asked. I was suddenly very interested in Aunt Lily.

'She wanted to live on her own and work on a farm. Aunt Elizabeth and Aunt Vidala said this was what came of reading too early: she'd picked up wrong ideas at the Hildegard Library, before her mind had been strengthened enough to reject them, and there were a lot of questionable books that should be destroyed. They said she would have to have a more severe Correction to help her focus her thoughts.'

'What was it?' I was wondering if my own mind was strong enough, and whether I too would be given multiple Corrections.

'It was a month in the cellar, by herself, with only bread and water. When she was let out again she wouldn't speak to anyone except to say yes and no. Aunt Vidala said she was too weak-minded to be an Aunt, and would have to be married after all.

'The day before she was supposed to leave the

379

Hall she wasn't there at breakfast, and then not at lunch. Nobody knew where she had gone. Aunt Elizabeth and Aunt Vidala said she must have run away, and it was a breach of security, and there was a big search. But they didn't find her. And then the shower water started smelling strange. So they had another search, and this time they opened the rooftop rainwater cistern that we use for the showers, and she was in there.'

'Oh, that's terrible!' I said. 'Was she — did someone murder her?'

'The Aunts said so at first. Aunt Helena had hysterics, and they even gave permission for some Eyes to come into Ardua Hall and inspect it for clues, but there weren't any. Some of us Supplicants went up and looked at the cistern. She couldn't have simply fallen in: there's a ladder, then there's a little door.'

'Did you see her?' I asked.

'It was a closed coffin,' said Becka. 'But she must have done it on purpose. She had stones in her pockets — that was the rumour. She didn't leave a note, or if she did Aunt Vidala tore it up. At the funeral they said that she'd died of a brain aneurysm. They wouldn't want it to be known that a Supplicant had failed so badly. We all said prayers for her; I'm sure God has forgiven her.'

'But why did she do it?' I asked. 'Did she want to die?'

'No one wants to die,' said Becka. 'But some people don't want to live in any of the ways that are allowed.'

'But drowning yourself!' I said.

'It's supposed to be calm,' said Becka. 'You hear bells and singing. Like angels. That's what Aunt Helena told us, to make us feel better.'

★ ★ ★

After I'd mastered the Dick and Jane books, I was given *Ten Tales for Young Girls*, a book of rhymes by Aunt Vidala. This is one that I remember:

Just look at Tirzah! She sits there,
With her strands of vagrant hair;
See her down the sidewalk stride,
Head held high and full of pride.
See her catch the Guardian's glance,
Tempt him to sinful circumstance.
Never does she change her way,
Never does she kneel to pray!
Soon she into sin will fall,
And then be hanging on the Wall.

Aunt Vidala's tales were about things girls shouldn't do and the horrifying things that would happen to them if they did. I realize now that the tales were not very good poetry, and even at the time I didn't like hearing about these poor girls who made mistakes and were severely punished or even killed; but nevertheless I was thrilled to be able to read anything at all.

One day I was reading the Tirzah story out loud to Becka so she could correct any mistakes I was making when she said, 'That would never happen to me.'

'What wouldn't?' I said.

'I would never lead any Guardians on like that. I would never catch their eyes. I don't want to look at them,' said Becka. 'Any men. They're horrible. Including the Gilead kind of God.'

'Becka!' I said. 'Why are you saying that? What do you mean, the Gilead kind?'

'They want God to be only one thing,' she said. 'They leave things out. It says in the Bible we're in God's image, male and female both. You'll see, when the Aunts let you read it.'

'Don't say such things, Becka,' I said. 'Aunt Vidala — she'd think it was heresy.'

'I can say them to you, Agnes,' she said. 'I'd trust you with my life.'

'Don't,' I said. 'I'm not a good person, not like you.'

★ ★ ★

In my second month at Ardua Hall, Shunammite paid me a visit. I met her in the Schlafly Café. She was wearing the blue dress of an official Wife.

'Agnes!' she cried, holding out both hands. 'I'm so happy to see you! Are you all right?'

'Of course I'm all right,' I said. 'I'm Aunt Victoria now. Would you like some mint tea?'

'It's just that Paula implied that maybe you'd gone . . . that there was something wrong — '

'That I'm a lunatic,' I said, smiling. I'd noted that Shunammite was referring to Paula as a familiar friend. Shunammite now outranked her, which must have irked Paula considerably

— to have such a young girl promoted above her. 'I know she thinks that. And by the way, I should congratulate you on your marriage.'

'You're not mad at me?' she said, reverting to our schoolgirl tone.

'Why would I be 'mad at' you, as you say?'

'Well, I stole your husband.' Is that what she thought? That she'd won a competition? How could I deny this without insulting Commander Judd?

'I received a call to higher service,' I said as primly as I could.

She giggled. 'Did you really? Well, I received a call to a lower one. I have four Marthas! I wish you could see my house!'

'I'm sure it's lovely,' I said.

'But you really are all right?' Her anxiety on my behalf may have been partly genuine. 'Doesn't this place wear you down? It's so bleak.'

'I'm fine,' I said. 'I wish you every happiness.'

'Becka's in this dungeon too, isn't she?'

'It's not a dungeon,' I said. 'Yes. We share an apartment.'

'Aren't you afraid she'll attack you with the secateurs? Is she still insane?'

'She was never insane,' I said, 'just unhappy. It's been wonderful to see you, Shunammite, but I must return to my duties.'

'You don't like me anymore,' she said half seriously.

'I'm training to be an Aunt,' I said. 'I'm not really supposed to like anyone.'

49

My reading abilities progressed slowly and with many stumbles. Becka helped me a lot. We used Bible verses to practise, from the approved selection that was available to Supplicants. With my very own eyes I was able to read portions of Scripture that I had until then only heard. Becka helped me find the passage that I'd thought of so often at the time Tabitha died:

> For a thousand years in thy sight are but
> as yesterday when it is past, and as a
> watch in the night. Thou carriest them
> away as with a flood; they are as a sleep;
> in the morning they are like grass which
> groweth up. In the morning it flourisheth,
> and groweth up; in the evening it is cut
> down, and withereth.

Laboriously I spelled out the words. They seemed different when they were on the page: not flowing and sonorous, as I had recited them in my head, but flatter, drier.

Becka said that spelling was not reading: reading, she said, was when you could hear the words as if they were a song.

'Maybe I won't ever get it right,' I said.

'You will,' said Becka. 'Let's try reading some real songs.'

She went to the library — I wasn't allowed in there as yet — and brought back one of our Ardua Hall hymn books. In it was the childhood nighttime song that Tabitha used to sing to me in her voice like silver bells:

Now I lay me down to sleep,
I pray the Lord my soul to keep . . .

I sang it to Becka, and then after a while I was able to read it to her. 'That's so hopeful,' she said. 'I would like to think that there are two angels always waiting to fly away with me.' Then she said, 'I never had anyone sing to me at night. You were so lucky.'

★   ★   ★

Along with reading, I had to learn to write. That was harder in some ways, though less hard in others. We used drawing ink and straight pens with metal nibs, or sometimes pencils. It depended on what had been recently allocated to Ardua Hall from the storehouses reserved for imports.

Writing materials were the prerogative of the Commanders and the Aunts. Otherwise they were not generally available in Gilead; women had no use for them, and most men didn't either, except for reports and inventories. What else would most people be writing about?

We'd learned to embroider and paint at the

385

Vidala School, and Becka said that writing was almost the same as that — each letter was like a picture or a row of stitching, and it was also like a musical note; you just had to learn how to form the letters, and then how to attach them together, like pearls on a string.

She herself had beautiful handwriting. She showed me how, often and with patience; then, once I could write, however awkwardly, she selected a series of Biblical mottoes for me to copy.

> And now abideth Faith, Hope, Charity, these
>   three; but the greatest of these is Charity.
> Love is as strong as Death.
> A bird of the air shall carry the voice, and
>   that which hath wings shall tell the matter.

I wrote them over and over. By comparing the different written versions of the same sentence, I could see how much I had improved, said Becka.

I wondered about the words I was writing. Was Charity really greater than Faith, and did I have either? Was Love as strong as Death? Whose was the voice that the bird was going to carry?

Being able to read and write did not provide the answers to all questions. It led to other questions, and then to others.

★   ★   ★

In addition to learning to read, I managed to successfully perform the other tasks assigned to me during those first months. Some of these

386

tasks were not onerous: I enjoyed painting the skirts and sleeves and head coverings on the little girls in the Dick and Jane books, and I did not mind working in the kitchen, chopping up turnips and onions for the cooks and washing dishes. Everyone at Ardua Hall had to contribute to the general welfare, and manual labour was not to be sneered at. No Aunt was considered above it, though in practice the Supplicants did most of the heavy hauling. But why not? We were younger.

Scrubbing the toilets was not enjoyable, however, especially when you had to scrub them again even when they were perfectly clean the first time, and then again for a third time. Becka had warned me that the Aunts would demand this repetition — it wasn't about the state of the toilets, she said. It was a test of obedience.

'But making us clean a toilet three times — that's unreasonable,' I said. 'It's a waste of valuable national resources.'

'Toilet cleaner is not a valuable national resource,' she said. 'Not like pregnant women. But unreasonable — yes, that's why it's a test. They want to see if you'll obey unreasonable demands without complaining.'

To make the test harder, they would assign the most junior Aunt to supervise. To be given stupid orders by someone almost your age is a lot more irritating than having that person be old.

'I hate this!' I said after the fourth week in a row of toilet-cleaning. 'I truly hate Aunt Abby! She's so mean, and pompous, and . . .'

'It's a test,' Becka reminded me. 'Like Job,

being tested by God.'

'Aunt Abby isn't God. She only thinks she is,' I said.

'We must try not to be uncharitable,' said Becka. 'You should pray for your hatred to go away. Just think of it as flowing out of your nose, like breath.'

Becka had a lot of these control-yourself techniques. I tried to practise them. They worked some of the time.

★ ★ ★

Once I'd passed my sixth-month examination and had been accepted as a permanent Supplicant, I was allowed into the Hildegard Library It's hard to describe the feeling this gave me. The first time I passed through its doors, I felt as if a golden key had been given to me — a key that would unlock one secret door after another, revealing to me the riches that lay within.

Initially I had access only to the outer room, but after a time I was given a pass to the Reading Room. In there I had my own desk. One of my assigned tasks was to make fair copies of the speeches — or perhaps I should call them sermons — that Aunt Lydia delivered on special occasions. She reused these speeches but changed them each time, and we needed to incorporate her handwritten notes into a legible typescript. By now I had learned how to type, although slowly.

While I was at my desk, Aunt Lydia would sometimes pass me going through the Reading

Room on her way to her own special room, where she was said to be doing important research that would make Gilead a better place: that was Aunt Lydia's lifetime mission, said the senior Aunts. The precious Bloodlines Genealogical Archives kept so meticulously by the senior Aunts, the Bibles, the theological discourses, the dangerous works of world literature — all were behind that locked door. We would be granted access only when our minds were sufficiently strengthened.

The months and years went by, and Becka and I became close friends, and told each other many things about ourselves and our families that we'd never told anyone else. I confessed how much I'd hated my stepmother, Paula, although I'd tried to overcome that feeling. I described the tragic death of our Handmaid, Crystal, and how upset I'd been. And she told me about Dr. Grove and what he'd done, and I'd told her my own story about him, which upset her on my behalf. We talked about our real mothers and how we wanted to know who they'd been. Perhaps we ought not to have shared so much, but it was very comforting.

'I wish I had a sister,' she said to me one day. 'And if I did, that person would be you.'

50

I've described our life as peaceful, and to the outward eye it was; but there were inner storms and turmoils that I have since come to learn are not uncommon among those seeking to dedicate themselves to a higher cause. The first of my inner storms came about when, after four years of reading more elementary texts, I was finally granted reading access to the full Bible. Our Bibles were kept locked up, as elsewhere in Gilead: only those of strong mind and steadfast character could be trusted with them, and that ruled out women, except for the Aunts.

Becka had begun her own Bible reading earlier — she was ahead of me, in priority as well as in proficiency — but those already initiated into these mysteries were not allowed to talk about their sacred reading experiences, so we had not discussed what she had learned.

The day came when the locked wooden Bible box reserved for me would be brought out to the Reading Room and I would finally open this most forbidden of books. I was very excited about it, but that morning Becka said, 'I need to warn you.'

'Warn me?' I said. 'But it's holy.'

'It doesn't say what they say it says.'

'What do you mean?' I asked.

'I don't want you to be too disappointed.' She paused. 'I'm sure Aunt Estée meant well.' Then she said, 'Judges 19 to 21.'

That was all she would tell me. But when I got to the Reading Room and opened the wooden box and then the Bible, that was the first place I turned to. It was the Concubine Cut into Twelve Pieces, the same story that Aunt Vidala had told us so long ago at school — the one that had disturbed Becka so much when she was little.

I remembered it well. And I remembered, too, the explanation that Aunt Estée had given us. She'd said that the reason the concubine had got killed was that she was sorry for having been disobedient, so she sacrificed herself rather than allowing her owner to be raped by the wicked Benjaminites. Aunt Estée had said the concubine was brave and noble. She'd said the concubine had made a choice.

But now I was reading the whole story. I looked for the brave and noble part, I looked for the choice, but none of that was there. The girl was simply shoved out the door and raped to death, then cut up like a cow by a man who'd treated her like a purchased animal when she'd been alive. No wonder she'd run away in the first place.

It came as a painful shock: kind, helpful Aunt Estée had lied to us. The truth was not noble, it was horrible. This was what the Aunts meant, then, when they said women's minds were too weak for reading. We would crumble, we would fall apart under the contradictions, we would not be able to hold firm.

Up until that time I had not seriously doubted the rightness and especially the truthfulness of Gilead's theology. If I'd failed at perfection, I'd concluded that the fault was mine. But as I discovered what had been changed by Gilead, what had been added, and what had been omitted, I feared I might lose my faith.

If you've never had a faith, you will not understand what that means. You feel as if your best friend is dying; that everything that defined you is being burned away; that you'll be left all alone. You feel exiled, as if you are lost in a dark wood. It was like the feeling I'd had when Tabitha died: the world was emptying itself of meaning. Everything was hollow. Everything was withering.

I told Becka some of what was taking place within me.

'I know,' she said. 'That happened to me. Everyone at the top of Gilead has lied to us.'

'How do you mean?'

'God isn't what they say,' she said. She said you could believe in Gilead or you could believe in God, but not both. That was how she had managed her own crisis.

I said that I wasn't sure I would be able to choose. Secretly I feared that I would be unable to believe in either. Still, I wanted to believe; indeed I longed to; and, in the end, how much of belief comes from longing?

51

Three years later, an even more alarming thing happened. As I've said, one of my tasks at the Hildegard Library was to make fair copies of Aunt Lydia's speeches. The pages for the speech I was to work on that day would be left on my desk in a silver folder. One morning I discovered, tucked in behind the silver folder, a blue one. Who had put it there? Had there been some mistake?

I opened it. The name of my stepmother, Paula, was at the top of the first page. What followed was an account of the death of her first husband, the one she'd had before she'd married my so-called father, Commander Kyle. As I've told you, her husband, Commander Saunders, had been killed in his study by their Handmaid. Or that was the story that had circulated.

Paula had said that the girl was dangerously unbalanced, and had stolen a skewer from the kitchen and killed Commander Saunders in an unprovoked attack. The Handmaid had escaped, but had been caught and hanged, and her dead body had been displayed on the Wall. But Shunammite had said that her Martha had said there had been an unlawful and sinful liaison — the Handmaid and the husband had been in the habit of fornicating in his study. That was what had given the Handmaid the opportunity to kill him, and that was also why she'd done it: the demands he'd been making of her had driven her over the edge of sanity. The rest of Shunammite's story was the same: Paula's discovery of the corpse, the capture of the Handmaid, the hanging. Shunammite had added a detail about Paula getting a lot of blood on herself while putting the dead Commander's trousers back on him to save appearances.

But the story in the blue folder was quite different. It was augmented by photographs, and transcripts of many secretly recorded conversations. There had been no illicit liaison between Commander Saunders and his Handmaid — only the regular Ceremonies as decreed by law. However, Paula and Commander Kyle — my erstwhile father — had been having an affair even before Tabitha, my mother, had died.

Paula had befriended the Handmaid and offered to help her escape from Gilead since she knew how unhappy the girl was. She'd even provided her with a map and directions, and the names of several Mayday contacts along the way. After the Handmaid had set out, Paula had skewered Commander Saunders herself. That was why she'd had so much blood on her, not from putting his trousers back on. In fact, he had never taken them off, or not on that night.

She'd bribed her Martha to back up the murderous Handmaid story, combining the bribe with threats. Then she'd called the Angels and accused the Handmaid, and the rest had followed. The unfortunate girl was found wandering the streets in despair, since the map was inaccurate and the Mayday contacts turned out not to exist.

The Handmaid had been interrogated. (The transcript of the interrogation was attached, and it was not comfortable reading.) Although admitting to her escape attempt and revealing Paula's part in it, she'd maintained her innocence of the murder — indeed, her ignorance of the murder — until the pain had become too much, and she'd made a false confession.

She was clearly innocent. But she was hanged anyway.

The Aunts had known the truth. Or at least one of them had known. There was the evidence, right in the folder in front of me. Yet nothing had happened to Paula. And a Handmaid had been hanged for the crime instead.

★   ★   ★

I was bedazzled, as if struck by lightning. But not only was I astounded by this story, I was mystified as to the reason it had been placed on my desk. Why had an unknown person given me such dangerous information?

Once a story you've regarded as true has turned false, you begin suspecting all stories. Was an effort being made to turn me against Gilead? Was the evidence faked? Was it Aunt Lydia's threat to reveal Paula's crime that had caused my stepmother to abandon her efforts to marry me to Commander Judd? Had this terrible story bought me my place as an Aunt at Ardua Hall? Was this a way of telling me that my mother, Tabitha, had not died of a disease but had been murdered in some unknown way by Paula, and possibly even by Commander Kyle? I didn't know what to believe.

There was no one I could confide in. Not even Becka: I didn't want to endanger her by making her complicit. The truth can cause a lot of trouble for those who are not supposed to know it.

I finished my work for the day, leaving the blue folder where I'd found it. The next day there was a new speech for me to work on, and the blue folder of the day before was gone.

$$\star \quad \star \quad \star$$

Over the course of the following two years, I found a number of similar folders waiting for me on my desk. They all held evidence of various crimes. Those containing the crimes of Wives were blue, of Commanders black, of professionals — such as doctors — grey, of Econopeople striped, of Marthas dull green. There were none containing the crimes of Handmaids, and none for those of Aunts.

Most of the files left for me were either blue or black, and described multiple crimes. Handmaids had been forced into illegal acts, then blamed for them; Sons of Jacob had plotted against one another; bribes and favours had been exchanged at the highest levels; Wives had schemed against other Wives; Marthas had eavesdropped and collected information, and then sold it; mysterious food poisonings had occurred, babies had changed hands from Wife to Wife on the basis of scandalous rumours that were, however, unfounded. Wives had been hanged for adulteries that had never occurred because a Commander wanted a different, younger Wife. Public trials — meant to purge traitors and purify the leadership — had turned on false confessions extracted by torture.

Bearing false witness was not the exception, it was common. Beneath its outer show of virtue and purity, Gilead was rotting.

★ ★ ★

Apart from Paula's, the file that most immediately concerned me was that of Commander Judd. It was a thick file. Among other misdemeanours, it contained evidence pertaining to the fates of his previous Wives, those he had been married to before my short-lived engagement to him.

He had disposed of them all. The first had been pushed down the stairs; her neck was broken. It was said that she'd tripped and fallen. As I knew from my reading of other files, it was not difficult to make such things look like accidents. Two of his Wives were said to have died in childbirth, or shortly thereafter; the babies were Unbabies, but the deaths of the Wives had involved deliberately induced septicemia or shock. In one case, Commander Judd had refused permission to operate when an Unbaby with two heads had lodged in the birth canal. Nothing could be done, he'd said piously, because there had still been a fetal heartbeat.

The fourth Wife had taken up flower-painting as a hobby at the suggestion of Commander Judd, who had thoughtfully purchased the paints for her. She'd then developed symptoms attributable to cadmium poisoning. Cadmium, the file noted, was a well-known carcinogenic, and the fourth Wife had succumbed to stomach cancer shortly thereafter.

I'd narrowly avoided a death sentence, it seemed. And I'd had help avoiding it. I said a prayer of gratitude that night: despite my doubts, I continued to pray. Thank you, I said. Help thou my unbelief. I added, And help Shunammite, for she will surely need it.

★   ★   ★

When I'd first begun reading these files, I was appalled and sickened. Was someone trying to cause me distress? Or were the files part of my education? Was my mind being hardened? Was I being prepared for the tasks I would later be performing as an Aunt?

This was what the Aunts did, I was learning. They recorded. They waited. They used their information to achieve goals known only to themselves. Their weapons were powerful but contaminating secrets, as the Marthas had always said. Secrets, lies, cunning, deceit — but the secrets, the lies, the cunning, and the deceit of others as well as their own.

If I remained at Ardua Hall — if I performed my Pearl Girls missionary work and returned as a full Aunt — this is what I would become. All of the secrets I had learned, and doubtless many more, would be mine, to use as I saw fit. All of this power. All of this potential to judge the wicked in silence, and to punish them in ways they would not be able to anticipate. All of this vengeance.

As I have said, there was a vengeful side to me that I had in the past regretted. Regretted but not expunged.

I would not be telling the truth if I said I was not tempted.

XIX

Study

The Ardua Hall Holograph

52

I had a disagreeable jolt last evening, my reader. I was scratching furtively away in the deserted library with my pen and my blue drawing ink, with my door open for air flow, when Aunt Vidala's head suddenly thrust itself around the corner of my private carrel. I did not startle — I have nerves of curable polymers, like those of plastinated corpses — but I coughed, a nervous reflex, and slid the closed *Apologia Pro Vita Sua* over the page I'd been writing on.

'Ah, Aunt Lydia,' said Aunt Vidala. 'I hope you're not catching a cold. Shouldn't you be in bed?' The big sleep, I thought: that's what you're wishing for me.

'Just an allergy,' I said. 'Many people have them at this time of year.' She could not deny this, being a major sufferer herself.

'I'm sorry for intruding,' she said untruthfully Her glance moved over Cardinal Newman's title. 'Always researching, I see,' she said. 'Such a notorious heretic.'

'Know your enemy,' I said. 'How may I help you?'

'I have something crucial to discuss. May I offer you a cup of warm milk at the Schlafly Café?' she said.

'How kind,' I replied. I replaced Cardinal Newman on my shelf, turning my back to her in order to slip my blue-inked page within.

Soon the two of us were sitting at a café table, me with my warm milk, Aunt Vidala with her mint tea. 'There was something odd about the Pearl Girls Thanks Giving,' she began.

'And what was that? I thought it all went much as usual.'

'That new girl, Jade. I am not convinced by her,' said Aunt Vidala. 'She seems unlikely.'

'They all seem unlikely at first,' I said. 'But they want a safe haven, protected from poverty exploitation, and the depredations of the so-called modern life. They want stability, they want order, they want clear guidelines. It will take her a little time to settle in.'

'Aunt Beatrice told me about that ridiculous tattoo on her arm. I suppose she told you as well. Really! God and Love! As if we could be taken in by such a crude attempt to curry favour! And such heretical theology! It reeks of an attempt to deceive. How do you know she's not a Mayday infiltrator?'

'We've been successful in detecting those in the past,' I said. 'As for the bodily mutilation, the youth of Canada are pagans; they have all kinds of barbaric symbols branded on themselves. I believe it shows a good intention; at least it is not a dragonfly or a skull or some such item. But we will keep a close eye on her.'

'We should have that tattoo removed. It's blasphemous. The word *God* is holy, it does not belong on an arm.'

'Removal would be too painful for her at the moment. It can wait until later. We don't want to discourage our young Supplicant.'

'If she is a true one, which I very much doubt. It would be typical of Mayday to attempt a ruse of this kind. I think she should be interrogated.' By herself, was what she meant. She does enjoy those interrogations a little too much.

'The more haste, the less speed,' I said. 'I prefer more subtle methods.'

'You didn't prefer them in the early days,' said Vidala. 'You were all for the primary colours. You didn't used to mind a little blood.' She sneezed. Perhaps we should do something about the mildew in this café, I thought. Then again, perhaps not.

⋆ ⋆ ⋆

It being late, I called Commander Judd in his office at home and requested a crash meeting, which was granted. I told my driver to wait for me outside.

The door was opened by Judd's Wife, Shunammite. She was not looking at all well: thin, white-faced, hollow-eyed. She'd lasted a comparatively long time for a Judd Wife; but at least she'd produced a baby, Unbaby though it had been. Now, however, her time appeared to be running out. I wondered what Judd had been putting in her soup. 'Oh, Aunt Lydia,' she said. 'Please come in. The Commander is expecting you.'

Why had she opened the door herself?

Door-opening is a Martha's job. She must have wanted something from me. I dropped my voice. 'Shunammite, my dear.' I smiled. 'Are you ill?' She had once been such a lively young girl, if brash and aggravating, but she was now a sickly wraith.

'I'm not supposed to say so,' she whispered. 'The Commander tells me it's nothing. He says I invent complaints. But I know there's something wrong with me.'

'I can have our clinic at Ardua Hall do an evaluation,' I said. 'A few tests.'

'I would have to get his permission,' she said. 'He won't let me go.'

'I will obtain his permission for you,' I said. 'Never fear.' There were tears then, and thank yous. In another age, she would have kneeled and kissed my hand.

★ ★ ★

Judd was waiting in his study. I have been there before, sometimes when he was in it, sometimes when he was not. It is a richly informative space. He should not bring work home with him from his office at the Eyes and leave it lying around so carelessly.

On the right wall — the one not visible from the door, as one must not shock the female inmates — there is a painting from the nineteenth century, showing a barely nubile girl without any clothes on. Dragonfly wings have been added to make her into a fairy, fairies having been known in those times to be averse to clothing. She has an amoral, elvish smile and is hovering over a mushroom. That's what Judd likes — young girls who can be viewed as not fully human, with a naughty core to them. That excuses his treatment of them.

The study is book-lined, like all these Commanders' studies. They like to accumulate, and to gloat over their acquisitions, and to boast to the others about what they have pilfered. Judd has a respectable collection of biographies and histories — Napoleon, Stalin, Ceauçsescu, and various other leaders and controllers of men. He has several highly valuable editions that I envy: Doré's *Inferno*, Dalí's *Alice's Adventures in Wonderland*, Picasso's *Lysistrata*. He has another kind of book, less respectable: vintage pornography, as I knew from having examined it. It is a genre that is tedious in bulk. The mistreatment of the human body has a limited repertoire.

'Ah, Aunt Lydia,' he said, half-rising from his chair in an echo of what was once considered gentlemanly behaviour. 'Do sit down and tell me what brings you out so late.' A beaming smile, not reflected in the expression of his eyes, which was both alarmed and flinty.

'We have a situation,' I said, taking the chair opposite.

His smile vanished. 'Not a critical one, I hope.'

'Nothing that cannot be dealt with. Aunt Vidala suspects the so-called Jade of being an infiltrator, sent to ferret out information and put us in a bad light. She wishes to interrogate the girl. That would be fatal to any productive future use of Baby Nicole.'

407

'I agree,' he said. 'We would not be able to televise her afterwards. What can I do to help you?'

'To help *us*,' I said. It is always good to remind him that our little privateer holds two. 'An order from the Eyes protecting the girl from interference until we know she may be credibly presented as Baby Nicole. Aunt Vidala is not aware of Jade's identity,' I added. 'And she should not be told. She is no longer fully reliable.'

'Can you explain that?' he said.

'For the moment, you'll have to trust me,' I said. 'And another thing. Your Wife, Shunammite, ought to be sent to the Calm and Balm Clinic at Ardua Hall for medical treatment.'

There was a long pause while we gazed into each other's eyes across his desk. 'Aunt Lydia, you read my mind,' he said. 'It would indeed be preferable for her to be in your care rather than in mine. In case anything might happen . . . in case she might develop a fatal illness.'

I will remind you here that there is no divorce in Gilead.

'A sage decision,' I said. 'You must remain above suspicion.'

'I depend on your discretion. I am in your hands, dear Aunt Lydia,' he said, rising from his desk. How true, I thought. And how easily a hand becomes a fist.

★   ★   ★

My reader, I am now poised on the razor's edge. I have two choices: I can proceed with my risky

408

and even reckless plan, attempt to transfer my packet of explosives by means of young Nicole, and, if successful, give both Judd and Gilead the first shove over the cliff. If I am unsuccessful, I will naturally be branded a traitor and will live in infamy; or rather die in it.

Or I could choose the safer course. I could hand Baby Nicole over to Commander Judd, where she would shine brilliantly for a moment before being snuffed out like a candle due to insubordination, as the chances of her meekly accepting her position here would be zero. I would then reap my reward in Gilead, which would potentially be great. Aunt Vidala would be nullified; I might even have her assigned to a mental institution. My control over Ardua Hall would be complete and my honoured old age secure.

I would have to give up the idea of retributive vengeance against Judd, as we would then be joined at the hip forever. Judd's Wife, Shunammite, would be a collateral casualty. I have placed Jade in the same dormitory space as Aunt Immortelle and Aunt Victoria, so once she was eliminated, their own fates would hang in the balance: guilt by association applies in Gilead, as it does elsewhere.

Am I capable of such duplicity? Could I betray so completely? Having tunnelled this far under the foundations of Gilead with my stash of cordite, might I falter? As I am human, it is entirely possible.

In that case, I would destroy these pages I have written so laboriously; and I would destroy you along with them, my future reader. One flare of a match and you'll be gone — wiped away as if you had never been, as if you will never be. I would deny you existence. What a godlike feeling! Though it is a god of annihilation.

I waver, I waver.

But tomorrow is another day.

XX

BLOODLINES

Transcript of Witness Testimony 369B

53

I'd made it into Gilead. I'd thought I knew a lot about it, but living a thing is different, and with Gilead it was very different. Gilead was slippery, like walking on ice: I felt off balance all the time. I couldn't read people's faces, and I often didn't know what they were saying. I could hear the words, I could understand the words themselves, but I couldn't translate them into meaning.

At that first meeting in the chapel, after we'd done the kneeling and the singing, when Aunt Beatrice took me to a pew to sit down, I looked back over the room full of women. Everyone was staring at me and smiling in a way that was part friendly and part hungry, like those scenes in horror movies where you know the villagers will turn out to be vampires.

Then there was an all-night vigil for the new Pearls: we were supposed to be doing silent meditation while kneeling. Nobody had told me about this: What were the rules? Did you put up your hand to go to the bathroom? In case you're wondering, the answer was yes. After hours of this — my legs were really cramping — one of the new Pearls, from Mexico I think, began crying hysterically and then yelling. Two Aunts picked her up and marched her out. I heard later that they'd turned her into a Handmaid, so it was a good thing I'd kept my mouth shut.

The following day we were given those ugly brown outfits, and the next thing I knewwe were being herded off to a sports stadium where we were seated in rows. No one had mentioned sports in Gilead — I'd thought they didn't have any — but it wasn't sports. It was a Particicution. They'd told us about those back in school, but they hadn't gone into too much detail, I guess, because they didn't want to traumatize us. Now I could understand that.

It was a double execution: two men literally torn apart by a mob of frenzied women. There was screaming, there was kicking, there was biting, there was blood everywhere, on the Handmaids especially: they were covered in it. Some of them held up parts — clumps of hair, what looked like a finger — and then the others yelled and cheered.

It was gruesome; it was terrifying. It added a whole new dimension to my picture of Handmaids. Maybe my mother had been like that, I thought: feral.

54

Becka and I did our best to instruct the new Pearl, Jade, as Aunt Lydia had requested, but it was like talking to the air. She did not know how to sit patiently, with her back straight and her hands folded in her lap; she twisted, squirmed, fidgeted with her feet. 'This is how women sit,' Becka would tell her, demonstrating.

'Yes, Aunt Immortelle,' she would say, and she would make a show of trying. But these attempts did not last long, and soon she was slouching again and crossing her ankles over her knees.

At Jade's first evening meal at Ardua Hall, we sat her between us for her own protection, because she was so heedless. Nonetheless, she behaved most unwisely. It was bread and an indeterminate soup — on Mondays they often mixed up the leftovers and added some onions — and a salad of pea vines and white turnip. 'The soup,' she said. 'It's like mouldy dishwater. I'm not eating it.'

'Shhh . . . Be thankful for what you are given,' I whispered back to her. 'I'm sure it's nutritious.'

The dessert was tapioca, again. 'I can't handle this.' She dropped her spoon with a clatter. 'Fish eyes in glue.'

'It's disrespectful not to finish,' said Becka.

'Unless you're fasting.'

'You can have mine,' said Jade.

'People are looking,' I said.

When she'd first arrived, her hair was greenish — that was the sort of mutilation they went in for in Canada, it seemed — but outside our apartment she had to keep her hair covered, so this had not been generally noticed. Then she began pulling hairs out of the back of her neck. She said this helped her think.

'You'll make a bald spot if you keep on doing that,' Becka said to her. Aunt Estée had taught us that when we were in the Rubies Premarital Preparatory classes: if you remove hairs frequently, they will not grow back. It is the same with eyebrows and eyelashes.

'I know,' said Jade. 'But nobody sees your hair around here anyway.' She smiled at us confidingly. 'One day I'm going to shave my head.'

'You can't do that! A woman's hair is her glory,' said Becka. 'It's been given to you as a covering. That's in Corinthians I.'

'Only one glory? Hair?' Jade said. Her tone was abrupt, but I don't think she meant to be rude.

'Why would you want to shame yourself by shaving your head?' I asked as gently as I could. If you were a woman, having no hair was a mark of disgrace: sometimes, after a complaint by a husband, the Aunts would cut off a disobedient or scolding Econowife's hair before locking her into the public stocks.

'To see what it's like to be bald,' said Jade. 'It's on my bucket list.'

416

'You must be careful what you say to others,' I told her. 'Becka — Aunt Immortelle and I are forgiving, and we understand that you are newly arrived from a degenerate culture; we are trying to help you. But other Aunts — especially the older ones such as Aunt Vidala — are constantly on the lookout for faults.'

'Yeah, you're right,' said Jade. 'I mean, Yes, Aunt Victoria.'

'What is a bucket list?' Becka asked.

'Stuff I want to do before I die.'

'Why is it called that?'

'It's from 'kick the bucket,'' said Jade. 'It's just a saying.' Then, seeing our puzzled looks, she continued. 'I think it's from when they used to hang people from trees. They'd make them stand on a bucket and then hang them, and their feet would kick, and naturally they would kick the bucket. Just my guess.'

'That's not how we hang people here,' said Becka.

Transcript of Witness Testimony 369B

55

I quickly realized that the two young Aunts in Doorway C didn't approve of me; but they were all I had because I wasn't on talking terms with anyone else. Aunt Beatrice had been kind when she'd been converting me, back in Toronto, but now that I was here I was no longer any concern of hers. She smiled at me in a distant way when I passed her, but that was all.

When I paused to think about it I was afraid, but I tried not to let fear control me. I was also feeling very lonely. I didn't have any friends here, and I couldn't contact anyone back there. Ada and Elijah were far away. There was no one I could ask for guidance; I was on my own, with no instruction book. I really missed Garth. I daydreamed about the things we'd done together: sleeping in the cemetery, panhandling on the street. I even missed the junk food we'd eaten. Would I ever get back there, and if I did, what would happen then? Garth probably had a girlfriend. How could he not have one? I'd never asked him because I didn't want to hear the answer.

But one of my biggest anxieties was about the person Ada and Elijah called the source — their contact inside Gilead. When would this person show up in my life? What if they didn't exist? If there was no 'source,' I'd be stuck here in Gilead because there wouldn't be anyone to get me out.

Transcript of Witness Testimony 369A

56

Jade was very untidy. She left her items in our
common room — her stockings, the belt of her
new Supplicants probationer uniform, sometimes even her shoes. She didn't always flush the
toilet. We'd find her hair combings blowing
around on the bathroom floor, her toothpaste
in the sink. She took showers at unauthorized
hours until firmly told not to, several times. I
know these are trivial things, but they can add up
in close quarters.

There was also the matter of the tattoo on her
left arm. It said GOD and LOVE, made into a
cross. She claimed it was a token of her conver-
sion to the true belief, but I doubted that, as
she'd let slip on one occasion that she thought
God was 'an imaginary friend.'

'God is a real friend, not an imaginary one,'
said Becka. There was as much anger in her
voice as she was capable of revealing.

'Sorry if I disrespected your cultural belief,'
Jade said, which did not improve things in the eyes
of Becka: saying God was a cultural belief was
even worse than saying he was an imaginary
friend. We realized that Jade thought we were stupid; certainly she thought we were superstitious.

'You should have that tattoo removed,' Becka

said. 'It's blasphemous.'

'Yeah, maybe you're right,' said Jade. 'I mean, Yes, Aunt Immortelle, thank you for telling me. Anyway, it's itchy as hell.'

'Hell is more than itchy,' said Becka. 'I will pray for your redemption.'

★ ★ ★

When Jade was upstairs in her room, we would often hear thumping noises and muffled shouts. Was it a barbarian form of prayer? I finally had to ask her what she was doing in there.

'Working out,' she said. 'It's like exercising. You have to keep strong.'

'Men are strong in body,' said Becka. 'And in mind. Women are strong in spirit. Though moderate exercise is allowed, such as walking, if a woman is of child-bearing age.'

'Why do you think you need to be strong in body?' I asked her. I was becoming more and more curious about her pagan beliefs.

'In case some guy aggresses you. You need to know how to stick your thumbs in their eyes, knee them in the balls, throw a heartstopper punch. I can show you. Here's how to make a fist — curl your fingers, wrap your thumb across your knuckles, keep your arm straight. Aim for the heart.' She slammed her fist into the sofa.

Becka was so astonished that she had to sit down. 'Women don't hit men,' she said. 'Or anyone, except when it's required by law, such as in Particicutions.'

'Well, that's convenient!' said Jade. 'So you

421

should just let them do whatever?'

'You shouldn't entice men,' said Becka. 'What happens if you do is partly your fault.'

Jade looked from one to the other of us. 'Victim-blaming?' she said. 'Really?'

'Pardon?' said Becka.

'Never mind. So you're telling me it's a lose-lose,' Jade said. 'We're screwed whatever we do.' The two of us gazed at her in silence; no answer is an answer, as Aunt Lise used to say.

'Okay,' she said. 'But I'm doing my workouts anyway.'

* * *

Four days after Jade's arrival, Aunt Lydia called Becka and me to her office. 'How is the new Pearl getting along?' she asked. When I hesitated, she said, 'Speak up!'

'She doesn't know how to behave,' I said.

Aunt Lydia smiled her wrinkly old-turnip smile. 'Remember, she is freshly come from Canada,' she said, 'so she doesn't know any better. Foreign converts are often like that when they arrive. It is your duty, for the moment, to teach her safer ways.'

'We've been trying, Aunt Lydia,' said Becka. 'But she's very — '

'Stubborn,' said Aunt Lydia. 'I am not surprised. Time will cure it. Do the best you can. You may go.' We went out of the office in the sideways manner we all used when leaving Aunt Lydia's office: it was impolite to turn your back on her.

422

★ ★ ★

The crime files continued to appear on my desk at the Hildegard Library. I could not decide what to think: one day I felt it would be a blessed state to be a full Aunt — knowing all the Aunts' carefully hoarded secrets, wielding hidden powers, doling out retributions. The next day I would consider my soul — because I did believe I had one — and how twisted and corrupted it would become if I were to act in that way. Was my soft, muddy brain hardening? Was I becoming stony, steely, pitiless? Was I exchanging my caring and pliable woman's nature for an imperfect copy of a sharp-edged and ruthless man's nature? I didn't want that, but how to avoid it if I aspired to be an Aunt?

★ ★ ★

Then something happened that changed my view of my position in the universe and caused me to give thanks anew for the workings of benign Providence.

Although I'd been granted access to the Bible and had been shown a number of dangerous crime files, I hadn't yet been given permission to access the Bloodlines Genealogical Archives, which were kept in a locked room. Those who'd been in there said this room contained aisles and aisles of folders. They were arranged on the shelves according to rank, men only: Economen, Guardians, Angels, Eyes, Commanders. Within those categories, the Bloodlines were filed by location, then by last name. The women were inside the folders of the men. The Aunts didn't have folders; their Bloodlines weren't recorded because they wouldn't be having any children. That was a secret sadness for me: I liked children, I'd always wanted children, I just hadn't wanted what came with them.

All Supplicants were given a briefing about the Archives' existence and purposes. They contained the knowledge of who the Handmaids had been before they were Handmaids, and who their children were, and who the fathers were: not only the declared fathers, but the illegal fathers also, since there were many women — both Wives and Handmaids — who were desperate to have babies in any way they could. But in all cases the Aunts recorded the Bloodlines: with so many older men marrying such young girls, Gilead could not risk the dangerous and sinful father-daughter inbreeding that might result if no one was keeping track.

But it was only after I'd done my Pearl Girls missionary work that I would have access to the Archives. I'd longed for the moment when I'd be able to trace my own mother — not Tabitha, but the mother who'd been a Handmaid. In those secret files, I'd be able to find out who she was, or had been — was she even still alive? I knew it was a risk — I might not like what I discovered — but I needed to try anyway. I might even be able to trace my real father, though that was less likely since he had not been a Commander. If I could find my mother, I would have a story instead of a zero. I would have a past beyond my own past, though I would not necessarily have a future with this unknown mother inside it.

One morning I found a file from the Archives on my desk. There was a small handwritten note paper-clipped to the front: *Agnes Jemima's Bloodline.* I held my breath as I opened the file. Inside was the Bloodlines record for Commander Kyle. Paula was in the folder, and their son, Mark. I wasn't part of that Bloodline, so I wasn't listed as Mark's sister. But through Commander Kyle's line I was able to discover the true name of poor Crystal — of Ofkyle, who'd died in childbirth — since little Mark was part of her Bloodline too. I wondered whether he would ever be told about her. Not if they could help it, was my guess.

At last I found the Bloodline on myself. It was not where it should have been — inside Commander Kyle's folder, in the time period relating to his first Wife, Tabitha. Instead it was at the back of the file in a sub-file of its own.

There was my mother's picture. It was a double picture, like the kind we'd see on Wanted posters for runaway Handmaids: the full face, the profile. She had light hair, pulled back; she was young. She was staring right into my own eyes: what was she trying to tell me? She wasn't smiling, but why would she smile? Her picture must have been taken by the Aunts, or else by the Eyes.

The name underneath had been blanked out, using heavy blue ink. There was an updated notation, however: *Mother of Agnes Jemima, now Aunt Victoria. Escaped to Canada.*

Currently working for Mayday terrorist intelligence. Two elimination attempts made (failed). Location currently unknown.

Underneath that, it said *Biological Father*, but his name, too, had been redacted. There was no picture. The notation said: *Currently in Canada. Said to be a Mayday operative. Location unknown.*

Did I look like my mother? I wished to think so.

Did I remember her? I tried to. I knew I should be able to, but the past was too dark.

Such a cruel thing, memory. We can't remember what it is that we've forgotten. That we have been made to forget. That we've had to forget, in order to pretend to live here in any normal way.

I'm sorry, I whispered. I can't bring you back. Not yet.

I placed my hand on top of my mother's picture. Did it feel warm? I wanted that. I wanted to think that love and warmth were radiating out of this picture — not a flattering picture, but that didn't matter. I wanted to think that this love was flowing into my hand. Childish make-believe, I know that. But it was comforting nonetheless.

⋆   ⋆   ⋆

I turned the page: there was another document. My mother had had a second child. That child had been smuggled into Canada as an infant. Her name was Nicole. There was a baby picture.

426

Baby Nicole.

Baby Nicole, whom we prayed for on every solemn occasion at Ardua Hall. Baby Nicole, whose sunny cherubic face appeared on Gilead television so often as a symbol of the unfairness being shown to Gilead on the international stage. Baby Nicole, who was practically a saint and martyr, and was certainly an icon — that Baby Nicole was my sister.

Underneath the last paragraph of text there was a line of wavery handwriting in blue ink: *Top Secret. Baby Nicole is here in Gilead.*

It seemed impossible.

I felt a rush of gratitude — I had a younger sister! But I also felt frightened: if Baby Nicole was here in Gilead, why hadn't everyone been told? There would have been widespread rejoicing and a huge celebration. Why had I myself been told? I felt entangled, though the nets around me were invisible. Was my sister in danger? Who else knew she was here, and what would they do to her?

By this time I knew that the person leaving these files for me must be Aunt Lydia. But why was she doing it? And how did she want me to react? My mother was alive, but she was also under sentence of death. She'd been deemed a criminal; worse, a terrorist. How much of her was in me? Was I tainted in some way? Was that the message? Gilead had tried to kill my renegade mother and had failed. Should I be glad about this, or sorry? Where should my loyalties lie?

Then, on impulse, I did a very dangerous

thing. Making sure no one was watching, I slipped the two pages with their glued-on pictures out of the Bloodlines file, then folded them several times and hid them in my sleeve. Somehow I could not bear to be parted with them. It was foolish and headstrong, but it was not the only foolish and headstrong thing I have ever done.

57

It was a Wednesday, the woe day. After the usual putrid breakfast, I received a message to go immediately to Aunt Lydia's office. 'What does it mean?' I asked Aunt Victoria.

'Nobody ever knows what Aunt Lydia might have in mind,' she said.

'Have I done something bad?' There was a big choice of bad things, that was for sure.

'Not necessarily,' she said. 'You might have done something good.'

Aunt Lydia was waiting for me in her office. The door was ajar, and she told me to come in even before I'd knocked. 'Close the door behind you and sit down,' she said.

I sat down. She looked at me. I looked at her. It's strange, because I knew she was supposed to be the powerful, mean old queen bee of Ardua Hall, but right then I didn't find her scary. She had a big mole on her chin: I tried not to stare at it. I wondered why she hadn't had it taken off.

'How are you enjoying it here, Jade?' she said. 'Are you adjusting?'

I should have said yes, or fine, or something, the way I'd been trained. Instead I blurted, 'Not well.'

She smiled, showing her yellowy teeth. 'Many

have regrets at first,' she said. 'Would you like to go back?'

'Like, how?' I said. 'Flying monkeys?'

'I suggest you refrain from making that kind of flippant remark in public. It could have painful repercussions for you. Do you have something to show me?'

I was puzzled. 'Like what?' I asked. 'No, I didn't bring — '

'On your arm, for instance. Under your sleeve.'

'Oh,' I said. 'My arm.' I rolled up the sleeve: there was GOD/LOVE, not looking very pretty.

She peered at it. 'Thank you for doing as I requested,' she said.

She was the one who'd requested it? 'Are you the source?' I asked.

'The what?'

Was I in trouble? 'You know, the one — I mean — '

She cut me off. 'You must learn to edit your thoughts,' she said. 'Unthink them. Now, next steps. You are Baby Nicole, as you must have been told in Canada.'

'Yeah, but I'd rather not be,' I said. 'I'm not happy about it.'

'I'm sure that is true,' she said. 'But many of us would rather not be who we are. We don't have unlimited choices in that department. Now, are you ready to help your friends back in Canada?'

'What do I have to do?' I asked.

'Come over here and place your arm on the desk,' she said. 'This won't hurt.'

She took a thin blade and made a nick in my tattoo, at the base of the O. Then, using a magnifying glass and a minute pair of tweezers, she slid something very small into my arm. She was wrong about it not hurting.

'No one would think of looking inside GOD. Now you're a carrier pigeon, and all we have to do is transport you. It's harder than it would have been once, but we'll manage it. Oh, and don't tell anyone about this until granted permission. Loose lips sink ships, and sinking ships kill people. Yes?'

'Yes,' I said. Now I had a lethal weapon in my arm.

'Yes, *Aunt Lydia*. Don't slip up on manners here, ever. You could trigger a denunciation, even for something so minor. Aunt Vidala loves her Corrections.'

Transcript of Witness Testimony 369A

58

Two mornings after I'd read my Bloodlines file I received a summons to Aunt Lydia's office. Becka had also been ordered to attend; we walked over together. We thought we were going to be asked again how Jade was getting along, whether she was happy with us, whether she was ready for her literacy test, whether she was firm in her faith. Becka said she was going to request that Jade be moved elsewhere because we'd been unable to teach her anything. She simply didn't listen.

But Jade was already in Aunt Lydia's office when we got there, sitting on a chair. She smiled at us, an apprehensive smile.

Aunt Lydia let us in, then looked up and down the corridor before closing the door. 'Thank you for coming,' she said to us. 'You may sit down.' We sat in the two chairs provided, one on either side of Jade. Aunt Lydia herself sat down, placing her hands on her desk to lower herself. Her hands were slightly tremulous. I found myself thinking, She's getting old. But that did not seem possible: surely Aunt Lydia was ageless.

'I have some information to share with you that will materially affect the future of Gilead,' Aunt Lydia said. 'You yourselves will have a crucial part to play. Are you brave enough? Do you stand ready?'

'Yes, Aunt Lydia,' I said, and Becka repeated the same words. The younger Supplicants were always being told they had a crucial part to play, and that bravery was required of them. Usually it meant giving up something, like time or food.

'Good. I will be brief. First, I must inform you, Aunt Immortelle, of something that the other two already know. Baby Nicole is here in Gilead.'

I was confused: why would the girl Jade have been told such an important piece of news? She could have no idea of what an impact the appearance of such an iconic figure would have among us.

'Really? Oh, praise be, Aunt Lydia!' said Becka. 'That is such wonderful news. Here? In Gilead? But why have we not all been told? It's like a miracle!'

'Control yourself, please, Aunt Immortelle. I must now add that Baby Nicole is the half-sister of Aunt Victoria.'

'No shit!' Jade exclaimed. 'I don't believe this!'

'Jade, I did not hear that,' said Aunt Lydia. 'Self-reverence, self-knowledge, self-control.'

'Sorry,' Jade mumbled.

'Agnes! I mean, Aunt Victoria!' Becka said. 'You have a sister! That is so joyful!! And it's Baby Nicole! You are so lucky, Baby Nicole is so adorable.' There was the standard picture of Baby Nicole on Aunt Lydia's wall: she was indeed adorable, but then, all babies are adorable. 'May I hug you?' Becka said to me. She was fighting hard to be positive. It must have been sad for her that I had a known relative but she did not have any: even her pretend father had just been shamefully executed.

'Calm, please,' said Aunt Lydia. 'Time has passed since Baby Nicole was a baby. She is now grown up.'

'Of course, Aunt Lydia,' said Becka. She sat down, folded her hands in her lap.

'But if she is here in Gilead, Aunt Lydia,' I said, 'where is she, exactly?'

Jade laughed. It was more like a bark.

'She is at Ardua Hall,' said Aunt Lydia, smiling. It was like a guessing game: she was enjoying herself. We must have looked mystified. We knew everyone at Ardua Hall, so where was Baby Nicole?

'She is in this room,' Aunt Lydia announced. She waved a hand. 'Jade here is Baby Nicole.'

'It can't be!' I said. Jade was Baby Nicole? Therefore Jade was my sister?

Becka sat with her mouth open, staring at Jade. 'No,' she whispered. Her face was woeful.

'Sorry about not being adorable,' Jade said. 'I tried, but I'm terrible at it.' I believe she meant it as a joke, to lighten the atmosphere.

'Oh — I didn't mean . . . ' I said. 'It's just . . . you don't look like Baby Nicole.'

'No she does not,' said Aunt Lydia. 'But she does look like you.' It was true, up to a point: the eyes yes, but not the nose. I glanced down at Jade's hands, folded for once in her lap. I wanted to ask her to stretch out her fingers so I could compare them to mine, but I felt that might be offensive. I didn't wish her to think I was demanding too much evidence of her genuine-ness, or else rejecting her.

'I'm very happy to have a sister,' I said to her politely, now that I was overcoming the shock. This awkward girl shared a mother with me. I'd have to try my best.

'You're both so lucky,' said Becka. Her voice was wistful.

'And you're like my sister,' I told her, 'so Jade is like your sister too.' I didn't want Becka to feel left out.

'May I hug you?' Becka said to Jade; or, as I suppose I should now call her in this account, Nicole.

'Yeah, I guess,' said Nicole. She then received a little hug from Becka. I followed suit. 'Thanks,' she said.

'Thank you, Aunts Immortelle and Victoria,' said Aunt Lydia. 'You are demonstrating an admirable spirit of acceptance and inclusion. Now I must trouble you for your full attention.'

We turned our faces towards her. 'Nicole will not be with us for long,' said Aunt Lydia. 'She will be leaving Ardua Hall shortly, and travelling back to Canada. She will be taking an important message with her. I want you both to help her.'

I was astonished. Why was Aunt Lydia letting her go back? No convert ever went back — it was treason — and if that person was Baby Nicole, it was treason ten times over.

'But, Aunt Lydia,' I said. 'That is against the law, and also God's will as proclaimed by the Commanders.'

'Indeed, Aunt Victoria. But as you and Aunt

Immortelle have now read a good many of the secret files I have been placing in your way, are you not aware of the deplorable degree of corruption that currently exists in Gilead?'

'Yes, Aunt Lydia, but surely . . . ' I had not been certain that Becka, too, had been treated to the crime files. Both of us had obeyed the TOP SECRET classification; but more importantly, each of us had wished to spare the other.

'The aims of Gilead at the outset were pure and noble, we all agree,' she said. 'But they have been subverted and sullied by the selfish and the power-mad, as so often happens in the course of history. You must wish to see that set right.'

'Yes,' said Becka, nodding. 'We do wish it.'

'Remember, too, your vows. You pledged yourselves to help women and girls. I trust you meant that.'

'Yes, Aunt Lydia,' I said. 'We did.'

'This will be helping them. Now, I don't want to force you to do anything against your will, but I must state the position clearly. Now that I have told you this secret — that Baby Nicole is here, and that she will soon be acting as a courier for me — every minute that passes in which you do not divulge this secret to the Eyes will count as treachery. But even if you do divulge it, you may still be severely punished, perhaps even terminated for having held back, even for an instant. Needless to say, I myself will be executed, and Nicole will soon be no better than a caged parrot. If she won't comply, they'll kill her, one way or another. They won't hesitate: you've read the crime files.'

'You can't do that to them!' Nicole said. 'That's not fair, it's emotional blackmail!'

'I appreciate your views, Nicole,' said Aunt Lydia, 'but your juvenile notions of fairness do not apply here. Keep your sentiments to yourself, and if you wish to see Canada again it would be wise to consider that a command.'

She turned to the two of us. 'You are, of course, free to make your own decisions. I will leave the room; Nicole, come with me. We wish to give your sister and her friend a little privacy in which to consider the possibilities. We will return in five minutes. At that time, I shall simply require a yes or a no from you. Other details regarding your mission will be supplied in good time. Come, Nicole.' She took Nicole by the arm and steered her out of the room.

Becka's eyes were wide and frightened, as mine must have been. 'We have to do it,' Becka said. 'We can't let them die. Nicole is your sister, and Aunt Lydia . . . '

'Do what?' I said. 'We don't know what she's asking for.'

'She's asking for obedience and loyalty,' said Becka. 'Remember how she rescued us — both of us? We have to say yes.'

★   ★   ★

After leaving Aunt Lydia's office, Becka went to the library for her day shift, and Nicole and I walked back to our apartment together.

'Now that we're sisters,' I said, 'you can call me Agnes when we're alone.'

'Okay, I'll try,' Nicole said.

We went into the main room. 'I have something I want to share with you,' I said. 'Just a minute.' I went upstairs. I'd been keeping the two pages from the Bloodlines files under my mattress, folded up small. When I returned, I unfolded them carefully and flattened them out. Once I'd laid them out on the table, Nicole — like me — couldn't resist placing her hand on the picture of our mother.

'This is amazing,' she said. She took her hand off, studied the picture again. 'Do you think she looks like me?'

'I wondered the same thing,' I said.

'Can you remember her at all? I must've been too young.'

'I don't know,' I said. 'Sometimes I think I can. I do seem to remember something. Was there a different house? Did I travel somewhere? But maybe it's wishful thinking.'

'What about our fathers?' she said. 'And why did they blank out the names?'

'Maybe they were trying to protect us in some way,' I said.

'Thanks for showing me,' said Nicole. 'But I don't think you should keep these around. What if you get caught with them?'

'I know. I tried to put the pages back, but the file wasn't there anymore.'

In the end, we decided to tear the pages up into small pieces and flush them down the toilet.

★　★　★

Aunt Lydia had told us we should strengthen our minds for the mission ahead of us. Meanwhile, we should continue on with life as usual, and not do anything to call attention to Nicole, or arouse suspicion. That was difficult, as we were anxious; I for one lived with a sense of dread: if Nicole were to be discovered, would Becka and I be accused?

Becka and I were due to leave on our Pearl Girls mission very soon. Would we even go, or did Aunt Lydia have some other destination in mind? We could only wait and see. Becka had studied the Pearl Girls standard guide of Canada, with the currency, the customs, and the methods of purchasing, including credit cards. She was much better prepared than I was.

When the Thanks Giving ceremony was less than a week away, Aunt Lydia called us to her office again. 'This is what you must do,' she said. 'I have arranged a room for Nicole at one of our country Retreat Houses. The papers are in order. But it is you, Aunt Immortelle, who will be going in Nicole's stead. She herself will take your place, and will travel as a Pearl Girl to Canada.'

'Then I won't be going?' said Becka, dismayed.

'You will go later,' said Aunt Lydia.

I suspected it was a lie, even then.

XXI

Fast and Thick

The Ardua Hall Holograph

59

I'd thought I had everything in order, but the best-laid plans gang aft agley, and trouble comes in threes. I write this in haste at the end of a very trying day. My office might as well have been Grand Central — before that venerable edifice was reduced to rubble during the War of Manhattan — so heavy was the foot traffic through it.

The first to make an appearance was Aunt Vidala, who turned up right after breakfast. Vidala and undigested porridge are a taxing combination: I vowed to imbibe some mint tea as soon as I might arrange it.

'Aunt Lydia, there is a matter to which I wish to draw your urgent attention,' she said.

I sighed inwardly. 'Of course, Aunt Vidala. Do sit down.'

'I won't take much of your time,' she said, settling herself in the chair in preparation for doing just that. 'It's about Aunt Victoria.'

'Yes? She and Aunt Immortelle are soon to set off on their Pearl Girls mission to Canada.'

'That is what I wish to consult you about. Are you sure they are ready for it? They are young for their ages — even more so than the other Supplicants of their generation. Neither of them have had any experience of the wider world, but some of the others have at least firmness of character that is lacking in these two. They are, you might say, malleable; they will be overly susceptible to the material temptations on offer in Canada. Also, in my opinion, Aunt Victoria is a defection risk. She has been reading some questionable material.'

'I trust you are not calling the Bible questionable,' I said.

'Certainly not. The material to which I refer is her own Bloodlines file from the Genealogical Archives. It will give her dangerous ideas.'

'She does not have access to the Bloodlines Genealogical Archives,' I said.

'Someone must have obtained the file for her. I happen to have seen it on her desk.'

'Who would have done that without my authorization?' I said. 'I must make inquiries; I cannot have insubordination. But I am sure Aunt Victoria is, by now, resistant to dangerous ideas. Despite your opinion of her juvenility, I believe she has achieved an admirable maturity and strength of mind.'

'A thin facade,' said Vidala. 'Her theology is very shaky. Her notion of prayer is fatuous. She was frivolous as a child and recalcitrant when it came to her school duties, especially the handicrafts. Also, her mother was — '

'I know who her mother was,' I said. 'The same can be said of many of our most respected younger Wives, who are the biological progeny of Handmaids. But degeneracy of that sort is not necessarily inherited. Her adoptive mother was a model of rectitude and patient suffering.'

'That is true as concerns Tabitha,' said Aunt Vidala. 'But, as we know, Aunt Victoria's original mother is a particularly flagrant case. Not only did she disregard her duty, abandon her appointed post, and defy those set in Divine Authority over her, but she was the prime mover in the stealing of Baby Nicole from Gilead.'

'Ancient history, Vidala,' I said. 'It is our mission to redeem, not to condemn on purely contingent grounds.'

'Certainly, as regards Victoria; but that mother of hers ought to be cut into twelve pieces.'

'No doubt,' I said.

'There is a credible rumour that she's working with Mayday Intelligence, in Canada, on top of her other treasons.'

'We win some, we lose some,' I said.

'That is an odd way of putting it,' said Aunt Vidala. 'It is not a sport.'

'It is kind of you to offer me your observations on acceptable speech,' I said. 'As for your insights on Aunt Victoria, the proof will be in the pudding. I am sure she will complete her Pearl Girls assignment most satisfactorily.'

'We shall see,' said Aunt Vidala with a half-smile. 'But if she defects, kindly remember that I warned you.'

★ ★ ★

Next to arrive was Aunt Helena, all apuff from limping over from the library. Increasingly her feet are a bother to her.

'Aunt Lydia,' she said. 'I feel you should be aware that Aunt Victoria has been reading her own Bloodlines file from the Genealogical Archives without authorization. I believe that, in view of her biological mother, it is most unwise.'

'I have just been informed of this fact by Aunt Vidala,' I said. 'She shares your view as to the feebleness of Aunt Victoria's moral fibre. But Aunt Victoria was well brought up, and has had the best education at one of our prime Vidala Schools. Is it your theory that nature will win out over nurture? In which case, the original sinfulness of Adam will assert itself in all of us despite our rigorous efforts to stamp it out, and I am afraid our Gilead project will be doomed.'

'Oh surely not! I didn't mean to imply that,' Helena said, alarmed.

'You've read Agnes Jemima's Bloodlines file yourself?' I asked her.

'Yes, many years ago. It was restricted at that time to the Founding Aunts.'

'We made the correct decision. Had the know-ledge that Baby Nicole was Aunt Victoria's half-sister been widely disseminated, it would have been detrimental to her development as a child. I now believe that some of the more unscrupulous within Gilead might have attempted to use her as a bargaining chip in their attempts to retrieve Baby Nicole, had they been aware of the relation-ship.'

'I had not thought of that,' said Aunt Helena. 'Of course you are right.'

'It may interest you to know,' I said, 'that Mayday is cognizant of the sisterly relationship;

they have had Baby Nicole within their grasp for some time. It is thought they may wish to reunite her with her degenerate mother, since her adoptive parents have died suddenly. In an explosion,' I added.

Aunt Helena twisted her claw-like little hands. 'Mayday is ruthless, they would think nothing of placing her in the care of a moral criminal such as her mother, or even of sacrificing an innocent young life.'

'Baby Nicole is quite safe,' I said.

'Praise be!' said Aunt Helena.

'Though she is as yet ignorant of the fact that she is Baby Nicole,' I said. 'But we hope soon to see her take her rightful place in Gilead. There is now a chance.'

'I rejoice to hear it. But should she indeed arrive among us, we must proceed carefully in the matter of her true identity,' said Aunt Helena. 'We must break it to her gently. Such revelations can destabilize a vulnerable mind.'

'My thoughts exactly. But in the meantime I would like you to observe the movements of Aunt Vidala. I fear it is she who has placed the Bloodlines file in the hands of Aunt Victoria, to what end I can't imagine. Possibly she wishes Aunt Victoria to be overwhelmed with despair at the news of her degenerate parentage, and be thrown into an unsettled spiritual state, and make some rash misstep.'

'Vidala never liked her,' said Aunt Helena. 'Even when she was at school.'

She limped away, happy to have been given a commission.

As I was sitting in the Schlafly Café having my late-afternoon cup of mint tea, Aunt Elizabeth hurried in. 'Aunt Lydia!' she wailed. 'There have been Eyes and Angels in Ardua Hall! It was like an invasion! You didn't sanction this?'

'Calm yourself,' I said. My own heart was beating fast and thick. 'Where, exactly, were they?'

'In the print shop. They confiscated all our Pearl Girls brochures. Aunt Wendy protested, and I am sorry to say she was arrested. They actually laid hands on her!' She shuddered.

'This is unprecedented,' I said, rising to my feet. 'I shall demand a meeting with Commander Judd immediately.'

I headed for my office, intending to use the red direct-line telephone, but there was no need: Judd was there before me. He must have simply barged in, pleading an emergency. So much for our agreed-on sacred separate sphere. 'Aunt Lydia. I felt an explanation of my action was in order,' he said. He was not smiling.

'I am sure there is an excellent one,' I said, allowing a little coldness into my voice. 'The Eyes and Angels have greatly overstepped the bounds of decency, not to mention those of custom and law.'

'All in the service of your good name, Aunt Lydia. May I sit down?' I gestured to the chair. We sat.

'After a number of dead ends, we came to the conclusion that the microdots I informed you about must have been passed to and fro between Mayday and an unknown contact here in Ardua Hall through the unwitting agency of the brochures that the Pearl Girls were distributing.' He paused to note my response.

'You astonish me!' I said. 'What effrontery!' I was wondering what had taken them so long. But then microdots are very small, and who would think to suspect our attractive and orthodox recruiting materials? No doubt the Eyes wasted a lot of time inspecting shoes and undergarments. 'Do you have proof?' I asked. 'And if so, who was the rotten apple in our barrel?'

'We raided the Ardua Hall print shop, and retained Aunt Wendy for questioning. It seemed the most direct path to the truth.'

'I cannot believe Aunt Wendy is implicated,' I said. 'That woman is incapable of devising such a scheme. She has the brain of a guppy. I suggest you release her immediately.'

'So we have concluded. She will recover from the shock in the Calm and Balm Clinic,' he said.

That was a relief to me. No pain unless necessary, but if necessary, pain. Aunt Wendy is a useful idiot but harmless as a pea. 'What did you discover?' I said. 'Were any of these microdots, as you call them, on those brochures that had been newly printed?'

'No, though an inspection of brochures recently returned from Canada yielded several dots containing maps and other items that must have been appended to them by Mayday. The unknown traitor within us must have realized that the elimination of The Clothes Hound end of the operation has rendered that pathway obsolete and has ceased to ornament the Pearl Girls brochures with classified information from Gilead.'

'I have long had my doubts about Aunt Vidala,' I said. 'Aunt Helena and Aunt Elizabeth also have clearance for the print shop, and I myself have always been the one to place the new brochures in the hands of our departing Pearl Girls, so I ought to be under suspicion as well.'

Commander Judd smiled at that. 'Aunt Lydia, you must have your little jokes,' he said, 'even at a time like this. Others had access as well: there were several apprentice printers. But there is no evidence of wrongdoing on any of their parts, and a substitute culprit will not do in this case. We must not leave the actual perpetrator at large.'

'So we remain in the dark.'

'Unfortunately. Very unfortunately for me, and thus very unfortunately for you as well, Aunt Lydia. My stock is falling rapidly with the Council: I've been promising them results. I sense the cold shoulders, the abrupt greetings. I detect the symptoms of an imminent purge: both you and I will be accused of laxness to the point of treachery for letting Mayday run rings around us, right under our noses here in Ardua Hall.'

'The situation is critical,' I said.

'There's a way to redeem ourselves,' he said. 'Baby Nicole must be produced immediately and put on full display. Television, posters, a large public rally.'

'I can see the virtue of that,' I said.

'It would be even more efficacious if I could announce her betrothal to myself, and have the subsequent wedding ceremony broadcast. You and I would be untouchable then.'

'Brilliant, as usual,' I said. 'But you are married.'

'How is the health of my Wife?' he asked, raising his eyebrows reproachfully.

'Better than it was,' I said, 'but not as good as it might be.' How can he have been so obvious as to have employed rat poison? Even in small quantities, it is so easily detectable. Dislikeable though Shunammite may have been as a schoolgirl, I have no wish to have her join Judd's Bluebeard's chamber of defunct brides. She is in fact making a recovery; however, her terror at the prospect of returning to the loving arms of Judd is impeding her progress. 'I fear she will have a relapse,' I said.

He sighed. 'I will pray for her release from suffering,' he said.

'And I am sure your prayers will be answered soon.' We gazed at each other across my desk.

'How soon?' he could not resist asking.

'Soon enough,' I said.

451

XXII

HEARTSTOPPER

Transcript of Witness Testimony 369A

60

Two days before Becka and I were supposed to receive our strands of pearls, we had an unexpected visit from Aunt Lydia during our private evening prayers. Becka opened the door.

'Oh, Aunt Lydia,' she said with some dismay. 'Praise be.'

'Kindly step back and shut the door behind me,' Aunt Lydia said. 'I'm in a hurry. Where is Nicole?'

'Upstairs, Aunt Lydia,' I said. While Becka and I did our praying, Nicole usually left the room and went off to practise her physical exercises.

'Please call her. There is an emergency,' said Aunt Lydia. She was breathing more quickly than usual.

'Aunt Lydia, are you well?' Becka asked anxiously. 'Would you like a glass of water?'

'Don't fuss,' she said. Nicole came into the room.

'Everything okay?' she asked.

'In point of fact, no,' said Aunt Lydia. 'We find ourselves in a tight corner. Commander Judd has just raided our printing press in search of treachery. Though he caused considerable distress to Aunt Wendy, he found nothing incriminating; but unfortunately he has learned that Jade is not

455

Nicole's true name. He has discovered that she is Baby Nicole, and is determined to marry her as soon as possible in order to increase his own prestige. He wishes the wedding to take place on Gilead television.'

'Triple shit!' said Nicole.

'Language, please,' said Aunt Lydia.

'They can't make me marry him!' said Nicole.

'They'd do it somehow,' said Becka. She'd turned very pale.

'This is terrible,' I said. From the file I'd read on Commander Judd, it was worse than terrible: it was a death sentence.

'What can we do?'

'You and Nicole must leave tomorrow,' said Aunt Lydia to me. 'As early as possible. A Gilead diplomatic plane will not be possible; Judd would hear of it and stop it. You'll have to take another route.'

'But we aren't ready,' I said. 'We don't have our pearls, or the dresses, or the Canadian money, or the brochures, or the silver back-packs.'

'I will bring the necessary items to you later tonight,' said Aunt Lydia. 'I have already arranged a pass identifying Nicole as Aunt Immortelle. Unfortunately, there will not be time for me to reschedule the sojourn at the Retreat House for Aunt Immortelle. Such a deception might not have lasted long enough in any case.'

'Aunt Helena will notice Nicole is gone,' I said. 'She always counts heads. And they'll wonder why Becka — why Aunt Immortelle — is still here.'

'Indeed,' said Aunt Lydia. 'Therefore I must ask you to perform a special service, Aunt Immortelle. Please conceal yourself for at least forty-eight hours after the other two have left. Perhaps in the library?'

'Not there,' said Becka. 'There are too many books. There isn't room for a person.'

'I'm sure you'll think of something,' said Aunt Lydia. 'Our entire mission, not to mention the personal safety of Aunt Victoria and Nicole, depends on you. It is a great deal of responsibility — a renewed Gilead can be possible only through you; and you would not want the others to be caught and hanged.'

'No, Aunt Lydia,' Becka whispered.

'Thinking cap on!' said Aunt Lydia brightly. 'Use your wits!'

'You're dumping too much on her,' said Nicole to Aunt Lydia. 'Why can't I just go alone? Then Aunt Immortelle and Agnes — Aunt Victoria — can make their trip together at the right time.'

'Don't be stupid,' I said. 'You can't. You'd be arrested immediately. Pearl Girls always go in twos, and even if you don't wear the uniform, a girl your age would never travel unaccompanied.'

'We should make it look as if Nicole has climbed over the Wall,' said Becka. 'That way they won't look inside Ardua Hall. I'll have to hide inside it somewhere.'

'What an intelligent idea, Aunt Immortelle,' said Aunt Lydia. 'Perhaps Nicole will oblige us by writing a note to that effect. She can say that she realizes she is unsuitable as an Aunt: that will

457

not be hard to believe. Then she can claim to have run off with an Economan — some lowly functionary doing repair work for us here — who has promised her marriage and a family. Such an intention would at least demonstrate an admirable desire to procreate.'

'As if. But no problem,' said Nicole.

'No problem what?' Aunt Lydia said crisply.

'No problem, Aunt Lydia,' said Nicole. 'I can write the note.'

* * *

At ten o'clock, when it was dark, Aunt Lydia reappeared at the door, carrying a bulky black cloth bag. Becka let her in. 'Blessed be, Aunt Lydia,' she said.

Aunt Lydia didn't bother with a formal greeting. 'I've brought everything you'll need. You will leave by the east gate at 6:30 a.m. precisely. There will be a black car waiting for you to the right of the gate. You will be driven out of this city as far as Portsmouth, New Hampshire, where you will take a bus. Here is a map, with the route marked. Get off at the X. The passwords there will be *May day* and *June moon*. The contact there will take you to your next destination. Nicole, if your mission is successful, those who murdered your adoptive parents will be revealed, if not held to account immediately. I can now tell both of you that if you do in fact reach Canada despite known obstacles, there is a not insignificant chance that you may — I say *may* — be reunited with your mother. She has been aware of that possibility for some time.'

'Oh, Agnes. Praise be — that would be so wonderful,' Becka said in a small voice. 'For both of you,' she added.

'I'm truly grateful to you, Aunt Lydia,' I said. 'I have prayed so long for such an outcome.'

'I said if you're successful. It's a big *if*,' said Aunt Lydia. 'Success is not a foregone conclusion. Excuse me.' She looked around, then sat down heavily on the sofa. 'I will trouble you for that glass of water now.' Becka went to get it.

'Are you all right, Aunt Lydia?' I asked.

'The minor infirmities of age,' she said. 'I hope you will live long enough to experience them. One more thing. Aunt Vidala is in the habit of taking an early-morning walk in the vicinity of my statue. If she sees you — dressed as Pearl Girls, as you will be — she will attempt to stop you. You must act quickly, before she can create a disturbance.'

'But what should we do?' I asked.

'You are strong,' said Aunt Lydia, looking at Nicole. 'Strength is a gift. Gifts should be employed.'

'You mean I should hit her?' said Nicole.

'That is a very direct way of putting it,' said Aunt Lydia.

★   ★   ★

After Aunt Lydia had gone, we opened the black cloth bag. There were the two dresses, the two sets of pearls, the two white hats, the two silver backpacks. There was a packet of brochures and an envelope with some Gilead food tokens, a bundle of Canadian paper money, and two credit cards. There were two passes to get us through the gates and checkpoints. There were also two bus tickets.

'Guess I'll write that note and go to bed,' said Nicole. 'See you in the a.m.' She was acting brave and unconcerned, but I could see she was nervous.

Once she was out of the room, Becka said, 'I really wish I was going with you.'

'I really wish you were coming too,' I said. 'But you'll be helping us. You'll be protecting us. And I'll find a way to get you out later, I promise.'

'I don't think there is a way,' said Becka. 'But I pray you are right.'

'Aunt Lydia said forty-eight hours. That means only two days. If you can hide that long . . .'

'I know where,' said Becka. 'On the roof. In the water cistern.'

'No, Becka! That's too dangerous!'

'Oh, I'll let all the water out first,' she said. 'I'll run it through the Doorway C bathtub.'

'They'll notice, Becka,' I said. 'In the A and B Doorways. If there isn't any water. They share our cistern.'

'They won't notice at first. We're not supposed to take baths or showers that early in the day.'

'Don't do it,' I said. 'Why don't I just not go?'

'You don't have a choice. If you stay here, what will happen to Nicole? And Aunt Lydia wouldn't want them interrogating you, and

460

making you tell about what she's planned. Or else Aunt Vidala would want to question you, and that would be the end.'

'Are you saying she'd kill me?'

'Eventually. Or someone would,' said Becka. 'It's what they do.'

'There must be a way we can take you,' I said. 'We can hide you in the car, or . . . '

'Pearl Girls only ever travel in twos,' she said. 'We wouldn't get far. I'll be with you in spirit.'

'Thank you, Becka,' I said. 'You *are* a sister to me.'

'I'll think of you as birds, flying away,' she said. 'A bird of the air will carry the voice.'

'I will pray for you,' I said. It did not seem adequate.

'And I for you.' She smiled slightly. 'I've never loved anyone but you.'

'I love you too,' I said. Then we hugged each other and cried a little.

'Get some sleep,' Becka said. 'You will need your strength for tomorrow.'

'You too,' I said.

'I will stay up,' she said. 'I'll do a vigil for you.' She went into her room, closing the door softly.

61

The next morning, Nicole and I slipped quietly out of Doorway C. The clouds in the east were pink and gold, the birds were chirping, the early-morning air was still fresh. There was no one else about. We walked quickly and quietly along the pathway in front of Ardua Hall, towards the statue of Aunt Lydia. Just as we got to it, Aunt Vidala came around the corner of the adjacent building, walking resolutely.

'Aunt Victoria!' she said. 'Why are you wearing that dress? The next Thanks Giving isn't until Sunday!' She peered at Nicole. 'And who is that with you? That's the new girl! Jade! She isn't supposed to — ' She reached out her hand and grabbed Nicole's strand of pearls, which broke.

Nicole did something with her fist. It was so fast I hardly saw it, but she hit Aunt Vidala in the chest. Aunt Vidala crumpled to the ground. Her face was pasty white, her eyes were closed.

'Oh no — ' I began to say.

'Help me,' said Nicole. She took Aunt Vidala by the feet and dragged her behind the base of the statue. 'Fingers crossed,' she said. 'Let's go.' She took me by the arm.

There was an orange on the ground. Nicole

picked it up and put it into her Pearl Girls dress pocket.

'Is she dead?' I whispered.

'Don't know,' said Nicole. 'Come on, we need to hurry.'

We reached the gate, we showed our passes, the Angels let us out. Nicole was holding her cloak shut so no one would see that her pearls were missing. There was a black car farther up the street to the right, as Aunt Lydia had said there would be. The driver did not turn his head as we got in.

'All set, ladies?' he said.

I said, 'Yes, thank you,' but Nicole said, 'We're not ladies.' I nudged her with my elbow.

'Don't talk to him like that,' I whispered.

'He's not a real Guardian,' she said. 'Aunt Lydia's not a moron.' She took the orange out of her pocket and began peeling it. The crisp scent of it filled the air. 'Want some?' she asked me. 'You can have half.'

'No thank you,' I said. 'It's not right to eat it.' It had been a sacred offering of a kind after all. She ate the whole orange.

She'll make a misstep, I was thinking. Someone will notice. She'll get us arrested.

62

I was feeling sorry that I'd punched Aunt Vidala, though not very sorry: if I hadn't hit her, she would have yelled and then we'd have been stopped. Even so, my heart was pounding. What if I'd actually killed her? But once they'd found her, dead or alive, there would be a hunt for us. We were in it up to the neck, as Ada would say.

Meanwhile, Agnes was acting offended in that silent, pinch-mouthed way the Aunts had of letting you know you'd crossed one of their lines. Most likely it was the orange. Maybe I shouldn't have taken it. Then I had a bad thought: dogs. Oranges are really scented. I started worrying about what to do with the peels.

My left arm had begun to itch again, around the O. Why was it taking so long to heal?

When Aunt Lydia was sticking the microdot into my arm, I'd thought her plan was brilliant, but now I felt it might not have been such a good idea. If my body and the message were one, what would happen if my body didn't make it to Canada? I could hardly cut off my arm and mail it.

★   ★   ★

Our car went through a couple of checkpoints — passports, Angels peering in the window to make sure we were us — but Agnes had told me to let the driver do the talking, and he did: Pearl Girls this and that, and how noble we were, and what sacrifices we were making. At one of them, the Angel said, 'Good luck on your mission.' At another one — farther out of town — they joked among themselves.

'Hope they don't bring back any ugly girls or sluts.'

'It's one or the other.' Laughs from both checkpoint Angels.

Agnes put her hand on my arm. 'Don't talk back,' she said.

When we'd reached the countryside and were on a highway, the driver handed us a couple of sandwiches: Gilead fake cheese. 'I guess this is breakfast,' I said to Agnes. 'Toe jam on white.'

'We should give thanks,' said Agnes in her pious Aunt's voice, so I guess she was still in a snit. It was weird to think of her as my sister; we were so unlike. But I hadn't really had time to figure any of that out.

'I'm glad to have a sister,' I said, to make peace.

'I'm glad too,' said Agnes. 'And I give thanks.' But she didn't sound very thankful.

'I give thanks too,' I said. Which was the end of that conversation. I thought of asking her how long we had to keep it up, this Gilead way of talking — couldn't we stop and act natural, now that we were escaping? But then, maybe for her it was natural. Maybe she didn't know another way.

*　　*　　*

In Portsmouth, New Hampshire, the driver of our car let us out at the bus station. 'Good luck, girls,' he said. 'Give 'em hell.'

'See? He's not a real Guardian,' I said, hoping to get Agnes talking again.

'Of course not,' she said. 'A real Guardian would never say 'hell.''

The bus station was old and crumbling, the women's washroom was a germ factory, and there was no place we could exchange our Gilead food tokens for anything a person would want. I was glad I'd eaten the orange. Agnes, however, was not squeamish, being used to the crap that passed for food at Ardua Hall, so she bought some kind of pretend doughnut with two of our tokens.

The minutes were ticking; I was getting jittery. We waited and waited, and finally a bus did come. Some people on board nodded at us when we got on, as they might to the military: a salute of the head. An older Econowife even said, 'God bless you.'

About ten miles along there was another checkpoint, but the Angels there were super polite to us. One of them said, 'You're very brave, heading into Sodom.' If I hadn't been so scared I might have laughed — the idea of Canada being Sodom was hilarious, considering how boring and ordinary it mostly was. It wasn't like there was a non-stop countrywide orgy going on.

Agnes squeezed my hand to tell me she would

466

do the talking. She had the Ardua Hall knack of keeping her face flat and calm. 'We are simply doing our service for Gilead,' she said in her underspoken robot Aunt's way, and the Angel said, 'Praise be.'

The ride got bumpier. They must have been keeping their road repair money for roads more people were likely to use: since trading with Canada was practically shut down nowadays, who'd want to go to North Gilead unless you lived there?

The bus wasn't full; everyone on it was Econoclass. We were on the scenic route, winding along the coast, but it wasn't all that scenic. There were a lot of closed-down motels and roadside restaurants, and more than one big red smiling lobster that was falling apart.

As we went north, the friendliness decreased: there were angry looks, and I had the feeling that our Pearl Girls mission and even the whole Gilead thing was leaking popularity. No one spat at us, but they scowled as if they would like to.

I wondered how far we had come. Agnes had the map that had been marked up by Aunt Lydia, but I didn't like to ask her to take it out: the two of us looking at a map would be suspicious. The bus was slow, and I was getting more and more anxious: How soon before someone noticed we weren't in Ardua Hall? Would they believe my bogus note? Would they call ahead, set up a roadblock, stop the bus? We were so conspicuous.

Then we took a detour, and it was one-way traffic, and Agnes started fidgeting with her hands. I nudged her with my elbow. 'We need to look serene, remember?' She gave me a wan smile and folded her hands in her lap; I could feel her taking deep breaths and letting them out slowly. They did teach you a few useful things at Ardua Hall, and self-control was one of them. *She who cannot control herself cannot control the path to duty. Do not fight the waves of anger, use the anger as your fuel. Inhale. Exhale. Sidestep. Circumvent. Deflect.*

I would never have made it as a real Aunt.

⋆ ⋆ ⋆

It was around five in the afternoon when Agnes said, 'We get off here.'

'Is this the border?' I said, and she said no, it was where we were supposed to meet our next ride. We took our backpacks off the rack and stepped down out of the bus. The town had boarded-up storefronts and smashed windows, but there was a fuel station and a shabby convenience store.

'This is encouraging,' I said gloomily

'Follow me and don't say anything,' Agnes said.

Inside, the store smelled like burnt toast and feet. There was hardly anything on the shelves, only a row of preserved food items with the lettering blacked out: canned goods and crackers or cookies. Agnes went up to the coffee counter — one of those red ones with bar stools — and sat down, so I did the same. There was a dumpy middle-aged Economan working the counter. In

Canada, it would've been a dumpy middle-aged woman.

'Yeah?' the man said. Clearly he wasn't impressed by our Pearl Girls outfits.

'Two coffees, please,' said Agnes.

He poured the coffees into mugs and shoved them across the counter. The coffee must have been sitting around all day because it was the worst I'd ever tasted, worse even than at Carpitz. I didn't want to annoy the guy by not drinking it, so I put in a packet of sugar. If anything, that made it worse.

'It's warm for a May day,' said Agnes.

'It's not May,' he said.

'Of course not,' she said. 'My mistake. There's a June moon.'

Now the guy was smiling. 'You need to use the washroom,' he said. 'Both of youse. It's through that door. I'll unlock it.'

We went through the door. It wasn't a washroom, it was an outside shed with old fishnets, a broken axe, a stack of buckets, and a back door. 'Don't know what took you so long,' said the man. 'Fucking bus, it's always late. Here's your new stuff. There's flashlights. Put your dresses in those backpacks, I'll dump them later. I'll be outside. We need to get a move on.'

The clothes were jeans and long T-shirts and wool socks and hiking boots. Plaid jackets, fleece pull-on hats, waterproof jackets. I had a little trouble with the left T-shirt sleeve — something caught on the O. I said, 'Fucking shit' and then, 'Sorry.' I don't think I've ever changed clothes so fast in my life, but once I got the silver dress off and those clothes on I began to feel more like myself.

63

I found the clothing provided for us disagreeable in the extreme. The underwear was very different from the plain, sturdy variety worn at Ardua Hall: to me it felt slippery and depraved. Over that there were male garments. It was disturbing to feel that rough cloth touching the skin of my legs, with no intervening petticoat. Wearing such clothing was gender treachery and against God's law: last year a man had been hanged on the Wall for dressing in his Wife's undergarments. She'd discovered him and turned him in, as was her duty.

'I have to take these off,' I said to Nicole. 'They're men's garments.'

'No, they're not,' she said. 'Those are girls' jeans. They're cut differently, and look at the little silver Cupids. Definitely girls'.'

'They'd never believe that in Gilead,' I said. 'I'd be flogged or worse.'

'Gilead,' said Nicole, 'is not where we're going. We've got two minutes to join our buddy outside. So suck it up.'

'Pardon?' Sometimes I could not make out what my sister was saying.

She laughed a little. 'It means 'be brave,'' she said.

We are going to a place where she will understand the language, I thought. And I will not.

* * *

The man had a battered pickup. The three of us squashed into the front seat. It was beginning to drizzle.

'Thank you for all you are doing for us,' I said. The man grunted.

'I get paid,' he said. 'For putting my neck in the noose. I'm too old for this.'

The driver must have been drinking while we were changing our clothes: I could smell the alcohol. I remembered that smell from the dinner parties Commander Kyle would have when I was young. Rosa and Vera used to finish up what was left in the glasses sometimes. Zilla, not as much.

Now that I was about to leave Gilead forever, I was feeling homesick for Zilla and Rosa and Vera, and for my former home, and for Tabitha. In those early times I was not motherless, but now I felt that I was. Aunt Lydia had been a mother of sorts, although a harsh one, and I would not see her again. Aunt Lydia had told Nicole and me that our real mother was alive and waiting for us in Canada, but I wondered if I would die on the way there. If so, I would never meet her at all in this life. Right then she was only a torn-up picture. She was an absence, a gap inside me.

Despite the alcohol, the man drove well and

472

quickly. The road was winding, and slick because of the drizzle. The miles went by; the moon had risen above the clouds, silvering the black outlines of the treetops. There was the occasional house, either dark or with only a few lights on. I made a conscious effort to quell my anxieties; then I fell asleep.

I dreamed of Becka. She was there beside me in the front of the truck. I couldn't see her, though I knew she was there. I said to her in the dream, 'So you came with us after all. I'm so happy.' But she didn't answer.

Transcript of Witness Testimony 369B

64

The night slid by in silence. Agnes was asleep, and the guy driving was not what you'd call talkative. I guess he thought of us as cargo to be delivered, and who ever talked to the cargo?

After a while we turned down a narrow side road; water glinted ahead. We pulled in beside what looked like a private dock. There was a motorboat with someone sitting in it.

'Wake her up,' the driver said. 'Take your stuff, there's your boat.'

I poked Agnes in the ribs and she started awake.

'Rise and shine,' I said.

'What time is it?'

'Boat time. Let's go.'

'Have a good trip,' said our driver. Agnes started thanking him some more, but he cut her off. He tossed our new backpacks out of the truck and was gone before we were halfway to the boat. I was using my flashlight so we could see the path.

'Turn out the light,' the person in the boat called softly. It was a man, wearing a waterproof with the hood up, but the voice sounded young. 'You can see okay. Take it slow. Sit on the middle seat.'

'Is this the ocean?' Agnes asked.

He laughed. 'Not yet,' he said. 'This is the Penobscot River. You'll get to the ocean soon enough.'

The motor was electric and very quiet. The boat went right down the middle of the river; there was a crescent moon, and the water was reflecting it.

'Look,' Agnes whispered. 'I've never seen anything so beautiful! It's like a trail of light!' At that moment I felt older than her. We were almost outside Gilead now, and the rules were changing. She was going to a new place where she wouldn't know how things were done, but I was going home.

'We're right out in the open. What if anyone sees us?' I asked the man. 'What if they tell them? The Eyes?'

'People around here don't talk to the Eyes,' he said. 'We don't like snoops.'

'Are you a smuggler?' I said, remembering what Ada had told me. My sister nudged me: bad manners again. You avoided blunt questions in Gilead.

He laughed. 'Borders — lines on a map. Things move across, people too. I'm just the delivery boy.'

The river got wider and wider. The mist was rising; the shores were vague.

'There she is,' the man said finally I could see a darker shadow, out on the water. 'The *Nellie J. Banks*. Your ticket to paradise.'

XXIII

Wall

The Ardua Hall Holograph

65

Aunt Vidala was discovered lying behind my statue in a comatose condition by elderly Aunt Clover and two of her septuagenarian gardeners. The conclusion the paramedics came to was that she'd had a stroke, a diagnosis confirmed by our doctors. Rumour sped round Ardua Hall, sad shakes of the head were exchanged, and prayers for Aunt Vidala's recovery were promised. A broken Pearl Girls necklace was found in the vicinity: someone must have lost it at some point, a wasteful oversight. I will issue a memorandum about vigilance in regard to those material objects it is our duty to safeguard. Pearls do not grow on trees, I will say, even artificial ones; nor should they be cast before swine. Not that there are any swine at Ardua Hall, I will add coyly.

I paid Aunt Vidala a visit in the Intensive Care Unit. She was lying on her back with her eyes closed and a tube going into her nose and another one going into her arm. 'How is our dear Aunt Vidala?' I asked the nursing Aunt on duty.

'I have been praying for her,' said Aunt Something. I can never remember the names of the nurses: it is their fate. 'She's in a coma: that may aid the healing process. There may be some paralysis. They're afraid her speech might be affected.'

'If she recovers,' I said.

'When she recovers,' the nurse said reproachfully. 'We don't like to voice anything negative within the hearing of our patients. They may appear to be asleep, but frequently they are fully aware.'

I sat beside Vidala until the nurse had gone. Then I made a rapid inspection of the pharmaceutical aids available. Should I up the anaesthetic? Tamper with the tube feeding into her arm? Pinch off her oxygen supply? I did none of these. I believe in effort, but not in unnecessary effort: Aunt Vidala was most likely negotiating her exit from this world all on her own. Before leaving the Intensive Care Unit, I pocketed a small vial of morphine, foresight being a cardinal virtue.

★ ★ ★

While we were taking our lunchtime places in the Refectory, Aunt Helena commented on the absence of Aunt Victoria and Aunt Immortelle. 'I believe they are fasting,' I said. 'I glimpsed them in the Hildegard Library Reading Room yesterday, studying their Bibles. They are hoping for guidance during their upcoming mission.'

'Commendable,' said Aunt Helena. She continued her discreet head-counting. 'Where is our new convert, Jade?'

'Perhaps she is ill,' I said. 'A female complaint.'

'I will go and see,' said Aunt Helena. 'Perhaps she needs a hot water bottle. Doorway C, is it?'

'How kind of you,' I said. 'Yes. I believe hers is the garret room on the third floor.' I hoped Nicole had left her elopement note in a prominent location.

Aunt Helena hurried back from her visit to Doorway C, giddy with the excitement of her discovery: the girl Jade had eloped. 'With a plumber named Garth,' Aunt Helena added. 'She claims to be in love.'

'That is unfortunate,' I said. 'We shall have to locate the pair, administer a reprimand, and make sure that the marriage has been properly performed. But Jade is very uncouth; she would not have made a reputable Aunt. Look on the bright side: the population of Gilead may well be augmented by this union.'

'But how could she have met such a plumber?' said Aunt Elizabeth.

'There was a complaint about a lack of bathwater this morning from Doorway A,' I said. 'They must have called in the plumber. Clearly it was love at first sight. Young people are impetuous.'

'No one in the Hall is supposed to take baths in the morning,' said Aunt Elizabeth. 'Unless someone has been breaking the rules.'

'That is not out of the question, unfortunately,' I said. 'The flesh is weak.'

'Oh yes, so weak,' Aunt Helena agreed. 'But how did she get out through the gate? She doesn't have a pass, it wouldn't have been allowed.'

'Girls of that age are very agile,' I said. 'I expect she climbed over the Wall.'

We continued with lunch — dry sandwiches and something ruinous that had been done to tomatoes, and a dessert of runny blancmange — and by the end of our humble meal the girl Jade's premature flight, her acrobatic feat of Wall-climbing, and her headstrong choice to fulfill her womanly destiny in the arms of an enterprising Economan plumber were general knowledge among us.

XXIV

THE *NELLIE J. BANKS*

66

We pulled up beside the ship. On the deck were three shadows; a flashlight shone briefly. We climbed up the rope ladder.

'Sit on the edge, swing your feet over,' said a voice. Someone took my arm. Then we were standing on the deck.

'Captain Mishimengo,' said the voice. 'Let's get you inside.' There was a low hum and I felt the ship moving.

We went into a little cabin with blackout curtains on the windows and some controls and what was likely a ship's radar, though I didn't have a chance to look at it closely.

'Glad you made it,' said Captain Mishimengo. He shook our hands; he had two fingers missing. He was stocky, about sixty, with tanned skin and a short black beard. 'Now here's our story, supposing you're asked: this is a cod schooner, solar, with fuel backup. Flag of convenience is Lebanon. We've delivered a cargo of cod and lemons by special licence, which means the grey market, and now we're heading back out. You'll need to stay out of sight during the day: I heard from my contact, via Bert who dropped you at the dock, that they're bound to be looking for you soon. There's a place for you to sleep, in the hold. If there's an inspection, coast guard, it won't be thorough, it's guys we know.' He rubbed his fingers together, which I knew meant money.

'Have you got any food?' I asked. 'We haven't eaten much all day.'

'Right,' he said. He told us to wait there and came back with a couple mugs of tea and some sandwiches. They were cheese, but it wasn't Gilead cheese, it was real cheese: goat cheese with chives, a kind Melanie had liked.

'Thank you,' said Agnes. I'd started eating but I mumbled thanks with my mouth full.

'Your friend Ada says hello, and see you soon,' Captain Mishimengo said to me.

I swallowed. 'How do you know Ada?'

He laughed. 'Everyone's related. Around here, anyways. We used to go deer-hunting in Nova Scotia together, back in the day.'

★ ★ ★

We reached our sleeping place by going down a ladder. Captain Mishimengo went first, turning on the lights. There were some freezers in the hold, and some big oblong metal boxes. On the side of one of the boxes was a hinged flap, and inside were two sleeping bags that didn't look very clean: I guess we weren't the first people to use them. The whole place smelled of fish.

'You can keep the box door open as long as there's no problems,' said Captain Mishimengo. 'Sleep tight, don't let the bugs bite.' We heard his steps receding.

'This is kind of awful,' I whispered to Agnes.

486

'The fish smell. These sleeping bags. I bet they have lice.'

'We should be grateful,' she said. 'Let's go to sleep.'

My GOD/LOVE tattoo was bothering me, and I had to lie on my right side to avoid squashing it. I wondered if I had blood poisoning. If so, I was in trouble because there was definitely not a doctor on board.

★ ★ ★

We woke up when it was still dark because the ship was rocking. Agnes climbed out of our metal box and went up the ladder to see what was happening. I wanted to go too but I really wasn't feeling well.

She came back down with a thermos of tea and two hard-boiled eggs. We'd reached the ocean, she said, and the waves were rocking the ship. She'd never imagined waves that big, though Captain Mishimengo said they were nothing much.

'Oh God,' I said. 'I hope they won't get any bigger. I hate throwing up.'

'Please do not use the name of God as a casual swear word,' she said.

'Sorry,' I said. 'But if you don't mind me saying, supposing there is a God, he has totally effed up my life.'

I thought she'd get angry then, but all she said was, 'You are not unique in the universe. No one has an easy time in life. But maybe God has effed up — as you put it — your life for a reason.'

'And I can hardly fucking wait to find out what that is,' I said. The pain in my arm was making me very irritable. I shouldn't have been so sarcastic, and I shouldn't have sworn at her.

'But I thought you grasped the true goal of our mission,' she said. 'The salvation of Gilead. The purification. The renewal. That is the reason.'

'You think that festering shitheap can be renewed?' I said. 'Burn it all down!'

'Why would you want to harm so many people?' she asked gently. 'It's my country. It's where I grew up. It's being ruined by the leaders. I want it to be better.'

'Yeah, okay,' I said. 'I get it. Sorry. I didn't mean you. You're my sister.'

'I accept your apology' she said. 'Thank you for understanding.'

We sat in the dark silence for a few minutes. I could hear her breathing, and a few sighs.

'You think this is going to work?' I asked finally. 'Will we get there?'

'It's not in our hands,' she said.

67

By the beginning of our second day, I was very worried about Nicole. She claimed she wasn't ill, but she had a fever. I recalled what we'd been taught at Ardua Hall about caring for the sick, and I attempted to keep her hydrated. There were some lemons on board, and I was able to mix some of their juice with tea and salt and a little sugar. I was finding it easier now to go up and down the ladder that led to our sleeping quarters, and reflected that it would have been much harder in a long skirt.

It was quite foggy. We were still in Gileadean waters, and around noon there was a coast guard inspection. Nicole and I shut the door of our metal box from the inside. She took hold of my hand and I squeezed it hard, and we stayed absolutely quiet. We heard footsteps tramping around, and voices, but the sounds dwindled and my heart stopped beating so quickly.

Later that day there was engine trouble, which I discovered when I went up for more lemon juice. Captain Mishimengo seemed worried: the tides in this region were very high and fast, he said, and without power we'd be swept out to sea, or else we'd be drawn into the Bay of Fundy and wrecked on the Canadian shore, and the ship would be impounded and the crew arrested. The ship was drifting south; did this mean we would be taken right back into Gilead?

I wondered if Captain Mishimengo was wishing he hadn't agreed to take us. He'd told me that if the ship should be pursued and captured, and we were found, he'd be accused of woman-smuggling. His ship would be seized, and since he himself was originally from Gilead and had escaped from the Gilead National Homelands via the Canadian border, they'd claim him as a citizen and put him on trial as a smuggler, and that would be the end of him.

'We're putting you in too much danger,' I said when I heard this. 'Don't you have an arrangement with the coast guard? About the grey market?'

'They'd deny it, there's nothing in writing,' he said. 'Who wants to be shot for taking bribes?'

* * *

For supper there were chicken sandwiches, but Nicole wasn't hungry and wanted to sleep.

'Are you very ill? May I feel your forehead?' Her skin was burning hot. 'I would just like to say that I'm grateful for you in my life,' I told her. 'I'm happy you are my sister.'

'I am too,' she said. After a minute she asked, 'Do you think we'll ever see our mother?'

'I have faith that we will.'

'Do you think she'll like us?'

'She will love us,' I said to soothe her. 'And we will love her.'

490

'Just because people are related to you doesn't mean you love them,' she murmured.

'Love is a discipline, like prayer,' I said. 'I'd like to pray for you, so you'll feel better. Would you mind?'

'It won't work. I won't feel any better.'

'But I will feel better,' I said. So she said yes.

'Dear God,' I said, 'may we accept the past with all its flaws, may we move forward into a better future in forgiveness and loving kindness. And may we each be thankful for our sister, and may we both see our mother again, and our two different fathers as well. And may we remember Aunt Lydia, and may she be forgiven for her sins and faults, as we hope we may be forgiven for ours. And may we always feel gratitude to our sister Becka, wherever she may be. Please bless all of them. Amen.'

By the time I'd finished, Nicole was asleep.

I tried to sleep myself, but it was stuffier than ever in the hold. Then I heard footsteps coming down the metal ladder. It was Captain Mishimengo. 'Sorry about this, but we need to offload you,' he said.

'Now?' I said. 'But it's night.'

'Sorry,' Captain Mishimengo said again. 'We got the motor going, but we're low on power. We're now in Canadian waters but nowhere close to where we were supposed to take you. We can't get to a harbour, it's too dangerous for us. The tide is against us.'

He said we were off the east shore of the Bay of Fundy. All Nicole and I had to do was reach that shore and we'd be fine; whereas he couldn't risk his ship and crew.

Nicole was sound asleep; I had to shake her awake.

'It's me,' I said. 'It's your sister.'

Captain Mishimengo repeated the same story to her: we had to leave the *Nellie J. Banks* right now.

'So, you want us to swim?' said Nicole.

'We'll put you in an inflatable,' he said. 'I've called ahead, they'll be expecting you.'

'She's not well,' I said. 'Can't it be tomorrow?'

'Nope,' said Captain Mishimengo. 'The tide's turning. Miss this window and you'll be swept out to sea. Warmest clothes, be on deck in ten minutes.'

'Warmest clothes?' said Nicole. 'Like we brought an Arctic wardrobe.'

We put on all the clothes we had. Boots, fleece hats, our waterproofs. Nicole went up the ladder first: she wasn't very steady, and she was using only her right arm.

On deck Captain Mishimengo was waiting for us with one of the crew members. They had some life jackets and a thermos for us. On the left side of the ship a wall of fog was rolling towards us.

'Thank you,' I said to Captain Mishimengo. 'For everything you've done for us.'

'Sorry it's not as planned,' he said. 'Godspeed.'

'Thank you,' I said again. 'And Godspeed to you.'

'Keep out of the fog if you can.'

'Great,' said Nicole. 'Fog. That's all we need.'

'It may be a blessing,' I said.

They lowered us down in the inflatable. There was a little solar motor: it was really simple to operate, Captain Mishimengo said: Power, Idle, Forward, Reverse. There were two oars.

'Shove off,' said Nicole.

'Pardon?'

'Push our boat away from the *Nellie*. Not with your hands! Here — use an oar.'

I did manage to push, but not very well. I'd never held an oar. I felt very clumsy. 'Goodbye, *Nellie J. Banks*,' I said. 'God bless!'

'Don't bother waving, they can't see you,' said Nicole. 'They must be glad to be rid of us, we're toxic cargo.'

'They were nice,' I said.

'You think they're not making big piles of money?'

The *Nellie J. Banks* was moving away from us. I hoped they'd have good luck.

I could feel the tide gripping the inflatable. Head in at an angle, Captain Mishimengo had said: cutting straight across the tide was dangerous, the inflatable could flip.

'Hold my flashlight,' Nicole said. She was fiddling with the buttons on the motor, using her right hand. The motor started. 'This tide's like a river.' We were indeed moving quickly. There were some lights on the shore to our left, very far away. It was cold, the kind of cold that goes right through all your clothing.

'Are we getting there?' I said after a while. 'To the shore?'

'I hope so,' said Nicole. 'Because if not, we'll

soon be back in Gilead.'

'We could jump overboard,' I said. We could not go back to Gilead, no matter what: they must have discovered by now that Nicole was missing, and had not gone with an Economan. We couldn't betray Becka and all she had done for us. It would be better to die.

'Fucking hell,' said Nicole. 'The motor just kakked.'

'Oh no,' I said. 'Can you . . . '

'I'm trying. Shit and fuck!'

'What? What is it?' I had to raise my voice: the fog was all around us, and the sound of the water.

'Electrical short, I think,' said Nicole. 'Or low battery.'

'Did they do that on purpose?' I said. 'Maybe they want us to die.'

'No way!' said Nicole. 'Why would they kill the customers? Now we have to row.'

'Row?' I said.

'Yeah, with the oars,' said Nicole. 'I can only use my good arm, the other one's like a puffball, and don't fucking ask me what a puffball is!'

'It's not my fault I don't know such things,' I said.

'You want to have this conversation right now? I am fucking sorry, but we are in a hot mess emergency here! Now, grab the oar!'

'All right,' I said. 'There. I have hold of it.'

'Put it in the oarlock. The oarlock! This thing! Now, use both hands. Okay, now watch me! When I say go, put the oar in the water and pull,' said Nicole. She was shouting.

'I don't know how. I feel so useless.'

'Stop crying,' said Nicole. 'I don't care how you feel! Just do it! Now! When I say go, pull the oar towards you! See the light? It's nearer!'

'I don't think it is,' I said. 'We're so far out. We'll be swept away.'

'No we won't,' said Nicole. 'Not if you try. Now, go! And, go! That's it! Go! Go! Go!'

XXV

Wakeup

The Ardua Hall Holograph

68

Aunt Vidala has opened her eyes. She has not yet said anything. Does she have a mind in there? Does she remember seeing the girl Jade wearing a silver Pearl Girls dress? Does she remember the blow that must have knocked her out? Will she say so? If yes to the first, then yes to the second. She'll put two and two together — who but I could have facilitated this scenario? Any denunciation she makes of me to a nurse will go straight to the Eyes; and then the clock will stop. I must take precautions. But what and how?

Rumour at Ardua Hall has it that her stroke was not spontaneous but was the result of some shock, or even of some attack. From the heel marks in the soil, it would appear that she was dragged around to the back of my statue. She has been removed from the Intensive Care Unit to a recovery ward, and Aunt Elizabeth and Aunt Helena are taking turns sitting beside her bed, waiting for her first words, each suspicious of the other; so it is not possible for me to be with her alone.

The elopement note has been the subject of much speculation. The plumber was an excellent touch: such a convincing detail. I am proud of Nicole's ingenuity, and trust it will stand her in good stead in the immediate future. The ability to concoct plausible lies is a talent not to be underestimated.

Naturally my opinion was sought as to the proper procedure. Should there not be a search? The girl's present location did not matter much, I said, so long as marriage and progeny were the goals; but Aunt Elizabeth said that the man may have been a lecherous imposter, or even a Mayday agent who'd infiltrated the Ardua Hall grounds in disguise; in either case, he would take advantage of the girl Jade and then abandon her, after which she would be fit for nothing more than the life of a Handmaid; so we should find her at once and arrest the man for interrogation.

Had there been an actual man, this would have been a favoured course of action: sensible girls do not elope in Gilead and well-meaning men do not elope with them. So I had to acquiesce, and a search team of Angels was sent out to sift through the houses and streets in the vicinity. They were less than enthusiastic: chasing after deluded young girls was not their idea of heroism. Needless to say, the girl Jade was not found; nor was any Mayday false plumber unearthed.

Aunt Elizabeth gave it as her opinion that there was something very suspicious about the whole affair. I agreed with her, and said I was as puzzled as she was. But what — I asked her — could be done? A cold trail was a cold trail. We must await developments.

★　★　★

500

Commander Judd was not so easily deflected. He called me into his office for an emergency meeting. 'You've lost Baby Nicole.' He was trembling with suppressed rage, and also fear: to have had Baby Nicole within his grasp, and to have let her slip — this would not be forgiven by the Council. 'Who else knows her identity?'

'No one else,' I said. 'You. Me. And Nicole herself, of course — I did see fit to share that information with her, in order to convince her of her high destiny. No one else.'

'They mustn't find out! How could you let this happen? To bring her in to Gilead, then allow her to be whisked away . . . The reputation of the Eyes will suffer, not to mention that of the Aunts.'

It was more enjoyable than I can well express to watch Judd writhe, but I put on a dismal face. 'We were taking every precaution,' I said. 'Either she really has absconded, or she's been abducted. If the latter, those responsible must be working with Mayday.'

I was buying time. One is always buying something.

★　★　★

I counted the hours as they passed. The hours, the minutes, the seconds. I had good reason to hope that my messengers were well on their way, carrying with them the seeds of Gilead's collapse. Not for nothing had I been photographing the Ardua Hall top-classification crime files over so many years.

Two Pearl Girls backpacks were discovered beside the entrance to a disused hiking trail in Vermont. Inside them were two Pearl Girls dresses, some orange peels, and one string of pearls. A search of the area was instituted, with sniffer dogs. No result.

Red herrings, so distracting.

★ ★ ★

The Works Department has investigated the shortage of water complained of by the Aunts living in Doorways A and B and has discovered poor Aunt Immortelle in the cistern, blocking the outlet. The frugal child had removed her outer clothing so as to save it for someone else's future use; it was found, neatly folded, on the top rung of the ladder. She'd retained her undergarments for purposes of modesty. It's how I would have expected her to behave. Don't think I am not saddened by her loss; but I remind myself that it was a willing sacrifice.

This news caused another outbreak of speculation: the rumour was that Aunt Immortelle had been murdered, and who more likely to have done it than the missing Canadian recruit known as Jade? Many of the Aunts — among them those who had greeted her arrival with such joy and satisfaction — were now saying that they'd always believed there was something fraudulent about her.

'It's a terrible scandal,' said Aunt Elizabeth. 'It reflects so badly on us!'

'We will cover it up,' I said. 'I shall take the

view that Aunt Immortelle was simply trying to investigate the faulty cistern, in order to spare valuable manpower that chore. She must have slipped, or fainted. It was an accident in the course of selfless duty. That is what I shall say at the dignified and laudatory funeral we will now proceed to have.'

'That is a stroke of genius,' said Aunt Helena dubiously.

'Do you think anyone will believe it?' Aunt Elizabeth asked.

'They will believe whatever is in the best interests of Ardua Hall,' I said firmly. 'Which is the same as their own best interests.'

★   ★   ★

But speculation grew. Two Pearl Girls had passed through the gate — the Angels on duty swore to that — and their papers were in order. Was one of them Aunt Victoria, who still had not appeared for meals? If not, where was she? And if so, why had she left early on her mission, before the Thanks Giving? She had not been accompanied by Aunt Immortelle, so who was the second Pearl Girl? Could it be that Aunt Victoria was complicit in a double escape? For, increasingly, it was looking like an escape. It was concluded that the elopement note had been part of it: intended to deceive, and to delay pursuit. How devious and cunning young girls could be, the Aunts whispered — especially foreigners.

Then news came that two Pearl Girls had been

spotted at the Portsmouth bus station in New Hampshire. Commander Judd ordered a search operation: these imposters — he called them that — must be captured and brought back for interrogation. They must not be allowed to speak to anyone but himself. In the case of a probable escape, the orders were to shoot to kill.

'That is somewhat harsh,' I said. 'They are inexperienced. They must have been misled.'

'Under the circumstances, a dead Baby Nicole is much more useful to us than a living one,' he said. 'Surely you realize that, Aunt Lydia.'

'I apologize for my stupidity,' I said. 'I believed that she was genuine; I mean, genuine in her desire to join us. It would have been a marvellous coup, had that been the case.'

'It's clear she was a plant, inserted into Gilead under false pretenses. Alive, she could pull both of us down. Don't you understand how vulnerable we would be if anyone else got hold of her and she were made to talk? I would lose all credibility. The long knives will come out, and not just for me: your reign at Ardua Hall will be over, and so — quite frankly — will you.'

He loves me, he loves me not: I am assuming the status of a mere tool, to be used and discarded. But that's a two-handed game.

'Very true,' I said. 'Some in our country are unfortunately obsessed with vengeful payback. They do not believe that you have always acted for the best, especially in your winnowing operations. But in this matter you have chosen the wisest option, as ever.'

That got a smile out of him, albeit a tense one.

I had a flashback, not for the first time. In my brown sackcloth robe I raised the gun, aimed, shot. A bullet, or no bullet?

A bullet.

★ ★ ★

I went to visit Aunt Vidala again. Aunt Elizabeth was on duty, knitting one of the little caps for premature babies that are in fashion nowadays. I remain deeply grateful that I have never learned to knit.

Vidala's eyes were closed. She was breathing evenly: worse luck.

'Has she spoken yet?' I asked.

'No, not a word,' said Aunt Elizabeth. 'Not while I've been here.'

'Good of you to be so attentive,' I said, 'but you must be tired. I'll spell you off. Go and get a cup of tea.' She threw me a suspicious look, but she went.

Once she was out of the room I leaned over and spoke loudly into Vidala's ear. 'Wake up!'

Her eyes opened. She focused on me. Then she whispered, with no slurring: 'You did this, Lydia. You'll hang for it.' Her expression was both vindictive and triumphant: finally she had an accusation that would stick, and my job was very nearly hers.

'You're tired,' I said. 'Go back to sleep.' She closed her eyes again.

I was rummaging in my pocket for the vial of morphine I'd brought with me when Elizabeth walked in. 'I forgot my knitting,' she said.

'Vidala spoke. When you were out of the room.'

'What did she say?'

'She must have some brain damage,' I said. 'She's accusing you of having struck her. She said you were in league with Mayday.'

'But no one can possibly believe her,' Elizabeth said, blanching. 'If anyone hit her, it must have been that Jade girl!'

'Belief is hard to predict,' I said. 'Some might find it expedient to have you denounced. Not all of the Commanders appreciated the ignominious exit of Dr. Grove. I have heard it said that you are unreliable — if you accused Grove, who else might you accuse? — in which case they will accept Vidala's testimony against you. People like a scapegoat.'

She sat down. 'This is a disaster,' she said.

'We've been in tight spots before, Elizabeth,' I said mildly. 'Remember the Thank Tank. We both made it out of that. Since then, we have done what was necessary.'

'You are so bolstering, Lydia,' she said.

'Such a shame about Vidala's allergies,' I said. 'I hope she won't suffer an asthmatic attack while sleeping. Now I must rush off, as I have a meeting. I will leave Vidala in your nurturing hands. I notice that her pillow needs rearranging.'

Two birds with one stone: if so, how satisfactory in ways both aesthetic and practical, and a diversion that will create more runway. Though not ultimately for me, as there is scant chance I myself will escape unscathed from the revelations that are sure to follow once Nicole appears on the television news in Canada and the cache of evidence she is carrying for me is displayed.

★ ★ ★

The clock ticks, the minutes pass. I wait. I wait.

Fly well, my messengers, my silver doves, my destroying angels. Land safely.

XXVI

LANDFALL

Transcript of Witness Testimony 369A

69

I don't know how long we were in the inflatable. It felt like hours. I'm sorry I can't be more precise.

There was fog. The waves were very high, and spray and water were coming in on top of us. It was cold as death. The tide was fast, and it was sweeping us out to sea. I was more than frightened: I thought we were going to die. The inflatable would be swamped, we would be thrown into the ocean, we would sink down and down. Aunt Lydia's message would be lost, and all the sacrifices would be for nothing.

Dear God, I prayed silently. Please help us get safe to land. And, If someone else has to die, let it be only me.

We were rowing and rowing. We each had an oar. I'd never been in a boat before so I didn't know how to do it. I felt weak and tired, and my arms were cramping with the pain.

'I can't,' I said.

'Keep going!' Nicole shouted. 'We're okay!'

The sound of the waves hitting the shore was close, but it was so dark I couldn't see where the shore was. Then a very big wave came right into the boat, and Nicole called, 'Row! Row for your life!'

There was a crunch, which must have been gravel, and another big wave came, and the inflatable tipped sideways, and we were hurled up onto the land. I was on my knees in the water, I was knocked over by another wave, but I managed to right myself, and Nicole's hand reached down out of the dark and pulled me up over some large boulders. Then we were standing, out of the reach of the ocean. I was shivering, my teeth were chattering together, my hands and feet were numb. Nicole threw her arms around me.

'We made it! We made it! I thought we were dead!' she shouted. 'I sure as hell hope this is the right shore!' She was laughing but also gasping for air.

I said in my heart, Dear God. Thank you.

Transcript of Witness Testimony 369B

70

It was really close. We almost kicked the bucket. We could have been swept out with the tide and ended up in South America, but more likely picked up by Gilead and strung up on the Wall. I'm so proud of Agnes — after that night she was really my sister. She kept on going even though she was at the end. There was no way I could have rowed the inflatable by myself.

The rocks were treacherous. There was a lot of slippery seaweed. I couldn't see very well because it was so dark. Agnes was beside me, which was a good thing because by that time I was delirious. My left arm felt as if it wasn't mine — as if it was detached from me and was just held on to my body by the sleeve.

We clambered over big rocks and sloshed through pools of water, slipping and sliding. I didn't know where we were going, but as long as we went uphill it would be away from the waves. I was almost asleep, I was so tired. I was thinking, I've made it this far and now I'm going to lose it and fall and brain myself. Becka said, *It's not much farther.* I couldn't remember her being in the inflatable but she was beside us on the beach, I couldn't see her because it was too dark. Then she said, *Look up there. Follow the lights.*

Someone shouted from a cliff overhead. There were lights moving along the top, and a voice yelled, 'There they are!' And another one called, 'Over here!' I was too tired to yell back. Then it got sandier, and the lights moved down a hill towards us along to the right.

Holding one of them was Ada. 'You did it,' she said, and I said, 'Yeah,' and then I fell over. Someone picked me up and started carrying me. It was Garth. He said, 'What'd I tell you? Way to go! I knew you'd make it.' That made me grin.

We went up a hill and there were bright lights and people with television cameras, and a voice said, 'Give us a smile.' And then I blacked out.

★   ★   ★

They airlifted us to the Campobello Refugee Medical Centre and stuffed antibiotics into me, so when I woke up my arm wasn't so puffy and sore.

My sister, Agnes, was there beside the bed, wearing jeans and a sweatshirt that said RUN FOR OUR LIFE, HELP FIGHT LIVER CANCER. I thought that was funny because that's what we'd been doing: running for our lives. She was holding my hand. Ada was there beside her, and Elijah, and Garth. They were all grinning like mad.

My sister said to me, 'It's a miracle. You saved our lives.'

'We're really proud of both of you,' said Elijah. 'Though I'm sorry about the inflatable — they were supposed to take you into the harbour.'

514

'You're all over the news,' said Ada. ' "Sisters defy the odds.' 'Baby Nicole's daring escape from Gilead.'"

'Also the document cache,' said Elijah. 'That's been on the news too. It's explosive. So many crimes, among the top brass in Gilead — it's much more than we've ever hoped for. The Canadian media are releasing one disruptive secret after another, and pretty soon heads will roll. Our Gilead source really came through for us.'

'Is Gilead gone?' I said. I felt happy but also unreal, as if it hadn't been me doing the things we'd done. How could we have taken those risks? What had carried us through?

'Not yet,' said Elijah. 'But it's the beginning.'

'Gilead News is saying it's all fake,' said Garth. 'A Mayday plot.'

Ada gave a short growly laugh. 'Of course that's what they'd say.'

'Where's Becka?' I asked. I was feeling dizzy again, so I closed my eyes.

'Becka's not here,' Agnes said gently. 'She didn't come with us. Remember?'

'She did come. She was there on the beach,' I whispered. 'I heard her.'

★ ★ ★

I think I went to sleep. Then I was awake again. 'Does she still have a fever?' said a voice.

'What happened?' I said.

'Shh,' said my sister. 'It's all right. Our mother is here. She's been so worried about you. Look,

515

she's right beside you.'

I opened my eyes, and it was very bright, but there was a woman standing there. She looked sad and happy, both at once; she was crying a little. She looked almost like the picture in the Bloodlines file, only older.

I felt it must be her, so I reached up my arms, the good one and the healing one, and our mother bent over my hospital bed, and we gave each other a one-armed hug. She only used the one arm because she had her other arm around Agnes, and she said, 'My darling girls.'

She smelled right. It was like an echo, of a voice you can't quite hear.

And she smiled a little and said, 'Of course you don't remember me. You were too young.'

And I said, 'No. I don't. But it's okay.'

And my sister said, 'Not yet. But I will.'

Then I went back to sleep.

XXVII

Sendoff

The Ardua Hall Holograph

71

Our time together is drawing short, my reader. Possibly you will view these pages of mine as a fragile treasure box, to be opened with the utmost care. Possibly you will tear them apart, or burn them: that often happens to words.

Perhaps you'll be a student of history, in which case I hope you'll make something useful of me: a warts-and-all portrait, a definitive account of my life and times, suitably footnoted; though if you don't accuse me of bad faith I will be astonished. Or, in fact, not astonished: I will be dead, and the dead are hard to astonish.

I picture you as a young woman, bright, ambitious. You'll be looking to make a niche for yourself in whatever dim, echoing caverns of academia may still exist by your time. I situate you at your desk, your hair tucked back behind your ears, your nail polish chipped — for nail polish will have returned, it always does. You're frowning slightly, a habit that will increase as you age. I hover behind you, peering over your shoulder: your muse, your unseen inspiration, urging you on.

You'll labour over this manuscript of mine, reading and rereading, picking nits as you go, developing the fascinated but also bored hatred

519

biographers so often come to feel for their subjects. How can I have behaved so badly, so cruelly, so stupidly? you will ask. You yourself would never have done such things! But you yourself will never have had to.

* * *

And so we come to my end. It's late: too late for Gilead to prevent its coming destruction. I'm sorry I won't live to see it — the conflagration, the downfall. And it's late in my life. And it's late at night: a cloudless night, as I observed while walking here. The full moon is out, casting her equivocal corpse-glow over all. Three Eyes saluted me as I passed them: in moonlight their faces were skulls, as mine must have been to them.

They will come too late, the Eyes. My messengers have flown. When worst comes to worst — as it will very soon — I'll make a quick exit. A needleful or two of morphine will do it. Best that way: if I allowed myself to live, I would disgorge too much truth. Torture is like dancing: I'm too old for it. Let the younger ones practise their bravery. Though they may not have a choice about that, since they lack my privileges.

But now I must end our conversation. Goodbye, my reader. Try not to think too badly of me, or no more badly than I think of myself.

In a moment I'll slot these pages into Cardinal Newman and slide it back onto my shelf. In my end is my beginning, as someone once said. Who was that? Mary, Queen of Scots, if history does not lie. Her motto, with a phoenix rising from its ashes, embroidered on a wall hanging. Such excellent embroiderers, women are.

The footsteps approach, one boot after another. Between one breath and the next the knock will come.

The Thirteenth Symposium

The Thirteenth Symposium

HISTORICAL NOTES
Being a partial transcript of the proceedings of the Thirteenth Symposium on Gileadean Studies, International Historical Association Convention, Passamaquoddy, Maine, June 29–30, 2197.

CHAIR: *Professor Maryann Crescent Moon, President, Anishinaabe University, Cobalt, Ontario.*
KEYNOTE SPEAKER: *Professor James Darcy Pieixoto, Director, Twentieth- and Twenty-First-Century Archives, Cambridge University, England.*

CRESCENT MOON: First, I would like to acknowledge that this event is taking place on the traditional territory of the Penobscot Nation, and I thank the elders and ancestors for permitting our presence here today. I would also like to point out that our location — Passamaquoddy, formerly Bangor — was not only a crucial jumping-off point for refugees fleeing Gilead but was also a key hub of the Underground Railroad in antebellum times, now more than three hundred years ago. As they say, history does not repeat itself, but it rhymes.

What a pleasure to welcome you all here to the Thirteenth Symposium on Gileadean Studies!

How our organization has grown, and with such good reason. We must continue to remind ourselves of the wrong turnings taken in the past so we do not repeat them.

A little housekeeping: for those who would like some Penobscot River fishing, there are two excursions planned; please remember your sunscreen and insect repellent. Details of these expeditions, and of the Gilead Period town architectural tour, are in your symposium files. We have added a Recreational Gilead Period Hymn Sing at the Church of Saint Jude, in company with three of the town's school choirs. Tomorrow is Period Costume Re-enactment Day, for those who have come equipped. I do ask you not to get carried away, as happened at the Tenth Symposium.

Now please welcome a speaker familiar to us all, both from his written publications and from his recent fascinating television series, *Inside Gilead: Daily Life in a Puritan Theocracy*. His presentation of objects from museum collections around the world — especially the handcrafted textile items — has been truly spellbinding. I give you: Professor Pieixoto.

PIEIXOTO: Thank you, Professor Crescent Moon, or should I say Madam President? We all congratulate you on your promotion, a thing that would never have happened in Gilead. (*Applause.*) Now that women are usurping leadership positions to such a terrifying extent, I hope you will not be too severe on me. I did take to heart your comments about my little jokes at the Twelfth Symposium — I admit some of them were not in the best of

526

taste — and I will attempt not to reoffend. (*Modi-fied applause.*)

It is gratifying to see such a large turnout. Who would have thought that Gilead Studies — neglected for so many decades — would suddenly have gained so greatly in popularity? Those of us who have laboured in the dim and obscure corners of academe for so long are not used to the bewildering glare of the limelight. (*Laughter.*)

You will all remember the excitement of a few years ago, when a footlocker containing the collection of tapes attributed to the Gilead Handmaid known as 'Offred' was discovered. That find was made right here in Passamaquoddy, behind a false wall. Our investigations and our tentative conclusions were presented at our last symposium, and have already given rise to an impressive number of peer-reviewed papers.

To those who have questioned this material and its dating, I can now say with assurance that half a dozen independent studies have verified our first assumptions, though I must qualify that somewhat. The Digital Black Hole of the twenty-first century that caused so much information to vanish due to the rapid decay rate of stored data — coupled with the sabotage of a large number of server farms and libraries by agents from Gilead bent on destroying any records that might conflict with their own, as well as the populist revolts against repressive digital surveillance in many countries — means that it has not been possible to date many Gileadean materials precisely. A margin of error of between ten and thirty years must be assumed. Within that range, however, we are as confident as any historian can usually be. (*Laughter.*)

Since the discovery of those momentous tapes, there have been two other spectacular finds, which, if authentic, will add substantially to our understanding of this long-gone period in our collective history.

First, the manuscript known as *The Ardua Hall Holograph*. This series of handwritten pages was discovered inside a nineteenth-century edition of Cardinal Newman's *Apologia Pro Vita Sua*. The book was purchased at a general auction by J. Grimsby Dodge, lately of Cambridge, Massachusetts. His nephew inherited the collection and sold it to a dealer in antiques who recognized its potential; thus it was brought to our attention.

Here is a slide of the first page. The handwriting is legible to those trained in archaic cursive; the pages have been trimmed to fit within the excavation in the Cardinal Newman text. The carbon dating of the paper does not exclude the Late Gilead period, and the ink used in the first pages is a standard drawing ink of the period, black in colour, though after a certain number of pages blue is employed. Writing was forbidden for women and girls, with the exception of the Aunts, but drawing was taught at schools to the daughters of elite families; so a supply of such inks was available.

The Ardua Hall Holograph claims to have been composed by a certain 'Aunt Lydia,' who features somewhat unflatteringly in the series of tapes discovered in the footlocker. Internal evidence suggests that she may also have been the 'Aunt Lydia' identified by archaeologists as the main subject of a large and clumsily executed statue discovered in an abandoned chicken battery farm seventy years after the fall of Gilead. The nose of the central figure had been broken off, and one of the other figures was headless, suggesting vandalism. Here is a slide of it; I apologize for the lighting. I took this picture myself, and I am not the world's best photographer. Budgetary constraints precluded my hiring a professional. (*Laughter.*)

The 'Lydia' personage is referenced in several debriefings of deep-cover Mayday agents as having been both ruthless and cunning. We have been unable to find her in the scant amount of televised material surviving from the period, though a framed photograph with 'Aunt Lydia' handwritten on the back was unearthed from the rubble of a girls' school bombed during the collapse of Gilead.

Much points to the same 'Aunt Lydia' as our holograph author. But as always we must be cautious. Suppose the manuscript is a forgery; not a clumsy attempt made in our own times to defraud — the paper and ink would quickly expose such a deception — but a forgery from within Gilead itself; indeed, from within Ardua Hall.

What if our manuscript were devised as a trap, meant to frame its object, like the Casket Letters used to bring about the death of Mary, Queen of Scots? Could it be that one of 'Aunt Lydia's' suspected enemies, as detailed in the holograph itself — Aunt Elizabeth, for instance, or Aunt Vidala — resentful of Lydia's power, craving her position, and familiar with both her handwriting and her verbal style, set out to compose this incriminating document, hoping to have it discovered by the Eyes?

It is remotely possible. But, on the whole, I incline to the view that our holograph is authentic. Certainly it is a fact that someone within Ardua Hall supplied the crucial microdot to the two half-sister fugitives from Gilead whose journey we will examine next. They themselves claim that this personage was Aunt Lydia: why not take them at their word?

Unless, of course, the girls' story of 'Aunt Lydia' is itself a misdirection, intended to protect the identity of the real Mayday double agent in the case of any treachery stemming from within Mayday. There is always that option. In our profession, one mysterious box, when opened, so often conceals another.

This leads us to a pair of documents that are almost certainly authentic. These are labelled as transcriptions of witness testimonies from two young women who, from their own accounts, discovered through the Bloodlines Genealogical Archives kept by the Aunts that they were half-sisters. The speaker who identifies herself as 'Agnes Jemima' purports to have grown up inside Gilead. The one styling herself as 'Nicole' appears to have been some eight or nine years younger. In her testimony she describes how she learned from two Mayday agents that she was smuggled out of Gilead as an infant.

'Nicole' might seem too young, in years but also in experience, to have been assigned to the hazardous mission the two of them appear to have carried out so successfully, but she was no younger than many involved in resistance operations and spywork over the course of the centuries. Some historians have even argued that persons of that age are especially suitable for such escapades, as the young are idealistic, have an underdeveloped sense of their own mortality and are afflicted with an exaggerated thirst for justice.

The mission described is thought to have been instrumental in initiating the final collapse of Gilead, since the material smuggled out by the younger sister — a microdot embedded in a scarified tattoo, which I must say is a novel method of information delivery (*laughter*) — revealed a great many discreditable personal secrets pertaining to various high-level officials. Especially noteworthy is a handful of plots devised by Commanders to eliminate other Commanders.

The release of this information touched off the so-called Ba'al Purge that thinned the ranks of the elite class, weakened the regime, and instigated a military putsch as well as a popular revolt. The civil strife and chaos that resulted enabled a campaign of sabotage coordinated by the Mayday Resistance and a series of successful attacks from within certain parts of the former United States, such as the Missouri hill country, the areas in and around Chicago and Detroit, Utah — resentful of the massacre of Mormons that had taken place there — the Republic of Texas, Alaska, and most parts of the West Coast.

But that is another story — one that is still being pieced together by military historians.

★   ★   ★

My focus will be on the witness testimonies themselves, recorded and transcribed most likely for the use of the Mayday Resistance movement. These documents were located in the library of the Innu University in Sheshatshiu, Labrador. No one had discovered them earlier — possibly because the file was not labelled clearly, being entitled 'Annals of the *Nellie J. Banks*: Two Adventurers.' Anyone glancing at that group of signifiers would have thought this was an account of ancient liquor smuggling, the *Nellie J. Banks* having been a famous rum-running schooner of the early twentieth century.

It was not until Mia Smith, one of our graduate students in search of a thesis topic, opened the file that the true nature of its contents became apparent. When she passed the material along to me for evaluation, I was very excited by it, since first-hand narratives from Gilead are vanishingly rare — especially any concerning the lives of girls and women. It is hard for those deprived of literacy to leave such records.

But we historians have learned to interrogate our own first assumptions. Was this double-bladed narrative a clever fake? A team of our graduate students set out to follow the route described by the supposed witnesses — first plotting their probable course on maps both terrestrial and marine, then travelling this route themselves in hopes of uncovering any extant clues. Maddeningly, the texts themselves are not dated. I trust that if you yourselves are ever involved in an escapade such as this, you will be more helpful to future historians and will include the month and year. (*Laughter.*)

After a number of dead ends and a rat-plagued night spent in a derelict lobster canning factory in New Hampshire, the team interviewed an elderly woman residing here in Passamaquoddy. She said her great-grandfather told a story about transporting people to Canada — mostly women — on a fishing boat. He'd even kept a map of the area that the great-granddaughter gifted to us, saying she was about to throw out that old junk so no one would have to tidy it up after she was dead.

I'll just bring up a slide of this map.

Using the laser pointer, I will now trace the most likely route taken by our two young refugees: by car to here, by bus to here, by pickup truck to here, by motorboat to here, and then on the *Nellie J. Banks* to this beach near Harbourville, Nova Scotia. From there they appear to have been airlifted to a refugee processing and medical centre on Campobello Island, New Brunswick.

Our team of students next visited Campobello Island, and on it the summer home built by the family of Franklin D. Roosevelt in the nineteenth century within which the refugee centre was temporarily located. Gilead wished to sever any ties with this edifice, and blew up the causeway from the Gilead mainland to prevent any land-based escapes by those hankering after more democratic ways. The house went through some rough times in those days but has since been restored and is run as a museum; regrettably, much of the original furniture has vanished.

Our two young women may have spent at least a week in this house, as by their own accounts both were in need of treatment for hypothermia and exposure, and, in the case of the younger sister, for sepsis due to an infection. While searching the building, our enterprising young team discovered some intriguing incisions in the woodwork of a second-storey windowsill.

Here they are on this slide — painted over but still visible.

This is an N, for 'Nicole' perhaps — you can trace the upstroke, here — and an A, and a G: could these refer to 'Ada' and 'Garth'? Or does the A point to 'Agnes'? There is a V — for 'Victoria'? — slightly below it, here. Over here, the letters AL, referring possibly to the 'Aunt Lydia' of their testimonies.

Who was the mother of these two half-sisters? We know there was a fugitive Handmaid who was an active field agent with Mayday for some years. After surviving at least two assassination attempts, she worked for some years under triple protection at their intelligence unit near Barrie, Ontario, which posed as an organic hemp products farm. We have not definitively excluded this individual as the author of the 'Handmaid's Tale' tapes found in the footlocker; and, according to that narrative, this individual had at least two children. But jumping to conclusions can lead us astray, so I depend on future scholars to examine the matter more closely, if possible.

For the use of interested parties — at the moment, an opportunity available only to symposium attendees, though, depending on funding, we hope to extend it for the benefit of a broader readership — my colleague Professor Knotly Wade and I have prepared a facsimile edition of these three batches of materials, which we have interleaved in an order that made approximate narrative sense to us. You can take the historian out of the storyteller, but you can't take the storyteller out of the historian! (*Laughter, applause.*) We have numbered the sections to aid in searches and references: needless to say, no such numbers appear on the originals. Copies of the facsimile may be requested at the registration desk; no more than one each, please, as supplies are limited.

Travel well on your journey into the past; and while you are there, ponder the meaning of the cryptic windowsill markings. I will confine myself to suggesting that the correspondence of the initial letters to several key names in our transcripts is highly evocative, to say the least.

★ ★ ★

I will conclude with one more fascinating piece of the puzzle.

The group of slides I am about to show you portrays a statue located at present on the Boston Common. Its provenance suggests it is not from the Gilead period: the name of the sculptor corresponds to that of an artist who was active in Montreal some decades after the collapse of Gilead, and the statue must have been transferred to its present position some years after the post-Gilead chaos and subsequent Restoration of the United States of America.

The inscription would appear to name the principal actors cited in our materials. If this is so, our two young messengers must indeed have lived not only to tell their tale but also to be reunited with their mother and their respective fathers, and to have children and grandchildren of their own.

I myself take this inscription to be a convincing testament to the authenticity of our two witness transcripts. The collective memory is notoriously faulty, and much of the past sinks into the ocean of time to be drowned forever; but once in a while the waters part, allowing us to glimpse a flash of hidden treasure, if only for a moment. Although history is rife with nuance, and we historians can never hope for unanimous agreement, I trust you will be able to concur with me, at least in this instance.

As you can see, the statue depicts a young woman wearing the costume of the Pearl Girls: note the definitive cap, the strand of pearls, and the backpack. She is carrying a bouquet of small flowers identified by our ethno-botanist consultant as forget-me-nots; on her right shoulder there are two birds, belonging, it would seem, to the pigeon or dove family.

Here is the inscription. The lettering is weathered and difficult to read on the slide, so I took

536

the liberty of transcribing it on the following slide, here. And on this last note I will close.

IN LOVING MEMORY OF

BECKA, AUNT IMMORTELLE

THIS MEMORIAL WAS ERECTED BY
HER SISTERS
AGNES AND NICOLE
AND THEIR MOTHER, THEIR TWO FATHERS,
THEIR CHILDREN AND THEIR
GRANDCHILDREN.

AND IN RECOGNITION OF THE INVALUABLE
SERVICES PROVIDED BY A.L.

*A BIRD OF THE AIR SHALL CARRY THE
VOICE, AND THAT WHICH HATH WINGS
SHALL TELL THE MATTER.
LOVE IS AS STRONG AS DEATH.*

Acknowledgements

The Testaments was written in many places: in the dome car of a train stuck on a siding due to a mudslide, on a couple of ships, in a number of hotel rooms, in the middle of a forest, in the centre of a city, on park benches, and in cafés, with words inscribed on the proverbial paper napkin, in notebooks, and on a laptop. The mudslide was beyond my control, as were some of the other events affecting the writing venues. Others were entirely my own fault.

But before the actual placing of words on pages, *The Testaments* was written partly in the minds of the readers of its predecessor, *The Handmaid's Tale*, who kept asking what happened after the end of that novel. Thirty-five years is a long time to think about possible answers, and the answers have changed as society itself has changed, and as possibilities have become actualities. The citizens of many countries, including the United States, are under more stresses now than they were three decades ago.

One question about *The Handmaid's Tale* that came up repeatedly is: How did Gilead fall? *The Testaments* was written in response to this question. Totalitarianisms may crumble from within, as they fail to keep the promises that brought them to power; or they may be attacked from without; or both. There are no sure-fire formulas, since very little in history is inevitable.

★   ★   ★

My thanks first to the readers of *The Handmaid's Tale:* their interest and curiosity has been inspiring. And many thanks to the large team who brought the book to life as a gripping, beautifully made, and award-winning MGM and Hulu television series: Steve Stark, Warren Littlefield, and Daniel Wilson on the producing end; show-runner Bruce Miller and his excellent writing room; the fine directors; and the amazing cast, for whom this was definitely not just another show: Elisabeth Moss, Ann Dowd, Samira Wiley, Joseph Fiennes, Yvonne Strahovski, Alexis Bledel, Amanda Brugel, Max Minghella, and so many others. The television series has respected one of the axioms of the novel: no event is allowed into it that does not have a precedent in human history.

Every published book is a group effort, so many thanks are due to the wild posse of editors and first readers on both sides of the Atlantic who have helped with this thought experiment in countless ways, from *I love that!* to *You can't get away with this!* to *I don't understand, tell me more.* This group includes, but is not limited to, Becky Hardie of Chatto/Penguin Random House U.K.; Louise Dennys and Martha Kanya-Forstner of Penguin Random House Canada; Nan Talese and LuAnn Walther of Penguin Random House U.S.; Jess Atwood Gibson, who is ruthless; and Heather Sangster of Strong Finish, the demon copy editor who picks every nit, including those yet unhatched. And thanks to the proofreading and production teams led by Lydia Buechler and Lorraine Hyland at Penguin Random House U.S. and Kimberlee Hesas at Penguin Random House Canada.

Thanks also to Todd Doughty and Suzanne Herz of Penguin Random House U.S.; to Jared Bland and Ashley Dunn of Penguin Random House Canada; and to Fran Owen, Mari Yamazaki, and Chloe Healy of Penguin Random House U.K.

To my now-retired agents, Phoebe Larmore and Vivienne Schuster; to Karolina Sutton, and to Caitlin Leydon, Claire Nozieres, Sophie Baker, and Jodi Fabbri of Curtis Brown; to Alex Fane, David Sabel, and the team at Fane Productions; and to Ron Bernstein of ICM.

In the special services department: to Scott Griffin for sailing advice; to Oberon Zell Ravenheart and Kirsten Johnsen; to Mia Smith, whose name appears in the text as a result of an auction in aid of the charity Freedom from Torture; and to the several Second World War resistance members from France, Poland, and the Netherlands whom I have known over the years. The character Ada was named for my aunt-by-marriage, Ada Bower Atwood Brannen, who was one of the first female hunting and fishing guides in Nova Scotia.

To those who keep me trundling through time and who remind me what day it is, including Lucia Cino of O. W. Toad Limited and Penny Kavanaugh; to V. J. Bauer, who designs and tends the website; to Ruth Atwood and Ralph Siferd; to Evelyn Heskin; and to Mike Stoyan and Sheldon Shoib, to Donald Bennett, to Bob Clark and Dave Cole.

To Coleen Quinn, who makes sure I get out of the Writing Burrow and onto the open road; to Xiaolan Zhao and Vicky Dong; to Matthew Gibson, who fixes stuff; and to Terry Carman and the Shock Doctors, for keeping the lights on.

And as always to Graeme Gibson, my partner in many strange and wonderful adventures for almost fifty years.

We do hope that you have enjoyed reading this large print book.

Did you know that all of our titles are available for purchase?

We publish a wide range of high quality large print books including:
Romances, Mysteries, Classics
General Fiction
Non Fiction and Westerns

Special interest titles available in large print are:
The Little Oxford Dictionary
Music Book
Song Book
Hymn Book
Service Book

Also available from us courtesy of Oxford University Press:
Young Readers' Dictionary
(large print edition)
Young Readers' Thesaurus
(large print edition)

For further information or a free brochure, please contact us at:
Ulverscroft Large Print Books Ltd.,
The Green, Bradgate Road, Anstey,
Leicester, LE7 7FU, England.
Tel: (00 44) 0116 236 4325
Fax: (00 44) 0116 234 0205